World Greatest Short Stories

45 MASTERPIECE

Indian, Chinese, Herbew, Italian, Persian, Arabian, Classical, etc.

Edited by

J.A. Hammerton

INDIANA
PUBLISHING HOUSE

2/13 Ansari Road, Darya Ganj,
New Delhi-110 002

45 MASTERPIECE

ISBN 81-242-0478-0

9788124204788

Published by:
Indiana Publishing House
2/13, Ansari Road, Darya Ganj
New Delhi - 110 002 (India)

Printed by:
Saurabh Printers Pvt. Ltd.
A-16, Sector-4, Noida (UP)

Editorial Board

Editorial Note

A SHORT story may be a mere anecdote of three hundred words or a work of ten or fifteen thousand. In content it may be anything from a glimpse of character, an incident, to a highly finished picture of life. But it should be a complete work of imagination, its effect achieved with a minimum of personages and events.

To select the best thousand examples was a task that could be achieved only on arbitrary lines. As to length, three thousand words was the ideal average, but this excluded some of the finest stories, so exceptions had to be allowed. National characteristics also had consideration. Another test was the value of a story as illustrating the development of the art.

PROBLEMS of arrangement were not entirely solved by classification according to the country of each writer's origin. This puts Richard Steele into the Irish volume and separates those ideal literary partners Agnes and Egerton Castle. But it is the best possible arrangement for the work, and the index makes reference easy. The inclusion of a series of stories of the War became possible when the War itself ruled out all modern German work.

A WORD as to the method of selection. The general editor prepared a trial list of titles, which was submitted to all the members of the Editorial Board, who rejected and added according to their individual tastes and knowledge, These individual lists were then collated and the final list evolved. The thousand stories selected are therefore representative of the combined opinion of the whole group of editors. A very few modifications of the final list were made necessary by difficulties of copyright and considerations of Anglo-Saxon taste in certain translations from foreign literatures.

MOST of the foreign stories have been specially translated, and all copyrights, in both stories and translations, the use of which authors and publishers have courteously permitted, are duly credited at the end of each volume.

J.A. HAMMERTON

Contents

CONTENTS

The Early Story-Tellers

IT is doubtful if any other form of art has so long interesting, and picturesque a history as the Short Story. It is one of the most important elements in the fabric of human life. It is the medium of the highest spiritual gospel: it is the chief weapon of all great reformers since at least the days of the Buddha: it is the source from which Shakespeare drew much of his inspiration; and though it changes in outward fashion from age to age, the art of the short story will not vanish until man does. For it is as perennial as life itself. To trace its origin, we should have to go back to the time when some strange, curious, ape-like creatures came down from the shelter of the forest trees and began to communicate with each other in articulate speech.

We cannot go back as far as that. But in the tales told by the nomad Bushmen of the South African desert, and by the black fellows of the Australian wilderness, we can get fairly close to the brief prose tale in its primitive form. And in this stage it is far from being a trivial thing. A modern man would be surprised by its importance, if he were unacquainted with the weird, shifting world of imagination in which the lower savages fearfully live. Many a wild, wandering hunter would give his finest weapon—the thing by which he wins food for himself and family—to learn some of these tales from the cunning old men who keep the tribal mysteries. For to him the tales are of high practical value. They contain magical secrets, by means of which a man can become the master of the whole world, and call the rain-clouds up to him, and charm the birds of the air and the beasts of the wood, and bring them all within his power.

Then there are stories that give a man a wonderful knowledge of the gods and spirits and totems; and with this knowledge he can make them all his servants. So he becomes the medicine-man or witch-doctor of his tribe. From the white frozen wastes around the Pole, where the Eskimo ranges, to the hot, steaming forests of the Congo, where the pigmy moves like a shadow through the bush, the magical art of the short story flourishes. And alongside this development of superstition, the kindly play of humorous fancy and interest in the character of one's neighbours goes on. The common people, dragooned and oppressed and terrified by their chiefs, elders, and witch-doctors, turn for relief to the short story, and weave around their camp-fires amusing and satirical anecdotes about some humble creature of the wilds who triumphs over all his powerful enemies. So we get that brilliant, shrewd, and entertaining series of little animal stories, where the rabbit, the fox, or some other small animal wins by trick and cunning what he cannot gain by force. The American Negro tales of Brer Rabbit are classic examples of this form of the primitive short story.

MANY of our old genuine fairy-tales have come down to us from the Stone Ages. That is why they appeal so delightfully to the minds of children. The imagination of the savage and the child are partly of the same power and quality. They float in a world of wonder, in which the wildest wishes become realities and the most impossible fancies wear the look of truth, especially when they are given form and substance by the art of the story-teller. But what is only a charming entertainment to our children was often a solemn belief to our barbaric forefathers two thousand years ago. The talking animals of our fairy-tales, for instance, are faint, outworn traditions of the mysterious guardian spirits, who assumed the shape of beasts and watched over the tribesmen who reverenced them as totems. "Puss-in-Boots" in his first form may have been the sacred totem of the Wild Cat clan; and quite likely the original beast in "Beauty and the Beast" was also one of these animal deities who fell in love with a mortal maiden, and was under a taboo not to reveal himself in human shape.

Thus the fairy-tale has a curious importance in the history of both savage and civilised races. Unhappily, many of the best known and prettiest of these tales have been worked over by brilliant French men and women of the seventeenth and eighteenth centuries. So they have become neither one thing or the other. It is best to go back to the earliest, genuine source of stories of magic and enchantment; and surprisingly early in date is the tale with which we open.

ABOUT 6800 years ago—according to one method of reckoning—Khufu, or Cheops, the greatest of the pyramid-builders, was lord of Egypt. Egypt was then a land with a high civilisation, a great school of builders and sculptors, and royal lovers of literature. It was Khufu's custom to call his sons round his throne and bid them tell him tales of the old magicians. The stories were recorded in their present shape by a scribe who lived about 3459 B.C.; but he attributes the first tale to King Khafri—the successor to Cheops and the second of the great pyramid-builders. Khafri may have reigned 1500 years before the scribe. Thus the modern short-story writer can claim one of the most ancient kings in the world as the father of his art—one who lived long before Homer or any known poet.

Khafri came of a line that intended to take over the priesthood of the sun-god, and make themselves the popes as well as the monarchs of their people. Perhaps the trouble that Khafri took to collect the old traditions of the magicians was part of a political scheme. He wanted to know as much as the priests did about the superstitious practices and hypnotic spells that were still used in Egyptian religion. The tale he relates is like its author. There is more in it than appears on the surface. It seems to be a common story of an unfaithful wife and an avenging husband. But fully understood, it is one of the great documents of civilisation. In primitive Egypt the women held the property, and all a man earned or inherited was made over to his wife. It was the age of what is known as mother-right. Possibly woman, having invented farming while man was hunting for food for the family, kept agriculture and its profits in her hands. When she wanted to marry, she sent a man a gift of clothes, as the woman does in Khafri's tale. When she tired of one husband, she obtained another by a second gift of clothing—a method of wooing followed by some savage girls at the present day.

The Tale of Khafri

The priestesses of Amon retained this privilege of choosing their spouses for some thousands of years. But the general laws of marriage and property were changed when kingship was established in Egypt—possibly by a virile race of invaders. Thus the erring wife in Khafri's tale is not a common offender, but the militant suffragette of her time, contending for the revival of the old woman's rights. But the husband puts a crocodile in the lake where her lover comes to bathe, and the wife is burnt at the stake, to discourage other women from attempting to revert to an obsolete custom.

THE next Egyptian story, " The Tale of Ahuri," carries us down to the days of Rameses the Great, under whose rule Moses possibly lived. The manuscript is in the writing of the late Greek period of Egyptian history, but the story dates back to 1320 B.C. Prince Setna, a son of Rameses, has the same ambition as Khafri had, and he sets out to gather the magical secrets of the priesthood. In particular, he seeks after a book of magic written by the god Thoth, by which a man could learn the speech of all living creatures and bend the heavens and earth to his will. In his search, Setna breaks open a kingly tomb, and finds it inhabited by the spirits of a royal brother and sister, who in their life-time had also sought after the book of Thoth. It rests by their side. But when Setna stoops to take it, Princess Ahuri bids him listen to the tale of her life, in which she tells how Thoth took vengeance upon her and her brother when they tried to use his book. Possibly the tale was written by some priestly scribe with a view to deterring some prince like Setna from prying too closely into the secrets of hypnotic suggestion, by means of which the Egyptian sorcerers performed their apparent miracles.

The Tale of Ahuri

In addition to this curious study in magic, there is a strange human interest in " Ahuri's Tale." Most readers will be repelled by it. For the romance in the life of the Princess turns on the difficulties put in her way when she fell in love with her brother and wished to marry him. But we must bear in mind that in her own eyes she was a virtuous heroine. The ancient Egyptians favoured brother and sister marriages, especially in their royal family. Even in modern Egypt it is a man's duty to marry his first cousin or some one in the family. Ahuri's father objected to her following the usual custom, merely because he wanted to found two lines of descendants. Having only two children, he desired the girl to marry a general's son, and the boy to marry a general's daughter. The marriage of Ahuri to her brother left only one line of royal descendants, and endangered the succession to the throne. Such was the native view of this extraordinary story.

Stories of the Buddha

BETWEEN the time when Ahuri lived and the time when her story was written in its present shape, a new form of the short prose tale was developed during a popular movement of religion in Ancient India. Gautama, the son of a chieftain in South Nepal, arose in the sixth century B.C., with a democratic, mystical creed, that he preached alike to king and pariah, with a view to uniting all castes in a common system of spiritual salvation. He became known as the Buddha, or Enlightened One, and none of the high-caste orthodox priests was able to appeal to the minds of the people as he did. Possessing a shrewd wit and a telling humour, he drove home his ideas by means of entertaining fables and tales—such as the quaint and surprising story of " The Monkey and the Queen's Jewels," and the charming " Tale of the Princess Sambula." His disciples adopted this method of preaching, and almost every popular story in Northern India—to the number of five hundred and fifty—was adapted by the Buddhists and collected after the death of the great reformer.

The tales spread from India to Persia and from Syria to Greece ; and some of them were transcribed by Planudes, a Greek monk, in the fourteenth century, and attributed by him to Aesop. Thus under the forged title of *Aesop's Fables* a few of the shorter and lighter animal stories told by the Buddha have become a popular element in our culture. But as will be seen by a reference to the original fable of " The Ass in the Lion's Skin," the ancient version remains superior to its various modern recensions. As Buddha told the tale, it is a vivid little picture of Hindu village life, with no shadow of improbability about it. Even in fables in which birds and animals use human speech —such as " The Talkative Tortoise "—the thing happens in a reasonable manner. For it is connected with the central doctrine of the Buddhist creed. According to Buddha, when a man dies he is born again. If he has been very wicked, he comes to life as a deadly snake or a wild beast, or something still more dreadful. But if he has accumulated a store of good actions, he is born to high rank and wealth. All life is one, and a holy man like the Buddha could win such spiritual power as to be able to remember his former births. The original stories indeed profess to be a record of the five hundred and fifty and more births of the Buddha and of his experiences in animal, bird, and human form. So these tales are known as the " Jatakas " or " Birth Stories." One of them—" The Judgment of the Buddha "—is an interesting problem. It is practically identical with the Scriptural story of the " Judgment of Solomon," and scholars are still disputing whether the Hindus came into contact with the Hebrews during the Babylonian Captivity.

The Pancha-tantra

WHEN the Buddhist's tales were written down, somewhere about 350 B.C., the orthodox, priestly Brahmans, who stood for the old caste system, suddenly became aware of the literary value and lively charm of the " Birth Stories." With a view to combating the growing influence of the new sect, the Brahmans stole some of the best tales, and made a book of them, entitled the *Pancha-tantra.* This dates back to 200 B C., and it contains the remarkable character study and amusing narrative of " The Brahman of Vain Dreams." This is clearly a Buddhist satire on the gluttony and foolishness of the orthodox high-caste priesthood, and it is surprising that the priests themselves should have included it in their version. Probably they could not resist its humour.

Tales from the Hitopadesa

The Brahmans did not appeal to the people, but aimed at overthrowing their rivals by winning over kings and inducing them to drive the Buddhists from India at the point of the sword. And to gain the favour of the men of royal rank, they used some of the stories they took from the Buddhists in compiling a work of statecraft, known as the *Hitopadesa*, or book of princely instruction. The tale of " The Rajah's Son and the Merchant's Wife " is a good example of the pieces in this book. It gives a rather low view of human nature, especially of feminine human nature. The attacks on the character of women contained in all these Hindu tales exerted for some thousands of years an influence upon the European mind, and assisted in bringing about that slanderous view of the character of the mothers of our race that largely prevailed in the Middle Ages. " The Faithful Servant," from the same Sanscrit classic, moves in a higher moral atmosphere, and though the miraculous element seems absurd to Western readers, it must be remembered that to the people for whom it was written it would not by any means appear ridiculous.

Polycrates and his Ring

EVEN in the lifetime of the Buddha, the leaders of Western civilisation had little to learn from the Hindu ascetics in regard to the frailty of women. For the ancient Greeks had a remarkable collection of anecdotes of a loose kind, which were known as Milesian Tales. They arose amid the luxury and licence of manners in the Greek cities of Asia Minor, and a lost work by Aristides contained many of them. But it is to another Asiatic Greek, Herodotus, born in Halicarnassus about 490 B.C., that we owe our earliest extant examples of the short tale in Greek prose. He wandered about the ancient world, talking with every man of importance he met, and recorded all the stories in his famous history, written when he settled in Italy. His kinsmen had been killed by a Greek tyrant in Asia, and this perhaps led him to write with a vehement passion for free government. In the tale of "Polycrates and His Ring" he gives a dramatic legend of one of the old Greek tyrants who made himself hated by his freedom-loving race. But his masterpiece in the art of the short story is "The Treasure of King Rhampsinitus." It is a tradition of Rameses the Great, and was no doubt told to the writer by one of the Egyptian priests he met in his travels in the Fayum.

The Treasure of Rhampsinitus

None of the Athenians in the Golden Age of Greek literature wrote any prose tales that have come down to us. They were occupied almost entirely with the drama, the study of history and philosophy. It is from Sicily in the Silver Age of Greek letters that we get our first short story of actual life from the hand of a great writer—Theocritus. He was born at Syracuse about 300 B.C., and in his sketch of "The Ladies of Syracuse" he gives a fresh, charming, and lively picture of the life of his native city. The plot is very slight, but the character-drawing and the beauty of the diction make it a thing of gold. Even Anatole France has done nothing finer; for it has the best qualities of the modern French *conte*, together with an exquisite loveliness beyond the reach of any modern novelist.

The Ladies of Syracuse

The amazing Greeks were our masters in every form of art. We excel them only where they did not compete with us, as in the long novel of manners with a well-defined plot. Yet even here the classic writers have some astonishing things to show us what they could have done had they wished. The modern realistic tale is a timid study of the depths of life in comparison with the works of some of the later Greek and Latin authors. Petronius, the brilliant libertine dandy of Rome who taught Nero his worst vices and committed suicide when he fell out of favour, wrote a satirical romance, of which two chapters have come down to us. In these is embedded a little jewel of ironic humour—"The Widow of Ephesus." It is probably a late version of one of the Milesian Tales that originated in Asia Minor. There is a still more amusing short story in the work of Petronius; but by reason of its character it cannot be included in a collection of tales for the general reader of modern times.

The Widow of Ephesus

For the same reason we have had to exclude the "True Story" by Lucian—the most brilliant of all satirists, ancient and modern. He was born about 125 A.D. at Samosata in Syria. Lucian was the solvent of his age—a witty, brilliant sceptic who laughed at everything, and prepared the way for the triumph of Christianity by bringing all the current forms of Pagan belief to ridicule.

Opposed to Lucian was a contemporary Latin writer, Apuleius, who was also born about 125 A.D. at Madaura in Northern Africa. Apuleius was a man of wealth who wandered about Asia enquiring into the mystic religions against which the Christians were struggling. In his gay, picturesque, rambling romance, "The Golden Ass," he shows a strong leaning to the worship

Cupid and Psyche

of Isis, and in the short story, "Cupid and Psyche," he takes up a charming old folk-tale and transforms it into one of the loveliest and most spiritual things in the history of fiction. For there can be little doubt that Psyche represents the human soul wooed by the Spirit of Divine Love.

Tragic Love, or Cnemon's Story

IT is strange to pass from the last of the Pagan story-tellers to the first of the Christian writers of romance, and find that the best short tale by Bishop Heliodorus is far more heathen in character than "Cupid and Psyche." Heliodorus lived towards the end of the fourth century of the present era. He is said to have been Bishop of Tricca, and a late tradition runs that a synod gave him the choice either to burn his romance or renounce his bishropic; the prelate preferred to keep his book from the flames. His short story of "Cnemon," which has here been entitled "Tragic Love," is remarkably well told. The extraordinary situation, derived from the old legend of Phaedra and Hippolytus, is developed in a rapid, dramatic manner, the dialogue is natural and easy, and the characters are drawn in swift and expressive strokes. The longer love romance by the same writer is much inferior to his shorter work; it is verbose, intricate and dull in parts. The dreadful atmosphere of dullness rests on most of the Greek romances written by later writers. Only Longus in his lovely pastoral, "Daphnis and Chloe," infuses life and beauty and freshness into the declining art of fiction; but the work of Longus is a novel rather than a short story.

IN the meantime, the great sacred writers of the Hebrews had built up in the Old Testament a monument of religious literature without parallel in the world. Besides containing the highest and clearest revelation of the Divine Power in the universe, the more ancient part of our Bible was a magnificent collection of poetry, drama, and narrative. The man who wrote the Book of Job was a greater poet than Aeschylus, Milton, or Dante; the scribe who set forth the Book of Ruth was one of the supreme masters in the art of narration. But it is in the New Testament that the loveliest of all short stories appear. Even as Jesus was greater than Buddha in spiritual things, so was He a more powerful, direct, and winning preacher. Appealing to the lowly, the poor and outcast, He spoke with a divine simplicity and power that make His parables the consummate flower of the art of narration. The Parable of the Prodigal Son is most beautiful as a work of art as well as a message of hope and joy to the sinner sunk in actual misery by his sin. And the story of the woman taken in adultery, which reveals so overwhelming and yet divinely pitiful a view of the weakness of all human nature, is perhaps the finest short story in the world. If our modern Theosophists and modern Buddhists would but study the Bible of their fathers with the attention they devote to the obscure and inartistic productions of the Indian mind, they would find that, both as literature and as a vehicle for the highest spiritual teaching, the Bible is incomparable.

Even in the books which some of the Reformed Churches regard as uncanonical, there are admirable examples of the narrative art of the Hebrews; and it is from these that we have taken the stories of "Tobit," and "Susanna," and "Bel and the Dragon." The three narratives were probably composed in the second and first centuries before Christ, but the traditions on which they are built go back some hundreds of years to the days of the Assyrian captivity. The story of Susanna is now the most famous of these three stories. It is thought to have been written in its present form about 100 B.C., when Simon ben Shetach was president of the Sanhedrin. Simon was anxious to reform the criminal law, especially in regard to false witnesses. His own son was falsely accused of a capital offence, and he let him die in the hope that the death of an innocent man would help him to save many more innocent lives. And it may have been Simon himself who brought out the old story of Susanna, after the death of his son, with a view to influencing public opinion, and getting a law passed that all perjurers should undergo the punishment that might have fallen on the person they wrongly accused.

Tobit, Susanna, and Bel and the Dragon

UNLIKE the nations of the old Mediterranean world, the ancient Chinese were not distinguished by their mastery of the narrative arts. Both the novels and the dramas of China are of modern origin; and even now they are scarcely regarded as literature by the Chinese scholars. The earliest masterpiece of the Chinese story-teller is the charming, delicate allegory, "The Peach-Blossom Fountain," written by Tao Chien in his old age, about 420 A.D. He was a lover of good wine and country-life, and his enchanted land with its exquisite beauty is merely the ordinary world as he saw it in memory with the magic eyes of youth. There is more drama and quite as much beauty in "The Lute-Girl's Lament," by another famous Chinese writer, Pŏ Chü-Yi, born in 772 A.D. He rose to high office in the state, and afterwards was banished to a petty post, where he gave himself up to poetry and philosophy. While he was travelling to his post of banishment he fell ill, and met on the river the deserted lute-girl, whose sad life he so beautifully depicts. This little work is accounted one of the highest things in the literature of his country; such is the exquisiteness of its original diction, that an admiring critic says that it wrought him into the state of ecstasy that the Buddhists practise.

The Peach-Blossom Fountain

The Lute-Girl's Lament

IN our country in the Middle Ages there was floating about a far larger number of vivid tales of every kind than those which remained ungathered in China. From the days of the Norman Kings to the days of the Tudors, all the material accumulated by the story-tellers of the world—Hindus, Persians, Arabs, Syrians, and even Egyptians—was carried across Europe and woven into the fabric of the common culture of Christendom. The bards of Ireland in the seventh century were the first to produce a tale of

The Fate of Deirdre

immortal beauty in "The Fate of Deirdre." This is one of the high things of man's making. Deirdre herself ranks beside Helen of Troy and Gudrun of Iceland; but she has not yet found a man of fine genius to cast her lovely, tragic story into a classic form of art. We must wait for this until Ireland produces a great narrative poet or a great dramatic master of music.

While the Gaels of Erin were moulding their national stories roughly into shape, the Cymri of Wales were developing their splendid body of myth and romance. A striking example of the early Welsh mythic romance is "The Dream of Maxen Wledig"—which is one of the tales by the old Welsh bards that Lady Charlotte Guest translated under the title of the *Mabinogion*. It is a very faint portrait of the Roman Emperor Maximus, seen through the haze of the fairy-tale and the romance of the later age of chivalry.

The Dream of Maxen Wledig

Far more interesting, however, are the stories of King Arthur and his knights. These were first formed on a base of historic fact by the bards of Cornwall, South Wales, and Strathclyde, towards the end of the sixth century. Coloured with romance, they passed to the Welsh-speaking people of Brittany, and they were afterwards taken over by the minstrels of Normandy and spread through France and Italy. Some of the Arthurian tales of the Welsh bards are found in the *Mabinogion*; but the more important romances have been worked over by Norman and Breton poets of the twelfth century, and finely transformed by them into the supreme literature of Christian chivalry. The best stories are Welsh in structure but French in spirit, like the earliest tale of Lancelot, "The Knight of the Cart," composed by Chrestien de Troyes about 1164. We possess an exquisite version of this story in "Queen Guenever's Maying," from the *Morte D'Arthur* of Sir Thomas Malory. Malory wove the works of the old French poets into a magnificent prose epic in the fifteenth century, but all his tales are more ancient than his day.

Queen Guenever's Maying

It was the French who carried the vogue of the Arthurian romances into Germany, where, long afterwards, Wagner dramatised the best of them and set it to music. The French also took over the romances of the Greeks of Byzantium, with which they became familiar during the first two Crusades. Permanent bonds of culture were established between the French and the Greeks by intermarriage, commerce, and the conquest of Constantinople; and many Greek tales of which the originals are now lost survive—like that of "King Coustans"—in a French version. This famous tale of the man who was born to be king has spread to Arabia and Abyssinia, and become part of the folklore of Europe. It was composed in French in the twelfth century.

The Tale of King Coustans

Towards the end of that century there was a French minstrel of Hainault, who, it has but recently been discovered, is one of the supreme masters of literature. From a new reading of the manuscript, his name seems to have been Old Antif, and his work is the exquisite song-story "Aucassin and Nicolette," that bears comparison with "Romeo and Juliet" as a love-tale of immortal beauty. The story is of Moorish origin; for Aucassin bears, in a slightly altered form, the name of a Mohammedan ruler of Cordova in the eleventh century, and the curious manner of telling a tale partly in verse and partly in prose is also a Mohammedan characteristic. Perhaps Old Antif fell into the hands of Moorish pirates, and as a slave learnt their ways. He has, too, a first-hand knowledge of Provence, where he stages the tale. For he remembers the strange, scandalous allegation made against the people of Aigue-Mortes that the men lay in child-bed when their wives had children. The Basques of the Pyrenees used to do this in ancient times, and savages in various parts of the world still act like the King of Torelore in "Aucassin and Nicolette." The English rendering of this famous romance given in our collection is the work of the present writer.

Aucassin and Nicolette

WHILE Old Antif and other minstrels were entertaining the castle folk with romances of chivalry, the parsons and friars were using the short story to attract the people to church, where the sermon became in many instances as picturesque and lively a vehicle of religious instruction as the miracle play. Everything of quick, human interest was matter for the popular art of the preachers. They took an Oriental apologue, like "The Hermit and the Treasure," which an unknown Italian first published, and gave it a Christian air and a brilliant concision. They ransacked the remains of antiquity for stories, and developed charming legends, such as we find in "King Philip and his Greek Slave," and in "The Humbling of Jovinian," which latter is a version of the well-known tale of King Robert of Sicily. From a collection of Arabian stories made by Petrus Alphonsus, a Christian Jew who rose to high honour in Spain in the eleventh century, they obtained the beautiful story of "The Knights of Egypt and Baldac"—the last word being mediaeval English for Bagdad, the romantic scene of the *Arabian Nights' Entertainments.* And from the English legend of Guy, Earl of Warwick, the story of "Guido and Tyrius" was derived.

Tales from the Gesta Romanorum

A hundred and more of these tales were formed into a book entitled *Gesta Romanorum*; and very likely it was an Englishman who produced this famous work towards the end of the thirteenth century or the beginning of the fourteenth. Among the stories included in it are the delightful romance of "The Husband of Aglaes," and "The Three Caskets" that Shakespeare used in "The Merchant of Venice." The ingenious "Three Maxims" is an excellent version of a tale that is found from England to China; and in "Theodosus of Rome" we have one of the early forms of the tale of King Lear, which is of British origin.

IN the days when the tales in the *Gesta Romanorum* were being penned, the old Vikings of Iceland, giving over war for the peaceful occupation of sheep-farmers, were producing round the hearth on dark winter evenings some of the most glorious things in the litera ture of the world. Their finest tale, "Gudrun," is too long to be called a short story, but we have many examples of the mastery which the old Norsemen won in the brief story. There is the old folk-story of "The Werewolf," which, for the sake of variety, we give in a Swedish version. Then there is the longer tale of "Frithiof the Bold," written by an Icelander in the fourteenth century, but full of brave and vivid memories of the wild age of the sea rovers. From the mainland come the ancient tales of "Glob and Alger"—a romance of barbarism—and "The Ness King," which is equally fine.

Tales from Scandinavia

THEN from Iceland and the Northlands we pass to the enchanted city of Bagdad in the days of the good Haroun Alraschid. The *Arabian Nights' Entertainments* is a late collection of all the popular tales of the lands of Islam. It is the *Gesta* of the mediaeval Mohammedan world, but immeasurably superior in romantic qualities and literary power to the popular collection of Christian tales. "The Fisherman and the Genie" comes from India. The tale of "The One-eyed Calender" may have been told to Haroun Alraschid; but long before his time it was known to the popular story-tellers, who still tell it on feast-days, sitting on a bench outside the café, with the townsmen gathered round smoking their long chibouks. These nameless story-tellers are probably the best men at their art that ever lived: they throw themselves with passion into their tales, and the emotions they simulate act on their imagination. Their best story is the now world-famous "Ali Baba and the Forty Thieves," which the Persians handed on to the Arabs. For drama, romance, and unexpected movement this is unequalled. Even the famous Syrian story of "Aladdin" cannot compare with it. Then, in "The Story of the Little Hunchback," we have a grimly amusing tale of the Turkestan city of Kashgar, the plot for which probably came over the passes from India.

The Arabian Nights

THE *Arabian Nights' Entertainments* in its first form was translated from the old Persian into Arabic as early as the tenth century. Then the popular wandering story-tellers worked upon it, and it was cast into its modern shape about four hundred years ago. The Persians still possess many stories that deserve to be included in the great work. Some of them are tales of common life, like the story of "The Pilgrim and the Robbers," in which is related an ordinary adventure of desert travel such as occurs week after week in modern Persia. The next story, "The Kazi of Emessa," probably goes back many hundreds of years. Besides the light it casts on Persian life and manners, it is remarkable for containing the central idea of "The Merchant of Venice" and also the first sketch of Shylock. Very likely the story is the original source of the tale from which Shakespeare drew his plot. "The Envious Vizier" is another Oriental narrative which has spread over Asia and Europe,

Persian Stories

and the German poet, Schiller, has versified one of the European versions. Most of these Persian tales are calculated to amuse a reader as much by their style as by their matter. They are full of extravagant and fanciful rhetorical flourishes, and they afford a first-hand example of the wildly florid diction of the Persian man of letters.

THE next and most important stage in the evolution of the art of the short story brings us back to Europe in the fourteenth century, when the first of the modern story-tellers, Giovanni Boccaccio of Florence, took some of the best things in the *Gesta Romanorum*, and some new tales of his own invention or his own arrangement, and composed his great classic, the *Decameron*. This work is the crown of mediaeval prose fiction. It looks back to the masters of Greek prose, in the vivid and terrible description of the Black Death in Florence, with which the book opens, and which is modelled on Thucydides' picture of Athens under the plague. It resumes and expands the craft of the best tellers of tales in the Middle Ages. It looks forward to the modern methods of art of brief narrative, inspiring Chaucer, Dryden, and later narrative poets with both ideas and form.

Tales from Boccaccio

Boccaccio has a wonderful range of vision and execution. He is the Shakespeare of the short story. He is coarse and delicate, humorous and tragic, superficial and profound by turns. All human life is his province. The fable of "The Three Rings" is worthy of Lucian at his best: it is an old anecdote to which he gives a keener edge and a direct significance. It announces the Renaissance. Then, in his delightful comedy of "Gillette of Narbonne," he has supplied Shakespeare with the plot of "All's Well that ends Well"; and in the strange tragedy of "Tancred of Salerno" he has done one of those rare high things in prose from which great painters as well as great poets have drawn inspiration. The wild love-story of "Cimon and Iphigenia" is almost as fine, and it is truer to fact than is the softened version that Dryden produced. The haunted pine-forest in the next story of "Anastasio" was visited by Byron out of love for the varied art of Boccaccio, who is as masterly in supernatural romance as he is in witty gallantries and tragic horrors.

With a happy sense of contrast he follows this eerie tale of the faithful lover with an ordinary story about the same subject. In "Federigo and the Falcon" he relies entirely upon his knowledge of the human heart, when a strong passion is working in it without anything to oppose it. This natural simple tale of gallantry and generosity is the most winning thing in the *Decameron*. But in popularity it is quite obscured by the story of the patient wife, "Griselda," which is the most famous of all Boccaccio's tales. As a piece of art it is inferior to some of his other stories, but its subject-matter—the fidelity of the married women of Europe—transformed it into a sort of evangel, and the European women prized it passionately, because it defended them against the slanders that, spreading from the Orient, had lowered them to the level of the prisoners of the zenana and harem. " Griselda," like the " Nut-Brown Maid " of our old English ballad, was a splendid weapon for the rehabilitation of the character of the mothers of Christendom.

Sacchetti and Ser Giovanni

FRANCO SACCHETTI, a follower of Boccaccio and a native of Florence, where he was born in 1330, is only one of the little masters of the *conte*. He described the daily life of his native city on its lighter side, and, as his "Blind Beggar of Orvieto" shows, he aimed only at provoking a ripple of amusement at the frailty and cunning of poor human nature. Ser Giovanni, the Florentine, who lived about the same time, is a writer of a higher stamp. He was an old notary with a charming strain of ironic humour; and for grace and sweetness of style he is scarcely inferior to Boccaccio. His first story, "Galgano and Minoccia," is one of the most beautiful triumphs of honour ever recorded. And his vivacious narrative of " Bucciolo and his Tutor " was the foundation of some of the scenes in Shakespeare's " Merry Wives of Windsor."

E. W.

EGYPTIAN
4800 B.C.

THE TALE OF KHAFRI

KING KHAFRI

I WILL tell your Majesty a wonderful thing that happened in the time of your father, King Nebka the Just, when he went to the temple of Ptah, the master of Memphis.

Now, one day His Majesty went into the temple of Ptah and with his train visited the house of his scribe and chief magician, Ubauaner. And the wife of Ubauaner saw a vassal standing behind the King, and as soon as she saw him, her heart longed after him, and she sent her maid to him with a gift of beautiful garments. And the maid brought the man back with her. Now the chief magician had a lodge on his lake, and after several days had passed, the vassal said to the wife of Ubauaner:

" There is a lodge on the lake. If it pleases thee, we will stay there together a little while."

Then the wife of the magician said to the steward who had charge of the lake:

" Let the lodge on the lake be prepared for me."

He did as she said, and she stayed there drinking with the vassal till the sun set. And when evening fell, the man went down into the lake to bathe, and the maid told the steward what had passed between her mistress and the vassal. And when daylight broke over the land and the second day had passed, the steward sought out the chief magician and told him what had happened in the lodge.

" Bring me my casket of ebony inlaid with vermilion containing my book of magic," said the magician to his steward.

And when Ubauaner obtained it, he fashioned a crocodile of wax, seven inches long, and chanted over it something from his book of magic.

" When that vassal goes down to bathe in my lake," he chanted, " then drag him into the depths of the water ! "

He gave the crocodile to the steward and said to him : " When the vassal goes down to the lake to bathe, as he does every day, throw this crocodile of wax into the water behind him ! "

The steward then departed, taking the waxen crocodile with him. And the wife of Ubauaner said to the steward:

"Let the lodge on the lake be prepared for me; for I wish to rest in it."

So the lodge was filled with all good things, and the woman came and made merry there with the vassal. When evening fell, the vassal went, as was his custom every day, to bathe in the lake, and the steward threw the crocodile of wax into the water after him. And the crocodile changed into a crocodile seven ells in length, and seized the vassal and carried him under the water.

Now the chief magician, Ubauaner, stayed seven days with Nebka the Just, King of Upper and Lower Egypt, while the vassal remained under the water without breathing. When the seven days were over, and Nebka the Just came to the temple, the chief magician came before him and said:

"Would it please your Majesty to come and see the marvel that has happened in regard to one of your vassals?"

So His Majesty went with Ubauaner to the lake, and Ubauaner called to the crocodile:

"Bring the man out of the water!"

And the crocodile came from the lake with the vassal, and the magician cried, "Stop!" And he laid a spell on the creature, and made it halt before the King.

"Oh, how terrible this crocodile is!" said Nebka the Just.

But his chief magician stooped and seized the monster, and it became in his hands only a little thing of wax. Ubauaner then told the King what the vassal had done in his house to his wife.

"Take what belongs to thee!" said the King to the crocodile.

And the crocodile plunged into the depths of the lake with its prey, and no man has ever known what became of him.

Then Nebka the Just, King of Upper and Lower Egypt, ordered that the wife of Ubauaner be brought forth to the north side of the palace; and there she was burnt and her ashes were cast into the river.

EGYPTIAN
1300 B.C.

THE TALE OF AHURI

Ziharpto

I AM Ahuri, daughter of the King Mineb-Ptah. The man thou seest by my side is my brother, Nenoferke-Ptah. We were born of the same father and the same mother, and our parents had no other children but us. When the time came for me to marry, I was led before the King at the hour when he was being entertained by his harem. I was greatly adorned, and I was beautiful.

" Look ! Ahuri, our daughter, is grown into a woman ! " said the King. " It is time to marry her. To whom shall we marry her, Ahuri, our daughter ? "

Now I deeply loved my brother, and I desired no other husband but him. I told my mother this, and she sought out the King, and said to him :

" Ahuri, our daughter, loves her brother. Let us marry them together, according to the custom ! "

But when the King heard all the words that my mother said, he replied :

" You have only two children, and yet you wish them to marry each other ! Would it not be better to wed Ahuri to the son of a commander of our foot-soldiers, and marry Nenoferke-Ptah to the daughter of another commander of the army ? "

" So you wish to start quarrelling with me ! " cried the Queen. " Even though I have no other children but these two, is it not the law that brother and sister should marry ? "

" I shall wed the boy to the daughter of one of my generals," said the King. " That will turn more to the benefit of our line ! "

When it was time for the women to appear before Pharaoh, they came and sought for me, and led me to the festival. But I was deeply troubled, and I could not bear myself joyfully as I had done the evening before. Pharaoh said to me :

" Was it not thou who sent to me that foolish message : " Let me marry my brother ? "

" Very well," I said, " marry me to the son of one commander of foot-soldiers, and marry Nenoferke-Ptah to the daughter of another commander of foot-soldiers, and may it turn out well for our family ! "

I laughed and Pharaoh laughed ; and he said to the chief of the royal house :

" Let Ahuri be led this very night to her brother's palace, and let her take with her all kinds of splendid gifts ! "

So I was led as bride to the palace of Nenoferke-Ptah, and Pharaoh commanded his people to bring me a great dowry in gold and silver, and all the folk of the royal house came to me with gifts. Then Nenoferke spent the day feasting with me, and received all the folk of the royal house, and he remained with me that night. And soon I was with child, and the news was carried to Pharaoh and his heart was gladdened by it ; and he took all sorts of precious objects from his royal treasures and sent me very beautiful presents in gold and silver and cloths of fine linen. And when the time came for me to take to my bed, I gave birth to this little child that thou seest before me. He was given the name of Maihet, and he was entered on the registers of the double house of life.

And many days after this, Nenoferke-Ptah seemed to have nothing on earth to do but wander amid the graves of Memphis, reading the writings on the tombs of the Pharaohs and on the gravestones of the scribes of the double house of life. For he took an extreme interest in these writings. And afterwards there was a procession in honour of the god Ptah, and Nenoferke-Ptah went into the temple to pray. But while he was walking behind the procession, deciphering the writings on the chapels of the gods, an old man saw him and laughed.

" Why are you laughing at me ? " said Nenoferke-Ptah.

" I am not laughing at you," said the priest, " but how can I help smiling when you come here to read writings without any power ? If truly you desire to read a writing, come to me, and I will send you to a place where there is that book that Thoth wrote himself with his own divine hand when he came down here with the other gods. There are two formulas written in it. On reciting the first, you will enchant the heavens and the earth, the land of night, the mountains and the waters. You will understand what the birds of the air and the reptiles say, and you will see the fishes of the abyss, for a divine force will rest on the water above them. If you read the second formula, then, though you are in your grave, you will recover the form that you had on earth. Yes ! you will even see again the sun rise over heaven with his divine train, and the moon in the form she puts on when she really appears ! "

" By the life of the King ! " said Nenoferke-Ptah to the priest, " tell me all that you wish for, and I will give it to you, if you lead me to the spot where this book is."

" Give me, then, a hundred pieces of silver for my burial, and have two coffins made for me as for a rich priest ! "

Nenoferke-Ptah ordered a page to give the priest a hundred pieces of silver, and had the two coffins made for the old man.

" The book in question," said the priest then, " is in the middle of the Nile at Coptos, in an iron chest. In the iron chest is a bronze box. In the bronze box is a box of cinnamon wood. In the box of cinnamon wood is a box of ivory and ebony. In the box of ivory and ebony is a silver box ; in the silver box is a golden box, and in this is the book. There is a vast mass of serpents, scorpions, and all kinds of reptiles round the chest containing the book, and an immortal snake is twined about it."

So astounded was Nenoferke-Ptah at hearing these words that he did not know in what part of the world he was. He left the temple and told me all that had happened.

" I shall go to Coptos," he said, " and bring back the book. Then I shall not leave the northern land again."

But I rose against the priest.

" Pray Amon to guard thee," I said, " for what thou hast said to Nenoferke-Ptah. For thou hast led me into this feud ; thou hast brought this war upon me ; and I find the spirit of the land of Thebes an enemy of my happiness ! "

I raised my hand against my brother so that he should not go to Coptos ; but he would not listen to me, but went before Pharaoh and related all that the priest had said.

" What is the wish of your heart ? " said Pharaoh.

" To be given the royal ship, all equipped. I will take Ahuri, my sister, and Maihet, her baby, to the south with me : I will bring back this book, and then I will never leave this land."

He was given the ship, well equipped, and we went on it, and made the voyage to Coptos.

And the chief priest and the priests of Isis of Coptos came down before us : and the men went without delay and stood in front of my brother, and their women came down and stood before me. We landed and went to the temple of Isis and of Harpocrates, and Nenoferke-Ptah had a bull, a goose, and wine brought, and presented an offering and a libation before Isis and Harpocrates. Then we were led into a house that was very beautiful and full of all sorts of good things. My brother spent four days of entertainment with the priests, while their wives held festival with me.

The morning after, Nenoferke-Ptah had a large quantity of pure wax brought before him. With it he fashioned a boat, filled with rowers and sailors, and over them he chanted a spell and gave them life and breath. He filled the royal ship with sand, and taking leave of me, he went on board. And I fixed my biding-place on the water of Coptos, saying, " I will know what happens to him ! "

" Rowers," he said, " row for me to the spot where the book is ! "

And they rowed for him. night and day ; and in three days he reached the spot, and threw out the sand and made an empty place in the river. He found a vast mass of serpents, scorpions, and all kind of reptiles round a chest of iron, and he saw a snake coiled around the chest. Chanting a spell, he took the life out of the serpents, scorpions, and reptiles. Then he attacked the great snake and killed it. It came to life again in a new form ; and again he attacked it and killed it. Once more the snake came to life ; but he cut it into two halves and placed sand in between each portion, and the snake died, and did not resume its former shape.

Nenoferke-Ptah then went to the spot where the chest was, and saw it was made of iron. Opening it, he found a box of bronze. Opening this, he found a box of cinnamon wood. Opening this, he found a box of ivory and ebony. Opening this, he found a box of silver, and opening this, he found a casket of gold with a book within it.

He drew the book from the golden casket, and recited the formula that was written in it. He enchanted the heavens and the earth, the land of night, the mountains and the waters. He understood all that was said by the birds of the air, the fish of the water, and the beasts of the heights. He recited the other formula of the writing, and he saw the sun rise into heaven with his train of gods, and the ascending moon, and the stars in their form. And he saw the fishes of the abyss, for a divine power rested on the water above them ; and chanting a spell on the water he made it resume its early form.

Then embarking once more, he said to the rowers, " Row for me to the place where Ahuri is ! "

They rowed for him, night and day; and in three days he came to the spot at which I was, and found me sitting by the water of Coptos. I did not drink: I did not eat: I never stirred: I was like a person who had come to the house of death.

"By the life of the King!" I said to Nenoferke-Ptah, "let me see this book, for which we have taken all these pains!"

He put the book in my hand. I read a formula of the writing in it, and I enchanted the heavens and the earth, the land of night, the mountains and the waters. I understood all that was said by the birds of the air, the fishes of the abyss, and the four-footed beasts. I recited another formula of the writing, and I saw the sun appear in the sky with his train of gods, and the risen moon, and all the stars of heaven in their form. I saw the fishes of the water; for there was a divine power that rested on the water above them.

As I could not write very much, in comparison with my brother, who was an accomplished scribe and a very learned man, he called for a piece of virgin papyrus, and wrote on it all the words there were in the book; and he soaked it in beer and let it all dissolve in a drink. Then he drank it up, and thus knew everything there was in the writing.

The same day we returned to Coptos, and held a feast before Isis and Harpocrates. Then we returned to the ship, and sailed away to the north. But Thoth knew what had happened to his book, and he hastened to plead before the sun-god, Ra.

"My law and my canon are now with Nenoferke-Ptah, son of King Mineb-Ptah!" he said. "He has penetrated into my lodge and pillaged it, and taken my casket with my book of incantations, and killed my watchman that guarded the casket."

"He is thine, he and all that is his—all!" said the great god, making a divine power come down from the heavens, and saying, "Let not Nenoferke-Ptah arrive in safety at Memphis, nor any that is with him!"

And at that very moment my child Maihet crawled from under the awning of the royal ship and fell into the river, fulfilling the good pleasure of Ra. All those on deck cried out. My brother came out of the cabin and recited a spell on the baby and made him arise; for there was a divine power resting on the water above him. Again he said a spell over the little child, and made him relate all that had happened to him, and the accusation that Thoth had laid before Ra.

We returned to Coptos with our dead son, and took him to the embalming-house, and placed people by him for the funeral ceremonies; we had him embalmed as became a royal prince, and we laid him in his coffin in the cemetery of Coptos.

"Let us go!" said my brother. "Let us not delay to return before the King hears what has befallen us, and his heart becomes troubled."

We returned to the ship and sailed away and came to the place where our little child Maihet had fallen in the river. I came forth from under the awning of the royal ship, and fell into the water, and fulfilled the good pleasure of Ra. And all who were on deck gave a loud cry.

Nenoferke-Ptah was told, and he came from under the awning, and recited a spell over me; and a divine force rested upon the water, and made me rise up. Drawing me out of the river, he said another spell over me, and made me relate all that happened and the accusation that Thoth had laid before Ra.

My brother then returned to Coptos with me, and led me to the house of the dead, and put people around me for the funeral services, and had me embalmed as became my high greatness, and then laid me in the tomb where my little child Maihet already reposed. Then sailing away, he came to the place where we had fallen in the river. There he talked to his own heart.

"Would it not be better," he said, "to go to Coptos and stay with them? For if I return to Memphis, and Pharaoh questions me about his children, what shall I say to him? Can I tell him, 'I took your children with me towards the land of Thebes, and I killed them and I live, and I return to Memphis still living'?"

He called for a piece of fine royal linen which belonged to him, and he made a magic band out of it. In this band he tied the book, and put it on his breast, and there fixed it firmly. Then he came from under the awning of the royal ship, and fell into the water, and fulfilled the good pleasure of Ra.

"Oh, what a great misfortune!" cried the sailors. "What a lamentable misfortune! He is gone, the excellent scribe, the wise man who had no equal!"

The ship of Pharaoh sailed on, before anybody knew where Nenoferke-Ptah lay. It arrived at Memphis, and Pharaoh was told, and he came down before the ship. He was in a mantle of mourning; and all the soldiers of Memphis were in mantles of mourning, and the great priest of Ptah, and the priests, and all the courtiers. And lo! they saw

Nenoferke-Ptah, caught against the helm oars of the royal ship, by reason of his excellent knowledge of magic. When he was raised from the water, the book was seen on his breast.

" Take that book away from his breast ! " said Pharaoh.

" Oh, our great master—may thy life be as long as Ra's !—he was an excellent scribe, a man of much wisdom was Nenoferke-Ptah," cried the courtiers and the priests of Ptah, and the high priest.

And, for fear, the King did not touch the book of Thoth. He placed his son for sixteen days in the embalming-house : he clad him in linen for thirty-five days, and shrouded him for seventy days ; and then had him laid in his tomb amid the houses of rest. Such were the misfortunes that befell us by reason of the book of Thoth.

INDIAN
Circa 560 B.C.

THE MONKEY AND THE QUEEN'S JEWELS

THE BUDDHA

ONCE on a time, when Brahmadatta was reigning in Benares, the future Buddha, having perfected his education, became one of the King's Ministers. One day the King, with a large following, went into his pleasaunce, and, after walking about the woods, felt a desire to disport himself in the water. So he went down into the royal tank and sent for his harem. The women of the harem, removing the jewels from their heads and necks and so forth, laid them aside with their upper garments in boxes under the charge of female slaves, and then went down into the water. Now, as the Queen was taking off her jewels and ornaments, and laying them with her upper robe on a box, she was watched by a female monkey, which was hidden in the branches of a tree hard by. Conceiving a longing to wear the Queen's pearl necklace, this monkey watched for the slave in charge to be off her guard. At first the girl kept looking all about her in order to keep the jewels safe; but as time wore on she began to nod. As soon as the monkey saw this, quick as the wind she jumped down, and quick as the wind she was up the tree again, with the pearls round her own neck. Then, for fear the other monkeys should see it, she hid the string of pearls in a hole in the tree, and sat on guard over her spoils as demurely as though nothing had happened. By and by the slave awoke, and, terrified at finding the jewels gone, saw nothing else to do but to scream out, "A man has run off with the Queen's pearl necklace."

Up ran the guards from every side, and, hearing this story, told it to the King.

"Catch the thief," said His Majesty; and away went the guards, searching high and low for the thief in the pleasaunce.

Hearing the din, a poor superstitious rustic took to his heels in alarm.

"There he goes," cried the guards, catching sight of the runaway; and they followed him up till they caught him, and with blows demanded what he meant by stealing such precious jewels.

Thought he, " If I deny the charge, I shall die with the beating I shall get from these ruffians. I'd better say I took it." So he confessed to the theft and was hauled off a prisoner to the King.

" Did you take those precious jewels ? " asked the King.

" Yes, your Majesty."

" Where are they now ? "

" Please, your Majesty, I'm a poor man ; I've never in my life owned anything, even a bed or a chair, of any value,—much less a jewel. It was the Treasurer who made me take that valuable necklace ; and I took it and gave it to him. He knows all about it."

Then the King sent for the Treasurer, and asked whether the rustic had passed the necklace on to him.

" Yes, sire," was the answer.

" Where is it, then ? "

" I gave it to your Majesty's Chaplain."

Then the Chaplain was sent for, and interrogated in the same way. And he said he had given it to the Chief Musician, who in his turn said he had given it to a courtesan as a present. But she, being brought before the King, utterly denied ever having received it.

Whilst the five were thus being questioned, the sun set.

" It's too late now," said the King ; " we will look into this to-morrow." So he handed the five over to his Ministers and went back into the city.

Hereupon the future Buddha, or Bodhisatta, fell a-thinking. " These jewels," thought he, " were lost inside the grounds, whilst the rustic was outside. There was a strong guard at the gates, and it was impossible for any one inside to get away with the necklace. I do not see how any one, whether inside or out, could have managed to secure it. The truth is, this poor wretched fellow must have said he gave it to the Treasurer merely in order to save his own skin ; and the Treasurer must have said he gave it to the Chaplain in the hope that he would get off if he could mix the Chaplain up in the matter. Further, the Chaplain must have said he gave it to the Chief Musician because he thought the latter would make the time pass merrily in prison ; whilst the Chief Musician's object in implicating the courtesan was simply to solace himself with her company during imprisonment. Not one of the whole five has anything to do with the theft. On the other hand, the grounds swarm with monkeys, and the necklace must have got into the hands of one of the female monkeys."

When he had arrived at this conclusion, the Bodhisatta went to the King with the request that the suspects might be handed over to him, and that he might be allowed to examine personally into the matter.

"By all means, my wise friend," said the King, "examine into it."

Then the Bodhisatta sent for his servants and told them where to lodge the five prisoners, saying, "Keep strict watch over them; listen to everything they say, and report it all to me." And his servants did as he bade them.

As the prisoners sat together, the Treasurer said to the rustic, "Tell me, you wretch, where you and I ever met before this day; tell me when you gave me that necklace."

"Worshipful sir," said the other, "it has never been mine to own aught so valuable even as a stool or bedstead that wasn't rickety. I thought that with your help I should get out of this trouble, and that's why I said what I did. Be not angry with me, my lord."

Said the Chaplain in his turn to the Treasurer, "How then came you to pass on to me what this fellow had never given to you?"

"I only said so because I thought that if you and I, both high officers of state, stand together, we can soon put the matter right."

"Brahmin," now said the Chief Musician to the Chaplain, "when, pray, did you give the jewels to me?"

"I only said I did," answered the Chaplain, "because I thought you would help to make the time pass more agreeably."

Lastly the courtesan said, "Oh, you wretch of a musician, you know you never visited me, nor I you. So when could you have given me the necklace, as you say?"

"Why be angry, my dear?" said the Musician; "we five have got to keep house together for a bit; so let us put a cheerful face on it and be happy together."

This conversation being reported to the Bodhisatta by his agents, he felt convinced the five were all innocent of the robbery, and that a female monkey had taken the necklace. "And I must find a means to make her drop it," said he to himself. So he had a number of bead necklaces made. Next he had a number of monkeys caught and turned loose again, with strings of beads on their necks, wrists, and ankles. Meantime, the guilty monkey kept sitting in the trees watching her treasure. Then the Bodhisatta ordered a number of men carefully to observe every monkey in the grounds, till they saw one wearing the missing pearl necklace, and then frighten her into dropping it.

Tricked out in their new splendour, the other monkeys strutted about till they came to the real thief, before whom they flaunted their finery. Jealousy overcoming her prudence, she exclaimed, " They're only beads ! " and put on her own necklace of real pearls. This was at once seen by the watchers, who promptly made her drop the necklace, which they picked up and brought to the Bodhisatta. He took it to the King, saying, " Here, sire, is the necklace. The five prisoners are innocent ; it was a female monkey in the pleasaunce that took it."

" How came you to find that out ? " asked the King ; " and how did you manage to get possession of it again ? "

Then the Bodhisatta told the whole story, and the King thanked the Bodhisatta, saying, " You are the right man in the right place." And he uttered this stanza in praise of the Bodhisatta :

For war men crave the hero's might,
For counsel sage sobriety,
Boon comrades for their jollity,
But judgment when in parlous plight.

Over and above these words of praise and gratitude, the King showered treasures upon the Bodhisatta like a storm-cloud pouring rain from the heavens. After following the Bodhisatta's counsels through a long life spent in charity and good works, the King passed away to fare thereafter according to his deserts.

THE TALE OF THE PRINCESS SAMBULA

The Buddha

ONCE upon a time King Brahmadatta had a son named Sotthisena, and when he had come of age the King set him up as viceroy. His chief consort, Sambula by name, was extremely beautiful, and gifted with so radiant a form that she appeared like a lamp-flame shining in a sheltered spot. By and by leprosy showed itself in Sotthisena, and the physicians failed to cure it. When the sore discharged he became so loathsome that in his depression he cried:

" What is my kingdom to me ? I shall perish without a friend in the wilderness."

And, bidding them tell the King, he left his harem and departed. Sambula, though he made many attempts to stop her, refused to return, saying, " I will watch over you, my lord, in the forest," went forth from the city with him.

On entering the forest, he built a hut of leaves and took up his abode in a shady and well-watered spot, where wild fruit abounded. How then did the royal lady watch over him ? Why, she rose up early in the morning, swept out his hermitage, set some water for him to drink, furnished him with a tooth-stick and water to wash his mouth, and when his mouth was cleansed she ground various simples and anointed his sores, and gave him luscious fruits to eat ; when he had rinsed his mouth and washed his hands, she saluted him and said, " Be earnest in well-doing, my lord."

Then taking a basket, a spade, and a hook, she went into the forest to gather wild fruit, and she brought and set it on one side, and fetching water in a jar she with various powders and clay washed Sotthisena and again offered him wild fruit. And when he had finished his meal, she brought him scented water and herself partook of the fruit. Then she arranged a board with a coverlet, and as he lay down on it she bathed his feet, and after dressing and cleaning his head and back and feet, she came and lay down by the side of the bed. In this way did she watch over her lord.

One day, as she was bringing fruit from the forest, she espied a mountain cave, and putting down the basket from her head, she stood on the edge of the cave, and stepping down to bathe, she rubbed her body all over with yellow dye and took a bath. After washing herself she climbed up again and put on her bark garment and stood on the edge of the pool. And the whole forest was lighted up with the radiance that was shed from her person.

At that moment a goblin, going forth to find his prey, caught sight of her, and falling in love with her, he repeated a couple of stanzas :

" Tied to the spot and trembling as in fear,
Who in this rocky cave is standing here ?
Tell us, I pray, O slender-waisted dame,
Who may thy kinsmen be, and what thy name.

" Who art thou, lady, ever fair and bright,
And what thy birth that thou canst flood with light
This grove, fit home of every beast of prey ?
An ogre, I to thee due homage pay."

On hearing what he said, she replied in three stanzas :

" Prince Sotthisena, know full well, is heir to Kāsi throne,
And I, this Prince's wedded wife, as Sambula am known.

" Videha's royal son is sick and in the forest lies;
Alone I tend him, mad with pain, or else he surely dies.

" This savoury bit of venison I picked up in the wood,
And bear it to my lord to-day, now faint for want of food."

This was followed by stanzas spoken alternately by the goblin and the lady :

" What good is this sick lord of thine, O Sambula, to thee ?
No wife, but nurse is what he craves. I will thy husband be."

" With sorrow worn, a wretch forlorn, no beauty can I claim,
If thou art fain a bride to gain, go woo some fairer dame."

" Four hundred wives have I to grace my home on yonder hill ;
O lady, deign o'er them to reign, and each fond wish fulfil.
Fair maid so bright with golden light, whate'er is dear to thee
Is mine to give, so come and live a life of joy with me.
But if denied to me as bride, thou art my lawful prey,
And wilt be good to serve as food to break my fast to-day."

(That ogre grim with his seven tufts inspiring dread alarm,
Found helpless Sambula astray and seized her by the arm.

Thus held by him, that ogre grim, her lustful, cruel foe,
She still deplored her absent lord, nor e'er forgot his woe.)

" No grief to me that I should be this hateful ogre's prey,
But that the love of my dear lord from me should fall away.
No gods are here, but absent far they flee,
Nor any guardians of the world I see,
To check the course of outrage and suppress
All acts of unrestrained licentiousness."

Then was the abode of Sakka shaken by the efficacy of her virtue, and his throne of yellow marble showed signs of heat. Sakka, on reflection, discovered the cause, and, taking his thunderbolt, he came with all speed, and, standing above the goblin, spoke another stanza :

" 'Mongst women folk the chief in fame,
She's wise and perfect, bright as flame,
Shouldst thou eat her, thy skull be riven,
O goblin, into fragments seven.
So harm her not ; let her go free,
For a devoted wife is she."

On hearing this the goblin let Sambula go. Sakka thought, " This goblin will be guilty of the same thing again," and so he bound him with celestial chains and let him loose on the third mountain from thence, that he might not return ; and after earnestly exhorting the royal lady, he departed to his own abode. And the Princess, after sunset, by the light of the moon reached the hermitage.

There, to explain the matter, she recited the following eight stanzas :

" Escaped from ogre, to her hut she fled,
As bird returning finds its fledglings dead,
Or cow, robbed of her calf, laments an empty shed.

" Thus Sambula, of royal fame, made moan,
Wild-eyed and helpless, in the wood, alone.

" Hail, priests and Brahmins, righteous sages too,
Deserted, I for refuge fly to you.

" All hail, ye lions and ye tigers fell,
And other beasts that in the woodland dwell.

" All hail, ye grasses, herbs and plants that creep,
All hail, ye forests green and mountains steep.

" All hail to Night, bedecked with stars on high,
Dark as blue lotus of the deepest dye.

"All hail to Ganges: mother of rivers she,
Known amongst men as famed Bhagirathi.

"Hail, Himavat, of all the mountains king,
Huge rocky pile, o'ertopping everything."

Regarding her, as she uttered this lamentation, Sotthisena thought, "She is overdoing her lamentation: I do not quite know what it all means. If she were acting thus for love of me, her heart would be broken. I will put her to the test."

And he went and sat at the door of his hut

She, still lamenting, came to the door, and, making a low obeisance, said, "Where has my lord been?"

"Lady," he said, "on other days you have never come at this hour; to-day you are very late," and in the form of a question he spoke this stanza:

"Illustrious lady, why so late to-day?
What favoured lover led to this delay?"

Then she made answer, "My lord, I was returning with my fruit when I beheld a goblin, and he fell in love with me, and seizing me by the hand, he cried, 'Unless you obey my words, I will eat you alive.' And at that moment, sorrowing for you only, I uttered this lament"; and she repeated this stanza:

"Seized by my foe, I, full of woe, these words to him did say,
'No grief to me that I should be a hateful ogre's prey,
But that the love of my dear lord from me should fall away!'"

Then she told him the rest of the story, saying:

"So when I was seized by this goblin, and was unable to make him let me go, I acted so as to excite the attention of the god. Then Sakka came, thunderbolt in hand, and, standing in the air, he threatened the goblin and made him release me. And he bound him with magic chains and deposited him on the third mountain range from here, and so departed. Thus was I saved by means of Sakka."

Sotthisena, on hearing this, replied:

"Well, lady, it may be so. With womenkind it is hard to discover the truth. In the Himalaya region dwell many foresters, ascetics, and magicians. Who shall believe you?". And so saying, he repeated a stanza:

"You jades are ever by far too clever,
Truth among such is a great rarity,
Ways of the sex are enough to perplex,
E'en as the course of a fish in the sea."

On hearing his words, she said :

" My lord, though you do not believe me, by virtue of the truth I speak I will heal you." So, filling a pot of water and performing an Act of Truth, she poured the water on his head and spoke this stanza :

> " May Truth for aye my shelter be,
> As I love no man more than thee,
> And by this Act of Truth, I pray,
> May thy disease be healed to-day."

When she had thus performed an Act of Truth, no sooner was the water sprinkled over Sotthisena than the leprosy straightway left him, as it were copper rust washed in some acid. After staying a few days there, they departed from the forest, and, coming to Benares, entered the park.

The King, being apprised of their arrival, went to the park, and there and then bade the royal umbrella to be raised over Sotthisena, and ordered that Sambula, by sprinkling, should be raised to the position of chief Queen. Then conducting them into the city, he himself adopted the ascetic life and took up his abode in the park, but he still constantly took his meals in the palace.

And Sotthisena merely conferred on Sambula the rank of chief consort, but no honour was paid her, and he ignored her very existence and took his pleasure with other women.

Sambula, through jealousy of her rivals, grew thin and pale of countenance and her veins stood out upon her body. One day when her father-in-law, the ascetic, came to have a meal, to get rid of her grief she came to him when he had finished eating, and saluting him, sat down on one side.

On seeing her in this languid condition, he repeated a stanza :

> " Seven hundred elephants by night and day
> Are guarding thee, all ready for the fray,
> Hundreds of archers shielding thee from harm ;
> Whence come the foes to fill thee with alarm ? "

On hearing his words she said, " Your son, my lord, is no longer the same to me," and she repeated five stanzas :

> " Fair as a lotus are the maids he loves,
> Their swan-like voice his deepest passion moves,
> And as he listens to their measured strain,
> In his affections I no longer reign.
>
> " In human shape but like to nymphs divine,
> Adorned with ornaments of gold they shine,

Of perfect form the noble maidens lie
In graceful pose, to charm the royal eye.

"If I once more might wander in the wood,
To glean a portion for his daily food,
Once more I should a husband's love regain,
And quit the court in forest realms to reign.

"A woman may in softest robes be drest,
And be with food in rich abundance blest,
Fair though she be, yet if an unloved wife,
Best fix a rope and put an end to life.

"Yea, the poor wretch on bed of straw that lies,
If she find favour in her husband's eyes,
Enjoys a happiness unknown to one,
Rich in all else, but poor in love alone."

When she had thus explained to the ascetic the cause of her thus pining away, he summoned the King and said :

" Dear Sotthisena, when you were crushed by the disease of leprosy and hid yourself in the forest, she went with you and ministered to your wants, and by the power of truth healed your sickness, and now after she has been the means of your being established on the throne, you do not even know the place of her sitting and uprising ; this is very wrong of you. An act of treachery to a friend like this is a sin," and reproving his son, he repeated this stanza :

"A loving wife is ever hard to find,
As is a man that to his wife is kind :
Thy wife was virtuous and loving too ;
Do thou, O King, to Sambula be true."

After he had thus reproved his son, he got up and went away. The King, when his father was gone, called for Sambula and said, " My dear, forgive the wrong I have done you this long time. Henceforth I confer on you all power," and he repeated the final stanza :

"Shouldst thou, with wealth in great abundance blest,
Still pine away, by jealousy opprest,
I and these maidens, creatures of thy hand,
Will be obedient to thy command."

Thenceforth the pair lived happily together, and after a life of charity and good works they departed to fare according to their deeds. The ascetic, after entering upon ecstatic meditation, passed to the heaven of Brahma.

THE ASS IN THE LION'S SKIN

The Buddha

IN the days when Brahmadatta was King of Benares, the future Buddha was born the son of a peasant ; and when he grew up he gained his living by tilling the ground.

And at that time a hawker used to go from village to village, selling goods that he carried on an ass. And whenever he was near a village, he took his pack from the back of his ass, and dressed the beast in a lion's skin, and turned it loose to feed in the fields of rice and barley. And when the watchmen in the fields saw the ass amid the grain, they dared not drive it away, thinking it was a lion.

One day the hawker was stopping by a certain village, and while his own breakfast was cooking, he dressed the ass in the lion's skin and turned it loose in a barley field. The watchmen did not dare to approach the animal, but ran home, crying out the news. Then all the villagers came forth with weapons in their hands, and blowing chanks and beating drums, they went as near as they dared to the barley field, and shouted. And being frightened by the noise the ass roared back—but it was the bray of a donkey !

And when the Buddha knew what sort of animal it was he made the first verse :

" This is not a lion roaring,
Nor a tiger nor a panther—
Only a poor wretched donkey,
Braying in a lion's skin ! "

And when the villagers saw that the creature was only an ass, they beat it till they broke its bones, and carrying off the lion's skin, they returned home. Then the hawker came from his hiding-place, and seeing into what a plight the ass had fallen, he made the second verse :

" All your life, you foolish donkey,
Could you feed on rice and barley,
Dressed up as a mighty lion—
But your braying broke the spell ! "

And while he was still speaking, the donkey died on the spot.

THE TALKATIVE TORTOISE

THE BUDDHA

IN the days when Brahmadatta was King of Benares, the future Buddha was born the son of a minister, and when he grew to manhood he became the King's counsellor.

Now the King was very talkative: while he was speaking, no one else could put in a word. And the Buddha wished to cure this talkativeness and was always casting about for some means of doing so.

At that time a tortoise was living in a lake in the Himalaya Mountains, and two young wild ducks, who came to feed there, made friends with him. And one day, when they were talking together in friendly fashion, the ducks said to the tortoise:

"Friend tortoise! we live at the Cave of Gold on Beautiful Mountain in the Himalaya country. It is a delightful place! Will you come there with us?"

"But how can I get there?"

"We can take you, if only you keep quiet and say not a word to anybody. Can you hold your tongue?"

"Yes, of course I can. Take me with you."

"That is well," said the ducks.

And making the tortoise grip hard on a stick with his teeth, they took the two ends in their beaks and flew high up in the air.

And some villagers saw the strange sight, and shouted:

"Look at those two ducks carrying a tortoise along on a stick!"

And the angry tortoise opened his mouth to say:

"If my friends choose to carry me, what is that to do with you, you miserable slaves!"

So just when the swift flight of the wild ducks had brought him over the King's palace in Benares, he let go the stick he was biting, and fell into the courtyard, and there broke in two. And everybody began to cry out in wonder:

"A tortoise has fallen from the sky in the royal courtyard and broken in two."

The King went to the spot with his courtiers, and took the Buddha with him.

" Tell me, my teacher," he said to the Buddha, " how this tortoise has fallen from the sky ? "

Then the Buddha thought to himself :

" Long have I sought for some means of admonishing the King. This tortoise must have been a friend to the wild ducks, and they must have made him bite on the stick, and have flown up into the air to carry him to the mountains. And being one of those creatures who cannot hold his tongue when some one else is talking, he must have wanted to say something, and letting go the stick he must have fallen from the sky and lost his life."

And then turning to the King he said aloud :

" Here, in truth, O King ! you see how the chatterbox, whose words have no end, comes to grief."

And he made these verses :

" The tortoise held the stick between his teeth,
While his friends carried him along the sky :
But opening his mouth to utter speech,
By one word out of season was he killed.

" Behold him then, O excellent in strength !
And speak wise words in measure and due time !
You see how, by his talking overmuch,
The wretched tortoise talked himself to death ! "

The King saw that the lesson was meant for him, and said :

" My teacher ! are you speaking of us ? "

And the Buddha then spoke openly :

" O great King ! " he said, " any man who talks beyond measure—king or peasant—meets at last with some misfortune like to this ! "

And from that time the King controlled himself and became a man of few words.

THE JUDGMENT OF THE BUDDHA

The Buddha

ONE day a woman took her child to the bathing-pond of the Buddha. And after bathing the child, she went down into the water to bathe herself.

Then a ghoul saw the child and craved to eat it. And taking the form of a woman, she came to the bathing-pond.

"This is a very beautiful child!" she said to the mother. "Is it yours?"

And when she learnt that it was, she asked if she might nurse it: and the mother agreeing, she nursed it a little while and then hastened away with it.

But the mother saw her, and ran after her, and caught hold of her, crying out:

"What are you doing with my child?"

"Where did you get the child from?" said the ghoul. "It is mine!"

And quarrelling loudly, they passed the Judgment Hall of the Buddha, and hearing the noise, he enquired into the dispute and asked them if they would abide by his decision. And they agreed. He ordered a line to be drawn on the ground, and told the ghoul to seize the child by the arms and the mother to take it by the legs:

"The child shall be hers who drags it over the line," he said.

But the child cried when its tender body was pulled, and the mother saw how her young one suffered, and it grieved her till her heart nigh broke. And letting go, she stood by weeping.

Then said the Buddha to the bystanders:

"Who is it that have hearts tender to babes? Those who have borne children, or those who have not?"

"Sir!" they answered, "the hearts of mothers are tender."

"Which of these two then is the mother?" he said. "She who has the child in her arms, or she who let it go?"

"She who let it go is the mother," they said.

"Then do you all think that the other is a thief?"

" Sir, we cannot tell," they said.

" Verily," he said, " this is a ghoul, who took the child to eat it."

" Oh, sir ! " they cried, " how did you know that ? "

" Because," he said, " her red eyes did not wink, and she knew no fear and had no pity." And turning to the thief he said, " Who are you ? "

" Lord ! I am a ghoul," she replied.

" Why did you take away this child ? " he asked.

" I desired to eat it, O my lord," she said.

" O foolish woman ! " thus he rebuked her, " for the sins in your former birth have you been born an evil spirit, and yet you still sin ! "

And laying a vow upon her to keep the five commandments, he let her go. But the mother of the child glorified the future Buddha, and said, " O my lord ! O great physician ! long life to you ! " Then she went away with her babe clasped to her breast.

INDIAN

Circa 300 B.C.

THE BRAHMAN OF VAIN DREAMS

THE PANCHA-TANTRA

CLOSE to the town of Nirmala Patna lies an *agrahra* called Darmapuri. There lived a Brahman named Soma Sarma, who for children had only one son. Yagna Sarma, as the young man was called, followed his studies with great success, and after he had become familiar with every kind of knowledge taught to persons of his condition, he sought a living in wandering about the neighbouring country, where his learning and his winning manner enabled him to find everywhere an abundance of alms which he shared with his family.

One day, having learnt that a neighbouring Brahman was giving a feast to celebrate the anniversary of the death of some kinsmen, he hastened to the house to take part in the feasting. Although the guests were many in number, they each received more than enough to satisfy them, and the feast was of the most splendid sort.

When it was over, Yagna Sarma, who had taken care to fill his belly well, turned down the road to his home. On the way, he heard that another Brahman, some distance away, was also giving that same day a feast for the same object as that at which he had already assisted. So he hastened to the second festival, and arrived at the moment when the guests were sitting in a file to be served. The master of the house saw him appear, and knowing that he had already taken part in the first feast given that day, and that he had eaten more than any other guest of the costly foods placed before him, he began to laugh. And looking with a mocking face at Yagna Sarma, he said to him :

" After having done so well at the feast given this morning, do you think you will find sufficient empty space in your belly to do honour to this feast ? "

But Yagna Sarma was not troubled by this reproach, and sitting down very quietly with the other guests, he ate with as good an appetite as if he had been fasting all day.

When the feast was over, the master of the house gave his guests gifts of *ghee* and butter and flour to take home with them. Yagna Sarma received his share, and put it in some earthen pots, and departed.

Having gone some distance, he stopped to consider the gifts he had received, and putting the pots in a row, he looked at them with great satisfaction :

" Here I am now at my ease," he said. " To-day I have a good bellyful ; to-morrow I can go without eating. But what shall I do with all these provisions ? I must sell them. And then what shall I do with the money I get ? I must buy a she-goat with it. And this she-goat ? She will bring forth kids for me, and in a little time I shall have a flock of them. I sell my flock, and with my money I buy a cow and a mare. My mare and my cow produce calves and foals, and these I sell for a good price, and in this way I find myself a man of considerable wealth. Everybody is talking about my fortune, one of my neighbouring Brahmans gives me his daughter. After the marriage, my wife is led to my house—great feasts given by my father-in-law and many presents. My wife soon reaches the age of child-bearing, and gives me a numerous posterity. My children must have the best teachers. I wish them to learn at an early age the sacred verses and the high knowledge. Rich as I am, it is also becoming that my wife and children should have an abundance of coloured garments and jewels of every sort.

" But if my wife, in all this happiness, forgets her duties ! If she takes it into her head to go out of the house from time to time, without my permission, and to visit neighbouring houses for the pleasure of chattering with other women ! Just look at the state of things ! During her absence, the children she has left all alone, amuse themselves by running about wildly. Look ! they are going to run under the feet of the cows, and get lame for life ! Come ! Run to the house ! Ah, Great Gods ! What do I see ? My youngest child is injured ! Thou ! imprudent woman, thou ! art the cause of this ! Was ever so careless a creature seen ? But thou shalt answer for it ! I will teach thee to be more thoughtful in the future ! Take that ! . . ."

And saying these words, Yagna Sarma gripped his pilgrim staff, and, brandishing it about with all his might, he struck the earthen pots in which were his *ghee* and milk and flour. So his provisions were scattered and lost. The fool overturned in a moment the foundation of his vain dreams. When he saw all his hopes vanish quicker than they had been formed, he groaned in secret over his shortsightedness, and, covered with shame, turned home.

INDIAN
600 A.D.

THE RAJAH'S SON AND THE MERCHANT'S WIFE

THE HITOPADESA

IN the country of Kanya-kubja there was a Rajah whose name was Veera-sena, by whom his royal son, by name Tungavala, had been appointed Yuva-rajah over the city of Veera-pura. He was young and possessed of great riches. Once upon a time, as he was walking about his own city, he took notice of a certain merchant's wife, who was in the very prime of youth, and so beautiful that she was, as it were, the standard of conquest of Makara-ketu. She also, whose name was Lavanyavatee, having observed him, her breast was rent in pieces by the destructive arrows of the god of love, and she gladly became of one mind with him. It is said:

" Unto women no man is to be found disagreeable, no one agreeable. They may be compared to a heifer on the plain that still longeth for fresh grass.

" Infidelity, violence, deceit, envy, extreme avariciousness, a total want of good qualities are the innate faults of womankind."

The young Rajah being returned to his palace, with a heart quite occupied with love, sent a female messenger to her, to whose words having attended, Lavanyavatee made such a reply as was calculated to deceive. Said she:

" I am faithful to my husband, and I am not accustomed even to touch another man; for 'She is not worthy to be called a wife in whom the husband delighteth not. The husband is the asylum of women; and of his honour the fire beareth testimony.

" 'The beauty of the Kokila is his voice; the beauty of a wife is constancy to her husband; the beauty of the ill-favoured is science; the beauty of the penitent is patience.

" 'She is a wife who is clever in the house; she is a wife who is fruitful in children; she is a wife who is the soul of her husband; she is a wife who is obedient to her husband.'

" And according to this doctrine, I make it a rule to do whatever the lord of my life directs, without examination."

To this the messenger replied, " It is right."

And Lavanyavatee observed that it was even so.

The messenger, having heard the whole of what Lavanyavatee had to say, reported it to Tungavala, who observed that he would invite her with that dear husband of hers, and, in his presence, pay her great attention and respect. To this the messenger replied:

"This is impracticable. Let art be used; for it is said, '*That which cannot be effected by force may be achieved by cunning.' An elephant was killed by a jackal, by going over a swampy place.*"

Then the young Rajah, by the advice of his messenger, sent for the husband of Lavanyavatee, and, having treated him with great marks of attention, took him into his service, and employed him in the most confidential affairs. One day, when the young Rajah had bathed and had anointed himself, and was clothed in robes of gold, he said to the husband:

"Charudanta, I am going to give a feast to the goddess Gowree, which will last for a month, and this evening it shall commence. Go then, and just before night, bring to me a young maiden of singular beauty, and when she hath been presented, she shall have due respect paid to her, according to what is ordained."

Charudanta did as he was commanded, and brought to his master such a young woman as he had described; and having delivered her, he privately resolved to find out how she was treated. The young Rajah, Tungavala, caused the young woman to sit down upon a rich sofa, and having entertained her with costly presents of cloth and garments, and given her a keepsake, he, that instant, sent her to her own house. Charudanta, having been a spectator of all which had passed, said to himself:

"This is a man of strict principle, who regardeth the woman of another as his own mother."

So after that, through the confidence created by this stratagem, his mind being biased by the lust of gain, he fetched his own wife and presented her; and the young Rajah, upon beholding Lavanyavatee, the delight of his heart, exclaimed:

"Dear Lavanyavatee! whither art thou going?"

Saying this, he got up from his seat, and, quite forgetful who was present, began to embrace her; whilst Charudanta, the miserable husband, stood gazing at her, motionless as a statue.

And thus was a fool, by his own contrivance, plunged into the greatest distress.

THE FAITHFUL SERVANT

The Hitopadesa

ONE day a young man, whose name was Veera-vara, and who proved to be a Rajah-putra come from some distant country, presented himself before the porter who stood at the King's gate, and addressed him in the following words :

" I am a soldier in search of employment ; pray procure me a sight of the King."

The porter went to his master, and, bowing, told him that there was a soldier at the gate, just arrived from some distant country, who said his name was Veera-vara ; and the King, Subhraka, commanded him to be introduced. Accordingly the porter conducted the stranger into the presence of his master ; to whom, respectfully bowing, he addressed himself as follows :

" Sir, if thou hast any occasion for my service, let my pay be fixed."

The King asked him, " How much ? " and he replied, " Four hundred suvarnas a day."

" What weapons hast thou ? " demanded the King.

" My two arms," replied the soldier, " and my sword, which makes a third."

" This will not do," concluded the King ; upon which the soldier bowed, and took his leave.

The Minister happening to be present, said :

" Please your Highness, give him four days' pay, and learn what sort of a man he is, and what assistance he can be of."

According to the Minister's advice, the man being called back, they gave him Tamboola,[1] and four days' pay in advance ; to the expenditure of which the King very privately attended, and found that he gave one moiety to the gods and the Brahmans, one-fourth to the poor, and spent the remainder in food and amusements ; and that, after performing these several praiseworthy actions, he attended sword in hand at the King's gate day and night, and never went to his lodgings without his master's express permission.

[1] Betel leaf—a token of friendship.

On the fourteenth night of what is called the dark side of the moon, the King heard a noise like one bitterly crying, upon which he called out to know who was waiting at the door, and his faithful Veera-vara answering that he was there, he ordered him to pursue the crying which they heard; so, saying, "I obey your Highness's commands," away he ran.

In the meantime, the King reflected in this manner:

"I have done wrong to send this soldier away by himself in such a dark cloudy night. I will even go too and see what is the matter."

So saying, he took his sword, and thus followed till he got without the city; and presently after he saw the soldier with a female endued with perfect youth and beauty, and richly attired, who was weeping.

"Who art thou, and why dost thou weep?" demanded Veera-vara.

"I am," said the female, "the goddess Sree, the fortune of King Subhraka's dominions, who hath long dwelt happily under the shadow of his wings; but, alas! I am now about to flee to some other place of refuge."

"What, O goddess," said the soldier, "will induce thee to tarry still longer here?"

"If," replied the goddess, "thou wilt offer up thy own son Sakti-vara, who is distinguished by two-and-thirty marks, to the goddess who presideth over the welfare of all nature, then will I remain here for a much longer period of time"; and saying this, she vanished from his sight.

Veera-vara now went home, and called up his son and his wife, who were both asleep; who having risen accordingly, he related to them everything which had passed with the goddess. His son, the moment he had concluded, exclaimed in a transport of joy:

"O how fortunate I am, who can thus be the means of preserving my Sovereign and his dominions! Then, O father, what occasion is there for any further hesitation or delay; since the assistance of this body is at all times ready upon such an occasion as this? For they say:

"'A good man should forsake wealth, and even life itself, for another. It is good to sacrifice one's self for a holy person upon the approach of his destruction.'

"This simple saying belongs particularly to our tribe; then if I am not permitted to do so, by what other act will the preservation of the prosperity of this great country be secured?"

Having considered this proposal, they all went to the temple of the goddess; and when they had worshipped her image, the father Veera-vara addressed her in these words:

"O goddess! let Subhraka our Sovereign be prosperous! and let this victim be accepted!"

Saying which, he cut off his son's head.

"Thus," said he to himself, "have I earned the wages which I received from my Sovereign; and now let me pay the forfeit of my son's life!" and instantly he cut off his own head.

His wife too, overpowered with grief for her husband and son, followed their example. The King, filled with astonishment at the scene before him, said to himself:

"Such little animals as myself come into life, and die away without end; but there never has been, nor ever will be, in this world one like unto him!"

"Oh, I can have no further enjoyment of these my dominions!"

Saying this, he lifted up his sword to cut off his head also; but on the instant, she on whom dependeth the happiness of all, making herself evident under human form, seized him by the hand, and said: "My son, forbear this rashness! At present thy kingdom is not subdued!"

The King prostrated himself before her, and said: "O goddess! of what use to me is dominion, or even life? If thou hast any compassion for me, O let Veera-vara, with his family, be restored to life; or if it be not thy will, permit me to pursue the path wherein I was found by thee!"

The goddess replied: "I am well pleased with this thy noble generosity and tenderness; then go thy ways, and prosper; and let this man, his wife, and son, all rise up and live!"

The King rendered thanks, and returned unobserved to an apartment of his palace to sleep. Veera-vara too being restored to life, together with his wife and son, he conducted them home.

Veera-vara being again on guard at the King's door, and being questioned by him respecting the person who was heard crying, replied, that upon her being seen she became invisible, and that there were no further tidings of her. The King was exceedingly well pleased at this.

and said within himself : " What a praiseworthy man he was," repeating these lines :

" ' He should speak kindly, without meanness ; he should be valiant, without boasting ; he should be generous, shedding his bounty into the dish of the worthy ; he should be resolute, but not harsh.'

" This is the character of a great man ! In this there is all ! "

In the morning early the King assembled a special council ; and when he had publicly proclaimed the proceedings of the night, he bestowed the government of Karnatta upon his generous deliverer.

HERODOTUS
485–425 B.C.

THE TREASURE OF KING RHAMPSINITUS

RHAMPSINITUS, King of Egypt, possessed a great quantity of money, such as no one of the succeeding kings was able to surpass, or even nearly come up to; and he, wishing to treasure up his wealth in safety, built a chamber of stone, of which one of the walls adjoined the outside of the palace. But the builder, forming a plan against it, devised the following contrivance: he fitted one of the stones so that it might be easily taken out by two men, or even one. When the chamber was finished, the King laid up his treasures in it; but in course of time the builder, finding his end approaching, called his sons to him, for he had two, and described to them how (providing for them that they might have abundant sustenance) he had contrived when building the King's treasury; and having clearly explained to them everything relating to the removal of the stone, he gave them its dimensions, and told them, if they would observe his instructions, they would be stewards of the King's riches. He accordingly died, and the sons were not long in applying themselves to the work; but having come by night to the palace, and having found the stone in the building, they easily removed it, and carried off a great quantity of treasure.

When the King happened to open the chamber, he was astonished at seeing the vessels deficient in treasure; but he was not able to accuse any one, as the seals were unbroken, and the chamber well secured. When therefore, on his opening it two or three times, the treasures were always evidently diminished (for the thieves did not cease plundering), he adopted the following plan: he ordered traps to be made, and placed them round the vessels in which the treasures were. But when the thieves came as before, and one of them had entered, as soon as he went near a vessel, he was straightway caught in the trap; perceiving, therefore, in what a predicament he was, he immediately called to his brother, and told him what had happened, and bade him enter as quick as possible, and cut off his head, lest, if he was seen and recognised, he should ruin him also : the other thought that he spoke well, and did as he was advised ; then, having fitted in the stone, he returned home, taking with him his brother's head.

When day came, the King having entered the chamber, was astonished at seeing the body of the thief in the trap without the head, but the chamber secure, and without any means of entrance or exit. In this perplexity he contrived the following plan : he hung up the body of the thief from the wall, and having placed sentinels there, he ordered them to seize and bring before him whomsoever they should see weeping or expressing commiseration at the spectacle.

The mother was greatly grieved at the body being suspended, and coming to words with her surviving son, commanded him, by any means he could, to contrive how he might take down and bring away the corpse of his brother ; but, should he neglect to do so, she threatened to go to the King, and inform him that he had the treasures.

When the mother treated her surviving son harshly, and when with many entreaties he was unable to persuade her, he contrived the following plan : having got some asses, and having filled some skins with wine, he put them on the asses, and then drove them along ; but when he came near the sentinels that guarded the suspended corpse, having drawn out two or three of the necks of the skins that hung down, he loosened them ; and when the wine ran out, he beat his head, and cried out aloud, as if he knew not to which of the asses he should turn first ; but the sentinels, when they saw wine flowing in abundance, ran into the road, with vessels in their hands, caught the wine that was being spilt, thinking it all their own gain ; but the man, feigning anger, railed bitterly against them all ; however, as the sentinels soothed him, he at length pretended to be pacified, and to forgo his anger ; at last he drove his asses out of the road, and set them to rights again. When more conversation passed, and one of the sentinels joked with him and moved him to laughter, he gave them another of the skins ; and they, just as they were, lay down and set to to drink, and joined him to their party, and invited him to stay and drink with them : he was persuaded, forsooth, and remained with them ; and as they treated him kindly during the drinking, he gave them another of the skins ; and the sentinels, having taken very copious draughts, became exceedingly drunk, and being overpowered by the wine, fell asleep on the spot where they had been drinking.

But he, as the night was far advanced, took down the body of his brother, and by way of insult shaved the right cheeks of all the sentinels; then, having laid the corpse on the asses, he drove them home, having performed his mother's injunctions.

The King, when he was informed that the body of the thief had been stolen, was exceedingly indignant, and, resolving by any means to find out the contriver of this artifice, had recourse, *as it is said,* to the following plan, a design which to me seems incredible: he ordered his own daughter to go to a house of ill-fame and there receive all suitors for her favours, first compelling each one to tell her what he had done during his life most clever and most wicked, and whosoever should tell her the facts relating to the thief, she was to seize, and not suffer him to escape.

When, therefore, the daughter did what her father commanded, the thief, having ascertained for what purpose this contrivance was had recourse to, and being desirous to outdo the King in craftiness, did as follows: Having cut off the arm of a fresh corpse at the shoulder, he took it with him under his cloak, and having gone in to the King's daughter, and being asked the same questions as all the rest were, he related that he had done the most wicked thing when he cut off his brother's head who was caught in a trap in the King's treasury; and the most clever thing, when, having made the sentinels drunk, he took away the corpse of his brother that was hung up. She, when she heard this, endeavoured to seize him, but the thief in the dark held out to her the dead man's arm, and she seized it and held it fast, imagining that she had got hold of the man's own arm; then the thief, having let it go, made his escape through the door.

When this also was reported to the King, he was astonished at the shrewdness and daring of the man; and at last, sending throughout all the cities, he caused a proclamation to be made, offering a free pardon, and promising great reward to the man, if he would discover himself.

The thief, relying on this promise, went to the King's palace; and Rhampsinitus greatly admired him and gave him his daughter in marriage, accounting him the most knowing of all men; for that the Egyptians are superior to all others, but he was superior to the Egyptians.

POLYCRATES AND HIS RING

Herodotus

THE exceeding good fortune of Polycrates, King of Samos, did not escape the notice of Amasis, King of Egypt, but was the cause of uneasiness to him; and when his successes continued to increase, having written a letter in the following terms, he despatched it to Samos:

"Amasis to Polycrates says thus: It is pleasant to hear of the successes of a friend and ally. But your too great good fortune does not please me, knowing, as I do, that the divinity is jealous. As for me, I would rather choose that both I and those for whom I am solicitous, should be partly successful in our undertakings, and partly suffer reverses; and so pass life, meeting with vicissitudes of fortune, than be prosperous in all things. For I cannot remember that I ever heard of any man who, having been constantly successful, did not at last utterly perish. Be advised therefore by me, and act thus with regard to your good fortune. Having considered what you can find that you value most, and the loss of which would most pain your soul, this so cast away, that it may never more be seen of man; and if after this successes are not mingled interchangeably with reverses, again have recourse to the remedy I have suggested."

Polycrates, having read this letter, and conceived that Amasis had given him good advice, inquired of himself by the loss of which of his valuables he should most afflict his soul; and on inquiry, he discovered the following: he had a seal which he wore, set in gold, made of an emerald, and it was the workmanship of Theodorus, the son of Telecles, a Samian; when, therefore, he had determined to cast this away, he did as follows. Having manned a fifty-oared galley, he went on board it, and then gave orders to put out to sea; and when he was a considerable distance from the island, he took off the seal, and, in the sight of all on board, threw it into the sea. This done, he sailed back again; and having reached his palace, he mourned it as a great misfortune.

But on the fifth or sixth day after this, the following circumstance occurred: a fisherman, having caught a large and beautiful fish, thought it a present worthy to be given to Polycrates; he accordingly carried it to the gates, and said that he wished to be admitted to the presence of Polycrates; and when this was granted, he presented the fish, and said:

"O King, having caught this, I did not think it right to take it to market, although I get my living by hard labour; but it seemed to me worthy of you and your empire: I bring it, therefore, and present it to you."

He, pleased with these words, replied:

"You have done well, and I give you double thanks for your speech and your present, and I invite you to supper."

The fisherman, thinking a great deal of this, went away to his own home; but the servants, opening the fish, found the seal of Polycrates in its belly; and as soon as they had seen it, and taken it out, they carried it with great joy to Polycrates, and as they gave him the seal they acquainted him in what manner it had been found. But when it occurred to him that the event was superhuman, he wrote an account of what he had done, and of what had happened, and having written, he despatched the account to Egypt.

But Amasis, having read the letter that came from Polycrates, felt persuaded that it was impossible for man to rescue man from the fate that awaited him, and that Polycrates would not come to a good end, since he was fortunate in everything, and even found what he had thrown away; having therefore sent a herald to Samos, he said that he must renounce his friendship. He did this, lest if some dreadful and great calamity befel Polycrates, he might himself be grieved for him, as for a friend.

THEOCRITUS
300 B.C.

THE LADIES OF SYRACUSE

A COUPLE of Syracusan women, staying at Alexandria, agree on the occasion of a great religious solemnity,—the feast of Adonis,—to go together to the palace of King Ptolemy Philadelphus, to see the image of Adonis, which the Queen Arsinoe, Ptolemy's wife, has had decorated with peculiar magnificence. A hymn, by a celebrated performer, is to be recited over the image. The names of the two women are Gorgo and Praxinoe; their maids are called Eunoe and Eutychis. Gorgo has come by appointment to Praxinoe's house to fetch her.

Gorgo.—Is Praxinoe at home?

Praxinoe.—My dear Gorgo, at last! Yes, here I am. Eunoe, find a chair,—get a cushion for it.

Gorgo.—It will do beautifully as it is.

Praxinoe.—Do sit down.

Gorgo.—Oh, this gad-about spirit! I could hardly get to you, Praxinoe, through all the crowd and all the carriages. Nothing but heavy boots, nothing but men in uniform. And what a journey it is! My dear child, you really live *too* far off.

Praxinoe.—It is all that insane husband of mine. He has chosen to come out here to the end of the world, and take a hole of a place,—for a house it is not,—on purpose that you and I might not be neighbours. He is always just the same;—anything to quarrel with one! anything for spite!

Gorgo.—My dear, don't talk so of your husband before the little fellow. Just see how astonished he looks at you. Never mind, Zopyrio, my pet, she is not talking about papa.

Praxinoe.—Good heavens! the child does really understand.

Gorgo.—Pretty papa!

Praxinoe.—That pretty papa of his the other day (though I told him beforehand to mind what he was about), when I sent him to a shop to buy soap and rouge, brought me home salt instead;—stupid, great, big, interminable animal!

Gorgo.—Mine is just the fellow to him. . . . But never mind now, get on your things and let us be off to the palace to see the Adonis. I hear the Queen's decorations are something splendid.

Praxinoe.—In grand people's houses everything is grand. What things you have seen in Alexandria! What a deal you will have to tell to anybody who has never been here!

Gorgo.—Come, we ought to be going.

Praxinoe.—Every day is holiday to people who have nothing to do. Eunoe, pick up your work; and take care, lazy girl, how you leave it lying about again; the cats find it just the bed they like. Come, stir yourself, fetch me some water, quick! I wanted the water first, and the girl brings me the soap. Never mind; give it me. Not all that, extravagant! Now pour out the water;—stupid! why don't you take care of my dress? That will do. I have got my hands washed as it pleased God. Where is the key of the large wardrobe? Bring it here;—quick!

Gorgo.—Praxinoe, you can't think how well that dress, made full, as you have got it, suits you. Tell me, how much did it cost?—the dress by itself, I mean.

Praxinoe.—Don't talk of it, Gorgo; more than eight pieces of good hard money. And about the work on it I have almost worn my life out.

Gorgo.—Well, you couldn't have done better.

Praxinoe.—Thank you. Bring me my shawl, and put my hat properly on my head;—properly. No, child (*to her little boy*), I am not going to take you; there's a bogy on horseback, who bites. Cry as much as you like; I'm not going to have you lamed for life. Now, we'll start. Nurse, take the little one and amuse him; call the dog in, and shut the street door. (*They go out.*) Good heavens! what a crowd of people! How on earth are we ever to get through all this? They are like ants: you can't count them. My dearest Gorgo, what will become of us? here are the Royal Horse Guards. My good man, don't ride over me! Look at that bay horse rearing bolt upright; what a vicious one! Eunoe, you mad girl, do take care!—that horse will certainly be the death of the man on his back. How glad I am now, that I left the child safe at home!

Gorgo.—All right, Praxinoe, we are safe behind them; and they have gone on to where they are stationed.

Praxinoe.—Well, yes, I begin to revive again. From the time I was a little girl I have had more horror of horses and snakes than of anything in the world. Let us get on; here's a great crowd coming this way upon us.

Gorgo (*to an old woman*).—Mother, are you from the palace?

Old Woman.—Yes, my dears.

Gorgo.—Has one a chance of getting there?

Old Woman.—My pretty young lady, the Greeks got to Troy by dint of trying hard; trying will do anything in this world.

Gorgo.—The old creature has delivered herself of an oracle and departed.

Praxinoe.—Women can tell you everything about everything, Jupiter's marriage with Juno not excepted.

Gorgo.—Look, Praxinoe, what a squeeze at the palace gates!

Praxinoe.—Tremendous! Take hold of me, Gorgo; and you, Eunoe, take hold of Eutychis!—tight hold, or you'll be lost. Here we go in all together. Hold tight to us, Eunoe! Oh, dear! oh, dear! Gorgo, there's my scarf torn right in two. My good man, as you hope to be saved, take care of my dress!

Stranger.—I'll do what I can, but it doesn't depend upon me.

Praxinoe.—What heaps of people! They push like a drove of pigs.

Stranger.—Don't be frightened, we are all right.

Praxinoe.—May you be all right, my dear sir, to the last day you live, for the care you have taken of us! What a kind, considerate man! There is Eunoe jammed in a squeeze. Push, you goose, push! Capital! We are all of us the right side of the door, as the bridegroom said when he had locked himself in with the bride.

Gorgo.—Praxinoe, come this way. Do but look at that work, how delicate it is!—how exquisite! Why, they might wear it in heaven.

Praxinoe.—Heavenly patroness of needlewomen, what hands were hired to do that work? Who designed those beautiful patterns? They seem to stand up and move about, as if they were real;—as if they were living things, and not needlework. Well, man is a wonderful creature! And look, look, how charming he lies there on his silver couch, with just a soft down on his cheeks, that beloved Adonis,—Adonis, whom one loves even though he is dead!

Another Stranger.—You wretched women, do stop your incessant chatter! Like turtles, you go on for ever. They are enough to kill one with their broad lingo,—nothing but *ā, ā, ā.*

Gorgo.—Lord, where does the man come from? What is it to you if we *are* chatterboxes ? Order about your own servants ! Do you give orders to Syracusan women ? If you want to know, we came originally from Corinth, as Bellerophon did ; we speak Peloponnesian. I suppose Dorian women may be allowed to have a Dorian accent.

Praxinoe.—O, honey-sweet Proserpine, let us have no more masters than the one we've got ! We don't the least care for *you* ; pray don't trouble yourself for nothing.

Gorgo.—Be quiet, Praxinoe ! That first-rate singer, the Argive woman's daughter, is going to sing the *Adonis* hymn. She is the same who was chosen to sing the dirge last year. We are sure to have something first-rate from *her*. She is going through her airs and graces ready to begin.

Then the singer begins her hymn :—

" Mistress, who loveth the haunts of Golgi, and Idalium, and high-peaked Eryx, Aphrodite that playest with gold ! how have the delicate-footed Hours, after twelve months, brought thy Adonis back to thee from the ever-flowing Acheron ! Tardiest of the immortals are the boon Hours, but all mankind wait their approach with longing, for they ever bring something with them. O Cypris, Dione's child ! thou didst change—so is the story among men—Berenice from mortal to immortal, by dropping ambrosia into her fair bosom ; and in gratitude to thee for this, O thou of many names and many temples ! Berenice's daughter, Arsinoe, lovely Helen's living counterpart, makes much of Adonis with all manner of braveries.

" All fruits that the tree bears are laid before him, all treasures of the garden in silver baskets, and alabaster boxes, gold-inlaid, of Syrian ointment ; and all confectionery that cunning women make on their kneading-tray, kneading up every sort of flowers with white meal, and all that they make of sweet honey and delicate oil, and all winged and creeping things are here set before him. And there are built for him green bowers with wealth of tender anise, and little boy-loves flutter about over them, like young nightingales trying their new wings on the tree, from bough to bough. Oh, the ebony, the gold, the eagle of white ivory that bears aloft his cup-bearer to Kronos-born Zeus ! And up there, see ! a second couch strewn for lovely Adonis, scarlet coverlets softer than sleep itself (so Miletus and the Samian wool-grower will say) ; Cypris has hers, and the rosy-armed Adonis has his, that eighteen or nineteen-year-old bridegroom. His kisses will not wound, the hair on his lip is yet light.

" Now, Cypris, good-night, we leave thee with thy bridegroom; but to-morrow morning, with the earliest dew, we will one and all bear him forth to where the waves splash upon the sea-strand, and letting loose our locks, and letting fall our robes, with bosoms bare, we will set up this, our melodious strain:

" ' Beloved Adonis, alone of the demigods (so men say), thou art permitted to visit both us and Acheron! This lot had neither Agamemnon, nor the mighty moon-struck hero Ajax, nor Hector the first-born of Hecuba's twenty children, nor Patroclus, nor Pyrrhus who came home from Troy, nor those yet earlier Lapithæ and the sons of Deucalion, nor the Pelasgians, the root of Argos and of Pelops' isle. Be gracious to us now, loved Adonis, and be favourable to us for the year to come! Dear to us hast thou been at this coming, dear to us shalt thou be when thou comest again.' "

The hymn concluded, Gorgo says:

" Praxinoe, certainly women are wonderful things. That lucky woman to know all that! and luckier still to have such a splendid voice! And now we must see about getting home. My husband has not had his dinner. That man is all vinegar, and nothing else; and if you keep him waiting for his dinner, he's dangerous to go near. Adieu, precious Adonis, and may you find us all well when you come next year! "

PETRONIUS
1st Century A.D.

THE WIDOW OF EPHESUS

THERE was a married woman in Ephesus of such famous virtue that she drew women even from the neighbouring states to gaze upon her. So when she had buried her husband, the common fashion of following the procession with loose hair, and beating the naked breast in front of the crowd, did not satisfy her. She followed the dead man even to his resting-place, and began to watch and weep night and day over the body, which was laid in an underground vault in the Greek fashion. Neither her parents nor her relations could divert her from thus torturing herself and courting death by starvation ; the officials were at last rebuffed and left her ; every one mourned for her as a woman of unique character, and she was now passing her fifth day without food. A devoted maid sat by the failing woman, shed tears in sympathy with her woes, and at the same time filled up the lamp, which was placed in the tomb, whenever it sank. There was but one opinion throughout the city, every class of person admitting this was the one true and brilliant example of chastity and love.

At this moment the governor of the province gave orders that some robbers should be crucified near the small building where the lady was bewailing her recent loss. So on the next night, when the soldier who was watching the crosses to prevent any one taking down a body for burial, observed a light shining plainly among the tombs, and heard a mourner's groans, a very human weakness made him curious to know who it was and what he was doing. So he went down into the vault, and on seeing a very beautiful woman, at first halted in confusion, as if he had seen a portent or some ghost from the world beneath. But afterwards noticing the dead man lying there, and watching the woman's tears and the marks of her nails on her face, he came to the correct conclusion, that she found her regret for the lost one unendurable.

He therefore brought his supper into the tomb, and began to urge the mourner not to persist in useless grief, and break her heart with unprofitable sobs, for all men made the same end and found the same resting-place, and so on with the other platitudes which restore wounded spirits to health. But she took no notice of his sympathy, struck and tōre her breast more violently than ever, pulled out her hair, and laid it on the dead body. Still the soldier did not retire, but tried to give the poor woman food with similar encouragements, until the maid, who was no doubt seduced by the smell of his wine, first gave in herself, and put out her hand at his kindly invitation, and then, refreshed with food and drink, began to assail her mistress's obstinacy, and say:

"What will you gain by all this, if you faint away with hunger, if you bury yourself alive, if you breathe out your undoomed soul before Fate calls for it?

"Believest thou that the ashes or the spirit of the buried dead can feel thy woe? Will you not begin life afresh? Will you not shake off this womanish failing, and enjoy the blessings of the light so long as you are allowed? Your poor dead husband's body here ought to persuade you to keep alive."

People are always ready to listen when they are urged to take a meal or to keep alive. So the lady, being thirsty after several days' abstinence, allowed her resolution to be broken down, and filled herself with food as greedily as the maid, who had been the first to yield.

Well, you know which temptation generally assails a man on a full stomach. The soldier used the same insinuating phrases which had persuaded the lady to consent to live, to conduct an assault upon her virtue. Her modest eye saw in him a young man, handsome and eloquent. The maid begged her to be gracious, and then said:

"Wilt thou fight love even when love pleases thee? Or dost thou never remember in whose lands thou art resting?"

I need hide the fact no longer. The lady ceased to hold out, and the conquering hero won her over entire. So they passed not only their wedding night together, but the next and a third, of course shutting the door of the vault, so that any friend or stranger who came to the tomb would imagine that this most virtuous lady had breathed her last over her husband's body. Well, the soldier was delighted with the woman's beauty, and his stolen pleasure; he bought up all the fine things his means permitted, and carried them to the tomb the moment darkness fell. So the parents of one of the crucified, seeing that the watch was ill-kept, took their man down in the dark and administered the last rite to him. The next day the soldier, seeing one of the crosses without its corpse, was in terror of punishment and explained to the lady what had happened. He declared that he would not wait for a court-martial, but would punish his own neglect with a thrust of his sword. So she had better get ready a place for a dying man, and let the gloomy vault enclose both her husband and her lover.

The lady's heart was tender as well as pure. "Heaven forbid," she replied, "that I should look at the same moment on the dead bodies of two men whom I love. No, I would rather make a dead man useful, than send a live man to death."

After this speech she ordered her husband's body to be taken out of the coffin and fixed up on the empty cross. The soldier availed himself of this far-seeing woman's device, and the people wondered the next day by what means the dead man had ascended the cross.

APULEIUS
125 A.D.

CUPID AND PSYCHE

IN a certain city there lived a King and Queen, who had three daughters of remarkable beauty. The charms of the two elder —and they were very great—were still thought not to exceed all possible measure of praise; but as for the youngest sister, human speech was too poor to express, much less adequately to extol, her exquisite and surpassing loveliness. In fact, multitudes of the citizens, and of strangers, whom the fame of this extraordinary spectacle gathered to the spot, were struck dumb with astonishment at her unapproachable beauty, and paid her religious adoration, just as though she were the goddess Venus herself.

This extraordinary transfer of celestial honours to a mortal maiden greatly incensed the real Venus; and, unable to suppress her indignation, and shaking her head, in towering wrath, she thus soliloquized:

"Behold how the primal parent of all things, behold how the first source of the elements, behold how I, the genial Venus of the whole world, am treated! The honour belonging to my majesty shared by a mortal girl! But this creature, whosoever she be, shall not so joyously usurp my honours; for I will soon cause her to repent of her contraband good looks."

Thus saying, the goddess forthwith summons her son, that winged and very malapert boy; she points out Psyche to him (for that was the name of the maiden), and after telling him the whole story about that mortal's rivalry of her own beauty, groaning with rage and indignation, she said:

"I conjure you by the ties of maternal love, by the sweet wounds inflicted by your arrow, by the warmth, delightful as honey, of that torch, to afford your parent her revenge, ay, and a full one too, and as you respect myself, severely punish this rebellious beauty; and this one thing, above all, use all your endeavours to effect: let this maiden be seized with the most burning love for the lowest of mankind, one whom fortune has stripped of rank, patrimony, and even of personal safety; one so degraded, that he cannot find his equal in wretchedness throughout the whole world."

Having thus said, and long and tenderly kissed her son, she sought the neighbouring margin of the shore on which the waves ebb and flow, and, with rosy feet, brushing along the topmost spray of the dancing waters, behold! she took her seat on the watery surface of the main; where the powers of the deep, the instant that she conceived the wish, appeared at once, as though she had previously commanded their attendance.

In the meantime, Psyche, with all her exquisite beauty, derived no advantage whatever from her good looks; she was gazed on by all, praised by all, and yet no one, king, noble, or plebeian even, came to woo her for his bride. They admired, no doubt, her divine beauty, but then they all admired it as they would a statue exquisitely wrought. Long before this, her two elder sisters, whose more moderate charms had not been bruited abroad among the nations, had been wooed by kings, and happily wedded to them; but Psyche, forlorn virgin, sat at home, bewailing her lonely condition, faint in body and sick at heart; and hated her own beauty, though it delighted all the rest of the world.

The wretched father of this most unfortunate daughter, suspecting the enmity of the gods, and dreading their wrath, consulted the very ancient oracle of Apollo, and sought of that mighty divinity, with prayers and victims, a husband for the maiden whom no one cared to have. But Apollo, though a Grecian and an Ionian, by right of the founder of Miletus, delivered an oracle to the following effect:

> On some high mountain's craggy summit place
> The virgin, deck'd for deadly nuptial rites;
> Nor hope a son-in-law of mortal race,
> But a dire mischief, viperous and fierce;
> Who flies through æther, and with fire and sword
> Tires and debilitates whate'er exists,
> Terrific to the powers that reign on high.—*Taylor.*

The King, who had led a happy life till then, on hearing the announcement of the sacred oracle, returned home sad and slow, and disclosed to his wife the behests of inauspicious fate. Many days together were passed in grief and tears and lamentation. But time pressed, and the dire oracle had now to be fulfilled. The procession was formed for the deadly nuptials of the ill-fated maiden; and the weeping Psyche walks not to her nuptials, but to her obsequies. And while her woe-begone parents, overwhelmed with horror, strove to delay the execution of the abominable deed, the daughter herself thus exhorted them to compliance:

"Why torment your unfortunate old age with continual weeping? Why waste your breath, which is more dear to me than to you, with repeated lamentations? Too late do you perceive that you have been smitten by the deadly shaft of envy. Alas! then should you have wept and lamented, then bewailed me as lost, when tribes and nations celebrated me with divine honours, and when, with one consent, they styled me a new-born Venus. Now do I feel and see that through that name of Venus alone I perish. Lead me away, then, and expose me on the rock to which the oracle has devoted me; I am in haste to encounter these auspicious nuptials; I am in haste to see this noble bridegroom of mine. Why should I delay? Why avoid his approach, who has been born for the destruction of the whole world?"

The maiden, after these words, said no more, but with unfaltering steps, took her place in the multitudinous procession. They advanced to the destined rock on a lofty mountain, and left the maiden alone on the summit; the nuptial torches, with which they had lighted their way, were now extinguished in their tears, and thrown aside, the ceremony was at an end, and with drooping heads they took their homeward way. Meanwhile, as Psyche lay trembling and weeping in dismay on the summit of the rock, the mild breeze of the gently-blowing Zephyr played round her garments, fluttering and gradually expanding them till they lifted her up, and the god, wafting her with his tranquil breath adown the lofty mountain side, laid her softly on the flowery turf in the lap of the valley.

Psyche, therefore, delightfully reclining in this pleasant and grassy spot, upon a bed of dewy herbage, felt her extreme agitation of mind allayed, and sank into a sweet sleep, from which she awoke refreshed in body, and with a mind more composed. She then espied a grove, thick planted with vast and lofty trees; she likewise saw a fountain in the middle of the grove, with water limpid as crystal. Near the fall of the fountain there was a kingly palace, not raised by human hands, but by divine skill. You might know, from the very entrance of the palace, that you were looking upon the splendid and delightful abode of some god.

Invited by the delightful appearance of the place, Psyche approached it, and, gradually taking courage, stepped over the threshold. The beauty of what she beheld lured her on, and everything filled her with admiration. In another part of the palace, she beheld magnificent repositories, stored with immense riches. But not one human being could she see, she only heard words that were uttered; and had voices alone for the servants. An exquisite banquet was served up, some one entered, and sang unseen, while another struck the lyre, which was no more visible than himself. Then, a swell of voices, as of a multitude singing in full chorus, was wafted to her ears, though not one of the vocalists could she descry.

After these delights had ceased, the evening now persuading to repose, Psyche retired to bed; and when the night was far advanced, a certain gentle, murmuring sound fell upon her ears. Then, alarmed for her honour, in consequence of the profound solitude of the place, she trembled and was filled with terror, and dreaded that of which she was ignorant more than any misfortune. And now her unknown bridegroom ascended the couch, made Psyche his wife, and hastily left her before break of day. This course was continued for a length of time; and, as by nature it has been so ordained, the novelty, by its constant repetition, afforded her delight, and the sound of the voices was the solace of her solitude.

In the meantime, her parents were wasting their old age in sorrow and lamentation; and the report of her fate, becoming more widely extended, her elder sisters had learnt all the particulars; whereupon, leaving their homes in deep grief, they hastened to visit and comfort their parents. On that night did Psyche's husband thus address her —for she could discern his presence with her ears and hands, though not with her eyes:

" Most charming Psyche, dear wife, cruel fortune now threatens you with a deadly peril, which needs, I think, to be guarded against with the most vigilant attention. For ere long, your sisters, who are alarmed at the report of your death, in their endeavours to discover traces of you, will arrive at yonder rock. If, then, you should chance to hear their lamentations, make them no reply, no, nor even so much as turn your eyes towards them. By doing otherwise, you will cause most grievous sorrow to me, and utter destruction to yourself."

Psyche assented, and promised that she would act agreeably to her husband's desire. But when he and the night had departed together, she, inconsolable, consumed the whole day in tears and lamentations, exclaiming over and over again that she was now utterly lost, since, besides being thus confined in a splendid prison, deprived of human conversation, she was not even allowed to relieve the minds of her sisters, who were sorrowing for her, nor, indeed, so much as to see them.

Without having refreshed herself, therefore, with the bath or with food, or, in fact, with any solace whatever, but weeping plenteously, she retired to rest. Shortly afterwards, her husband, coming to her bed earlier than usual, embraced her as she wept, and thus expostulated with her:

"Is this, my Psyche, what you promised me? What am I, your husband, henceforth to expect of you? What can I now hope for, when neither by day nor by night, not even in the midst of our conjugal endearments, you cease to be distracted with grief? Very well, then, act now just as you please, and comply with the baneful dictates of your inclination. However, when you begin too late to repent, you will recall to mind my serious admonitions."

Upon this, she had recourse to prayers; and threatening that she would put an end to herself if her request were denied, she extorted from her husband a consent that she might see her sisters, to soothe their grief, and enjoy their conversation. This he yielded to the entreaties of his new-made wife, and he gave her permission, besides, to present her sisters with as much gold and as many jewels as she pleased; but he warned her repeatedly, and so often as to terrify her, never, on any occasion, to be persuaded by the pernicious advice of her sisters, to make any inquiries concerning the form of her husband; lest, by a sacrilegious curiosity, she might cast herself down from such an exalted position of good fortune, and never again feel his embraces.

She thanked her husband for his indulgence; and now, having quite recovered her spirits, "Nay," said she, "I would suffer death a hundred times rather than be deprived of your most delightful company, for I love you, yes, I adore you to desperation, whoever you are, ay, even as I love my own soul, nor would I give you in exchange for Cupid himself. But this also I beseech you to grant to my prayers; bid Zephyr, this servant of yours, convey my sisters to me, in the same manner in which he brought me hither."

Her husband, overcome by the power of love, yielded reluctantly, and promised all she desired. After this, upon the approach of morning, he again vanished from the arms of his wife.

Meanwhile, the sisters, having inquired the way to the rock on which Psyche was abandoned, hastened thither; and there they wept and beat their breasts till the rocks and crags resounded with their lamentations. They called to their unfortunate sister, by her own name, until the shrill sound of their voices descending the declivities of the mountain, reached the ears of Psyche, who ran out of her palace in delirious trepidation, and exclaimed:

"Why do you needlessly afflict yourselves with doleful lamentations? Here am I, whom you mourn; cease those dismal accents, and now at last dry up those tears that have so long bedewed your cheeks, since you may now embrace her whom you have been lamenting."

Then, summoning Zephyr, she acquaints him with her husband's commands, in obedience to which, instantly wafting them on his gentlest breeze, he safely conveys them to Psyche. Now do they enjoy mutual embraces, and hurried kisses; and their tears, that had ceased to flow, return, after a time, summoned forth by joy.

"Now come," said Psyche, "enter my dwelling in gladness, and cheer up your afflicted spirits with your Psyche."

Having thus said, she showed them the vast treasures of her golden palace, and sumptuously refreshed them in a most beautiful bath, and with the delicacies of a divine banquet; until, satiated with this copious abundance of celestial riches, they began to nourish envy in the lowest depths of their breasts. One of them, especially, very minute and curious, persisted in making inquiries about the master of this celestial wealth, what kind of person, and what sort of husband he made.

Psyche, however, would by no means violate her husband's injunctions, or disclose the secrets of her breast; but, devising a tale for the occasion, told them that he was a young man, and very good-looking, and that he was, for the most part, engaged in rural occupations, and hunting on the mountains. And lest, by any slip in the course of the protracted conversation, her secret counsels might be betrayed, having loaded them with ornaments of gold and jewelled necklaces, she called Zephyr, and ordered him at once to convey them back again.

This being immediately executed, these excellent sisters, as they were returning home, now burning more and more with the rancour of envy, conversed much with each other; at last one of them thus began:

"Do but see how blind, cruel, and unjust Fortune has proved! Were you, my sister, delighted to find that we, born of the same parents, had met with such a different lot? We, indeed, who are the elder, are delivered over as bondmaids to foreign husbands, and live in banishment from our home, our native land, and our parents ; and this, the youngest of us all, is raised to the enjoyment of such boundless wealth, and has a god for her husband, she who does not even know how to enjoy, in a proper manner, such an abundance of blessings ? While I, wretched creature, am tied to a husband who, in the first place, is older than my father ; and who, in the next place, is balder than a pumpkin, and more dwarfish than any boy, and who fastens up every part of his house with bolts and chains."

"But I," replied the other sister, "have got to put up with a husband who is tormented and crippled with gout ; and who, on this account, seldom honours me with his embraces, while I have to be everlastingly rubbing his distorted and chalky fingers with filthy fomentations, nasty rags, and stinking poultices ; scalding these delicate hands, and acting the part not of a wife, but of a female doctor. You, sister, seem to bear all this with a patient, or rather a servile spirit, but, for my part, I can no longer endure that such a fortunate destiny should have so undeservedly fallen to her lot. And then, recollect in what a haughty and arrogant manner she behaved towards us, and how, by her boasting and immoderate ostentations, she betrayed a heart swelling with pride, and how reluctantly she threw us a trifling portion of her immense riches ; and immediately after, being weary of our company, ordered us to be turned out, and to be puffed and whisked away. But may I be no woman, nor indeed may I breathe, if I do not hurl her down headlong from such mighty wealth. In the first place, then, let us not show these things that we have got, either to our parents or to any one else ; in fact, we are to know nothing at all about her safety. For the present, let us away to our husbands, and revisit our poor and plain dwellings, that, after long and earnest consideration, we may return the better prepared to humble her pride."

This wicked project was voted good by the two wicked sisters. Concealing those choice and sumptuous presents which they had received from Psyche, tearing their hair, and beating their faces, which well deserved such treatment, they redoubled their pretended grief. In this manner, too, hastily leaving their parents, after having set their sorrows bleeding afresh, they returned to their homes, swelling with malicious rage, and plotting wicked schemes, nay, actual murder against their innocent sister.

In the meantime, Psyche's unknown husband once more admonished her thus in their nocturnal conversation :

"Are you aware what a mighty peril Fortune is preparing to launch against you from a distance, one too, which, unless you take strenuous precautions against it, will ere long confront you, hand to hand ? Those perfidious she-wolves are planning base stratagems against you with all their might, to the end that they may prevail upon you to view my features, which, as I have often told you, if you once see, you will see no more. If, then, these most abominable vampires come again, armed with their baneful intentions, and that they will come I know full well, do not hold any converse whatever with them ; but if, through your natural frankness and tenderness of disposition, you are not able to do this, at all events be careful not to listen to or answer any inquiries about your husband. For before long we shall have an increase to our family, and infant as you are, you are pregnant with another infant, which, if you preserve my secret in silence, will be born divine, but if you profane it, will be mortal."

Radiant with joy at this news, Psyche exulted in the glory of this future pledge of love, and in the dignity of a mother's name.

But now those pests and most dire Furies, breathing viperous virulence, were hastening towards her with the speed of ruthless hate. Then again her husband warned his Psyche to this effect during his brief visit :

"The day of trial, and this most utter calamity, are now at hand. Your own malicious sex, and your own blood, in arms against you, have struck their camp, drawn up their forces in battle array, and sounded the charge. Now are your wicked sisters aiming with the drawn sword at your throat. Alas ! darling Psyche, by what mighty dangers are we now surrounded ! Take pity on yourself and on me ; and by an inviolable silence, rescue your home, your husband, yourself, and that little one of ours from this impending destruction. Shun those wicked women, whom, after the deadly hatred which they have conceived against you, and having trampled under foot the ties of blood, it were not right to call sisters ; neither see, nor listen to them, when, like Sirens, hanging over the crag, they shall make the rocks resound with their ill-omened voices."

Psyche, in accents interrupted by sobs and tears, thus replied :

"Already, methinks, you have experienced convincing proofs of my fidelity and power of keeping a secret. Only order Zephyr once again to discharge his duties, and at least grant me a sight of my sisters, by way of compensation for your own hallowed form. Indulge me with the gratification of embracing my sisters, and refresh with joyousness the soul of Psyche, who is so devoted and so dear to you. Then no longer I shall be anxious to view your features. Henceforth, not even the shades of night will have any effect on me. I clasp you in my arms, and you are my light."

Enchanted by these words, and by her honeyed embraces, her husband brushed away her tears with his locks, and assuring her that he would do as she wished, instantly anticipated the light of the dawning day by flight. But the pair of sisters who had engaged in this conspiracy, not having so much as visited their parents, direct their course with precipitate haste straight from the ships towards the rock, and not waiting for the presence of the buoyant breeze, leap into the abyss with ungovernable rashness. Zephyr, however, not forgetful of the royal commands, received them, though reluctantly, in the bosom of the breathing breeze, and laid them on the ground.

With rapid steps and without a moment's delay, they entered the palace, and deceitfully screening themselves under the name of sister, embraced their prey; then, covering a whole store-house of deeply hidden treachery beneath a joyous countenance, they thus addressed her in flattering terms:

"Psyche, you are not quite so slender as you used to be. Why, you will be a mother before long. Can you fancy with what exceeding joy you will gladden our whole house! O how delighted we shall be to nurse this golden baby, for if it only equals the beauty of its parents, it will be born a perfect Cupid."

Thus, by a false appearance of affection, they gradually stole upon the heart of their sister, while she, after making them sit awhile to recover from the fatigue of their journey and refresh themselves with warm baths, regaled them in a marvellously splendid manner with innumerable exquisite dainties.

But the malice of these wicked women was not softened or lulled to rest even by the dulcet sweetness of the music; but, shaping their conversation so as to lead Psyche into the intended snare, they began insidiously to inquire what sort of a person her husband was, and from what family he was descended. She, in her extreme simplicity, having forgotten her former account, invented a new story about her husband, and said he was a native of the adjoining province; that he was a merchant, with abundance of money, a man of middle age, with a few grey hairs sprinkled here and there on his head. Then, abruptly terminating the conversation, she again committed them to their windy vehicle, after having loaded them with costly presents.

While they were returning homewards, soaring aloft on the tranquil breath of Zephyrus, they thus interchanged their thoughts with each other:

" What are we to say, sister, of the monstrous lies of that silly creature ? At one time her husband is a young man, with the down just beginning to show itself on his chin ; at another he is of middle age, and his hair begins to be silvered with grey. Who can this be, whom a short space of time thus suddenly changes into an old man ? And yet, if she really is ignorant of the appearance of her husband, she must no doubt have married a god, and then through this pregnancy of hers she will be presenting us with a god. At all events, if she does happen, which heaven forbid ! to become the mother of a divine infant, I shall instantly hang myself."

The sisters, thus inflamed with passion, called on their parents in a careless and disdainful manner, and after being kept awake all night by the turbulence of their spirits, made all haste at morning to the rock, whence, by the usual assistance of the breeze, they descended swiftly to Psyche, and with tears squeezed out, by rubbing their eyelids, thus craftily addressed her:

" Happy indeed are you, and fortunate in your very ignorance of a misfortune of such magnitude. There you sit, without a thought upon your danger ; while we, who watch over your interests with the most vigilant care, are in anguish at your lost condition. For we have learned for a truth, nor can we, as being sharers in your sorrows and misfortunes, conceal it from you, that it is an enormous serpent, gliding along in many folds and coils, with a neck swollen with deadly venom, and prodigious gaping jaws, that secretly sleeps with you by night. Do for a moment recall to mind the Pythian oracle, which declared that you were destined to become the wife of a fierce and truculent animal. Besides, many of the husbandmen, who are in the habit of hunting all round the country, and ever so many of the neighbours, have observed him returning home from his feeding-place in the evening, and swimming across the shoals of the neighbouring stream. All declare, too, that he will not long continue to pamper you with delicacies, but that as soon as ever you are a mother he will devour you, as a most exquisite morsel."

Poor, simple, tender-hearted Psyche was aghast with horror at this dreadful story; and, quite bereft of her senses, lost all remembrance of her husband's admonitions and of her own promises, and hurled herself headlong into the very abyss of calamity. Trembling, therefore, with pale and livid cheeks, and with an almost lifeless voice, she faltered out these broken words:

"Dearest sisters, you have acted towards me as you ought, and with your usual affectionate care; and indeed it appears to me that those who gave you this information have not invented a falsehood. For, in fact, I have never yet beheld my husband's face, nor do I know at all whence he comes. I only hear him speak in an undertone by night, and have to bear with a husband of an unknown appearance, and one that has an utter aversion to the light of day: I consequently have full reason to be of your opinion, that he may be some monster or other. Besides, he is always terrifying me from attempting to behold him, and threatens some shocking misfortune as the consequence of indulging any curiosity to view his features. Now, therefore, if you are able to give any saving aid to your sister in this perilous emergency, defer it not for a moment."

Finding the approaches thus laid open, and their sister's heart exposed all naked to their attacks, these wicked women thought the time was come to sally out from their covered approach and attack the timorous thoughts of the simple girl with the drawn sword of deceit. Accordingly, one of them thus began:

"Since the ties of blood oblige us to have no fear of peril before our eyes when your safety is to be ensured, we will discover to you the only method which will lead to your preservation, and one which has been considered by us over and over again. On that side of the bed where you are accustomed to lie, secretly conceal a very sharp razor, one that you have whetted to a keen edge by passing it over the palm of your hand; and hide likewise under some covering of the surrounding tapestry a lamp, well trimmed and full of oil, and shining with a bright light. Make these preparations with the utmost secrecy, and after the monster has glided into the bed as usual, when he is now stretched out at length, fast asleep and breathing heavily, then slide out of bed, go softly along with bare feet and on tiptoe, free the lamp from its place of concealment in the dark, and borrow the aid of its light to execute your noble purpose; then at once, boldly raising your right hand, bring down the keen weapon with all your might, and cut off the head of the noxious serpent at the nape of the neck. Nor shall our assistance be wanting to you ; for we will keep anxious watch, and be with you the very instant you shall have effected your own safety by his death ; and then, immediately bringing you away with all these things, we will wed you, to your wish, with a human creature like yourself."

Having with such pernicious language inflamed the mind of their sister, and wrought her to a perfect pitch of determination, they deserted her, fearing exceedingly even to be in the neighbourhood of such a catastrophe ; and, being laid upon the rock by the wonted impulse of their winged bearer, they immediately hurried thence with impetuous haste, at once got on board their ships, and sailed away.

But Psyche, now left alone, except so far as a person who is agitated by maddening Furies is not alone, fluctuated in sorrow like a stormy sea ; and, though her purpose was fixed and her heart was resolute when she first began to make preparations for the impious work, her mind now wavers, and is distracted with numerous apprehensions at her unhappy fate.

The night came, and with it came her husband, and after their first dalliance was over, he fell into a deep sleep. Then Psyche, to whose weak body and spirit the cruel influence of fate imparted unusual strength, uncovered the lamp, and seized the knife with masculine courage. But the instant she advanced the lamp, and the mysteries of the couch stood revealed, she beheld the very gentlest and sweetest of all wild creatures, even Cupid himself, the beautiful God of Love, there fast asleep ; at sight of whom, the joyous flame of the lamp shone with redoubled vigour and the sacrilegious razor repented the keenness of its edge.

But as for Psyche, astounded at such a sight, losing the control of her senses, faint, deadly pale, and trembling all over, she fell on her knees, and made an attempt to hide the blade in her own bosom ; and this no doubt she would have done, had not the blade, dreading the commission of such a crime, glided out of her rash hand. And now, faint and unnerved as she was, she feels herself refreshed at heart by gazing upon the beauty of those divine features. She looks upon the genial locks of his golden head, the orbed curls that strayed over his milk-white neck and roseate cheeks, and fell gracefully entangled, some before, some behind ; causing the very light of the lamp itself to flicker by their radiant splendour. On the shoulders of the volatile god were dewy wings of brilliant whiteness ; and though the pinions were at rest, yet the tender down that fringed the feathers wantoned to and fro in tremulous unceasing play. At the foot of the bed lay his bow, his quiver, and his arrows, the auspicious weapons of the mighty god.

While with unsatiable wonder and curiosity Psyche is examining and admiring her husband's weapons, she draws one of the arrows out of the quiver, and touches the point with the tip of her thumb to try its sharpness; but happening to press too hard, for her hand still trembled, she punctured the skin, so that some tiny drops of rosy blood oozed forth; and thus did Psyche, without knowing it, fall in love with LOVE. Then, gazing passionately on his face, and fondly kissing him again and again, her only fear was lest he should wake too soon.

But while she hung over him bewildered with delight, the lamp, whether from treachery or baneful envy, or because it longed to touch, and to kiss, as it were, such a beautiful object, spirted a drop of scalding oil from the summit of its flame upon the right shoulder of the god.

The god, thus scorched, sprang from the bed, and seeing the disgraceful tokens of forfeited fidelity, without a word was flying away from the eyes and arms of his most unhappy wife. But Psyche, the instant he rose, seized hold of his right leg with both hands, and hung on to him, a wretched appendage to his flight through the regions of the air, till at last her strength failed her and she fell to the earth.

Her divine lover, however, not deserting her as she lay on the ground, alighted upon a neighbouring cypress tree, and thus angrily addressed her from its lofty top:

"O simple, simple Psyche, for you I have been unmindful of the commands of my mother Venus; for when she bade me cause you to be infatuated with passion for some base and abject man, I chose rather to fly to you myself as a lover. I, that redoubtable archer, have wounded myself with my own arrow, and have made you my wife, that I, forsooth, might be thought by you to be a serpent, and that you might cut off my head, which bears those very eyes which have so doated upon you. This was the danger that I told you again and again to be on your guard against, this was what I so benevolently forewarned you of. But as for those choice counsellors of yours, they shall speedily feel my vengeance for giving you such pernicious advice; but you I will punish only by my flight."

And so saying, he soared aloft, and flew away.

Meanwhile Psyche lay prostrate on the ground, gazing on the flight of her husband as long as ever he remained in sight, and afflicting her mind with the most bitter lamentations. But when the reiterated movement of his wings had borne her husband through the immensity of space till she saw him no more, she threw herself headlong from the bank of the adjacent river into its stream. But the gentle river, honouring the god, who is in the habit of imparting his warmth to the waters themselves, and fearing his power, bore her on the surface of a harmless wave to the bank, and laid her safe on its flowery turf.

Departing from the spot, after she had toiled some little way along the road, she came at last to an unknown by-path, and following it, she arrived at a certain city, of which the husband of one of her sisters was king. On learning this circumstance, Psyche requested that her arrival might be announced to her sister. Being immediately conducted to her, when they had mutually embraced, and the forms of salutation were over, on her sister inquiring the cause of her visit, she replied :

" Of course you remember the advice you gave me, when you persuaded me to destroy with a sharp razor the beast that lay with me under the assumed name of a husband, before he should swallow me, poor creature, in his voracious maw. I proceeded to do as we had arranged ; but as soon as ever I discerned his features by the light of the lamp, I beheld a sight truly wonderful and divine, the very son himself of the goddess Venus, Cupid I say, sunk in tranquil repose. Just, however, as, struck with astonishment at the sight of such a boundless blessing, and in utter ecstasy through an over-abundance of pleasure, I was at a loss how sufficiently to enjoy my fortune, by a most shocking accident, the lamp spirted out some scalding oil upon his right shoulder. Instantly awakened by the pain, and seeing me armed with the weapon and the light, ' For this shameful conduct,' said he, ' quit my bed this instant, I divorce you for ever. I will at once marry your sister,'—mentioning you expressly by name,—and then he ordered Zephyr to waft me beyond the precincts of the palace."

Scarcely had Psyche ended her narrative, when the other, goaded by maddening lust and baneful envy, deceived her husband by a story which she had ready invented, as though she had heard something about the death of her parents, and immediately embarking, proceeded to the same rock. When she arrived there, though another wind was blowing, yet, elated with blind hope, she exclaimed :

" Receive me, Cupid, a wife worthy of thee, and thou, Zephyr, acknowledge thy mistress."

Then with a great bound, she threw herself headlong from the mountain ; but neither alive nor dead was she able to reach the spot she sought. For her limbs were torn in pieces by the crags, and scattered here and there as she fell, her entrails were rent asunder, just as she deserved ; and so, furnishing a banquet for birds and beasts of prey, she perished.

Nor was the other sister's punishment long delayed ; for Psyche's wandering steps led her to another city, in which that sister dwelt ; and she also, deceived by the same tale, and impiously desirous of supplanting Psyche as a wife, hastened to the rock, and there met with her death in a similar manner.

In the meantime, while Psyche wandered through various nations, anxiously searching for Cupid, he himself, with the wound from the lamp, lay in his mother's chamber groaning. A snow-white sea-gull, the bird which skims along the waves of the sea, flapping them with its wings, dived down into the bosom of the ocean. There, approaching Venus, as she bathed and swam, he informed her that her son was confined to his bed by a severe burn, was in great pain, and his cure was doubtful: that all sorts of scandalous reports were flying about concerning the whole family of Venus ; and it was in everybody's mouth that mother and son had gone off, the one to a mountain, to carry on an intrigue with a girl ; the other to amuse herself with swimming in the sea.

Thus did this talkative and very meddling bird chatter in the ear of Venus, to lower her son in her estimation.

Venus, exceedingly enraged, instantly exclaimed :

" So then this hopeful son of mine has already got some mistress or other. Come, now, you who are the only one to serve me with true affection, what is the name of her who has thus decoyed the ingenuous and beardless boy ? "

The talkative bird was only too ready to reply :

" I am not quite sure, mistress. I think, though, if I remember right, he is said to have fallen desperately in love with a girl whose name is Psyche."

" What ! " exclaimed Venus, in a burst of indignation, " of all wenches in the world, is he in love with Psyche, the usurper of my beauty, and the rival of my fame ? And by way of additional insult, he takes me for a go-between, through whose instrumentality he made acquaintance with the girl."

Thus exclaiming, she forthwith emerged from the sea, and hastened to her golden chamber, where, finding her son lying ill, as she had been informed, she cried out as loud as ever she could before she entered the door:

"This is pretty conduct, indeed! and very becoming our dignified birth, and your sobriety of character. In the first place, to trample under foot the commands of your mother, your sovereign mistress, and refrain from tormenting my enemy with an ignoble love, and then at your age, a mere boy, to take her to your profligate and immature embraces, on purpose, I suppose, that I might endure the vexation of having my enemy for my daughter-in-law. But I will make you repent of these tricks of yours and that you shall find this match a sour and bitter one."

Having thus vented her wrath, she rushed impetuously out of doors, and was immediately accosted by Ceres and Juno, who, observing her angry countenance, asked her why she marred the beauty of her sparkling eyes by such a sullen frown.

"Most opportunely are you come," she replied, "to appease that violence which has taken possession of my raging bosom. Inquire for me, I beg, with the utmost care and diligence after that runaway vagabond, Psyche; for the infamous stories about my family, and the conduct of my son who does not deserve to be named, cannot be unknown to you."

The two goddesses, knowing what had happened, endeavoured lightly to mitigate the rage of Venus. But she, indignant that her injuries were not treated with more respect, turned her back upon them, and with hasty steps again betook herself to the ocean.

In the meantime Psyche wandered about, day and night, restlessly seeking her husband, and the more anxious to find him, because, though she had incurred his anger, she hoped to appease him, if not by the tender endearments of a wife, at least by entreaties as humble as a slave could urge. Perceiving a temple on the summit of a lofty mountain,

"How can I tell," said she, "but yonder may be the residence of my lord?"

And immediately she hastened thither, while, wayworn and exhausted as she was, hope and affection quickened her steps, and gave her vigour to climb the highest ridges of the mountain and enter the temple. There she saw blades of wheat, some in sheaves, some twisted into chaplets, and ears of barley also. There were scythes likewise, and all the implements of harvest, but all lying scattered about in confusion, just as such things are usually thrown down, in the heat of summer, from the careless hands of the reapers.

Psyche began carefully to sort all these things, and arrange them properly in their several places, deeming it her duty not to fail in respect for the temples and ceremonies of any deity, but to implore the benevolent sympathy of all the gods. Bounteous Ceres found her thus diligently employed in her temple, and cried to her, from a distance:

"Ah, poor unfortunate Psyche! Venus, full of rage, is eagerly tracking your footsteps, craving to inflict upon you the deadly penalties, and the whole force of her divine vengeance. And can you then busy yourself with my concerns, and think of anything else but your own safety?"

Psyche, prostrating herself before the goddess, moistening her feet with abundant tears, and sweeping the ground with her locks, besought her protection with manifold prayers.

"I implore thee," said she, "by thy fruit-bearing right hand, by the joyful ceremonies of harvest, by the winged car of the dragons thy servants, by the furrows of the Sicilian soil, by the chariot of Pluto, by the earth that closed upon him, by the dark descent and unlighted nuptials of Proserpine, by the torch-illumined return of thy recovered daughter, and by the other mysteries which Eleusis, the sanctuary of Attica, conceals in silence: succour, O succour the life of the wretched Psyche, thy suppliant! Suffer me, if for a few days only, to conceal myself in that heap of wheatsheaves, till the raging anger of the mighty goddess be mitigated by the lapse of time; or at least until my bodily powers, weakened by long-continued labour, be renewed by an interval of rest."

"I am touched by your tears and entreaties," Ceres replied, "and fain would render you assistance; but I cannot provoke the displeasure of my relative, to whom I am also united by ties of friendship of old date, and who besides is a very worthy lady. Begone, therefore, from this temple directly, and be very thankful that I do not seize and detain you as a prisoner."

Psyche, thus repulsed, contrary to her expectations, and afflicted with twofold grief, retraced the way she came, and presently espied in a gloomy grove of the valley below the mountain a temple of exquisite structure. Unwilling to omit any chance of better fortune, though ever so remote, but resolving rather to implore the protection of the god, whoever he might be, she approached the sacred doors. There she beheld splendid offerings, and garments embroidered with golden letters, fastened to the branches of trees and to the door-posts of the temple, upon which was recorded the name of the goddess to whom they had been dedicated, and also the particulars of the favour received.

Then Psyche fell upon her knees, and with her hands embracing the yet warm altar, having first wiped away her tears, she thus offered up a prayer :

"O sister and consort of mighty Jove! be thou, Juno Sospita, a protectress to me in these my overwhelming misfortunes, and deliver me, worn out with long sufferings, from the fear of my impending danger ; for I know that thou art accustomed readily to succour women in time of peril."

While Psyche thus prayed, Juno appeared before her, in all the august majesty of her divinity, and said :

"How readily would I lend an ear to your entreaties ; but propriety will not permit me to act contrary to the wishes of Venus, my daughter-in-law, whom I have always loved as my own child. Then, besides, the laws forbid me to receive into my protection any fugitive servant, without the consent of her mistress."

Dismayed by this second shipwreck of her fortunes, and being no longer able to make search for her volatile husband, Psyche gave up all hopes of safety, and thus communed with herself :

"What other relief for my sorrows can now be looked for or procured, since even goddesses cannot, though willing, afford me any assistance ? In what direction shall I once more bend my wandering steps, entangled, as I am, in snares so inextricable ? Concealed in what habitations, in what darkness even, can I escape the ever-vigilant eyes of the mighty Venus ? Assume, then, a masculine courage, my soul, boldly renounce vain hopes, voluntarily surrender yourself into the hands of your mistress, and try, though late, to soften her rage by submissive behaviour. Besides, who knows whether you may not perhaps find in his mother's house him whom you have been so long seeking in vain."

Thus prepared for this doubtful experiment of duty, or rather for certain destruction, she considered with herself how she was to preface her entreaties.

Venus, meanwhile, declining to employ earthly means in pursuing her inquiries after Psyche, returned to heaven. She ordered the chariot to be got ready, which Vulcan had constructed with exquisite skill, and presented to her before the celebration of her marriage.

Then straightway went Venus to the royal citadel of Jove, and with a haughty air demanded, as especially necessary, the services of the crier god; nor did the azure brow of Jupiter refuse its assent. Exulting Venus, accompanied by Mercury, immediately descended from heaven, and thus anxiously addressed him:

"My Arcadian brother, you well know that your sister, Venus, never did anything without the presence of Mercury, nor are you ignorant how long I have been unable to find my absconded female slave. Nothing remains, therefore, to be done but for you to proclaim her in public, and announce a reward to him who shall find her. Take care, therefore, that my commands are speedily executed, and clearly describe the marks by which she may be recognised; that no one may excuse himself on the plea of ignorance, if he incurs the crime of unlawfully concealing her."

So saying, she gave him a little book, in which were written Psyche's name and sundry particulars. This done, she immediately returned home. Nor did Mercury neglect her commands; for going about among all nations, he thus performed his duties as crier:

"If any one can seize in her flight, and bring back, a fugitive daughter of a king, a handmaid of Venus, and by name Psyche, or discover where she has concealed herself, let such person repair to Mercury, and receive, by way of reward, for the discovery, seven sweet kisses from Venus herself, and one exquisitely delicious touch of her charming tongue."

Mercury having thus made proclamation, the desire of obtaining such a reward excited the emulous endeavours of all mankind, and this circumstance it was that quite put an end to all Psyche's hesitation. She was already near her mistress's gates, when she was met by one of the retinue of Venus, whose name was HABIT, and who immediately cried out, as loud as she could bawl:

"So, you most good-for-nothing wench, have you at last begun to discover that you have a mistress? And do you pretend, too, in your abundant assurance, that you don't know what immense trouble we have had in endeavouring to find you out? But it is well that you have fallen into my hands, of all others, and have got within the very jaws of Orcus, to receive, without delay, the penalty of such obstinate contumacy."

So saying, she instantly twisted her hands in Psyche's hair, and dragged the unresisting captive along. But Venus, the moment she was dragged into her presence, burst into a loud laugh, such as people laugh who are furiously angry; and shaking her head and scratching her right ear:

"At length," said she, "have you deigned to pay your respects to your mother-in-law? Or rather, are you come to see your sick husband, who is yet dangerously ill from the wound you gave him? But make yourself easy; for I shall at once give you a reception such as a good mother-in-law ought to give. Where," she cried, "are those servants of mine, ANXIETY and SORROW?"

These attending, at her call, she delivered her to them to be tormented. Thereupon, in obedience to the commands of their mistress, they scourged and inflicted other torments on the wretched Psyche, and after they had tortured her, brought her back again into the presence of Venus.

"Just look at her," said Venus, again setting up a laugh; "her interesting state quite moves my compassion, since it is through that, forsooth, that she is to make me a happy grandmother. And the son of a vile handmaid is to hear himself called the grandson of Venus! And yet I talk nonsense in calling him my grandson; for ill-assorted marriages, contracted, too, in a country place, without any witnesses, and without the father's consent, cannot possibly be deemed legitimate; consequently this child will be a bastard, even if I do suffer you to bring it into the light at all."

Having thus said, she flew upon her, tore ner clothes in a great many places, pulled out her hair, shook her by the head, and grievously maltreated her. Then taking wheat, barley, millet, poppy, vetches, lentils, and beans, and mixing them all together in one heap, she said to her:

"You seem to me, such an ugly slave as you now are, to be likely to gain lovers in no other way than by diligent drudgery. I will, therefore, myself, for once, make trial of your industrious habits. Take and separate this promiscuous mass of seeds, and having properly placed each grain in its place, and so sorted the whole, give me a proof of your expedition, by finishing the task before evening."

Then having delivered over to her the vast heap of seeds, she at once took her departure for a nuptial banquet.

But Psyche, astounded at the stupendous task, sat silent and stupefied, and did not move a hand to the confused and inextricable mass. Just then, a tiny little ant, one of the inhabitants of the fields, became aware of this prodigious difficulty; and pitying the distress of the partner of the mighty god, and execrating the mother-in-law's cruelty, it ran busily about, and summoned together the whole tribe of ants in the neighbourhood, crying to them:

"Take pity on her, ye active children of the all-producing earth! Take pity, and make haste to help the wife of Love, a pretty damsel, who is now in a perilous situation."

Immediately the six-footed people came rushing in whole waves one upon another, and with the greatest diligence separated the whole heap, grain by grain; then, having assorted the various kinds into different heaps, they vanished forthwith.

At nightfall, Venus returned home and saw with what marvellous expedition the task had been executed.

"This is no work of your hands, wicked creature," she said, "but his whom you have charmed, to your own sorrow and his"; and throwing her a piece of coarse bread, she went to bed.

Meanwhile, Cupid was closely confined in his chamber, partly that he might not inflame his wound by froward indulgence, and partly lest he should associate with his beloved. The lovers, thus separated from each other under one roof, passed a miserable night. But as soon as Aurora had ushered in the morning, Venus called Psyche, and thus addressed her:

"Do you see yonder grove, stretching along the margin of a river, whose deep eddies receive the waters of a neighbouring fountain? There shining sheep of a golden colour wander about, feeding without a shepherd. I desire that you bring me immediately a flock of that precious wool, get it how you may."

Psyche willingly set out, not with any intention of executing this command, but to procure rest from her misfortunes, by hurling herself headlong from the rock into the river. But when she came to the brink, a green reed, the nurse of sweet music, divinely inspired by a gentle breath of air, thus prophetically murmured:

"Psyche! exercised in mighty sorrows, neither pollute my sacred waters by your most miserable death, nor venture yet to approach the formidable sheep on the opposite bank. While heated by the burning radiance of the sun, they are transported with savage rage, and are the destruction of mortals, either by their sharp horns, their stony foreheads, or their venomous bites. Therefore until the sun has declined from the meridian, and the serene spirit of the flood has lulled the animals to rest, you may hide yourself under yonder lofty plane tree, which drinks of the same river with myself; and as soon as the sheep have mitigated their fury, if you shake the branches of the neighbouring grove, you will find the woolly gold everywhere sticking to them."

Thus the artless and humane reed taught the wretched Psyche how to accomplish this dangerous enterprise with safety.

Psyche, therefore, observing all the directions, found her obedience was not in vain, but returned to Venus with her bosom full of the delicate golden fleece. Yet she was not able to win the approbation of her mistress by this her second perilous labour. But Venus, smiling bitterly with knitted brows, thus addressed her:

"I do not fail to perceive another's hand in the performance of this task also; but I will now try whether you are endowed with a courageous mind and singular prudence. Do you see the summit of yonder lofty mountain? From that peak fall the dusky waters of a black fountain, which, after being confined in the neighbouring valley, irrigate the Stygian marshes, and supply the hoarse streams of Cocytus? Bring me immediately in this little urn ice-cold water drawn from the very midst of the lofty fountain."

Thus speaking, she gave her a vessel of polished crystal, and at the same time threatened her more severely than before.

But Psyche started off with the utmost celerity to reach the very summit of the mountain, presuming that there, at least, she would find the period of her most miserable life. However, when she arrived at its confines, she saw the deadly difficulty of the stupendous undertaking. For a rock, enormously lofty and inaccessibly rugged, vomits from its middle the horrid waters of the fountain, which, immediately falling headlong, are carried unseen through a deep, narrow, and covered channel into the neighbouring valley. On the right and left hand they creep through hollow rocks, over which fierce dragons stretch out their long necks, and keep a perpetual watch with unwinking vigilance. And the vocal waters exclaim ever and anon as they roll along:

"Begone; what are you about? Mind what you do; take care; fly; you will perish."

Psyche, therefore, petrified through the impossibility of accomplishing the task, and being perfectly overwhelmed by the danger before her, was even deprived of the benefit of tears, the last solace of the wretched. But the sorrow of the innocent soul is not concealed from the penetrating eyes of Providence. The rapacious eagle, Jove's royal bird, on a sudden flew to her with expanded wings, remembering his ancient obligations to Cupid, who enabled him to carry the Phrygian cup-bearer up to Jove; therefore, in gratitude to the young god, the eagle deserted the lofty paths of Jupiter, and bringing seasonable assistance to Cupid's wife in her distress, he thus addressed her:

" Can you, simple as you are, and inexperienced in attempts of this kind, ever hope to steal one drop of this most holy and no less terrible fountain? Have you not heard, at least, that these Stygian waters are formidable even to Jupiter himself, and that as you swear by the divinity of the gods, so they are accustomed to swear by the majesty of Styx? But give me that little urn."

Snatching it in haste, he sailed away on his strong wings, steering his course to the right and to the left, between the rows of raging teeth, and the three-forked vibrating tongues of the dragons until he reached and drew the reluctant waters, which warned him to begone while he might in safety. But he pretended that Venus herself wanted some of the water, and had ordered him to procure it; and on this account his access to the fountain was somewhat facilitated.

Psyche, therefore, joyfully receiving the full urn, returned with all speed to Venus. Yet not even by the accomplishment of this dangerous enterprise could she appease the anger of the raging goddess. For designing to expose her to still more outrageous trials, Venus thus addressed her, a smile, the harbinger of ruin, accompanying her words:

" You appear to me to be a profound and malevolent sorceress, or you never could with so much dexterity have performed my commands: but there is one task more, my dear, which you must perform. Take this box," she said, delivering it to her, " and direct your course to the infernal regions and the deadly palace of Pluto. Then, presenting the box to Proserpine, say, Venus requests you to send her a small portion of your beauty, at least as much as may be sufficient for one short day; for she has consumed all the beauty she possessed, through the attention which she pays to her sick son. But return with the utmost expedition; for I must adorn myself with this beauty of Proserpine before I go to the theatre of the gods."

Psyche was now truly sensible that she was arrived at the extremity of her evil fortune; and clearly perceived that she was openly and undisguisedly impelled to immediate destruction, since she was forced to direct her steps to Tartarus and the shades below. Without any further delay, therefore, she proceeded towards a lofty tower, that she might thence hurl herself headlong; for she considered that she should thus descend by a straight and easy road to the infernal regions. But she was no sooner arrived there, than the tower suddenly addressed her in the following words:

"Why, O miserable creature, dost thou seek to destroy thyself by falling headlong hence? And why dost thou rashly sink under this thy last danger and endurance? For as soon as thy breath shall thus be separated from thy body, thou wilt indeed descend to profound Tartarus, but canst not by any means return thence. Listen, therefore, to me. Lacedaemon, a noble city of Achaia, is not far from hence. Near this city, concealed in devious places, is Tenarus, which you must seek; for there you will find a cavity, which is Pluto's breathing hole, and an untraversed road presents itself to the view through the yawning gap. As soon as you have passed the threshold of this cavity, you will proceed in a direct path to the palace of Pluto. You ought not, however, to pass through those shades with empty hands, but should take a sop of barley bread, soaked in hydromel, in each hand, and in your mouth two pieces of money. And when you have accomplished a good part of your deadly journey, you will meet a lame ass laden with wood, with a driver as lame as himself, who will ask you to reach him certain cords to fasten the burden which has fallen from the ass: but be careful that you pass by him in silence. Then, without any delay, proceed till you arrive at the dead river, where Charon, immediately demanding his fee, ferries the passengers over in his patched boat to the farthest shore.

"Avarice, it appears, lives among the dead; nor does Charon himself, nor the father Pluto, though so great a god, do anything gratuitously. To this squalid old man give one of the pieces of money which you carry with you; yet in such a manner, that he may take it with his own hand from your mouth. While you are passing over the sluggish river, a certain dead old man, floating on its surface, and raising his putrid hand, will entreat you to take him into the boat. Beware, however, of yielding to any impulse of unlawful pity. Having passed over the river, and proceeded to a little distance beyond it, you will see certain old women, weaving a web, who will request you to lend them a helping hand ; but it is not lawful for you to touch the web. For all these, and many other particulars, are snares prepared for you by Venus, that you may drop one of the sops out of your hands. But do not suppose that this would be a trifling loss ; since the want of only one of these sops would prevent your return to light. For a huge dog, with three large, fierce, and formidable necks and heads, barking with his thundering jaws, terrifies in vain the dead, whom he cannot injure ; and always watching before the threshold and black palace of Proserpine, guards the void Plutonian mansion.

" Having appeased this dog with one of your sops, you may easily pass by him, and then you will immediately enter the presence of Proserpine herself, who will receive you in a very courteous and benignant manner, desire you to repose on a soft seat, and persuade you to partake of a sumptuous banquet. But seat yourself on the ground, ask for a piece of common bread, and eat it ; then deliver your message, and having received what you came for, bribe the cruel dog with the remaining sop. Afterwards, having given to the avaricious ferryman the piece of money which you have reserved, and having passed his river, you will return by the way you came to the choir of the celestial stars. But, above all things, I warn you, be particularly cautious not to open or look on the box which you carry, or explore that concealed treasury of divine beauty."

In this manner, the propitious tower delivered its prophetic admonitions.

Psyche, therefore, without delay, proceeded to Tenarus, and duly taking her pieces of money and her sops, ran down the infernal avenue. Here, having passed by the lame ass in silence, given the ferryman his fee, neglected the entreaties of the floating corpse, despised the fraudulent prayers of the spinsters, and lulled the rage of the horrid dog with a sop, she entered the palace of Proserpine. Nor did she accept the delicate seat, or delicious banquet ; but humbly sat at the feet of Proserpine, and, contented with a piece of common bread, delivered her embassy from Venus. Immediately after this, she received the box secretly filled and shut ; and having stopped the barking mouth of the dog with the remaining sop, and given the ferryman the other piece of money, she returned from the infernal regions much more vigorous than before.

Having again beheld and adored the fair light of day, though she was in haste to finish her errand, she was seized with a rash curiosity :

" Behold," said she, " what a foolish bearer am I of divine beauty, who do not even take the least portion of it, that I may by this means appear pleasing in the eyes of my beautiful lover."

As she ended this soliloquy, she opened the box ; but it contained no beauty, nor indeed anything but an infernal and truly Stygian sleep, which, being freed from its confinement, immediately seizes her, suffuses all her members with a dense cloud of somnolence, and holds her prostrate on the very spot where she opened the box ; so that she lay motionless, and nothing else than a sleeping corpse.

But Cupid, being now recovered of his wound, and unable to endure the long absence of his Psyche, glided through the narrow window of the bedchamber in which he was confined. His wings, invigorated by repose, flew far more swiftly than before ; he hastened to his Psyche, and carefully brushing off the cloud of sleep and shutting it up again in its old receptacle, the box, he roused Psyche with an innocuous touch of one of his arrows.

" Behold," said he, " unhappy girl, again you have all but perished, a victim to curiosity. Now, however, strenuously perform the task imposed upon you by my mother, and I myself will take care of the rest."

Having thus spoken, the lover soared aloft on his wings, and Psyche immediately carried the present of Proserpine to Venus.

In the meantime, Cupid, wasting away through excess of love, and dreading his mother's sudden prudery, betakes himself to his usual weapons of craft, and having with rapid wings penetrated the summit of heaven, supplicates the mighty Jupiter, and defends his cause. Then Jupiter, stroking the little cheeks of Cupid, and kissing his hand, thus addressed him :

" Though you, my masterful son, never pay me that reverence which has been decreed me by the synod of the gods, but perpetually wound this breast of mine, nevertheless, remembering my own moderation, and that you have been nursed in these hands of mine, I will accomplish all that you desire."

Having thus spoken, he ordered Mercury immediately to summon an assembly of all the gods ; and at the same time to proclaim, that if any one of the celestials absented himself he should be fined ten thousand pieces of money. The fear of such a penalty caused the celestial theatre to be filled immediately; whereupon lofty Jupiter, sitting on his sublime throne, thus addressed the assembly:

"Ye conscript gods, whose names are registered in the white roll of the Muses, you are all well acquainted with that youth whom I have reared with my own hands, and the impetuous fire of whose juvenile years I deem it necessary to restrain by some bridle or other. He has made choice of a girl. Let him, therefore, hold her, let him possess her, and embracing Psyche, always enjoy the object of his love."

Then turning his face to Venus, "Nor do you, my daughter," said he, "be sorrowful on this occasion, nor fearful that your pedigree and rank will be disgraced by a mortal marriage; for I will now cause the nuptials not to be unequal, but legitimate, and agreeable to the civil law."

Immediately after this, he ordered Mercury to bring Psyche to heaven; and as soon as she arrived, extending to her a cup of ambrosia:

"Take this," said he, "Psyche, and be immortal; nor shall Cupid ever depart from your embrace, but these nuptials of yours shall be perpetual."

Then, without delay, a sumptuous wedding supper was served up. The husband, reclining at the upper end of the table, embraced Psyche in his bosom; in like manner, Jupiter was seated with Juno, and after them, the other gods and goddesses in their proper order. Thus Psyche came lawfully into the hands of Cupid; and at length, a daughter was born to them, whom we call PLEASURE.

HELIODORUS
400 A.D.

TRAGIC LOVE

The Story told by Cnemon

MY father's name was Aristippus, an Athenian, a member of the Upper Council, and possessed of a decent fortune. After the death of my mother, as he had no child but me, he began to think of a second marriage, esteeming it hard that he should live an unsettled life solely on my account; he married, therefore, a woman of polished manners, but a mischief-maker, called Demaeneta.

From the moment of her marriage she brought him entirely under her subjection, enticing him by her beauty and seeming attentions; for there never was a woman who possessed the arts of allurement in a greater degree: she would lament at his going out, run with joy to meet him at his return, blame him for his stay, and mingle kisses and embraces with the tenderest expostulations. My father, entangled in these wiles, was entirely wrapped up in her. At first she pretended to behave to me as if I had been her own son; this likewise helped to influence my father. She would sometimes kiss me, and constantly wished to enjoy my society. I readily complied, suspecting nothing, but was agreeably surprised at her behaving to me with so much maternal affection.

When, however, she approached me with more wantonness; when her kisses became warmer than those of a relation ought to be, and her glances betrayed marks of passion, I began to entertain suspicions, to avoid her company, and repress her caresses. I need not enumerate what artifices she used, what promises she employed to gain me over, how she called me darling, sweetest, breath of her life; how she mingled blandishments with these soft words; how, in serious affairs, she behaved really as a mother, in less grave hours but too plainly as a lover.

At length, one evening, after I had been assisting at the solemn Panathenaean festival (when a ship is sent to Minerva by land), and had joined in the hymns and usual procession, I returned home in my dress of ceremony, with my robe and crown. She, as soon as she saw me, ran up to me, embraced me, and called me her dear Theseus, her young Hippolytus: How do you imagine I then felt, who now blush even at the recital?

My father that night was to sup in the Prytanaeum, and, as it was a grand and stated entertainment, was not expected to return home till the next day. I had not long retired to my apartment when she followed me; but when she found that I resisted with horror, regardless of her allurements, her promises, or her threats, fetching a deep-drawn sigh, she retired; and the very next day, with uncommon wickedness, began to put her machinations in force against me.

She took to her bed; and, when my father returned and inquired the reason of it, she said she was indisposed, and at first would say no more. But when he insisted, with great tenderness, on knowing what had so disordered her, with seeming reluctance she thus addressed him:

"This dainty youth, this son of yours, whom I call the gods to witness I loved as much as you could do yourself, taking the opportunity of your absence, while I was advising and exhorting him to temperance, and to avoid drunkenness and loose companions (for I was not ignorant of his inclinations, though I avoided dropping the least hint of them to you, lest it should appear the calumny of a step-mother)—while, I say, I took this opportunity of speaking to him alone, that I might spare his confusion, I am ashamed to tell how he abused both you and me; nor did he confine himself to words; but assaulting me both with hands and feet, kicked me at last upon the stomach, and left me in a dreadful condition, in which I have continued ever since."

When my father heard this, he made no reply, asked no questions, framed no excuse for me; but, believing that she who had appeared so fond of me, would not, without great reason, accuse me, the next time he met me in the house he gave me a tremendous blow; and calling his slaves, he commanded them to scourge me, without so much as telling me the cause of it. When he had wreaked his resentment, "Now, at least," said I, "father, tell me the reason of this shameful treatment."

This enraged him the more. "What hypocrisy!" cried he; "he wants me to repeat the story of his own wickedness." And, turning from me, he hastened to Demaeneta. But this implacable woman, not yet satisfied, laid another plot against me.

She had a young slave called Thisbe, handsome enough, and skilled in music. She, by her mistress's orders, put herself in my way; and though she had before appeared hostile to me, she now made advances, in gestures, words, and behaviour. I, like a silly fellow as I was, began to be vain of my own attractions ; and, in short, made an appointment with her one night.

When, one day, as I was cautioning her to have a care lest her mistress found us out, she broke out :

" O Cnemon ! how great is your simplicity, if you think it dangerous for a slave like me to be discovered with you. What would you think this very mistress deserves, who, calling herself of an honourable family, having a lawful husband, and knowing death to be the punishment of her crime, yet entertains a lover ? "

" Be silent," I replied ; " I cannot give credit to what you say."

" What if I show you the lover in the very fact ? "

" If you can, do."

" Most willingly will I," says she, " both on your account, who have been so abused by her, and on my own, who am the daily victim of her jealousy. If you are a man, therefore, seize her paramour."

I promised I would, and she then left me.

The third night after this she awakened me from sleep, and told me that the intruder was in the house ; that my father, on some sudden occasion, was gone into the country, and that the lover had taken this opportunity of secretly visiting Demaeneta. Now was the time for me to punish him as he deserved ; and that I should go in, sword in hand, lest he should escape.

I did as Thisbe exhorted me ; and taking my sword, she going before me with a torch, went towards my mother's chamber. When I arrived there, and perceived there was a light burning within, my passion rising, I burst open the door, and, rushing in, cried out, " Where is the villain, the vile paramour of this paragon of virtue ? " and thus exclaiming, I advanced, prepared to transfix them both, when my father, O ye gods ! leaping from the couch, fell at my feet, and besought me, " O my son ! stay your hand, pity your father, and these grey hairs which have nourished you. I have used you ill, I confess, but not so as to deserve death from you. Let not passion transport you ; do not imbrue your hands in a parent's blood ! "

He was going on in this supplicatory strain, while I stood thunderstruck, without power either to speak or stir. I looked about for Thisbe, but she had withdrawn. I cast my eyes in amaze round the chamber, confounded and stupefied ; the sword fell from my hand.

Demaeneta, running up, immediately took it away ; and my father, now seeing himself out of danger laid hands upon me, and ordered me to be bound, his wife stimulating him all the time, and exclaiming, " This is what I foretold ; I bade you guard yourself from the attempts of this youth ; I observed his looks, and feared his designs."

" You did," he replied, " but I could not have imagined he would carry his wickedness to such a pitch."

He then kept me bound ; and though I made several attempts to explain the matter, he would not suffer me to speak.

When the morning was come, he brought me out before the people, bound as I was ; and flinging dust upon his head, thus addressed them : " I entertained hopes, O Athenians, when the gods gave me this son, that he would have been the staff of my declining age. I brought him up genteelly ; I gave him a good education ; I went through every step needful to procure him the full privileges of a citizen of Athens ; in short, my whole life was a scene of solicitude on his account. But he, forgetting all this, abused me first with words, and assaulted my wife with blows ; and at last broke in upon me in the night, brandishing a drawn sword, and was prevented from committing parricide only by a sudden consternation which seized him, and made the weapon drop from his hand. I have recourse, therefore, to this assembly for my own defence and his punishment. I might, I know, lawfully have punished him even with death myself ; but I had rather leave the whole matter to your judgment than stain my own hands with his blood " : and, having said this, he began to weep.

Demaeneta too accompanied him with her tears, lamenting the untimely but just death which I must soon suffer, whom my evil genius had armed against my parent ; and thus seeming to confirm by her lamentations the truth of her husband's accusations.

At length I desired to be heard in my turn, when the clerk, arising, put this pointed question to me : Did I attack my father with a sword ?

When I replied, " I did indeed attack him, but hear how I came so to do "—the whole assembly exclaimed that, after this confession, there was no room for apology or defence.

Some cried out I ought to be stoned ; others, that I should be delivered to the executioner, and thrown headlong into the Barathrum.

During this tumult, while they were disputing about my punishment, I cried out, " All this I suffer on account of my step-mother, who makes me to be condemned unheard."

A few of the assembly appeared to take notice of what I said, and to have some suspicions of the truth of the case ; yet even then I could not obtain an audience, so much were all minds possessed by the disturbance.

At length they proceeded to ballot : one thousand seven hundred condemned me to death ; some to be stoned, others to be thrown into the Barathrum. The remainder, to the number of about a thousand, having some suspicions of the machinations of my step-mother, adjudged me to perpetual banishment ; and this sentence prevailed : for though a greater number had doomed me to death, yet there being a difference in their opinions as to the kind of death, they were so divided that the numbers of neither party amounted to a thousand.

Thus, therefore, was I driven from my father's house and my country ; the wicked Demaeneta, however, did not remain unpunished ; in what manner you shall hear by and by.

I went immediately from the assembly to the Piraeus, and finding a ship ready to set sail for Aegina, I embarked in her, hearing there were some relations of my mother's there. I was fortunate enough to find them on my arrival, and passed the first days of my exile agreeably enough among them. After I had been there about three weeks, taking my accustomed solitary walk, I came down to the port ; a vessel was standing in ; I stopped to see from whence she came, and who were on board. The ladder was no sooner let down, when a person leapt on shore, ran up to me, and embraced me. He proved to be Charias, one of my former companions.

" O Cnemon ! " he cried out, " I bring you good news. You are revenged on your enemy : Demaeneta is dead."

" I am heartily glad to see you, Charias," I replied ; " but why do you hurry over your good tidings as if they were bad ones ? Tell me how all this has happened ; I fear she has died a natural death, and escaped that which she deserved."

" Justice," said he, " has not entirely deserted us ; and though she sometimes seems to wink at crime for a time, protecting her vengeance, such wretches rarely escape at last : neither has Demaeneta. From my connection with Thisbe, I have been made acquainted with the whole affair.

" After your unjust exile, your father, repenting of what he had done, retired from the sight of the world into a lonely villa, and there lived—' gnawing his own heart,' according to the poet. But the furies took possession of his wife, and her passion rose to a higher pitch in your absence than it had ever done before. She lamented your misfortunes and her own, calling day and night in a frantic manner upon Cnemon, her dear boy, her soul; insomuch that the women of her acquaintance, who visited her, wondered at and praised her; that, though a step-dame, she felt a mother's affection. They endeavoured to console and strengthen her; but she replied that her sorrows were past consolation, and that they were ignorant of the wound which rankled at her heart.

" When she was alone she abused Thisbe for the share she had in the business. ' How slow were you in assisting my love! How ready in administering to my revenge! You deprived me of him I loved above all the world, without giving me an instant to repent and be appeased.' And she gave plain hints that she intended some mischief against her.

" Thisbe, seeing her disappointed, enraged, almost out of her senses with love and grief, and capable of undertaking anything, determined to be beforehand with her; and, by laying a snare for her mistress, to provide for her own security. One day, therefore, she thus accosted her:

" ' Why, O my mistress, do you wrongfully accuse your slave? It has always been my study to obey your will in the best manner I could; if anything unlucky has happened, fortune is to blame; I am ready now, if you command me, to endeavour to find a remedy for your distress.'

" ' What remedy can you find?' cried she. ' He who alone could ease my torments is far distant; the unexpected lenity of his judges has been my ruin: had he been stoned or otherwise put to death, my hopes and cares would have been buried with him. Impossibility of gratification extinguishes desire, and despair makes the heart callous. But now I seem to have him before my eyes: I hear, and blush at hearing, him upbraid me with his injuries. Sometimes I flatter my fond heart that he will return again, and that I shall obtain my wishes; at other times I form schemes of seeking him myself, on whatever shore he wanders. These thoughts agitate, inflame, and drive me beside myself. Ye gods! I am justly served. Why, instead of laying schemes against his life, did I not persist in endeavouring to subdue him by kindness? He refused me at first, and it was but fitting he should do so; I was a stranger, and he reverenced his father's honour. Time and persuasion might have overcome his coldness; but I, unjust and inhuman as I was, more like a tyrant than his lover, cruelly punished his first disobedience. Yet with how much justice might he slight Demaeneta, whom he so infinitely surpassed in beauty! But, my dear Thisbe, what remedy is it you hint at?'

"The artful slave replied: 'O mistress, Cnemon, as most people think, in obedience to the sentence, has departed both from the city and from Attica; but I, who inquire anxiously into everything that you can have any concern in, have discovered that he is lurking somewhere about the town. You have heard perhaps of Arsinoë the singer: he has long been connected with her. After his misfortune, she promised to go into exile with him, and keeps him concealed at her house till she can prepare herself for setting out.'

"'Happy Arsinoë!' cried Demaeneta; 'happy at first in possessing the love of Cnemon, and now in being permitted to accompany him into banishment. But what is all this to me?'

"'Attend, and you shall hear,' said Thisbe. 'I will pretend that I am in love with Cnemon. I will beg Arsinoë, with whom I am acquainted, to introduce me some night to him in her room; you may, if you please, represent Arsinoë, and receive his visit instead of me. I will take care that he shall have drunk a little freely.'

"Demaeneta eagerly embraced the proposal, and desired her to put it into immediate execution. Thisbe demanded a day only for preparation; and going directly to Arsinoë, asked her if she knew Teledemus. Arsinoë replying that she did, 'Receive us then,' says she, 'this evening into your house; I have promised to meet him to-night: he will come first; I shall follow, when I have put my mistress to bed.'

"Then hastening into the country to Aristippus, she thus addressed him: 'I come, master, to accuse myself; punish me as you think fit. I have been the cause of your losing your son; not indeed willingly, but yet I was instrumental in his destruction: for when I perceived that my mistress led a dishonourable life, I began to fear for myself, lest I should suffer if she should be detected by anybody else. I pitied you too, who received such ill returns for all your affection; I was afraid, however, of mentioning the matter to you, but I discovered it to my young master; and coming to him by night, to avoid observation, I told him that my mistress had a lover. He, hurried on by resentment, mistook my meaning, and thought I said that the lover was then with her. His passion rose; he snatched a sword, and ran madly on towards her chamber. The rest you know. You have it in your power at least to clear the character of your banished son, and to punish her who has injured both of you ; for I will show you to-day Demaeneta with her paramour, in a strange house without the city.'

" ' If you can do that,' said Aristippus, ' your freedom shall be your reward. I shall, perhaps, take some comfort in life when I have got rid of this wicked woman. I have for some time been uneasy within myself : I have suspected her ; but, having no proofs, I was silent. But what must we do now ? '

" ' You know,' said she, ' the garden where is the monument of the Epicureans : come there in the evening, and wait for me.'

" And having so said, away she goes ; and coming to Demaeneta, ' Dress yourself,' she cries, ' immediately ; neglect nothing that can set off your person ; everything that I have promised you is ready.'

" Demaeneta did as she was desired, and adorned herself with all her skill ; and in the evening Thisbe attended her to the place of assignation. When they came near she desired her to stop a little ; and going forwards she begged Arsinoë to step into the next house, and leave her at liberty in her own ; for she wished to spare the young man's blushes, who was but lately initiated into love affairs ; and, having persuaded her, she returned, introduced Demaeneta, and took away the light (lest, forsooth, you, who were then safe at Aegina, should discover her).

" ' I will now go,' said she, ' and bring the youth to you ; he is drinking at a house in the neighbourhood.'

" Away she flies where Aristippus was waiting, and exhorts him to go immediately and bind the villain fast. He follows her, rushes into the house, and, by help of a little moonlight which shone, with difficulty finding Demaeneta, exclaims, ' I have caught you now, you abandoned creature ! '

" Thisbe immediately upon this exclamation bangs to the door on the other side, and cries out, ' What untoward fortune ! the paramour has escaped ; but take care at least that you secure the other.'

" ' Make yourself easy,' he replied ; ' I have secured this wicked woman, whom I was the most desirous of taking ' ; and seizing her, he began to drag her towards the city.

" But she, feeling deeply the situation she was in, the disappointment of her hopes, the ignominy which must attend her offences, and the punishment which awaited them, vexed and enraged at being deceived and detected, when she came near the pit which is in the Academy (you know the place where our generals sacrifice to the Manes of our heroes), suddenly disengaging herself from the hands of the old man, flung herself headlong in : and thus she died a wretched death, suited for a wretch like herself.

" Upon this Aristippus cried out, ' You have yourself anticipated the justice of the laws,' and the next day he laid the whole matter before the people ; and having with difficulty obtained his pardon, consulted his friends and acquaintance how best he could obtain your recall. What success he has met with I cannot inform you of ; for I have been obliged, as you see, to sail here on my own private business. But I think you have the greatest reason to expect that the people will consent to your return, and that your father will himself come to seek you, and conduct you home."

Here Charias ended his recital.

How I came to this place, and what have been my fortunes since, would take up more time and words than there is at present opportunity for.

HEBREW LITERATURE
Circa 200 B.C.

TOBIT

THE book of the words of Tobit, son of Tobiel, the son of Ananiel, the son of Aduel, the son of Gabael, of the seed of Asael, of the tribe of Naphtali; who in the time of Enemessar King of the Assyrians was led captive out of Thisbe, which is at the right hand of Kadesh Naphtali in Galilee above Aser.

I Tobit have walked all the days of my life in the way of truth and justice, and I did many almsdeeds to my brethren, and my nation, who came with me to Nineve, into the land of the Assyrians. And when I was in mine own country, in the land of Israel, being but young, all the tribe of Naphtali my father fell from the house of Jerusalem, which was chosen out of all the tribes of Israel, that all the tribes should sacrifice there, where the temple of the habitation of the Most High was consecrated and built for all ages. Now all the tribes which together revolted, and the house of my father Naphtali, sacrificed unto the heifer Baal. But I alone went often to Jerusalem at the feasts, as it was ordained unto all the people of Israel by an everlasting decree, having the first fruits and tenths of increase, with that which was first shorn; and them gave I at the altar to the priests the children of Aaron. The first tenth part of all increase I gave to the sons of Aaron, who ministered at Jerusalem: another tenth part I sold away, and went, and spent it every year at Jerusalem: and the third I gave unto them to whom it was meet, as Debora my father's mother had commanded me, because I was left an orphan by my father.

Furthermore, when I was come to the age of a man, I married Anna of mine own kindred, and of her I begat Tobias.

And when we were carried away captives to Nineve, all my brethren and those that were of my kindred did eat of the bread of the Gentiles. But I kept myself from eating; because I remembered God with all my heart. And the Most High gave me grace and favour before Enemessar, so that I was his purveyor. And I went into Media, and left in trust with Gabael, the brother of Gabrias, at Rages a city of Media ten talents of silver.

Now when Enemessar was dead, Sennacherib his son reigned in his stead; and in his time the highways were troubled, that I could not go into Media. And in the time of Enemessar I gave many alms to my brethren, and gave my bread to the hungry, and my clothes to the naked: and if I saw any of my nation dead, or cast about the walls of Nineve, I buried him. And if the King Sennacherib had slain any, when he was come, and fled from Judea, I buried them privily; for in his wrath he killed many; but the bodies were not found, when they were sought for of the King. And when one of the Ninevites went and complained of me to the King, that I buried them, and hid myself; understanding that I was sought for to be put to death, I withdrew myself for fear. Then all my goods were forcibly taken away, neither was there anything left me, beside my wife Anna and my son Tobias. And there passed not five and fifty days, before two of his sons killed him, and they fled into the mountains of Ararath; and Sarchedonus his son reigned in his stead; who appointed over his father's accounts, and over all his affairs, Achiacharus my brother Anael's son. And Achiacharus intreating for me, I returned to Nineve. Now Achiacharus was cupbearer, and keeper of the signet, and steward, and overseer of the accounts: and Sarchedonus appointed him next unto him: and he was my brother's son.

Now when I was come home again, and my wife Anna was restored unto me, with my son Tobias, in the feast of Pentecost, which is the holy feast of the seven weeks, there was a good dinner prepared me, in the which I sat down to eat. And when I saw abundance of meat, I said to my son, "Go and bring what poor man soever thou shalt find out of our brethren, who is mindful of the Lord; and, lo, I tarry for thee." But he came again, and said: "Father, one of our nation is strangled, and is cast out in the marketplace." Then before I had tasted of any meat, I started up, and took him up into a room until the going down of the sun. Then I returned, and washed myself, and ate my meat in heaviness, remembering that prophecy of Amos, as he said, Your feasts shall be turned into mourning, and all your mirth into lamentation. Therefore I wept: and after the going down of the sun I went and made a grave, and buried him. But my neighbours mocked me, and said: "This man is not yet afraid to be put to death for this matter: who fled away; and yet, lo, he burieth the dead again." The same night also I returned from the burial, and slept by the wall of my courtyard, being polluted, and my face was uncovered: and I knew not that there were sparrows in the wall, and mine eyes being open, the sparrows muted warm dung into mine eyes, and a whiteness came in mine eyes; and I went to the physicians, but they helped me not: moreover Achiacharus did nourish me, until I went into Elymais.

And my wife Anna did take women's works to do. And when she had sent them home to the owners, they paid her wages, and gave her also besides a kid. And when it was in my house, and began to cry, I said unto her: "From whence is this kid? is it not stolen? render it to the owners; for it is not lawful to eat anything that is stolen." But she replied upon me: "It was given for a gift more than the wages." Howbeit I did not believe her, but bade her render it to the owners: and I was abashed at her. But she replied upon me: "Where are thine alms and thy righteous deeds? behold, thou and all thy works are known."

Then I being grieved did weep, and in my sorrow prayed, saying: "O Lord, Thou art just, and all Thy works and all Thy ways are mercy and truth, and Thou judgest truly and justly for ever. Remember me, and look on me, punish me not for my sins and ignorances, and the sins of my fathers, who have sinned before Thee: for they obeyed not Thy commandments: wherefore Thou hast delivered us for a spoil, and unto captivity, and unto death, and for a proverb of reproach to all the nations among whom we are dispersed. And now Thy judgments are many and true: deal with me according to my sins and my fathers': because we have not kept Thy commandments, neither have walked in truth before Thee. Now therefore deal with me as seemeth best unto Thee, and command my spirit to be taken from me, that I may be dissolved, and become earth: for it is profitable for me to die rather than to live, because I have heard false reproaches, and have much sorrow: command therefore that I may now be delivered out of this distress, and go into the everlasting place: turn not Thy face away from me."

It came to pass the same day, that in Ecbatane, a city of Media, Sara the daughter of Raguel was also reproached by her father's maids; because that she had been married to seven husbands, whom Asmodeus the evil spirit had killed, before they had lain with her. "Dost thou not know," said they, "that thou hast strangled thine husbands? thou hast had already seven husbands, neither wast thou named after any of them. Wherefore dost thou beat us for them? if they be dead, go thy ways after them, let us never see of thee either son or daughter."

When she heard these things, she was very sorrowful, so that she thought to have strangled herself; and she said: "I am the only daughter of my father, and if I do this, it shall be a reproach unto him, and I shall bring his old age with sorrow unto the grave." Then she prayed toward the window, and said: "Blessed art Thou, O Lord my God, and Thine holy and glorious name is blessed and honourable for ever: let all Thy works praise Thee for ever. And now, O Lord, I set mine eyes and my face toward Thee, and say, Take me out of the earth, that I may hear no more the reproach. Thou knowest, Lord, that I am pure from all sin with man, and that I never polluted my name, nor the name of my father, in the land of my captivity: I am the only daughter of my father, neither hath he any child to be his heir, neither any near kinsman, nor any son of his alive, to whom I may keep myself for a wife: my seven husbands are already dead; and why should I live? but if it please not Thee that I should die, command some regard to be had of me, and pity taken of me, that I hear no more reproach."

So the prayers of them both were heard before the majesty of the great God. And Raphael was sent to heal them both, that is, to scale away the whiteness of Tobit's eyes, and to give Sara the daughter of Raguel for a wife to Tobias the son of Tobit; and to bind Asmodeus the evil spirit; because she belonged to Tobias by right of inheritance. The selfsame time came Tobit home, and entered into his house, and Sara the daughter of Raguel came down from her upper chamber.

In that day Tobit remembered the money which he had committed to Gabael in Rages of Media, and said with himself: "I have wished for death; wherefore do I not call for my son Tobias, that I may signify to him of the money before I die?"

And when he had called him, he said: "My son, when I am dead, bury me; and despise not thy mother, but honour her all the days of thy life, and do that which shall please her, and grieve her not. Remember, my son, that she saw many dangers for thee, when thou wast in her womb; and when she is dead, bury her by me in one grave. My son, be mindful of the Lord our God all thy days, and let not thy will be set to sin, or to transgress His commandments: do uprightly all thy life long, and follow not the ways of unrighteousness. For if thou deal truly, thy doings shall prosperously succeed to thee, and to all them that live justly. Give alms of thy substance; and when thou givest alms, let not thine eye be envious, neither turn thy face from any poor, and the face of God shall not be turned away from thee. If thou hast abundance, give alms accordingly: if thou have but a little, be not afraid to give according to that little: for thou layest up a good treasure for thyself against the day of necessity. Because that alms do deliver from death, and suffereth not to come into darkness. For alms is a good gift unto all that give it in the sight of the Most High. Beware of all whoredom, my son, and chiefly take a wife of the seed of thy fathers, and take not a strange woman to wife, which is not of thy father's tribe: for we are the children of the prophets, Noe, Abraham, Isaac, and Jacob: remember, my son, that our fathers from the beginning, even that they all married wives of their own kindred, and were blessed in their children, and their seed shall inherit the land. Now therefore, my son, love thy brethren, and despise not in thy heart thy brethren, the sons and daughters of thy people, in not taking a wife of them: for in pride is destruction and much trouble, and in lewdness is decay and great want: for lewdness is the mother of famine. Let not the wages of any man, which hath wrought for thee, tarry with thee, but give him it out of hand: for if thou serve God, He will also repay thee: be circumspect, my son, in all things thou doest, and be wise in all thy conversation. Do that to no man which thou hatest: drink not wine to make thee drunken: neither let drunkenness go with thee in thy journey. Give of thy bread to the hungry, and of thy garments to them that are naked; and according to thine abundance give alms; and let not thine eye be envious, when thou givest alms. Pour out thy bread on the burial of the just, but give nothing to the wicked. Ask counsel of all that are wise, and despise not any counsel that is profitable. Bless the Lord thy God alway, and desire of Him that thy ways may be directed, and that all thy paths and counsels may prosper: for every nation hath not counsel; but the Lord Himself giveth all good things, and He humbleth whom He will, as He will; now therefore, my son, remember my commandments, neither let them be put out of thy mind. And now I signify this to thee, that I committed ten talents to Gabael the son of Gabrias at Rages in Media. And fear not, my son, that we are made poor: for thou hast much wealth, if thou fear God, and depart from all sin, and do that which is pleasing in His sight."

Tobias then answered and said: "Father, I will do all things which thou hast commanded me: but how can I receive the money, seeing I know him not?" Then he gave him the handwriting, and said unto him: "Seek thee a man which may go with thee, whiles

I yet live, and I will give him wages: and go and receive the money." Therefore when he went to seek a man, he found Raphael that was an angel. But he knew not; and he said unto him: "Canst thou go with me to Rages? and knowest thou those places well?" To whom the angel said: "I will go with thee, and I know the way well; for I have lodged with our brother Gabael." Then Tobias said unto him: "Tarry for me, till I tell my father." Then he said unto him: "Go, and tarry not." So he went in and said to his father: "Behold, I have found one which will go with me." Then he said: "Call him unto me, that I may know of what tribe he is, and whether he be a trusty man to go with thee."

So he called him, and he came in, and they saluted one another. Then Tobit said unto him: "Brother, show me of what tribe and family thou art." To whom he said: "Dost thou seek for a tribe or family, or an hired man to go with thy son?"

Then Tobit said unto him: "I would know, brother, thy kindred and name." And he answered: "I am Azarias, the son of Ananias the great, and of thy brethren." Then Tobit said: "Thou art welcome, brother; be not now angry with me, because I have enquired to know thy tribe and thy family; for thou art my brother, of an honest and good stock: for I know Ananias and Jonathas, sons of that great Samaias, as we went together to Jerusalem to worship, and offered the firstborn, and the tenths of the fruits; and they were not seduced with the error of our brethren: my brother, thou art of a good stock. But tell me, what wages shall I give thee? Wilt thou a drachm a day, and things necessary, as to mine own son? Yea, moreover, if ye return safe, I will add something to thy wages." So they were well pleased. Then said he to Tobias: "Prepare thyself for the journey, and God send you a good journey." And when his son had prepared all things for the journey, his father said: "Go thou with this man, and God, which dwelleth in heaven, prosper your journey, and the angel of God keep you company." So they went forth both, and the young man's dog with them.

But Anna his mother wept, and said to Tobit: "Why hast thou sent away our son? is he not the staff of our hand, in going in and out before us? Be not greedy to add money to money: but let it be as refuse in respect of our child. For that which the Lord hath given us to live with doth suffice us." Then said Tobit to her: "Take no care, my sister; he shall return in safety, and thine eyes shall see him. For the good angel will keep him company, and his journey shall be prosperous, and he shall return safe." Then she made an end of weeping.

And as they went on their journey, they came in the evening to the river Tigris, and they lodged there. And when the young man went down to wash himself, a fish leaped out of the river, and would have devoured him. Then the angel said unto him: "Take the fish." And the young man laid hold of the fish, and drew it to land. To whom the angel said: "Open the fish, and take the heart and the liver and the gall, and put them up safely." So the young man did as the angel commanded him; and when they had roasted the fish, they did eat it: then they both went on their way, till they drew near to Ecbatane. Then the young man said to the angel: "Brother Azarias, to what use is the heart and the liver and the gall of the fish?" And he said unto him: "Touching the heart and the liver, if a devil or an evil spirit trouble any, we must make a smoke thereof before the man or the woman, and the party shall be no more vexed. As for the gall, it is good to anoint a man that hath whiteness in his eyes, and he shall be healed."

And when they were come near to Rages, the angel said to the young man: "Brother, to-day we shall lodge with Raguel, who is thy cousin; he also hath one only daughter, named Sara; I will speak for her, that she may be given thee for a wife. For to thee doth the right of her appertain, seeing thou only art of her kindred. And the maid is fair and wise: now therefore hear me, and I will speak to her father; and when we return from Rages we will celebrate the marriage: for I know that Raguel cannot marry her to another according to the law of Moses, but he shall be guilty of death, because the right of inheritance doth rather appertain to thee than to any other." Then the young man answered the angel: "I have heard, brother Azarias, that this maid hath been given to seven men, who all died in the marriage chamber. And now I am the only son of my father, and I am afraid, lest, if I go in unto her, I die, as the others before: for a wicked spirit loveth her, which hurteth nobody, but those which come unto her: wherefore I also fear lest I die, and bring my father's and my mother's life because of me to the grave with sorrow: for they have no other son to bury them." Then the angel said unto him: "Dost thou not remember the precepts which thy father gave thee, that thou shouldest marry a wife of thine own kindred? wherefore hear me, O my brother; for she shall be given thee to wife; and make thou no reckoning of the evil spirit; for this same night shall she be given thee in marriage. And when thou shalt come into the marriage chamber, thou shalt take the ashes of perfume, and shalt lay upon them some of the heart and liver of the fish, and shalt make a smoke with it: and the devil shall smell it, and flee away, and never come again any more: but when thou shalt come to her, rise up both of you, and pray to God which is merciful, who will have pity on you, and save you: fear not, for she is appointed unto thee from the beginning; and thou shalt preserve her, and she shall go with thee. Moreover I suppose that she shall bear thee children." Now when Tobias had heard these things, he loved her, and his heart was effectually joined to her.

And when they were come to Ecbatane, they came to the house of Raguel, and Sara met them: and after they had saluted one another, she brought them into the house. Then said Raguel to Edna his wife: "How like is this young man to Tobit my cousin!" And Raguel asked them: "From whence are ye, brethren?" To whom they said: "We are of the sons of Naphtali, which are captives in Nineve." Then he said to them: "Do ye know Tobit our kinsman?" And they said: "We know him." Then said he: "Is he in good health?" And they said: "He is both alive, and in good health": and Tobias said: "He is my father." Then Raguel leaped up, and kissed him, and wept, and blessed him, and said unto him: "Thou art the son of an honest and good man." But when he had heard that Tobit was blind, he was sorrowful, and wept. And likewise Edna his wife and Sara his daughter wept. Moreover they entertained them cheerfully; and after that they had killed a ram of the flock, they set store of meat on the table.

Then said Tobias to Raphael: "Brother Azarias, speak of those things of which thou didst talk in the way, and let this business be dispatched." So he communicated the matter with Raguel: and Raguel said to Tobias: "Eat and drink, and make merry: for it is meet that thou shouldst marry my daughter: nevertheless I will declare unto thee the truth. I have given my daughter in marriage to seven men, who died that night they came in unto her: nevertheless for the present be merry." But Tobias said: "I will eat nothing here, till we agree and swear one to another." Raguel said: "Then take her from henceforth according to the manner, for thou art her cousin, and she is thine, and the merciful God give you good success in all things." Then he called his daughter Sara, and she came to her father, and he took her by the hand, and gave her to be wife to Tobias, saying: "Behold, take her after the law of Moses, and lead her away to thy father." And he blessed them; and called Edna his wife, and took paper, and did write an instrument of covenants, and sealed it. Then they began to eat.

After Raguel called his wife Edna, and said unto her: "Sister, prepare another chamber, and bring her in thither." Which when she had done as he had bidden her, she brought her thither: and she wept, and she received the tears of her daughter, and said unto her: "Be of good comfort, my daughter; the Lord of heaven and earth give thee joy for this thy sorrow: be of good comfort, my daughter."

And when they had supped, they brought Tobias in unto her. And as he went, he remembered the words of Raphael, and took the ashes of the perfumes, and put the heart and the liver of the fish thereupon, and made a smoke therewith. The which smell when the evil spirit had smelled, he fled into the utmost parts of Egypt, and the angel bound him. And after that they were both shut in together, Tobias rose out of the bed, and said: "Sister, arise, and let us pray that God would have pity on us." Then began Tobias to say: "Blessed art Thou, O God of our fathers, and blessed is Thy holy and glorious name for ever; let the heavens bless Thee, and all Thy creatures. Thou madest Adam, and gavest him Eve his wife for an helper and stay: of them came mankind: Thou hast said, It is not good that man should be alone; let Us make unto him an aid like unto himself. And now, O Lord, I take not this my sister for lust, but uprightly: therefore mercifully ordain that we may become aged together." And she said with him: "Amen." So they slept both that night.

And Raguel arose, and went and made a grave, saying: "I fear lest he also be dead." But when Raguel was come into his house, he said unto his wife Edna: "Send one of the maids, and let her see whether he be alive: if he be not, that we may bury him, and no man know it." So the maid opened the door, and went in, and found them both asleep, and came forth, and told them that he was alive. Then Raguel praised God, and said: "O God, Thou art worthy to be praised with all pure and holy praise; therefore let Thy saints praise Thee with all Thy creatures; and let all Thine angels and Thine elect praise Thee for ever. Thou art to be praised, for Thou hast made me joyful; and that is not come to me which I suspected; but Thou hast dealt with us according to Thy great mercy. Thou art to be praised, because

Thou hast had mercy of two that were the only begotten children of their fathers: grant them mercy, O Lord, and finish their life in health with joy and mercy." Then Raguel bade his servants to fill the grave. And he kept the wedding feast fourteen days. For before the days of the marriage were finished, Raguel had said unto him by an oath, that he should not depart till the fourteen days of the marriage were expired; and then he should take the half of his goods, and go in safety to his father; and should have the rest when I and my wife be dead.

Then Tobias called Raphael, and said unto him: "Brother Azarias, take with thee a servant, and two camels, and go to Rages of Media to Gabael, and bring me the money, and bring him to the wedding. For Raguel hath sworn that I shall not depart. But my father counteth the days; and if I tarry long, he will be very sorry." So Raphael went out, and lodged with Gabael, and gave him the handwriting: who brought forth bags which were sealed up, and gave them to him. And early in the morning they went forth both together, and came to the wedding: and Tobias blessed his wife.

Now Tobit his father counted every day: and when the days of the journey were expired, and they came not, then Tobit said: "Are they detained? or is Gabael dead, and there is no man to give him the money?" Therefore he was very sorry. Then his wife said unto him: "My son is dead, seeing he stayeth long"; and she began to bewail him, and said: "Now I care for nothing, my son, since I have let thee go, the light of mine eyes." To whom Tobit said: "Hold thy peace, take no care, for he is safe." But she said: "Hold thy peace, and deceive me not; my son is dead." And she went out every day into the way which they went, and did eat no meat on the daytime, and ceased not whole nights to bewail her son Tobias, until the fourteen days of the wedding were expired, which Raguel had sworn that he should spend there.

Then Tobias said to Raguel: "Let me go, for my father and my mother look no more to see me." But his father-in-law said unto him: "Tarry with me, and I will send to thy father, and they shall declare unto him how things go with thee." But Tobias said: "No; but let me go to my father." Then Raguel arose, and gave him Sara his wife, and half his goods, servants, and cattle, and money: and he blessed them, and sent them away, saying: "The God of heaven give you a prosperous journey, my children." And he said to his daughter: "Honour thy father- and thy mother-in-law, which are now thy parents, that I may hear good report of thee." And he kissed her. Edna also said to Tobias: "The Lord of heaven restore thee, my dear brother, and grant that I may see thy children of my daughter Sara before I die, that I may rejoice before the Lord: behold, I commit my daughter unto thee of special trust; wherefore do not entreat her evil."

After these things Tobias went his way, praising God that He had given him a prosperous journey, and blessed Raguel and Edna his wife, and went on his way till they drew near unto Nineve. Then Raphael said to Tobias: "Thou knowest, brother, how thou didst leave thy father: let us haste before thy wife, and prepare the house. And take in thine hand the gall of the fish." So they went their way, and the dog went after them. Now Anna sat looking about toward the way for her son. And when she espied him coming, she said to his father: "Behold, thy son cometh, and the man that went with him." Then said Raphael: "I know, Tobias, that thy father will open his eyes. Therefore anoint thou his eyes with the gall, and being pricked therewith, he shall rub, and the whiteness shall fall away, and he shall see thee."

Then Anna ran forth, and fell upon the neck of her son, and said unto him: "Seeing I have seen thee, my son, from henceforth I am content to die." And they wept both. Tobit also went forth toward the door, and stumbled: but his son ran unto him, and took hold of his father: and he strake of the gall on his father's eyes, saying: "Be of good hope, my father." And when his eyes began to smart, he rubbed them; and the whiteness scaled away from the corners of his eyes: and when he saw his son, he fell upon his neck. And he wept, and said: "Blessed art Thou, O God, and blessed is Thy name for ever; and blessed are all Thine holy angels: for Thou hast scourged, and hast taken pity on me; for, behold, I see my son Tobias." And his son went in rejoicing, and told his father the great things that had happened to him in Media.

Then Tobit went out to meet his daughter-in-law at the gate of Nineve, rejoicing, and praising God: and they which saw him go marvelled, because he had received his sight. But Tobit gave thanks before them, because God had mercy on him. And when he came near to Sara his daughter-in-law, he blessed her, saying: "Thou art welcome, daughter: God be blessed, which hath brought thee unto us, and blessed be thy father and thy mother." And there was joy among all his brethren which were at Nineve. And Achiacharus, and Nasbas his brother's son, came: and Tobias' wedding was kept seven days with great joy.

Then Tobit called his son Tobias, and said unto him: "My son, see that the man have his wages, which went with thee, and thou must give him more." And Tobias said unto him: "O father, it is no harm to me to give him half of those things which I have brought: for he hath brought me again to thee in safety, and made whole my wife, and brought me the money, and likewise healed thee." Then the old man said: "It is due unto him." So he called the angel, and he said unto him: "Take half of all that ye have brought, and go away in safety." Then he took them both apart, and said unto them:

"Bless God, praise Him, and magnify Him, and praise Him for the things which He hath done unto you in the sight of all that live. It is good to praise God, and exalt His name, and honourably to show forth the works of God; therefore be not slack to praise Him. It is good to keep close the secret of a king, but it is honourable to reveal the works of God. Do that which is good, and no evil shall touch you. Prayer is good with fasting and alms and righteousness. A little with righteousness is better than much with unrighteousness. It is better to give alms than to lay up gold: for alms doth deliver from death, and shall purge away all sin. Those that exercise alms and righteousness shall be filled with life: but they that sin are enemies to their own life. Surely I will keep close nothing from you. For I said, It was good to keep close the secret of a king, but that it was honourable to reveal the works of God. Now therefore, when thou didst pray, and Sara thy daughter-in-law, I did bring the remembrance of your prayers before the Holy One: and when thou didst bury the dead, I was with thee likewise. And when thou didst not delay to rise up, and leave thy dinner, to go and cover the dead, thy good deed was not hid from me: but I was with thee. And now God hath sent me to heal thee and Sara thy daughter-in-law. I am Raphael, one of the seven holy angels, which present the prayers of the saints, and which go in and out before the glory of the Holy One."

Then they were both troubled, and fell upon their faces: for they feared. But he said unto them: "Fear not, for it shall go well with you; praise God therefore. For not of any favour of mine, but by the will of our God I came; wherefore praise Him for ever. All these days I did appear unto you; but I did neither eat nor drink, but ye did see a vision. Now therefore give God thanks: for I go up to Him that sent me; but write all things which are done in a book." And when they arose, they saw him no more. Then they confessed the great and wonderful works of God, and how the angel of the Lord had appeared unto them.

Then Tobit wrote a prayer of rejoicing, and said:

Blessed be God that liveth for ever,
And blessed be His kingdom.
For He doth scourge, and hath mercy:
He leadeth down to hell, and bringeth up again:
Neither is there any that can avoid His hand.
Confess Him before the Gentiles, ye children of Israel:
For He hath scattered us among them.
There declare His greatness,
And extol Him before all the living:
For He is our Lord,
And He is the God our Father for ever.
And He will scourge us for our iniquities, and will have mercy again,
And will gather us out of all nations, among whom He hath scattered us.
If ye turn to Him with your whole heart, and with your whole mind,
And deal uprightly before Him,
Then will He turn unto you,
And will not hide His face from you.
Therefore see what He will do with you,
And confess Him with your whole mouth,
And praise the Lord of might,
And extol the everlasting King.
In the land of my captivity do I praise Him,
And declare His might and majesty to a sinful nation.
O ye sinners, turn and do justice before Him:
Who can tell if He will accept you, and have mercy on you?
I will extol my God,
And my soul shall praise the King of heaven,
And shall rejoice in His greatness.
Let all men speak,
And let all praise Him for His righteousness.
O Jerusalem, the holy city,

He will scourge thee for thy children's works,
And will have mercy again on the sons of the righteous.
Give praise to the Lord, for He is good:
And praise the everlasting King,
That His tabernacle may be builded in thee again with joy,
And let Him make joyful there in thee those that are captives,
And love in thee for ever those that are miserable.
Many nations shall come from far to the name of the Lord God
With gifts in their hands, even gifts to the King of heaven;
All generations shall praise Thee
With great joy.
Cursed are all they which hate Thee,
And blessed shall all be which love Thee for ever.
Rejoice and be glad for the children of the just:
For they shall be gathered together,
And shall bless the Lord of the just.
O blessed are they which love Thee,
They shall rejoice in Thy peace:
Blessed are they which have been sorrowful for all Thy scourges;
For they shall rejoice for Thee,
When they have seen all Thy glory,
And shall be glad for ever.
Let my soul bless God the great King.
For Jerusalem shall be built up with sapphires, and emeralds, and precious stone:
Thy walls and towers and battlements with pure gold.
And the streets of Jerusalem shall be paved with beryl and carbuncle and stones of Ophir.
And all her streets shall say, Alleluia; and they shall praise him,
Saying, Blessed be God, which hath extolled it for ever.

So Tobit made an end of praising God. And he was eight and fifty years old when he lost his sight, which was restored to him after eight years: and he gave alms, and he increased in the fear of the Lord God, and praised Him. And when he was very aged, he called his son, and the six sons of his son, and said to him: "My son, take thy children; for, behold, I am aged, and am ready to depart out of this life. Go into Media, my son, for I surely believe those things which Jonas the prophet spake of Nineve, that it shall be overthrown; and that for a time peace shall rather be in Media; and that our brethren shall lie scattered in the earth from that good land: and Jerusalem shall be desolate, and the house of God in it shall be burned, and shall be desolate for a time; and that again God will have mercy on them, and bring them again into the land, where they shall build a temple, but not like to the first, until the time of that age be fulfilled; and afterward they shall return from all places of their captivity, and build up Jerusalem gloriously, and the house of God shall be built in it for ever with a glorious building, as the prophets have spoken thereof. And all nations shall turn, and fear the Lord God truly, and shall bury their idols. So shall all nations praise the Lord, and His people shall confess God, and the Lord shall exalt His people; and all those which love the Lord God in truth and justice shall rejoice, showing mercy to our brethren. And now, my son, depart out of Nineve, because that those things which the prophet Jonas spake shall surely come to pass. But keep thou the law and the commandments, and show thyself merciful and just, that it may go well with thee. And bury me decently, and thy mother with me; but tarry no longer at Nineve. Remember, my son, how Aman handled Achiacharus that brought him up, how out of light he brought him into darkness, and how he rewarded him again: yet Achiacharus was saved, but the other had his reward: for he went down into darkness. Manasses gave alms, and escaped the snares of death which they had set for him: but Aman fell into the snare, and perished. Wherefore now, my son, consider what alms doeth, and how righteousness doth deliver."

When he had said these things, he gave up the ghost in the bed, being an hundred and eight and fifty years old; and he buried him honourably. And when Anna his mother was dead, he buried her with his father. But Tobias departed with his wife and children to Ecbatane to Raguel his father-in-law, where he became old with honour, and he buried his father- and mother-in-law honourably, and he inherited their substance, and his father Tobit's. And he died at Ecbatane in Media, being an hundred and seven and twenty years old. But before he died he heard of the destruction of Nineve, which was taken by Nabuchodonosor and Assuerus: and before his death he rejoiced over Nineve.

SUSANNA AND THE ELDERS

HEBREW LITERATURE

THERE dwelt a man in Babylon, called Joakim: and he took a wife, whose name was Susanna, the daughter of Chelcias, a very fair woman, and one that feared the Lord. Her parents also were righteous, and taught their daughter according to the law of Moses. Now Joakim was a great rich man, and had a fair garden joining unto his house: and to him resorted the Jews; because he was more honourable than all others. The same year were appointed two of the ancients of the people to be judges, such as the Lord spake of, that wickedness came from Babylon from ancient judges, who seemed to govern the people. These kept much at Joakim's house: and all that had any suits in law came unto them.

Now when the people departed away at noon, Susanna went into her husband's garden to walk. And the two elders saw her going in every day, and walking; so that their lust was inflamed toward her. And they perverted their own mind, and turned away their eyes, that they might not look unto heaven, nor remember just judgments. And albeit they both were wounded with her love, yet durst not one show another his grief. For they were ashamed to declare their lust, that they desired to have to do with her. Yet they watched diligently from day to day to see her. And the one said to the other: "Let us now go home: for it is dinner time." So when they were gone out, they parted the one from the other, and turning back again they came to the same place; and after that they had asked one another the cause, they acknowledged their lust: then appointed they a time both together, when they might find her alone.

And it fell out, as they watched a fit time, she went in as before with two maids only, and she was desirous to wash herself in the garden: for it was hot. And there was nobody there save the two elders, that had hid themselves, and watched her. Then she said to her maids: "Bring me oil and washing balls, and shut the garden doors, that I may wash me." And they did as she bade them, and shut the garden doors, and went out themselves at privy doors to fetch the things that she had commanded them: but they saw not the elders, because they were hid.

Now when the maids were gone forth, the two elders rose up, and ran unto her, saying: "Behold, the garden doors are shut, that no man can see us, and we are in love with thee; therefore consent unto us, and lie with us. If thou wilt not, we will bear witness against thee, that a young man was with thee: and therefore thou didst send away thy maids from thee."

Then Susanna sighed, and said: "I am straitened on every side: for if I do this thing, it is death unto me: and if I do it not, I cannot escape your hands. It is better for me to fall into your hands, and not do it, than to sin in the sight of the Lord." With that Susanna cried with a loud voice: and the two elders cried out against her. Then ran the one, and opened the garden door. So when the servants of the house heard the cry in the garden, they rushed in at a privy door, to see what was done unto her. But when the elders had declared their matter, the servants were greatly ashamed: for there was never such a report made of Susanna.

And it came to pass the next day, when the people were assembled to her husband Joakim, the two elders came also full of mischievous imagination against Susanna to put her to death: and said before the people, Send for Susanna, the daughter of Chelcias, Joakim's wife. And so they sent. So she came with her father and mother, her children, and all her kindred.

Now Susanna was a very delicate woman, and beauteous to behold. And these wicked men commanded to uncover her face (for she was covered), that they might be filled with her beauty. Therefore her friends and all that saw her wept. Then the two elders stood up in the midst of the people, and laid their hands upon her head. And she weeping looked up toward heaven: for her heart trusted in the Lord. And the elders said: "As we walked in the garden alone, this woman came in with two maids, and shut the garden doors, and sent the maids away. Then a young man, who there was hid, came unto her, and lay with her. Then we that stood in a corner of the garden, seeing this wickedness, ran unto them. And when we saw them together, the man we could not hold: for he was stronger than we, and opened the door, and leaped out. But having taken this woman, we asked who the young man was, but she would not tell us: these things do we testify."

Then the assembly believed them, as those that were the elders and judges of the people: so they condemned her to death. Then Susanna cried out with a loud voice, and said: "O everlasting God, that knowest the secrets, and knowest all things before they be: Thou knowest that they have borne false witness against me, and, behold, I must die; whereas I never did such things as these men have maliciously invented against me."

And the Lord heard her voice. Therefore when she was led to be put to death, the Lord raised up the holy spirit of a youth, whose name was Daniel: who cried with a loud voice; "I am clear from the blood of this woman." Then all the people turned them toward him, and said: "What mean these words that thou hast spoken?"

So he standing in the midst of them said: "Are ye such fools, ye sons of Israel, that without examination or knowledge of the truth ye have condemned a daughter of Israel? Return again to the place of judgment: for they have borne false witness against her." Wherefore all the people turned again in haste, and the elders said unto him: "Come, sit down among us, and show it us, seeing God hath given thee the honour of an elder."

Then said Daniel unto them: "Put these two aside one far from another, and I will examine them." So when they were put asunder one from another, he called one of them, and said unto him: "O thou that art waxen old in wickedness, now thy sins which thou hast committed aforetime are come to light: for thou hast pronounced false judgment, and hast condemned the innocent, and hast let the guilty go free; albeit the Lord saith, The innocent and righteous shalt thou not slay. Now then, if thou hast seen her, tell me, Under what tree sawest thou them companying together?" Who answered: "Under a mastic tree." And Daniel said: "Very well; thou hast lied against thine own head; for even now the angel of God hath received the sentence of God to cut thee in two."

So he put him aside, and commanded to bring the other, and said unto him: "O thou seed of Canaan, and not of Juda, beauty hath deceived thee, and lust hath perverted thine heart. Thus have ye dealt with the daughters of Israel, and they for fear companied with you: but the daughter of Juda would not abide your wickedness. Now therefore tell me, Under what tree didst thou take them companying together?" Who answered: "Under an holm tree." Then said Daniel unto him: "Well; thou hast also lied against thine own head: for the angel of God waiteth with the sword to cut thee in two, that He may destroy you." With that all the assembly cried out with a loud voice, and praised God, who saveth them that trust in Him.

And they arose against the two elders, for Daniel had convicted them of false witness by their own mouth: and according to the law of Moses they did unto them in such sort as they maliciously intended to do to their neighbour: and they put them to death. Thus the innocent blood was saved the same day.

Therefore Chelcias and his wife praised God for their daughter Susanna, with Joakim her husband, and all the kindred, because there was no dishonesty found in her.

From that day forth was Daniel had in great reputation in the sight of the people.

BEL AND THE DRAGON

Hebrew Literature

AND King Astyages was gathered to his fathers, and Cyrus of Persia received his kingdom. And Daniel conversed with the King, and was honoured above all his friends. Now the Babylonians had an idol, called Bel, and there were spent upon him every day twelve great measures of fine flour, and forty sheep, and six vessels of wine. And the King worshipped it, and went daily to adore it: but Daniel worshipped his own God.

And the King said unto him: "Why dost not thou worship Bel?" Who answered and said: "Because I may not worship idols made with hands, but the living God, who hath created the heaven and the earth, and hath sovereignty over all flesh." Then said the King unto him: "Thinkest thou not that Bel is a living god? seest thou not how much he eateth and drinketh every day?" Then Daniel smiled, and said: "O King, be not deceived: for this is but clay within, and brass without, and did never eat or drink anything." So the King was wroth, and called for his priests, and said unto them: "If ye tell me not who this is that devoureth these expenses, ye shall die. But if ye can certify me that Bel devoureth them, then Daniel shall die: for he hath spoken blasphemy against Bel." And Daniel said unto the King: "Let it be according to thy word."

Now the priests of Bel were threescore and ten, beside their wives and children. And the King went with Daniel into the temple of Bel. So Bel's priests said: "Lo, we go out: but thou, O King, set on the meat, and make ready the wine, and shut the door fast, and seal it with thine own signet; and to-morrow when thou comest in, if thou findest not that Bel hath eaten up all, we will suffer death: or else Daniel, that speaketh falsely against us." And they little regarded it: for under the table they had made a privy entrance, whereby they entered in continually, and consumed those things. So when they were gone forth, the King set meats before Bel. Now Daniel had commanded his servants to bring ashes, and those they strewed throughout all the temple in the presence of the King alone: then went they out, and shut the door, and sealed it with the King's signet, and so departed.

Now in the night came the priests with their wives and children, as they were wont to do, and did eat and drink up all. In the morning betime the King arose, and Daniel with him. And the King said: "Daniel, are the seals whole?" And he said: "Yea, O King, they be whole." And as soon as he had opened the door, the King looked upon the table, and cried with a loud voice: "Great art thou, O Bel, and with thee is no deceit at all." Then laughed Daniel, and held the King that he should not go in, and said: "Behold now the pavement, and mark well whose footsteps are these." And the King said: "I see the footsteps of men, women, and children." And then the King was angry, and took the priests with their wives and children, who showed him the privy doors, where they came in, and consumed such things as were upon the table. Therefore the King slew them, and delivered Bel into Daniel's power, who destroyed him and his temple.

And in that same place there was a great dragon, which they of Babylon worshipped. And the King said unto Daniel: "Wilt thou also say that this is of brass? lo, he liveth, he eateth and drinketh; thou canst not say that he is no living god: therefore worship him." Then said Daniel unto the King: "I will worship the Lord my God: for He is the living God. But give me leave, O King, and I shall slay this dragon without sword or staff." The King said: "I give thee leave."

Then Daniel took pitch, and fat, and hair, and did seethe them together, and made lumps thereof: this he put in the dragon's mouth, and so the dragon burst in sunder: and Daniel said: "Lo, these are the gods ye worship." When they of Babylon heard that, they took great indignation, and conspired against the King, saying: "The King is become a Jew, and he hath destroyed Bel, he hath slain the dragon, and put the priests to death." So they came to the King, and said: "Deliver us Daniel, or else we will destroy thee and thine house." Now when the King saw that they pressed him sore, being constrained, he delivered Daniel unto them: who cast him into the lions' den: where he was six days. And in the den there were seven lions, and they had given them every day two carcases, and two sheep: which then were not given to them, to the intent they might devour Daniel.

Now there was in Jewry a prophet, called Habakkuk, who had made pottage, and had broken bread in a bowl, and was going into the field, for to bring it to the reapers. But the angel of the Lord said unto Habakkuk: "Go, carry the dinner that thou hast into Babylon unto Daniel, who is in the lions' den." And Habakkuk said: "Lord, I never saw Babylon; neither do I know where the den is." Then the angel of the Lord took him by the crown, and bare him by the hair of his head, and through the vehemency of his spirit set him in Babylon over the den. And Habakkuk cried, saying: "O Daniel, Daniel, take the dinner which God hath sent thee." And Daniel said: "Thou hast remembered me, O God: neither hast Thou forsaken them that seek Thee and love Thee." So Daniel arose, and did eat: and the angel of the Lord set Habakkuk in his own place again immediately.

Upon the seventh day the King went to bewail Daniel: and when he came to the den, he looked in, and, behold, Daniel was sitting. Then cried the King with a loud voice, saying: "Great art Thou, O Lord God of Daniel, and there is none other beside Thee." And he drew him out, and cast those that were the cause of his destruction into the den: and they were devoured in a moment before his face.

CHINESE
420 A.D.

THE PEACH-BLOSSOM FOUNTAIN

TAO CHIEN

TOWARDS the close of the fourth century, a certain fisherman of Wu-ling, who had followed up one of the river branches without taking note whither he was going came suddenly upon a grove of peach-trees in full bloom, extending some distance on each bank, with not a tree of any other kind in sight. The beauty of the scene and the exquisite perfume of the flowers filled the heart of the fisherman with surprise, as he proceeded onwards, anxious to reach the limit of this lovely grove. He found that the peach-trees ended where the water began, at the foot of a hill, and there he espied what seemed to be a cave with light issuing from it.

So he made fast his boat, and crept in through a narrow entrance, which shortly ushered him into a new world of level country, of fine houses, of rich fields, of fine pools, and of luxuriance of mulberry and bamboo. Highways of traffic ran north and south ; sounds of crowing cocks and barking dogs were heard around ; the dress of the people who passed along or were at work in the fields was of a strange cut ; while young and old alike appeared to be contented and happy.

One of the inhabitants, catching sight of the fisherman, was greatly astonished ; but, after learning whence he came, insisted on carrying him home, and killed a chicken and placed some wine before him. Before long, all the people of the place had turned out to see the visitor, and they informed him that their ancestors had sought refuge here, with their wives and families, from the troublous times of the House of Ch'in, adding that they had thus become finally cut off from the rest of the human race. They then inquired about the politics of the day, ignorant of the establishment of the Han dynasty, and of course of the later dynasties which had succeeded it. And when the fisherman told them the story, they grieved over the vicissitudes of human affairs.

Each in turn invited the fisherman to his home and entertained him hospitably, until at length the latter prepared to take his leave.

" It will not be worth while to talk about what you have seen to the outside world," said the people of the place to the fisherman, as he bade them farewell and returned to his boat, making mental notes of his route as he proceeded on his homeward voyage.

When he reached home, he at once went and reported what he had seen to the Governor of the district, and the Governor sent off men with him to seek, by the aid of the fisherman's notes, to discover this unknown region. But he was never able to find it again. Subsequently, another desperate attempt was made by a famous adventurer to pierce the mystery; but he also failed, and died soon afterwards of chagrin, from which time forth no further attempts were made.[1]

[1] The whole story is allegorical, and signifies that the fisherman had been strangely permitted to go back once again into the peach-blossom days of his youth.

CHINESE
772 A.D.

THE LUTE-GIRL'S LAMENT

PŎ CHŬ-YI

BY night, at the riverside, adieus were spoken: beneath the maple's flower-like leaves, blooming amid autumnal decay. Host had dismounted to speed the parting guest, already on board his boat. Then a stirrup-cup went round, but no flute, no guitar, was heard. And so, ere the heart was warmed with wine, came words of cold farewell, beneath the bright moon glittering over the bosom of the broad stream . . . when suddenly, across the water, a lute broke forth into sound. Host forgot to go, guest lingered on, wondering whence the music, and asking who the performer might be.

At this, all was hushed, but no answer given. A boat approached, and the musician was invited to join the party. Cups were refilled, lamps trimmed again, and preparations for festivity renewed.

At length, after much pressing, she came forth, hiding her face behind her lute; and twice or thrice, sweeping the strings, betrayed emotion ere her song was sung. Then every note she struck swelled with pathos deep and strong as though telling the tale of a wrecked and hopeless life, while with bent head and rapid finger she poured forth her soul in melody. Now softly, now slowly, her plectrum sped to and fro; now this air, now that, loudly, with the crash of falling rain, softly, as the murmur of whispered words; now loud and soft together, like the patter of pearls and pearlets dropping upon a marble dish. Or liquid, like the warbling of the mango-bird in the bush; trickling, like the streamlet on its downward course. And then like the torrent, stilled by the grip of frost, so for a moment was the music lulled, in a passion too deep for sound.[1] Then, as bursts the water from the broken vase, as clash the arms upon the mailed horseman, so fell the plectrum once more upon the strings with a slash like the rent of silk.

Silence on all sides: not a sound stirred the air. The autumn moon

[1] "The sure perception of the exact moment when the rest should be silence."

shone silver athwart the tide, as with a sigh the musician thrust her plectrum beneath the strings and quietly prepared to take leave.

" My childhood," said she, " was spent at the capital, in my home near the hills. At thirteen, I learnt the guitar, and my name was enrolled among the primas of the day. The maëstro himself acknowledged my skill: the most beauteous of women envied my lovely face. The youths of the neighbourhood vied with each other to do me honour. A single song brought me I know not how many costly bales. Golden ornaments and silver pins were smashed, blood-red skirts of silk were stained with wine, in oft-times echoing applause. And so I laughed on from year to year, while the spring breeze and autumn moon swept over my careless head.

" Then my brother went away to the wars: my mother died. Nights passed and mornings came; and with them my beauty began to fade. My doors were no longer thronged: but few cavaliers remained. So I took a husband, and became a trader's wife. He was all for gain, and little recked of separation from me. Last month he went off to buy tea, and I remained behind, to wander in my lonely boat on moon-lit nights over the cold wave, thinking of the happy days gone by, my reddened eyes telling of tearful dreams."

The sweet melody of the lute had already moved my soul to pity, and now these words pierced me to the heart again.

" O lady," I cried, " we are companions in misfortune, and need no ceremony to be friends. Last year I quitted the Imperial city, banished to this fever-stricken spot, where in its desolation, from year's end to year's end, no flute nor guitar is heard. I live by the marshy river-bank, surrounded by yellow reeds and stunted bamboos. Day and night no sounds reach my ears save the blood-stained note of the nightjar, the gibbon's mournful wail. Hill songs I have, and village pipes with their harsh discordant twang. But now that I listen to thy lute's discourse, methinks 'tis the music of the gods. Prithee sit down awhile and sing to us yet again, while I commit thy story to writing."

Grateful to me (for she had been standing long), the lute-girl sat down and quickly broke forth into another song, sad and soft, unlike the song of just now. Then all her hearers melted into tears unrestrained; and none flowed more freely than mine, until my bosom was wet with weeping.

CELTIC
7TH CENTURY

THE FATE OF DEIRDRE

KING CONOR and the nobles of Ulster went to a feast in the house of Feidlimid, the son of Dall, who was teller of tales to the King. And Conor and his men were joyful and light of heart, drinking their ale to the music of the minstrels, and listening to the chants of the bards, the tales of the story-tellers, and the prophecies of the druids and those who number the moon and the stars. And while the drinking-horns went round about the board and the revellers shouted in their mirth, the wife of Feidlimid bore a lovely and well-shaped daughter.

Cathbad, the chief druid of Erin, chanced to be in the house ; and he rose up, and took his ancient books, and went out into the field and looked at the clouds of the air and the position of the stars and moon, to see the fate and fortune of the child. And the signs were so terrible that he returned in haste to Conor and the nobles of the Red Branch, and told them the child would grow up into a fair woman who would bring woe upon Ulster.

" She will be tall, with long tresses of golden hair and smiling lips," cried the druid ; " and for her love many chiefs shall strive, and great kings shall sue for her favour. For her the heroes of Ulster shall war in their chariots, and many men will be slain. Deirdre shall be her name, and evil is the fate that will fall upon her ! "

" Let the child be slain ! " shouted the nobles of the Red Branch.

And they rose up in anger to put the little child to death : but Conor stayed them.

" This thing must not be done," said the King. " It is not seemly to fight against fate, and it is an accursed thing to destroy the life of an innocent babe. Look how beautiful the child is, and how pleasant her laugh ! Great shame would it be to quench her life, O ye nobles of Ulster and heroes of the Red Branch ! I will submit to the foretellings of the seer, but I will not submit to do a base deed to escape from what is to come. If you think that the fate the druid foretells cannot be avoided, then kill yourselves each with his own hand. But do not shed the blood of an innocent babe ; for that would bring a curse upon our land. I will take the girl under my care, and if she live and I last, she shall become my wife and my Queen. So I swear by the sun and the moon, to all the men of Erin, that if one of them attempts to destroy her, now or hereafter, he shall not live while I have life in my body ! "

And the nobles of Ulster listened in silence and stayed without speaking, till the heroes of the Red Branch rose up together and cried : " Right is thy judgment, high King of Ulster, and it is our duty to see thy will is done ! "

So Conor took the child under his protection, and she was brought up in a fortress of the Red Branch at some distance from the burg of Emain ; and an old woman, Levorcham, waited upon her, and fed her with rich meat and drink that she might grow tall and strong. And so that none of the men of Ulster might look upon her till the time came for her to marry the King, all the windows in the front of the fort were closed, and only the windows at the rear were opened. A beautiful orchard, full of fruit, grew behind the fort, and here Deirdre walked under the eye of her nurse at the beginning and the end of the day, beneath the shade of the fresh leaves and boughs, and by the side of a pleasant stream that wound softly through the middle of the orchard. And about the orchard was a high wall ; and four savage dogs, sent from Conor, guarded the walls, so that a man's life was in peril if he approached the place. For no man was allowed to come near Deirdre, save only Cailcin, her teacher, and King Conor himself.

And Deirdre grew like a young flowering tree, till her beauty was beyond that of any other woman. And when she was but fourteen years of age, she was ripe for marriage, and Conor thought to take her to his couch. It was in the winter-time, and the ground was covered with snow, and Cailcin killed a calf to prepare a roast for her, and the blood of the calf fell on the snow, and a raven flew down to drink it. This Deirdre marked as she sat by a window, gazing into the garden, and she sighed so deeply that her old nurse, Levorcham, heard her.

" Why are you sorrowful ? " said the nurse.

" A desire has come to me," said Deirdre. " One man only will I love—he who has the three colours that I see here. His hair must be as black as the raven, his cheeks red like the blood, and his body as white as the snow."

" Honour and all happiness to you ! " said Levorcham. " The

man you desire is not far away. He lives near at hand, and the name of him is Naisi, the son of Usnach."

" I shall never be happy again," said Deirdre, " till the time comes when I see him."

And on a certain day it happened that Naisi was alone on the wall of the neighbouring burg of Emain, and he sent his war-cry ringing in music over the land. Musical was the cry that the sons of Usnach were used to send forth. All the kine that heard their ringing melody gave two-thirds more milk than was their wont : and every man who heard their cry took pleasure in it and was made joyful. And wonderful was the play that these men made with their weapons. Had all the men of Ulster come up against them in one place, and had the sons of Usnach set their backs against each other, the men of Ulster would not have conquered these three men, so marvellously skilled were they in parry and guard. And swift were they of foot when they went hunting, for it was their practice to chase their quarry to its death.

Naisi went down into the plain of Emain, and Deirdre escaped from the fortress, and ran past him, and he did not know who she was.

" Fair is the young heifer that springs by me ! " he said.

" Well may the young heifers be fair," she said, " in a land where none of them can find a mate ! "

" Thou hast thy mate," said Naisi, knowing her at last by her great beauty—" the bull of the whole land of Ulster—Conor the King ! "

" I would choose between you two," she said, " and it is the younger I would take."

" No," said Naisi. " No ! I fear the prophecy of Cathbad ! "

" Do you mean to refuse me ? " she said.

" Yes, in truth," he replied.

But, springing upon him, Deirdre seized him by the ears and shook him.

" Two ears of shame shall you have," she cried, " two ears of shame and mockery, if you do not take me with you ! "

" Release me," he said. " Release me, O my wife ! "

Deirdre stood aside, and Naisi sent forth his ringing war-cry. The men of Ulster heard it, and one after another they sprang up and took their weapons ; and the sons of Usnach came out in haste to restrain their brother.

" What has happened ? " they cried. What is it you have done ?

Do not let war be made between us and the men of Ulster by any fault of yours."

Then Naisi told them all that had happened between him and Deirdre.

"Woe shall come on you for this," said his brothers, "and shame will rest on you all your life! We must take her to some other land. For there is no king in Erin who will fail to welcome us if we go to him."

And after talking together, they went away that night with a hundred and fifty fighting men, and the same number of women, hounds, and servants: and Deirdre went with them. For many days they roved through Erin, doing service to one king after another: and many times Conor of Ulster tried to bring about their death, laying ambushes for them and sending men to slay them while they were feasting or sleeping. And the sons of Usnach wandered to the west, and from there they went to the north-east; and at last the men of Ulster, coming in great strength, drove them out of Erin, and they sailed away to the land of Alba (Scotland). And in the wildernesses of Alba they dwelt. For a time they lived by chasing the deer upon the mountains, and when the wild game failed them, they raided the cattle of the men of Alba. Then the men of Alba gathered in force to destroy them, and to escape from death they did homage to the King of Alba, and he accepted them as his men, and they served him in his wars.

Fearing that the men of Alba might see Deirdre, and slay them all to obtain her, the sons of Usnach built a house for her in the fields by the King's burg, and set their dwelling-places around it. But the high steward of the King was out walking early one morning, and he made a round about the house, and looking in he saw Naisi sleeping by the side of Deirdre. And hastening back to the King of Alba, he awakened him.

"Unto this day," he said, "we have seen no woman worthy to be your Queen, but now we have found her. For Naisi, the son of Usnach, has a wife that would grace the Emperor of the western world. Slay the man and take his wife to yourself!"

"No," said the King, "I cannot do that. But you must go every day to her house and woo her for me in secret."

And this the steward did. But all that he said to Deirdre she straightway told to Naisi, and the King of Alba and his steward saw that nothing was to be obtained from her. So, by the order of the King, the sons of Usnach were sent continually into great perils and dangerous adventures and fierce wars, that they might be slain: but they bore themselves so bravely and skilfully in every combat that the King won no advantage over them. Then he gathered the men of Alba together to destroy the sons of Usnach, and the steward told Deirdre of this, and she brought the news to Naisi.

"Leave this place!" she said. "If you do not depart this very night, to-morrow you will all be done to death."

And the sons of Usnach marched away in the darkness, and settled on an island in the sea. Tidings of their misfortunes were brought to the men of Ulster, and they were sorry for the sons of Usnach.

"Sad is it, O Conor!" they said, "that the sons of Usnach should perish in a strange land for the sake of a bad woman! It were better for them to return to their own land and come under thy protection, than be slain by the hands of foes in a strange land!"

"Let them come to us, then," said Conor, "and let men go as sureties to them."

And the news was carried to the sons of Usnach.

"This is good news for us," they said, "and gladly will we return to Erin. Bring Fergus as our surety, and Dubhtach, and Cormac, the son of Conor."

And these three men went to them, and with them they came over the sea. But by the cunning of Conor, Fergus was asked to an ale-feast when he landed, and Dubhtach and Cormac stayed with him. But the sons of Usnach, being pledged to eat no meat till they had taken the food of Conor, went on with the son of Fergus, and came to the plain around Emain.

Now Conor had long been at war with Eogan, the son of Durthacht, and Eogan had come to Emain to make peace with him. And Conor now bade Eogan go out with the royal fighting men, and slay the sons of Usnach as they were coming to the King. The sons of Usnach stood on a level space in the plain, and the women sat on the walls of Emain. Eogan advanced with the King's fighting men across the plain, and the son of Fergus came and stood by the side of Naisi. All the greeting Eogan gave them was a fierce thrust of his spear. The son of Fergus sprang forward, and threw both arms about Naisi, and fell with him, spreading his body above him to shield and shelter him. But Eogan drove his spear through the bodies of both men, and it was thus that Naisi was slain, with the body of the son of Fergus above him. Then murder was done all along the plain, and none escaped the point of the spears or the edge of the swords but Deirdre. Her hands were bound behind her back, and she was given into the power of Conor.

But when Fergus and Dubhtach and Cormac, the sureties, heard what had happened, they hastened unto Emain and did great deeds. With one thrust of his spear, Dubhtach slew Mane, a son of Conor, and Fiachna, his grandson: and Fergus killed Traigthren and his brother. Conor was right angry at this, and he came forth to fight them. And upon that day three hundred of the men of Ulster fell, and Dubhtach killed the women of Ulster and Fergus set Emain on fire. Then the two heroes, with three thousand fighting men, left their own land and went to Connaught, where Ailill and Queen Maeve gave them shelter; and for sixteen years the cries and the lamentations of the people of Ulster did not cease. For every night Fergus and Dubhtach set out on a foray of vengeance, and made the Ulstermen tremble and wail.

For a year Deirdre lived on in the house of Conor. And all this time she smiled no smile of laughter nor raised her head from her knee. And little was the sleep she had or the food she took. And when they brought minstrels to cheer her, she sang a keen for the sons of Usnach:

"Though Conor the king of the North rejoices
In minstrel music of pipe and horn,
Sweeter to me were the sound of the voices
Of Usnach's sons in the early morn:
When Naisi sang like a wave of the sea,
With Ardan and Aindle in harmony,
Amid the bens and the glens of Alba,
From which I fled to be thus forlorn!

Of all men under the arch of heaven
Fairest to me was Usnach's son.
Beauty and strength to him were given,
And honour and daring till life was done.
Friendly to me was the comely face
Of Naisi, and loving was his embrace:
Now earth lies black on his fair, white body—
And I am Deirdre, the joyless one!"

And when Conor saw neither mirth nor kindness could win Deirdre and neither honours nor feastings gladdened her heart, he sent for Eogan, the son of Durthacht, who had slain Naisi in Emain plain. And Conor came with Eogan to the place where Deirdre was sitting.

"Deirdre," said the King, "whom do you hate more of the two men now before you?"

"You yourself," she said.

" Then you shall live with Eogan for a year," said Conor ; and he gave Deirdre into Eogan's hand

She was placed with Eogan in his chariot, and Conor entered the chariot and drove behind them. And as they were passing through the plain of Emain, Deirdre cast a fierce look at Eogan in front of her, and another at Conor behind her. For there was nothing in the world she hated more than these two men. And Conor saw this, as she looked at him and Eogan.

" Ah, Deirdre ! " he said. " It is the glance a ewe gives when she is between two rams, that you cast on me and Eogan ! " And when Deirdre heard this, she sprang up and gave a leap out of the chariot, and fell on a great rock in front of her, and shattered her head so that her brain was seen. Thus came Deirdre to her death.

THE DREAM OF MAXEN WLEDIG

Celtic

MAXEN WLEDIG was Emperor of Rome, and he was a comelier man, and a better and a wiser, than any emperor that had been before him. And one day he held a council of kings, and he said to his friends, " I desire to go to-morrow to hunt."

And the next day in the morning he set forth with his retinue, and came to the valley of the river that flowed towards Rome. And he hunted through the valley until mid-day. And with him also were two-and-thirty crowned kings, that were his vassals ; not for the delight of hunting went the Emperor with them, but to put himself on equal terms with those kings.

And the sun was high in the sky over their heads and the heat was great. And sleep came upon Maxen Wledig. And his attendants stood and set up their shields around him upon the shafts of their spears to protect him from the sun, and they placed a gold enamelled shield under his head ; and so Maxen slept.

And he saw a dream. And this is the dream that he saw. He was journeying along the valley of the river towards its source ; and he came to the highest mountain in the world. And he thought that the mountain was as high as the sky ; and when he came over the mountain, it seemed to him that he went through the fairest and most level regions that man ever yet beheld, on the other side of the mountain. And he saw large and mighty rivers descending from the mountain to the sea, and towards the mouths of the rivers he proceeded.

And as he journeyed thus, he came to the mouth of the largest river ever seen. And he beheld a great city at the entrance of the river, and a vast castle in the city, and he saw many high towers of various colours in the castle. And he saw a fleet at the mouth of the river, the largest ever seen. And he saw one ship among the fleet ; larger was it by far, and fairer, than all the others. Of such part of the ship as he could see above the water, one plank was gilded and the other silvered over. He saw a bridge of the bone of a whale from the ship to the land, and he thought that he went along the bridge, and came into the ship. And a sail was hoisted on the ship, and along the sea and the ocean was it borne.

Then it seemed that he came to the fairest island in the whole world, and he traversed the island from sea to sea, even to the farthest shore of the island. Valleys he saw, and steeps, and rocks of wondrous height, and rugged precipices. Never yet saw he the like. And thence he beheld an island in the sea, facing this rugged land. And between him and this island was a country of which the plain was as large as the sea, the mountain as vast as the wood. And from the mountain he saw a river that flowed through the land and fell into the sea.

And at the mouth of the river he beheld a castle, the fairest that man ever saw, and the gate of the castle was open, and he went into the castle. And in the castle he saw a fair hall, of which the roof seemed to be all gold, the walls of the hall seemed to be entirely of glittering precious gems, the doors all seemed to be of gold. Golden seats he saw in the hall, and silver tables. And on a seat opposite to him he beheld two auburn-haired youths playing at chess. He saw a silver board for the chess, and golden pieces thereon. The garments of the youths were of jet-black satin, and chaplets of ruddy gold bound their hair, whereon were sparkling jewels of great price, rubies, and gems, alternately with imperial stones. Buskins of new Cordovan leather on their feet, fastened by slides of red gold.

And beside a pillar in the hall he saw a hoary-headed man, in a chair of ivory, with the figures of two eagles of ruddy gold thereon. Bracelets of gold were upon his arms, and many rings were on his hands, and a golden torque about his neck ; and his hair was bound with a golden diadem. He was of powerful aspect. A chess-board of gold was before him, and a rod of gold, and a steel file in his hand. And he was carving out chessmen.

And he saw a maiden sitting before him in a chair of ruddy gold. Not more easy than to gaze upon the sun when brightest, was it to look upon her by reason of her beauty. A vest of white silk was upon the maiden, with clasps of red gold at the breast ; and a surcoat of gold tissue upon her, and a frontlet of red gold upon her head, and rubies and gems were in the frontlet, alternating with pearls and imperial stones. And a girdle of ruddy gold was around her. She was the fairest sight that man ever beheld.

The maiden arose from her chair before him, and he threw his arms about the neck of the maiden, and they two sat down together in the chair of gold; and the chair was not less roomy for them both, than for the maiden alone. And as he had his arms about the maiden's neck, and his cheek by her cheek, behold, through the chafing of the dogs at their leashing, and the clashing of the shields as they struck against each other, and the beating together of the shafts of the spears, and the neighing of the horses and their prancing, the Emperor awoke.

And when he awoke, nor spirit nor existence was left him, because of the maiden whom he had seen in his sleep, for the love of the maiden pervaded his whole frame. Then his household spake unto him.

"Lord," said they, "is it not past the time for thee to take thy food?"

Thereupon the Emperor mounted his palfrey, the saddest man that mortal ever saw, and went forth towards Rome.

And thus he was during the space of a week. When they of the household went to drink wine and mead out of golden vessels, he went not with any of them. When they went to listen to songs and tales, he went not with them there; neither could he be persuaded to do anything but sleep. And as often as he slept, he beheld in his dreams the maiden he loved best; but except when he slept he saw nothing of her, for he knew not where in the world she was.

One day the page of the chamber spake unto him; now, although he was page of the chamber, he was King of the Romans.

"Lord," said he, "all the people revile thee."

"Wherefore do they revile me?" asked the Emperor.

"Because they can get neither message nor answer from thee as men should have from their lord. This is the cause why thou art spoken evil of."

"Youth," said the Emperor, "do thou bring unto me the wise men of Rome, and I will tell them wherefore I am sorrowful."

Then the wise men of Rome were brought to the Emperor, and he spake to them.

"Sages of Rome," said he, "I have seen a dream. And in the dream I beheld a maiden, and because of the maiden is there neither life, nor spirit, nor existence within me."

"Lord," they answered, "since thou judgest us worthy to counsel thee, we will give thee counsel. And this is our counsel: that thou send messengers for three years to the three parts of the world to seek for thy dream. And as thou knowest not what day or what night good news may come to thee, the hope thereof will support thee."

So the messengers journeyed for the space of a year, wandering about the world, and seeking tidings concerning his dream. But when they came back at the end of the year, they knew not one word more than they did the day they set forth. And then was the Emperor exceeding sorrowful, for he thought that he should never have tidings of her whom best he loved.

Then spoke the King of the Romans unto the Emperor.

" Lord," said he, " go forth to hunt by the way thou didst seem to go, whether it were to the east, or to the west."

So the Emperor went forth to the hunt, and he came to the bank of the river.

" Behold," said he, " this is where I was when I saw the dream, and I went towards the source of the river westward."

And thereupon thirteen messengers of the Emperor's set forth, and before them they saw a high mountain, which seemed to them to touch the sky. Now this was the guise in which the messengers journeyed; one sleeve was on the cap of each of them in front, as a sign that they were messengers, in order that through what hostile land soever they might pass no harm might be done them. And when they were come over this mountain, they beheld vast plains, and large rivers flowing therethrough.

" Behold," said they, " the land which our master saw."

And they went along the mouths of the rivers, until they came to the mighty river which they saw flowing to the sea, and the vast city, and the many-coloured high towers in the castle. They saw the largest fleet in the world, in the harbour of the river, and one ship that was larger than any of the others.

" Behold again," said they, " the dream that our master saw."

And in the great ship they crossed the sea, and came to the Island of Britain. And they traversed the island until they came to Snowdon.

" Behold," said they, " the rugged land that our master saw."

And they went forward until they saw Anglesey before them, and until they saw Arvon likewise.

" Behold," said they, " the land our master saw in his sleep."

And they saw Aber Sain, and a castle at the mouth of the river. The portal of the castle saw they open, and into the castle they went, and they saw a hall in the castle. Then said they:

" Behold, the hall which he saw in his sleep."

They went into the hall, and they beheld two youths playing at chess on the golden bench. And they beheld the hoary-headed man beside the pillar, in the ivory chair, carving chessmen. And they beheld the maiden sitting on a chair of ruddy gold.

The messengers bent down upon their knees.

" Empress of Rome, all hail ! "

" Ha, gentles," said the maiden, " ye bear the seeming of honourable men, and the badge of envoys, what mockery is this ye do to me ? "

" We mock thee not, lady ; but the Emperor of Rome hath seen thee in his sleep, and he has neither life nor spirit left because of thee. Thou shalt have of us therefore the choice, lady, whether thou wilt go with us and be made Empress of Rome, or that the Emperor come hither and take thee for his wife ? "

" Ha, lords," said the maiden, " I will not deny what ye say, neither will I believe it too well. If the Emperor love me, let him come here to seek me."

And by day and night the messengers hied them back. And when their horses failed, they bought other fresh ones. And when they came to Rome, they saluted the Emperor, and asked their boon, which was given to them according as they named it.

" We will be thy guides, lord," said they, " over sea and over land, to the place where is the woman whom best thou lovest, for we know her name, and her kindred, and her race."

And immediately the Emperor set forth with his army. And these men were his guides. Towards the Island of Britain they went over the sea and the deep. And he conquered the Island from Beli the son of Manogan, and his sons, and drove them to the sea, and went forward even unto Arvon. And the Emperor knew the land when he saw it. And when he beheld the castle of Aber Sain :

" Look yonder," said he, " there is the castle wherein I saw the damsel whom I best love."

And he went forward into the castle and into the hall, and there he saw Kynan the son of Eudav, and Adeon the son of Eudav, playing at chess. And he saw Eudav the son of Caradawc, sitting on a chair of ivory carving chessmen. And the maiden whom he had beheld in his sleep, he saw sitting on a chair of gold.

" Empress of Rome," said he, " all hail ! "

And the Emperor threw his arms about her neck; and that night she became his bride.

And the next day, in the morning, the damsel asked her maiden portion. And he told her to name what she would. And she asked to have the Island of Britain for her father, from the Channel to the Irish Sea, together with the three adjacent Islands, to hold under the Empress of Rome; and to have three chief castles made for her, in whatever places she might choose in the Island of Britain. And she chose to have the highest castle made at Arvon. And they brought thither earth from Rome that it might be more healthful for the Emperor to sleep, and sit, and walk upon. After that the two other castles were made for her, which were Caerlleon and Caermarthen.

And one day the Emperor went to hunt at Caermarthen, and he came so far as the top of Brevi Vawr, and there the Emperor pitched his tent. And that encamping place is called Cadeir Maxen, even to this day. And because that he built the castle with a myriad of men, he called it Caervyrddin.

Then Helen bethought her to make high roads from one castle to another throughout the Island of Britain. And the roads were made. And for this cause are they called the roads of Helen Luyddawc, that she was sprung from a native of this island, and the men of the Island of Britain would not have made these great roads for any save for her.

Seven years did the Emperor tarry in this Island. Now, at that time, the men of Rome had a custom, that whatsoever Emperor should remain in other lands more than seven years should remain to his own overthrow, and should never return to Rome again.

So they made a new Emperor. And this one wrote a letter of threat to Maxen. There was nought in the letter but only this:

"If thou comest, and if thou ever comest to Rome."

And even unto Caerlleon came this letter to Maxen, and these tidings. Then sent he a letter to the man who styled himself Emperor in Rome. There was nought in that letter also but only this:

"If I come to Rome, and if I come."

And thereupon Maxen set forth towards Rome with his army, and vanquished France and Burgundy, and every land on the way, and sat down before the city of Rome.

A year was the Emperor before the city, and he was no nearer taking it than the first day. And after him there came the brothers of Helen

Luyddawc from the Island of Britain, and a small host with them, and better warriors were in that small host than twice as many Romans. And the Emperor was told that a host was seen, halting close to his army and encamping, and no man ever saw a fairer or better-appointed host for its size, nor more handsome standards.

And Helen went to see the host, and she knew the standards of her brothers. Then came Kynan the son of Eudav, and Adeon the son of Eudav, to meet the Emperor. And the Emperor was glad because of them, and embraced them.

Then they looked at the Romans as they attacked the city. Said Kynan to his brother:

" We will try to attack the city more expertly than this."

So they measured by night the height of the wall, and they sent their carpenters to the wood, and a ladder was made for every four men of their number. Now when these were ready, every day at mid-day the Emperors went to meat, and they ceased to fight on both sides till all had finished eating. And in the morning the men of Britain took their food, and they drank until they were invigorated. And while the two Emperors were at meat, the Britons came to the city, and placed their ladders against it, and forthwith they came in through the city.

The new Emperor had no time to arm himself when they fell upon him, and slew him, and many others with him. And three nights and three days were they subduing the men that were in the city and taking the castle. And others of them kept the city, lest any of the host of Maxen should come therein, until they had subjected all to their will.

Then spake Maxen to Helen Luyddawc.

" I marvel, lady," said he, " that thy brothers have not conquered this city for me."

" Lord, Emperor," she answered, " the wisest youths in the world are my brothers. Go thou thither and ask the city of them, and if it be in their possession thou shalt have it gladly."

So the Emperor and Helen went and demanded the city. And they told the Emperor that none had taken the city, and that none could give it him, but the men of the Island of Britain. Then the gates of the city of Rome were opened, and the Emperor sat on the throne, and all the men of Rome submitted themselves unto him.

The Emperor then said unto Kynan and Adeon:

" Lords," said he, " I have now had possession of the whole of my empire. This host give I unto you to vanquish whatever region ye may desire in the world."

So they set forth and conquered lands, and castles, and cities. And they slew all the men, but the women they kept alive. And thus they continued until the young men that had come with them were grown grey-headed, from the length of time they were upon this conquest.

Then spoke Kynan unto Adeon his brother:

" Whether wilt thou rather," said he, " tarry in this land, or go back into the land whence thou didst come forth ? "

Now he chose to go back to his own land, and many with him. But Kynan tarried there with the other part and dwelt there.

And they took counsel and cut out the tongues of the women, lest they should corrupt their speech. And because of the silence of the women from their own speech, the men of Armorica are called Britons. From that time there came frequently, and still comes, that language from the Island of Britain.

And this dream is called the Dream of Maxen Wledig, Emperor of Rome. And here it ends.

SIR THOMAS MALORY
Circa 1470 A.D.

QUEEN GUENEVER'S MAYING

IT passed on from Candlemas until after Easter, that the month of May was come, when every lusty heart beginneth to blossom, and to bring forth fruit; for like as herbs and trees bring forth fruit and flourish in May, in likewise every lusty heart that is in any manner a lover, springeth and flourisheth in lusty deeds. For it giveth unto all lovers courage, that lusty month of May, in something to constrain him to some manner of thing more in that month than in any other month, for diverse causes. For then all herbs and trees renew a man and woman, and in likewise lovers call again to their mind old gentleness and old service, and many kind deeds that were forgotten by negligence.

For like as winter rasure doth alway arase and deface green summer, so fareth it by unstable love in man and woman. For in many persons there is no stability; for we may see all day, for a little blast of winter's rasure, anon we shall deface and lay apart true love for little or nought, that cost much thing; this is no wisdom nor stability, but it is feebleness of nature and great disworship, whomsoever useth this.

Therefore, like as May month flowereth and flourisheth in many gardens, so in likewise let every man of worship flourish his heart in this world, first unto God, and next unto the joy of them that he promised his faith unto; for there was never worshipful man nor worshipful woman, but they loved one better than another; and worship in arms may never be foiled, but first reserve the honour to God, and secondly the quarrel must come of thy lady: and such love I call virtuous love. But nowadays men can not love seven night but they must have all their desires: that love may not endure by reason; for where they be soon accorded, and hasty heat, soon it cooleth. Right so fareth love nowadays, soon hot, soon cold: this is no stability. But the old love was not so; men and women could love together seven years, and no lycours lusts were between them, and then was love, truth, and faithfulness: and lo, in likewise was used love in King Arthur's days.

Wherefore I liken love nowadays unto summer and winter; for like as the one is hot and the other cold, so fareth love nowadays;

therefore all ye that be lovers call unto your remembrance the month of May, like as did Queen Guenever, for whom I make here a little mention, that while she lived she was a true lover, and therefore she had a good end.

So it befell in the month of May, Queen Guenever called unto her knights of the Table Round; and she gave them warning that early upon the morrow she would ride on Maying into woods and fields beside Westminster.

"And I warn you that there be none of you but that he be well horsed, and that ye all be clothed in green, either in silk outher in cloth; and I shall bring with me ten ladies, and every knight shall have a lady behind him, and every knight shall have a squire and two yeomen; and I will that ye all be well horsed."

So they made them ready in the freshest manner. And these were the names of the knights: Sir Kay le Seneschal, Sir Agravaine, Sir Brandiles, Sir Sagramore le Desirous, Sir Dodinas le Savage, Sir Ozanna le Cure Hardy, Sir Ladinas of the Forest Savage, Sir Persant of Inde, Sir Ironside, that was called the Knight of the Red Launds, and Sir Pelleas, the lover; and these ten knights made them ready in the freshest manner to ride with the Queen.

And so upon the morn they took their horses with the Queen, and rode on Maying in woods and meadows as it pleased them, in great joy and delights; for the Queen had cast to have been again with King Arthur at the furthest by ten of the clock, and so was that time her purpose.

Then there was a knight that hight Meliagrance, and he was son unto King Bagdemagus, and this knight had at that time a castle of the gift of King Arthur within seven mile of Westminster. And this knight, Sir Meliagrance, loved passing well Queen Guenever, and so had he done long and many years. And the book saith he had lain in a wait for to steal away the queen, but evermore he forbare for by cause of Sir Launcelot; for in no wise he would meddle with the Queen an Sir Launcelot were in her company, outher else an he were near hand her.

And that time was such a custom, the Queen rode never without a great fellowship of men of arms about her, and they were many good knights, and the most part were young men that would have worship; and they were called the Queen's Knights, and never in no battle, tournament, nor jousts, they bare none of them no manner of knowledging of their own arms, but plain white shields, and thereby they were called the Queen's Knights. And then when it happed any of them to be of great worship by his noble deeds, then at the next Feast of Pentecost, if there were any slain or dead, as there was none year that there failed but some were dead, then was there chosen in his stead that was dead, the most men of worship that were called the Queen's Knights. And thus they came up all first, or they were renowned men of worship, both Sir Launcelot and all the remnant of them.

But this knight, Sir Meliagrance, had espied the Queen well and her purpose, and how Sir Launcelot was not with her, and how she had no men of arms with her but the ten noble knights all arrayed in green for Maying. Then he purveyed him a twenty men of arms and an hundred archers for to destroy the Queen and her knights, for he thought that time was best season to take the Queen.

So as the Queen had Mayed and all her knights, all were bedashed with herbs, mosses and flowers, in the best manner and freshest. Right so came out of a wood Sir Meliagrance with an eight-score men well harnessed, as they should fight in a battle of arrest, and bade the Queen and her knights abide, for maugre their heads they should abide.

"Traitor knight," said Queen Guenever, "what cast thou for to do? Wilt thou shame thyself? Bethink thee how thou art a King's son, and knight of the Table Round, and thou to be about to dishonour the noble King that made thee knight; thou shamest all knighthood and thyself, and me I let thee wit shalt thou never shame, for I had lever cut mine own throat in twain rather than thou shouldst dishonour me."

"As for all this language," said Sir Meliagrance, "be it as it be may, for wit you well, madam, I have loved you many a year, and never or now could I get you at such an advantage as I do now, and therefore I will take you as I find you."

Then spake all the noble knights at once and said:

"Sir Meliagrance, wit thou well ye are about to jeopard your worship to dishonour, and also ye cast to jeopard our persons howbeit we be unarmed. Ye have us at a great avail, for it seemeth by you that ye have laid watch upon us; but rather than ye should put the Queen to a shame and us all, we had as lief to depart from our lives, for an if we other ways did, we were shamed for ever."

Then said Sir Meliagrance: "Dress you as well ye can, and keep the Queen."

Then the ten knights of the Table Round drew their swords, and the other let run at them with their spears, and the ten knights manly abode them, and smote away their spears that no spear did them none harm. Then they lashed together with swords, and anon Sir Kay, Sir Sagramore, Sir Agravaine, Sir Dodinas, Sir Ladinas, and Sir Ozanna were smitten to the earth with grimly wounds. Then Sir Brandiles, and Sir Persant, Sir Ironside, Sir Pelleas fought long, and they were sore wounded, for these ten knights, or ever they were laid to the ground, slew forty men of the boldest and the best of them.

So when the Queen saw her knights thus dolefully wounded, and needs must be slain at the last, then for pity and sorrow she cried Sir Meliagrance:

"Slay not my noble knights, and I will go with thee upon this covenant, that thou save them, and suffer them not to be no more hurt, with this, that they be led with me wheresomever thou leadest me, for I will rather slay myself than I will go with thee, unless that these my noble knights may be in my presence."

"Madam," said Meliagrance, "for your sake they shall be led with you into mine own castle, with that ye will be ruled, and ride with me."

Then the Queen prayed the four knights to leave their fighting, and she and they would not depart.

"Madam," said Sir Pelleas, "we will do as ye do, for as for me I take no force of my life nor death."

For as the French book saith, Sir Pelleas gave such buffets there that none armour might hold him.

Then by the Queen's commandment they left battle, and dressed the wounded knights on horseback, some sitting, some overthwart their horses, that it was pity to behold them. And then Sir Meliagrance charged the Queen and all her knights that none of all her fellowship should depart from her; for full sore he dread Sir Launcelot du Lake, lest he should have any knowledging. All this espied the Queen, and privily she called unto her a child of her chamber that was swiftly horsed, to whom she said:

"Go thou, when thou seest thy time, and bear this ring unto Sir Launcelot du Lake, and pray him as he loveth me that he will see me and rescue me, if ever he will have joy of me; and spare not thy horse," said the Queen, "neither for water, neither for land."

So the child espied his time, and lightly he took his horse with the spurs, and departed as fast as he might. And when Sir Meliagrance saw him so flee, he understood that it was by the Queen's commandment for to warn Sir Launcelot. Then they that were best horsed chased him and shot at him, but from them all the child went suddenly. And then Sir Meliagrance said to the Queen :

"Madam, ye are about to betray me, but I shall ordain for Sir Launcelot that he shall not come lightly at you."

And then he rode with her, and they all, to his castle, in all the haste that they might. And by the way Sir Meliagrance laid in an ambushment the best archers that he might get in his country, to the number of thirty, to await upon Sir Launcelot, charging them that if they saw such a manner of knight come by the way upon a white horse, that in any wise they slay his horse, but in no manner of wise have not ado with him bodily, for he is over-hard to be overcome.

So this was done, and they were come to his castle, but in no wise the Queen would never let none of the ten knights and her ladies out of her sight, but always they were in her presence ; for the book saith, Sir Meliagrance durst make no masteries, for dread of Sir Launcelot, insomuch he deemed that he had warning. So when the child was departed from the fellowship of Sir Meliagrance, within a while he came to Westminster, and anon he found Sir Launcelot.

And when he had told his message, and delivered him the Queen's ring :

"Alas," said Sir Launcelot, "now I am shamed for ever, unless that I may rescue that noble lady from dishonour."

Then eagerly he asked his armour ; and ever the child told Sir Launcelot how the ten knights fought marvellously, and how Sir Pelleas, and Sir Ironside, and Sir Brandiles, and Sir Persant of Inde fought strongly, but namely Sir Pelleas, there might none withstand him ; and how they all fought till at the last they were laid to the earth ; and then the Queen made appointment for to save their lives, and go with Sir Meliagrance.

"Alas," said Sir Launcelot, "that most noble lady, that she should be so destroyed ; I had lever," said Sir Launcelot, "than all France, that I had been there well armed."

So when Sir Launcelot was armed and upon his horse, he prayed the child of the Queen's chamber to warn Sir Lavaine how suddenly he was departed, and for what cause. And pray him as he loveth me, that he will hie him after me, and that he stint not until he come to the castle where Sir Meliagrance abideth, or dwelleth ; "for there," said

Sir Launcelot, " he shall hear of me an I am a man living, and rescue the Queen and the ten knights the which he traitorously hath taken, and that shall I prove upon his head, and all them that hold with him."

Then Sir Launcelot rode as fast as he might, and the book saith he took the water at Westminster Bridge, and made his horse to swim over Thames unto Lambeth. And then within a while he came to the same place thereas the ten noble knights fought with Sir Meliagrance. And then Sir Launcelot followed the track until that he came to a wood, and there was a straight way, and there the thirty archers bade Sir Launcelot turn again, and follow no longer that track.

" What commandment have ye thereto," said Sir Launcelot, " to cause me that am a knight of the Round Table to leave my right way ? "

" This way shalt thou leave, otherelse thou shalt go it on thy foot, for wit thou well thy horse shall be slain."

" That is little mastery," said Sir Launcelot, " to slay mine horse ; but as for myself, when my horse is slain, I give right nought for you, not an ye were five hundred more."

So then they shot Sir Launcelot's horse, and smote him with many arrows ; and then Sir Launcelot avoided his horse, and went on foot ; but there were so many ditches and hedges betwixt them and him that he might not meddle with none of them.

" Alas for shame," said Launcelot, " that ever one knight should betray another knight ; but it is an old saw, A good man is never in danger but when he is in the danger of a coward."

Then Sir Launcelot went a while, and then he was foul cumbered of his armour, his shield, and his spear, and all that longed unto him. Wit ye well he was full sore annoyed, and full loath he was for to leave anything that longed unto him, for he dread sore the treason of Sir Meliagrance. Then by fortune there came by him a chariot that came thither for to fetch wood.

" Say me, carter," said Sir Launcelot, " what shall I give thee to suffer me to leap into thy chariot, and that thou bring me unto a castle within this two mile ? "

" Thou shalt not come within my chariot," said the carter, " for I am sent for to fetch wood for my lord, Sir Meliagrance."

" With him would I speak."

" Thou shalt not go with me," said the carter.

Then Sir Launcelot leapt to him, and gave him such a buffet that he fell to the earth stark dead. Then the other carter, his fellow, was afeared, and weened to have gone the same way; and then he cried:

"Fair lord, save my life, and I shall bring you where ye will."

"Then I charge thee," said Sir Launcelot, "that thou drive me and this chariot even unto Sir Meliagrance's gate."

"Leap up into the chariot," said the carter, "and ye shall be there anon."

So the carter drove on a great wallop, and Sir Launcelot's horse followed the chariot, with more than a forty arrows broad and rough in him. And more than an hour and an half Dame Guenever was awaiting in a bay window with her ladies, and espied an armed knight standing in a chariot.

"See, madam," said a lady, "where rideth in a chariot a goodly armed knight; I suppose he rideth unto hanging."

"Where?" said the Queen.

Then she espied by his shield that he was there himself, Sir Launcelot du Lake. And then she was ware where came his horse ever after that chariot, and ever he trod his guts and his paunch under his feet.

"Alas," said the Queen, "now I see well and prove, that well is him that hath a trusty friend. Ha, ha, most noble knight," said Queen Guenever, "I see well thou art hard bestad when thou ridest in a chariot."

Then she rebuked that lady that likened Sir Launcelot to ride in a chariot to hanging.

"It was foul mouthed," said the Queen, "and evil likened, so for to liken the most noble knight of the world unto such a shameful death. O Jesu defend him and keep him," said the Queen, "from all mischievous end."

By this was Sir Launcelot come to the gates of that castle, and there he descended down, and cried, that all the castle rang of it:

"Where art thou, false traitor, Sir Meliagrance, and knight of the Table Round? now come forth here, thou traitor knight, thou and thy fellowship with thee; for here I am, Sir Launcelot du Lake, that shall fight with you."

And therewithal he bare the gate wide open upon the porter, and smote him under his ear with his gauntlet, that his neck brast in sunder.

When Sir Meliagrance heard that Sir Launcelot was there he ran unto Queen Guenever, and fell upon his knee, and said:

"Mercy, madam, now I put me wholly into your grace."

"What aileth you now?" said Queen Guenever; "forsooth, I

might well wit some good knight would revenge me though my lord Arthur wist not of this your work."

"Madam," said Sir Meliagrance, "all this that is amiss on my part shall be amended right as yourself will devise, and wholly I put me in your grace."

"What would ye that I did?" said the Queen.

"I would no more," said Meliagrance, "but that ye would take all in your own hands, and that ye will rule my lord Sir Launcelot; and such cheer as may be made him in this poor castle ye and he shall have until to-morn, and then may ye and all they return unto Westminster and my body and all that I have I shall put in your rule."

"Ye say well," said the Queen, "and better is peace than ever war, and the less noise the more is my worship."

Then the Queen and her ladies went down unto the knight, Sir Launcelot, that stood wroth out of measure in the inner court, to abide battle; and ever he bade:

"Thou traitor knight come forth."

Then the Queen came to him and said:

"Sir Launcelot, why be ye so moved?"

"Ha, madam," said Sir Launcelot, "why ask ye me that question? Meseemeth," said Sir Launcelot, "ye ought to be more wroth than I am, for ye have the hurt and the dishonour, for wit ye well, madam, my hurt is but little for the killing of a mare's son, but the despite grieveth me much more than all my hurt."

"Truly," said the Queen, "ye say truth; but heartily I thank you," said the Queen, "but ye must come in with me peaceably, for all thing is put in my hand, and all that is evil shall be for the best, for the knight full sore repenteth him of the misadventure that is befallen him."

"Madam," said Sir Launcelot, "sith it is so that ye been accorded with him, as for me I may not be again it, howbeit Sir Meliagrance hath done full shamefully to me, and cowardly. Ah, madam," said Sir Launcelot, "an I had wist ye would have been so soon accorded with him I would not have made such haste unto you."

"Why say ye so," said the Queen, "do ye forthink yourself of your good deeds? Wit you well," said the Queen, "I accorded never unto him for favour nor love that I had unto him, but for to lay down every shameful noise."

"Madam," said Sir Launcelot, "ye understand full well I was

never willing nor glad of shameful slander nor noise; and there is neither king, queen, nór knight, that beareth the life, except my lord King Arthur, and you, madam, should let me, but I should make Sir Meliagrance's heart full cold or ever I departed from hence."

"That wot I well," said the Queen, "but what will ye more? Ye shall have all thing ruled as ye list to have it."

"Madam," said Sir Launcelot, "so ye be pleased I care not, as for my part ye shall soon please."

Right so the Queen took Sir Launcelot by the bare hand, for he had put off his gauntlet, and so she went with him till her chamber; and then she commanded him to be unarmed. And then Sir Launcelot asked where were the ten knights that were wounded sore; so she showed them unto Sir Launcelot, and there they made great joy of the coming of him, and Sir Launcelot made great dole of their hurts, and bewailed them greatly. And there Sir Launcelot told them how cowardly and traitorly Meliagrance set archers to slay his horse, and how he was fain to put himself in a chariot. Thus they complained every each to other; and full fain they would have been revenged, but they peaced themselves by cause of the Queen.

Then, as the French book saith, Sir Launcelot was called many a day after le Chevaler du Chariot, and did many deeds, and great adventures he had. And so leave we of this tale le Chevaler du Chariot.

MEDIAEVAL FRENCH
12TH CENTURY

THE TALE OF KING COUSTANS THE EMPEROR

THE tale telleth us that there was erewhile an Emperor of Byzance, which as now is called Constantinople; but anciently it was called Byzance. There was in the said city an Emperor; pagan he was, and was held for wise as of his law. He knew well enough of a science that is called Astronomy, and he knew withal of the course of the stars, and the planets, and the moon: and he saw well in the stars many marvels, and he knew much of other things wherein the paynims much study, and in the lots they trow, and the answers of the Evil One, that is to say, the Enemy. This Emperor had to name Musselin; he knew much of lore and of sorceries, as many a pagan doth even yet.

Now it befell on a time that the Emperor Musselin went his ways a night-tide, he and a Knight of his alone together, amidst of the city which is now called Constantinople, and the moon shone full clear.

And so far they went, till they heard a Christian woman who travailed in child-bed in a certain house whereby they went. There was the husband of the said woman aloft in a high solar, and was praying to God one while that she might be delivered, and then again another while that she might not be delivered.

When the Emperor had hearkened this a great while, he said to the Knight: "Hast thou heard it of yonder churl how he prayeth that his wife may be delivered of her child, and another while prayeth that she may not be delivered? Certes, he is worser than a thief. For every man ought to have pity of women, more especially of them that be sick of childing. And now, so help me Mahoume and Termagaunt! if I do not hang him, if he betake him not to telling me reason wherefore he doeth it! Come we now unto him."

They went within, and said the Emperor: "Now, churl, tell me of a sooth wherefore thou prayedst thy God thus for thy wife, one while that she might be delivered, and another while that she might be delivered not. This have I will to wot."

"Sir," said he, "I will tell thee well. Sooth it is that I be a clerk, and know much of a science which men call Astronomy. Withal I wot of the course of the stars and of the planets; therefore saw I well that if my wife were delivered at the point and the hour whereas I prayed God that she might not be delivered, that if she were delivered at that hour, the child would go the way of perdition, and that needs must he be burned, or hanged, or drowned. But whenas I saw that it was good hour and good point, then prayed I to God that she might be delivered. And so sore have I prayed God, that He hath hearkened my prayer of his mercy, and that she is delivered in good point. God be heried and thanked!"

"Tell me now," said the Emperor, "in what good point is the child born?"

"Sir," said he, "of a good will; know sir, forsooth, that this child, which here is born, shall have to wife the daughter of the Emperor of this city, who was born but scarce eight days ago; and he shall be Emperor withal, and lord of this city, and of all the earth."

"Churl," said the Emperor, "this which thou sayest can never come to pass."

"Sir," said he, "it is all sooth, and thus it behoveth it to be."

"Certes," quoth the Emperor, "'tis a mighty matter to trow in."

But the Emperor and the Knight departed thence, and the Emperor bade the Knight go bear off the child in such wise, if he might, that none should see him therein. The Knight went and found there two women, who were all busied in arraying the woman who had been brought to bed. The child was wrapped in linen clothes, and they had laid him on a chair. Thereto came the Knight, and took the child and laid him on a board, and brought him to the Emperor, in such wise that none of the women wotted thereof. The Emperor did do slit the belly of him with a knife from the breast down to the navel, and said withal to the Knight, that never should the son of that churl have to wife his daughter, nor be Emperor after him.

Therewithal would the Emperor do the Knight to put forth his hand to the belly, to seek out the heart; but the Knight said to him: "Ah, sir, a-God's mercy, what wouldst thou do? It is nought meet to thee, and if folk were to wot thereof, great reproach wouldst thou get thee. Let him be at this present, for he is more than dead. And if it please thee that that one trouble more about the matter, I will bear him down to the sea to drown him."

"Yea," quoth the Emperor, "bear him away thither, for right sore do I hate him."

So the Knight took the child, and wrapped him in a cover-point of silk, and bore him down toward the sea. But therewith had he pity of the child, and said that by him should he never be drowned; so he left him, all wrapped up as he was, on a midden before the gate of a certain abbey of monks, who at that very nick of time were singing their matins.

When the monks had done singing their matins, they heard the child crying, and they bore him before the Lord Abbot. And the Abbot saw that the child was fair, and said that he would do it to be nourished. Therewith he did do unwrap it, and saw that it had the belly cloven from the breast down to the navel.

The Abbot, so soon as it was day, bade come leeches, and asked of them for how much they would heal the child; and they craved for the healing of him an hundred of bezants. But he said that it would be more than enough, for overmuch would the child be costing. And so much did the Abbot, that he made market with the surgeons for four-score bezants. And thereafter the Abbot did do baptize the child, and gave him to name Coustans, because him-seemed that he costed exceeding much for the healing of him.

The leeches went so much about with the child, that he was made whole: and the Abbot sought him a good nurse, and got the child to suckle, and he was healed full soon; whereas the flesh of him was soft and tender, and grew together swiftly one to the other, but ever after showed the mark.

Much speedily waxed the child in great beauty; when he was seven years old the Abbot did him to go to the school, and he learned so well, that he over-passed all his fellows in subtilty and science. When he was of twelve years, he was a child exceeding goodly; so it might nought avail to seek a goodlier. And whenas the Abbot saw him to be a child so goodly and gentle, he did him to ride abroad with him.

Now so it fell out, that the Abbot had to speak with the Emperor of a wrong which his bailiffs had done to the abbey. The Abbot made him a goodly gift, whereas the abbey and convent were subject unto him, for the Emperor was a Saracen. When the Abbot had given him his goodly gift, the Emperor gave him day for the third day thence, whenas he should be at a castle of his, three leagues from the city of Byzance.

The Abbot abode the day: when he saw the time at point to go to the Emperor, he mounted a-horseback, and his chaplain, and esquire, and his folk; and with him was Coustans, who was so well fashioned that all praised his great beauty, and each one said that he seemed well to be come of high kindred, and that he would come to great good.

So when the Abbot was come before the castle whereas the Emperor should be, he came before him and spake to and greeted him: and the Emperor said to him that he should come into the castle, and he would speak with him of his matter: the Abbot made him obeisance, and said to him: "Sir, a-God's name!" Then the Abbot called to him Coustans, who was holding of his hat while he spake unto the Emperor; and the Emperor looked on the lad, and saw him so fair and gentle as never before had he seen the like fair person. So he asked of the Abbot what he was; and the Abbot said him that he wotted not, save that he was of his folk, and that he had bred him up from a little child. "And if I had leisure with thee, I would tell thee thereof fine marvels."

"Yea," said the Emperor; "come ye into the castle, and therein shalt thou say me the sooth."

The Emperor came into the castle, and the Abbot was ever beside him, as one who had his business to do; and he did it to the best that he might, as he who was subject unto him. The Emperor forgat in nowise the great beauty of the lad, and said unto the Abbot that he should cause him come before him, and the Abbot sent for the lad, who came straightway.

When the child was before the Emperor, he seemed unto him right fair; and he said unto the Abbot, that great damage it was that so fair a lad was Christian. But the Abbot said that it was great joy thereof, whereas he would render unto God a fair soul. When the Emperor heard that, he fell a-laughing, and said to the Abbot that the Christian law was of no account, and that all they were lost who trowed therein. When the Abbot heard him so say, he was sore grieved; but he durst not make answer as he would, so he said much humbly: "Sir, if God please, who can all things, they are not lost; for God will have mercy of His sinners."

Then the Emperor asked of him whence that fair child was come; and the Abbot said that it was fifteen years gone since he had been found before their gate, on a midden, all of a night-tide. " And our monks heard him a-crying whenas they had but just said matins; and they went to seek the child, and brought him to me; and I looked on the babe, and beheld him much fair, and I said that I would do him to be nourished and baptized. I unwrapped him, for the babe was wrapped up in a cover-point of vermil sendel; and when he was unwrapped, I saw that he had the belly slit from the breast to the navel. Then I sent for leeches and surgeons, and made market with them to heal him for four-score bezants; and thereafter he was baptized, and I gave him to name Coustans, because he costed so much of goods to heal. So was the babe presently made whole: but never sithence might it be that the mark appeared not on his belly."

When the Emperor heard that, he knew that it was the child whose belly he had slit to draw the heart out of him. So he said to the Abbot that he should give him the lad. And the Abbot said that he would speak thereof to his convent, and that he should have him with their good-will. The Emperor held his peace, and answered never a word. But the Abbot took leave of him, and came to his abbey, and his monks, and told them that the Emperor had craved Coustans of him. " But I answered that I would speak to you if ye will yea-say it. Say, now, what ye would praise of my doing herein."

" What!" said the wisest of the convent; " by our faith, evil hast thou done, whereas thou gavest him not presently, even as he demanded of thee. We counsel thee send him straightway, lest the Emperor be wrath against us, for speedily may we have scathe of him."

Thereto was their counsel fast, that Coustans should be sent to the Emperor. So the Abbot commanded the Prior to lead Coustans thereto; and the Prior said: " A-God's name!"

So he mounted, and led with him Coustans, and came unto the Emperor, and greeted him on behalf of the Abbot and the convent; and then he took Coustans by the hand, and, on the said behalf, gave him to the Emperor, who received him as one who was much wrath that such a runagate and beggar churl should have his daughter to wife. But he thought in his heart that he would play him the turn.

When the Emperor had gotten Coustans, he was in sore imagination how he should be slain in such wise that none might wot word thereof. And it fell out so that the Emperor had matters on hand at the outer marches of his land, much long aloof thence, well a twelve days' journey. So the Emperor betook him to going thither, and had

Coustans thither with him, and thought what wise he might to do slay him, till at last he let write a letter to his Burgreve of Byzance.

"I, Emperor of Byzance and Lord of Greece, do thee to wit who abidest duly in my place for the warding of my land; and so soon as thou seest this letter thou shalt slay or let slay him who this letter shall bear to thee, so soon as he hath delivered the said letter to thee, without longer tarrying. As thou holdest dear thine own proper body, do straightway my commandment herein."

Even such was the letter which the fair child Coustans bore, and knew not that he bore his own death. The lad took the letter, which was close, and betook him to the road, and did so much by his journeys that he came in less time than fifteen days to Byzance, which is nowadays called Constantinople.

When the lad entered into the city, it was the hour of dinner; so, as God would have it, he thought that he would not go his errand at that nick of time, but would tarry till folk had done dinner: and exceeding hot was the weather, as is wont about St. John's-mass. So he entered into the garden all a-horseback. Great and long was the garden; so the lad took the bridle from off his horse and unlaced the saddle-girths, and let him graze; and thereafter he went into the nook of a tree; and full pleasant was the place, so that presently he fell asleep.

Now so it fell out, that when the fair daughter of the Emperor had eaten, she went into the garden with three of her maidens; and they fell to chasing each other about, as whiles is the wont of maidens to play; until at the last the fair Emperor's daughter came under the tree whereas Coustans lay a-sleeping, and he was all vermil as the rose. And when the damsel saw him, she beheld him with a right good will, and she said to herself that never on a day had she seen so fair a fashion of man. Then she called to her that one of her fellows in whom she had the most affiance, and the others she made to go forth from out of the garden.

Then the fair maiden, daughter of the Emperor, took her fellow by the hand, and led her to look on the lovely lad whereas he lay a-sleeping; and she spake thus: "Fair fellow, here is a rich treasure. Lo thou! the most fairest fashion of a man that ever mine eyes have seen on any day of my life. And he beareth a letter, and well I would see what it sayeth."

So the two maidens drew nigh to the lad, and took from him the letter, and the daughter of the Emperor read the same; and when she had read it, she fell a-lamenting full sore, and said to her fellow: " Certes here is a great grief! "

" Ha, my Lady! " said the other one, " tell me what it is."

" Of a surety," said the Maiden, " might I but trow in thee I would do away that sorrow! "

" Ha, Lady," said she, " hardly mayest thou trow in me, whereas for nought would I uncover that thing which thou wouldst have hid."

Then the Maiden, the daughter of the Emperor, took oath of her according to the paynim law; and thereafter she told her what the letter said; and the damsel answered her: " Lady, and what wouldest thou do? "

" I will tell thee well," said the daughter of the Emperor; " I will put in his pouch another letter, wherein the Emperor, my father, biddeth his Burgreve to give me to wife to this fair child here, and that he make great feast at the doing of the wedding unto all the folk of this land; whereas he is to wot well that the lad is a high man and a loyal."

When the damsel had heard that, she said that would be good to do. " But, Lady, how wilt thou have the seal of thy father? "

" Full well," said the Maiden, " for my father delivered to me four pair of scrolls, sealed of his seal thereon; he hath written nought therein; and I will write all that I will."

" Lady," said she, " thou hast said full well; but do it speedily, and haste thee ere he awakeneth."

" So will I," said the Maiden.

Then the fair Maiden, the daughter of the Emperor, went to her coffers, and drew thereout one of the said scrolls sealed, which her father had left her, that she might borrow moneys thereby, if so she would. For ever was the Emperor and his folk in war, whereas he had neighbours right felon, and exceeding mighty, whose land marched upon his. So the Maiden wrote the letter in this wise:

" I, King Musselin, Emperor of Greece and of Byzance the city, to my Burgreve of Byzance greeting. I command thee that the bearer of this letter ye give to my fair daughter in marriage according to our law; whereas I have heard and wot soothly that he is a high person, and well worthy to have my daughter. And thereto make ye great joy and great feast to all them of my city and of all my land."

In such wise wrote and said the letter of the fair daughter of the Emperor; and when she had written the said letter, she went back to the garden, she and her fellow together, and found that one yet asleep, and they put the letter into his pouch. And then they began to sing and make noise to awaken him. So he awoke anon, and was all astonied at the fair Maiden, the daughter of the Emperor, and the other one her fellow, who came before him; and the fair Maiden, daughter of the Emperor, greeted him; and he greeted her again right debonairly. Then she asked of him what he was, and whither he went; and he said that he bore a letter to the Burgreve, which the Emperor sent by him; and the Maiden said that she would bring him straightway whereas was the Burgreve. Therewith she took him by the hand, and brought him to the palace, where there was much folk, who all rose against the Maiden, as to her who was their Lady.

Now the Maiden demanded the Burgreve, and they told her that he was in a chamber; so thither she led the lad, and the lad delivered the letter, and said that the Emperor greeted him. But the Burgreve made great joy of the lad, and kissed the hand of him. The Maiden opened the pouch, and fell a-kissing the letter and the seal of her father for joy's sake, whereas she had not heard tidings of him a great while.

Thereafter she said to the Burgreve that she would hearken the letter in privy council, even as if she wotted nought thereof; and the Burgreve said that that were good to do. Then went the Burgreve and the Maiden into a chamber, and the Maiden unfolded the letter and read it to the Burgreve, and made semblance of wondering exceedingly; and the Burgreve said to her:

"Lady, it behoveth to do the will of my lord thy father, for otherwise we shall be blamed exceedingly."

The Maiden answered him: "And how can this be, that I should be wedded without my lord my father? A strange thing it would be, and I will do it in no manner."

"Ha, Lady!" said the Burgreve, "what is that thou sayest? Thy father has bidden thus by his letter, and it behoveth not to gainsay."

"Sir," said the Maiden (unto whom it was late till the thing were done), "thou shalt speak unto the barons and mighty men of this realm, and take counsel thereof. And if they be of accord thereto, I am she who will not go against it." Then the Burgreve said that she spake well and as one wise.

Then spake the Burgreve to the barons, and showed them the letter, and they accorded all to that that the matter of the letter must be accomplished, and the will of the Emperor done. Then they wedded the fair youth Coustans, according to the paynim law, unto the fair daughter of the Emperor; and the wedding endured for fifteen days: and such great joy was there at Byzance that it was exceeding, and folk did no work in the city, save eating and drinking and making merry.

Long while abode the Emperor in the land whereas he was; and when he had done his business, he went his ways back towards Byzance; and whenas he was but anigh two journeys thence, came to him a message of the messengers who came from Byzance. The Emperor asked of him what they did in the city; and the varlet said that they were making exceeding good cheer of eating and drinking and taking their ease, and that no work had they done therein these fifteen days.

"And wherefore is that?" said the Emperor.

"Wherefore, Sir! Wot ye not well thereof?"

"Nay, forsooth," said the Emperor, "but tell me wherefore."

"Sir," said the varlet, "thou sentest a youngling, exceeding fair, thy Burgreve, and badest him by thy letter to wed him to thy daughter the fair, and that he should be Emperor after thee, whereas he was a man right high, and well worthy to have her. But thy daughter would not take that before that the Burgreve should have spoken to the barons. And he spake to all them, and showed them thy letter; and they said that it behoved to do thy commandment. And when thy daughter saw that they were all of one accord thereon, she durst not go against them, but yea-said it. Even in such wise hath thy daughter been wedded, and such joy has been in the city as none might wish it better."

The Emperor, when he heard the messenger speak thus, was all astonied, and thought much of this matter; and he asked of the varlet how long it was since the lad had wedded his daughter, and whether or no he had lain by her?

"Sir," said the varlet, "yea; and she may well be big by now; because it is more than three weeks since he hath wedded her."

"Forsooth," said the Emperor, "in a good hour be it! for since it is so, it behoveth me to abide it, since no other it may be."

So far rode the Emperor till he came to Byzance, whereas they made him much fair feast; and his fair daughter came to meet him, and her husband Coustans, who was so fair a child that none might better be. The Emperor, who was a wise man, made of them much great joy, and laid his two hands upon their two heads, and held them there a great while ; which is the manner of benison amongst paynims.

That night thought the Emperor much on this marvel, how it could have come about ; and so much he pondered it, that he wotted full well that it had been because of his daughter. So he had no will to gainsay her, but he demanded to see the letter which he had sent, and they showed it unto him, and he saw his seal hanging thereto, and saw the letter which was written ; and by the manner whereby the thing had been done, he said to himself that he had striven against the things which behoved to be.

Thereafter, the Emperor made Coustans a knight, even his new son who was wedded unto his daughter, and he gave and granted to him all the whole land after his death. And the said Coustans bore him well and wisely, as a good knight, and a valiant and hardy, and defended him full well against his enemies. No long time wore ere his lord the Emperor died, and his service was done much richly, after the paynim law. Then was Coustans Emperor, and he loved and honoured much the Abbot who had nourished him, and he made him his very master. And the Emperor Coustans, by the counsel of the Abbot, and the will of God the all mighty, did do christen his wife, and all they of that land were converted to the law of Jesus Christ. And the Emperor Coustans begot on his wife an heir male, who had to name Constantine, who was thereafter a prudhomme much great. And thereafter was the city called Constantinople, because of his father, Coustans, who costed so much, but aforetime was it called Byzance.

Here withal endeth the Story of King Coustans the Emperor.

The said story was done out of the ancient French into English by William Morris.

AUCASSIN AND NICOLETTE

OLD ANTIF, 1280 A.D.

Hear a tale of joy and grief
By the minstrel Old Antif,
Telling how two lovers met,
Aucassin and Nicolette,
And the dolours undergone,
And the deeds of prowess done
By a lad of noble race
For a lady fair of face!

Sweet is the tale and finely told.
Though a man be ill and old,
Sick of body, sad of mind,
And to moody thought inclined,
If he hear it, he shall be
Healed and filled with jollity.
It is so sweet!

SO great, so marvellous, and so mortal was the war Count Bougars of Valence made on Count Garin of Beaucaire, that never a day broke but there were a hundred knights and ten thousand men-at-arms, foot and horse, at the gates and walls and barriers of the town. He burnt and wasted his lands and killed his men.

Count Garin of Beaucaire was old and feeble and at the end of his life. He had no heir, son or daughter, but one boy. This young man was such as I shall tell you. Aucassin was his name: tall, handsome, and charming he was, with well-shaped legs and feet and body and arms. His fair hair fell in little curls, his eyes were laughing and sparkling, his face a bright oval, with a high well-cut nose. And so full was he of good qualities, there was no room for anything bad in him. But Love, who conquers all, had so taken him captive that he would not become a knight, or put on armour, or ride to tourney or do any of his duties.

"Son," said his father and mother, "arm and mount your horse, and defend your lands and help your men. If they see you among themselves, they will fight the better for their own lives and goods, and for your lands and mine."

"Father," said Aucassin, "how can you talk only about this

matter. May God never grant me anything I pray for, if I become knight, or mount horse, or ride forth to battle to slay or to be slain, without you give me Nicolette, my sweetheart, whom I love so much!"

"Son," said the father, "this cannot be! You must let Nicolette alone. She is only a captive brought from a strange land, and purchased by the Viscount of my town from the Saracens. He has led her here and brought her up, and baptized her, and made her his god-child; and one of these days he will give her to some young fellow who will keep her in food in an honourable way. With all this you have nothing to do. But if you want a wife I will give you the daughter of a count or a king. There is no man so great in France but that if you want his daughter to wife, you shall have her."

"Oh, father!" said Aucassin, "where is there on earth so high a seat of honour that Nicolette, my sweetest love, would not worthily fill? Were she Empress of Constantinople or Germany, or Queen of France or England, it would be very little for her. So noble is she and courtly, and of good race, and endowed with all fine qualities."

Of the castle of Beaucaire
Gallant Aucassin was heir;
And no power or pleading moved him
To desert the maid that loved him;
Though his father looked full grim,
And his mother threatened him:
"Go to, fool! How can you rave
For a pretty, wanton slave,
Cast from a heathen town in Spain
And sold by pagan sailormen?
Since you want to take a wife,
Choose a girl of noble life!"
"Mother, on this my mind is set—
Nobly born is Nicolette,
Lovely and sweet in every part;
Her beauty lights up all my heart.
Good it is to win such bliss,
So sweet she is!"

When Count Garin of Beaucaire saw that he could not draw Aucassin away from his love Nicolette, he went to the Viscount of the town, who was his vassal, and spoke to him:

"Sir Viscount, take away your god-child, Nicolette. Cursed be the land from which she was brought into our country! For through her am I losing Aucassin. He will not become a knight or do any of his duties. And take heed of this thing—If I catch the girl I will burn her at the stake, and you yourself will be in fear of your life!"

"Sir," said the Viscount, "it pains me to see that he comes and goes here, and talks with her. I have purchased Nicolette with my money, and brought her up and baptized her, and one of these days I shall give her to a young man who can win food for her in an honourable way. With all this your son Aucassin has nothing to do. But since it is your will and pleasure, I will send her far away so that he shall never see her again."

"Look well to it," said Count Garin. "Great troubles may happen to you over this matter!"

He went away. The Viscount was a very powerful man in the town, and he had a splendid palace by the side of a garden. In a chamber on a top story he imprisoned Nicolette, with an old woman to keep her company; and he sent them the bread, meat, wine, and other things they needed. Then he had the door sealed, so that no one could go in or out; and there was only a very small window overlooking the garden, through which a little fresh air came.

In the vault where Nicolette
Prisoned is, may no one get.
Pleasant is the place to see,
Carved and painted wondrously;
But no pleasure can she find
In the room, for grief of mind.
Look! for she is leaning still
From the marble window-sill!
Delicate brows and yellow hair
She has, and delicately fair
Her face is, and no man can see
On earth a lovelier thing than she.
In the woodland far below
She can see the roses blow,
And the pretty birds that sing,
While she is reft of everything.
"Ah me! Poor slave!" she cries. "Ah me!
Why should I a prisoner be?
Aucassin! My lord! My knight!
Heart's desire, and eyes' delight!
Because you do not hate me, I
In a prison cell must lie,
All with grief and pain fordone.
But, by God, sweet Mary's Son,
Here for long I will not stay:
Love shall find a way.

The rumour went through all the land that Nicolette was lost. Some said she had fled from the country, and others said that Count Garin of Beaucaire had had her put to death. If there was a man who had joy in the news, Aucassin was not that man; and he went to the Viscount of the town, and spoke to him.

"Sir Viscount! What have you done with Nicolette, my sweetest sweetheart, the thing I love most in the whole world? Have you stolen her away from me and hidden her? You must know well that if I die through it, my blood will be required of you, and justly so. For you will have slain me with your two hands, by stealing from me the one thing in this world that I love most."

"Fair sir," said the Viscount, "let this matter be! Nicolette is a slave brought by me from a strange land, and purchased with my own money from the Saracens. I have brought her up, and baptized her, and made her my god-child, and fed her, and one of these days I will give her to some young fellow who will keep her in an honourable way. With all this you have nothing to do, but to take to wife the daughter of a count or of a king. Moreover, what would you have won, had you made her your mistress and taken her to your bed? Very little would you have gained by it; for all the days of your life your body would have been dishonoured, and afterwards your soul would have gone to hell, and never would you have entered heaven!"

"What have I to do in heaven?" said Aucassin. "I have no desire to enter it; but only to have Nicolette, my very sweet love, whom I long for so much. For into heaven there go only such folk as I will tell you. There go old priests and maimed, old cripples who squat all day and all night before altars and in crypts: those who wear worn-out mantles and old tattered garments: those go who are naked, with bare feet and with bare rumps, who are dying of hunger and thirst, and cold and wretchedness. These are the folk that go to heaven, and with such as them have I nothing to do! But to hell gladly will I go. For to hell go the handsome clerks and the gallant knights who are slain in the tourneys and the splendid wars, and the good squires and the men of noble birth. And with them I desire to go. And to hell go the lovely, courteous ladies, who have two or three lovers besides their husbands, and there go our gold and our silver, our ermine and our furs, and the harpers and the minstrels and the kings of our age. Gladly with them will I go, if only I have Nicolette, my sweetest love, with me!"

"Faith!" said the Viscount, "all your talk is in vain, and never shall you see the girl. And if I spoke to you about her and your father knew of it, he would burn me and her in a fire, and your own life too would be in peril."

"This gives me great pain," said Aucassin, and very sorrowfully he left the Viscount.

Sadly Aucassin departs,
With the heaviest of hearts.
Strength or solace finds he none,
Now that Nicolette is gone.
Sadly homeward he repairs,
Sadly mounts the castle stairs
To his chamber, where he lies
Weeping, and on his love he cries:
"Sweet wert thou, my Nicolette,
In all thy movements! Sweeter yet
In laughing talk and loving ways!
Sweetest to kiss and to embrace!
Now I am so sorely tried,
I care not if to-day I died,
For then would all my sorrows end,
Sister, sweet friend!"

While Aucassin was in his chamber, sorrowing for his sweetheart Nicolette, Count Bougars of Valence did not forget that he had to bring his war to an end. So he called out his men, foot and horse, and drew up to the castle to assail it. And the cries and rumours spread; knights and squires armed themselves and sought the gates and the walls to defend the castle, the townsmen climbed to the galleries of the ramparts and flung paving-stones and sharpened stakes upon the assailers.

While the assault was spreading all around and growing very fierce, Count Garin of Beaucaire came into the room where Aucassin was grieving and bewailing Nicolette, his sweetest darling, whom he loved so much.

"Ha, my son!" said he. "What a coward and miserable creature you are to look on, when an enemy is storming your best and strongest castle! If you lose it, you are a ruined man! Son, take your arms and mount your horse, and defend your lands and help your men. Go forth to the battle. You need not even strike or be struck. If only our vassals see you among them, they will fight better for their own lives and goods, and for your lands and mine. And you are so tall and so strong, you could easily do this thing, and it is your duty to do it."

"Father," said Aucassin, "how can you talk only about this one matter. May God never grant me anything I pray for, if I become knight or mount horse and go forth to battle to slay or be slain, without you give me Nicolette, my sweetheart, whom I love so much ! "

" Son," said the father, " that cannot be. Rather would I endure to be wholly ruined and lose everything I have, than that you should take her for your mistress or your wife."

He turned away, and when Aucassin saw him going, he called him back.

" Father ! " said Aucassin. " Come, I will make a good bargain with you."

" What, fair son ? "

" I will arm myself and go into the fight on one condition. If God bring me back safe and sound, you will let me see Nicolette, my sweet darling, long enough to speak two or three words to her, and give her one kiss."

" I agree," said the father.

So he made the bargain, and Aucassin was joyful.

A hundred thousand pounds of gold
Would not make a man more bold
Than was Aucassin to get
One sweet kiss from Nicolette.
Shouting for his armour, he
Dons his hauberk joyfully ;
Laces a helm upon his head ;
Girds on his sword ; bestrides his steed ;
Couches his lance, and grips his shield ;
Gallantly he takes the field.
Calling his sweetheart to his mind,
He spurs his horse, and, like the wind,
Sweeps through the town-gate, and his foes
Around him close.

Aucassin was armed and horsed as you have heard. God ! how he sat—the shield on his neck, the helm on his head, and the sword-belt on his left hip ! The lad was tall and strong, handsome and charming, and very powerful ; the horse on which he sat was fleet and mettlesome, and the boy put him skilfully through the gate. But do not fancy that he was thinking of taking spoil of oxen, cows and goats, or of striking down his enemies or being struck down by them. Not at all ! It never came into his mind ; for he thought so much on Nicolette, his sweet darling, that he forgot his reins, and all that he had to do. And his horse, still smarting from the spur, carried him into the thick of the fight, and dashed him into the midst of his foes. And on all sides they man-handled him, and wrested his shield and lance from him, and quickly led him a prisoner, and began to discuss in what way they should put him to death.

"Ha, God!" said Aucassin, when he overheard them. "Sweet Jesus! Are these my mortal enemies, who hale me about and talk of cutting off my head forthwith? But if I get my head struck off I shall never speak again to my sweetheart Nicolette, whom I love so much. Yet here am I still with a good sword, sitting on a fresh horse. If I do not protect myself now for her sake, may God never help her if she goes on loving me!"

The lad was big and strong, and the horse beneath him was eager; and putting his hand to his sword, he began to strike out, left and right, and slash through helms and nose-guards, hands and arms—making such a carnage round him as a wild boar does when he stands at bay before the dogs in a forest. He struck down ten knights and wounded seven more, and then charged suddenly out of the crowd of foes, riding back full gallop, sword in hand.

Count Bougars of Valence heard that his men were about to hang Aucassin, his enemy, and he came to the spot and Aucassin did not overlook him. Gripping his sword, he smote him right through the helm, and battered in his head. He was so stunned that he tumbled to the earth, and Aucassin stretched out his hand, and seized him by the nose-guard, and led him a prisoner to his father.

"Father," said Aucassin, "see, here is your enemy who has warred against you so long and done you so much evil! Twenty years has this war lasted, and no man could bring it to an end!"

"Fair son," said the father, "it is well you have done your first deeds of knightly courage, and given over dreaming of foolish things!"

"Father," said Aucassin, "don't start lecturing me, but let me have my part of the bargain we made."

"Bah! what bargain, fair son?"

"Oh, father! have you forgotten your promise? By my head I do not mean to forget it, whoever else does, so deeply it goes to my heart. Did you not bargain with me, when I took my arms and went out to the fight, that, if God brought me back safe and sound, you would let me see my sweetheart, Nicolette, long enough for me to speak two or three words to her and give her one kiss? This was the bargain you made with me, and I wish you to keep it!"

"I keep it?" said his father. "May God never help me if I keep such a bargain with you. If the girl were here now I would burn her in a fire, and you yourself might not escape it ! "

" Is that all you have to say ? " said Aucassin.

" So help me God," said his father, " yes ! "

" Faith ! " said Aucassin, " I am very sorry that a man of your age should be a liar. Count of Valence, you are my prisoner ? "

" That is so, sir," said Count Bougars.

" Then give me your hand," said Aucassin.

" Willingly, sir."

So he put his hand in the lad's.

" This pledge shall you make me," said Aucassin, " that never, in all the days that you have to live, shall it be within your power to bring shame on my father, or injure him in body or goods, and you will not do it ! "

" For God's sake, sir," said the Count, " do not mock me, but set me to ransom. There is nothing you can ask me—gold or silver, war-horses or palfreys, ermines or sables, hounds or hawks—that I will not give you."

" What ! " said Aucassin, " Do you not know that I took you prisoner ? "

" Yes, sir," said Count Bougars.

" So help me God, then," said Aucassin, " if you will not give me that pledge I will send your head flying from your shoulders ! "

" God's name ! " he said. " I'll give any pledge you please ! "

So he pledged him, and Aucassin set him on a horse and mounted another, and conducted him to a place of safety.

Seeing that his only son,
Aucassin, could not be won
From Nicolette, the bright-faced maid,
Count Garin was sore dismayed ;
And in anger had him thrown
In a dungeon of grey stone
Under the ground ; and there the lad
For lonely grief went well-nigh mad.
Listen, and you will hear him cry,
Like a man about to die :
" Nicolette of the bright face,
Lily of love and rose of grace !
Sweeter than grapes my sweetheart is,
Or wine in carven chalices !
It was but the other day
That a pilgrim came this way—
Weak and poor and travel-worn—
Who in Limousin was born.

With the falling sickness, he
Stricken was full grievously,
Full of pain and well-nigh dead,
When you passed before his bed.
Lifting your train and ermine gown
And smock, your fair, white leg was shown,
And the pilgrim, seeing it,
Rose up from his deadly fit—
Rose up cured of all disease,
And went home joyful and at ease!
Wonder of the world! I will
Worship you and praise you still,
For the beauty of your face,
For the joy of your embrace,
For the rapture of your kiss,
And your body's sweetnesses!
For you am I in prison bound,
In this dungeon underground:
Where I rage in such mad fear,
I must die in darkness here,
For you, my dear!"

Aucassin was put in prison as you have heard, and Nicolette, on the other hand, was shut in a vaulted chamber. It was in the summer-time, in the month of May when the days are warm, long, and bright, and the nights quiet and serene. Nicolette lay one night in her bed, and saw the moon shine white through the window, and heard the nightingale sing in the garden below, and she thought on Aucassin, her friend, whom she loved so much. Then she fell to thinking of Count Garin of Beaucaire, who hated her to death, and she thought she would not remain any longer there; since if she were betrayed, and Count Garin learnt where she was, he would put her to death in a terrible way. She touched the old woman who was with her, and found she was asleep. She rose up and put on a fine mantle of cloth of silk, and took the bed-clothes and the towels and tied them together, and made as long a rope as she was able, and fastened it to the pillar of the window, and so lowered herself into the garden. Then lifting her mantle, with one hand in front and the other behind, she kilted it, because she saw that the dew was heavy on the grass. And so she went down the garden.

Her yellow hair fell in little curls; her eyes were blue and laughing; and her face finely curved, with a proud, shapely little nose; her little lips were more tenderly red than cherries and roses are in summer-time; her teeth were white and small; and her firm little breasts swelled beneath her mantle like two nuts of a walnut-tree. So slim was her waist that you could have clipped her in your two hands; and the daisies that snapped beneath her toes as she passed, and fell on the arch of her foot, looked quite black beside her feet and legs. So very white the maiden was.

She reached the postern gate, and, unfastening it, passed out into the streets of Beaucaire, keeping on the shadowy side: for the moon was shining very bright; and she wandered on until she came to the tower where her lover was imprisoned. The tower was cracked here and there, and she crouched against one of the buttresses, and wrapped her mantle about her, and put her head through one of the cracks in the old ruin; and there she heard Aucassin within, weeping and making great sorrow, and lamenting for his sweet darling whom he loved so much. And when she had listened enough to him, she began to speak.

Leaning on a moonlit pier,
Lovely Nicolette could hear
Aucassin, in his dark cell,
Weep for her he loved too well,
And desire her love again.
So she spoke him frank and plain:
" Aucassin, young, valiant knight,
Born to honour and delight!
All in vain you weep for me,
Since betrothed we cannot be;
For your kinsmen hate me sore,
And your father hates me more.
For your sake I now must flee
To some land across the sea."
Cutting off a lock of hair,
She cast it through the window, where
Her lover took the yellow tress
To kiss and fondle it and press
Close to his sad and loving heart;
And weeping still he would not part
From his sweetheart.

When Aucassin heard Nicolette say that she wished to go away to another country, he was very angry.

" Sweet, lovely friend," he said, " you must not go away; for if you do, you will kill me. The first man who set eyes on you and had the power, would at once seize you, and put you in his bed, and make you his mistress. And if you lay in any man's bed but mine, do not think I should wait till I found a knife to stab myself to the heart and die. No, no! I would not wait so long as that. I would just fling myself against the first wall or grey stone, and beat my head till I knocked my eyes out and my brains. Sooner would I die such a death than learn you had been in any other man's bed but mine!"

" Ah ! " she said, " I do not believe you love me as much as you say. I love you more than you love me ! "

" Oh, my sweet, lovely darling," said Aucassin, " it is not possible you should love me as much as I love you. Woman cannot love man as much as man does woman. For the love of a woman lies in her eye, and in the nipple of her breast, and in the toe of her foot ; but the love of a man is planted in his heart, and from there it cannot escape ! "

While Aucassin and Nicolette were talking together, the town watch came along the street with their drawn swords under their cloaks. For Count Garin had ordered them to put the girl to death as soon as ever they took her. And the watchman on the tower saw them coming, and heard them talking of Nicolette and threatening to kill her.

" God ! " he said, " what a great pity it would be if they slew so lovely a maid ! It would be a mighty good piece of work if I could tell her without them knowing it, so that she could guard herself against them. For, if they kill her, my young lord Aucassin will die of it, and that will be a great pity."

Wise the watchman was, and brave,
Kind to warn and quick to save !
Making up a merry tune,
Loud he sang beneath the moon :
" Lassie with the noble heart,
Winsome form and winning art,
Grey-blue eyes and yellow hair,
Talking with your lover there—
I can see you where you stand !
Listen now and understand !
Run from the soldiers ! Run ! for they
Quickly come along this way.
With bare swords they seek you out,
Fiercely searching round about.
Great the hurt that will betide you !
So hide you ! hide you !

" Ha ! " said Nicolette. " May the soul of your father and your mother rest in blessed peace for the kindness and courtesy you have shown me ! Please God I shall escape from them, and may God Himself be my guard ! "

Wrapping herself in her mantle, she stayed in the shadow of the buttress until the men had passed, and then she took leave of Aucassin, and ran till she came to the castle wall. There was a breach in the rampart that had been repaired with wattles and earth, and she climbed over this, and got between the wall and the ditch, and looking down she saw that the ditch fell sheer and deep, and she was mightily afraid.

"Ha, sweet God!" she said, "if I let myself fall I shall break my neck; if I stay here they will take me to-morrow and burn me in a fire. Yet would I rather die here now than have the people staring at me at the stake to-morrow!"

She crossed herself, and let herself slip down the ditch, and when she came to the bottom, her lovely feet and her lovely hands, that had not known what wounds were, were bruised and skinned, and the blood spurted from them in a dozen places Yet she felt neither hurt nor pain, because of the terror she was in. And if she was hurt in getting into the ditch, she was still more hurt in getting out of it. But she thought it would do her no good to linger there, and finding a sharpened stake that the townsmen had thrown when defending the castle, she hacked out steps, one above the other, and climbed with great difficulty till she reached the top.

Now, two bow-shots away was the forest, that stretched thirty leagues in length and breadth, and within it were wild beasts and deadly snakes. She was afraid they would kill her if she went in the forest. But then she remembered that if she were found by the ramparts, she would be taken back to the town to be burnt.

Nicolette of the bright face,
Climbing from the perilous place,
Began to cry in bitter fear
And call on Christ to succour her:
"Father, King of majesty!
I cannot tell what way to flee!
In the leafy forest I
By lion or wild boar will die.
Here, if I bide till morning break,
Men will lead me to the stake,
And to the fire shall I be doomed,
And all my body be consumed.
Yet, by the majesty of God,
Rather will I be wild beasts' food
Than by the city stay and burn!
Back I'll not turn!"

Nicolette cried sorely as you have heard. Then commending herself to God, she wandered on till she came into the forest. But she was afraid to enter the deep wood, because of the wild beasts and the snakes, and she crept into a thick bush, and there sleep fell upon her. And she slept till the morrow at high prime, when the herd-boys came from the town, and drove their beasts between the wood and the river. And they turned aside to a very beautiful spring that rose on the edge of the forest, and there they spread out a cloak, and put their bread on it. While they were eating, Nicolette was awakened by the songs of the birds and the shouts of the herd-boys, and she sprang towards them.

"Fair children!" said she, "may the Lord God help you!"

"God bless you!" said one who was readier of speech than the others.

"Good boys," she said, "do you know Aucassin, the son of Count Garin of Beaucaire?"

"Yes, we know him well."

"So God help you, good boys!" she said, "tell him that there is a beast in this forest, and that he must come and hunt it down. And if he can capture it, he will not give a limb of it for a hundred pounds of gold! No, not for five hundred pounds or for any wealth!"

And the herd-boys stared at her; and when they saw how lovely she was, they were amazed.

"How can I tell Aucassin that?" said the boy who was readier of speech than the others. "God's curse on him who shall carry such a tale! It is some ghastly thing you speak about. For there is no beast of price in this forest—stag, lion, or wild boar—with a limb worth more than twopence or threepence at the most. Yet you speak of such great wealth! God's curse on him who believes you, or carries your tale. You are a fairy woman, and we do not want your company! So keep your own ways."

"Ha! good boys," said she, "this thing you must do. The beast has such a medicine that it will cure Aucassin of all his sickness. And I have five shillings in my purse, and you can take them if you will give him my message. Within three days must he set out on the hunt, and if in three days he does not find the beast, never shall any one see him cured of his sickness."

"My faith!" said the herd-boy, "we will take the money, and if he comes by this spring we will tell him; but we cannot go searching for him."

"In God's name!" she said. Then she took leave of the herd-boys, and went away.

Leaving the herd-boys by the spring,
Nicolette went wandering
Through the deep foliage, till she stood

Right in the middle of the wood,
Where the track branched out in a maze
Of seven long, dim forest ways.
And there she thought to try her love
And see how faithful he would prove.
So with lily and heather flower
And boughs, she built a bonny bower—
A bonnier bower was never seen!
" By God!" she said, " if Aucassin
Come this way, and will not rest,
For love's sake, in my flowery nest,
He shall not have my lips to kiss,
Nor I have his!"

As you have heard, Nicolette made her bower very pretty and very dainty, and lined it without and within with flowers and foliage, and then she lay down under a thick bush close by, to see what Aucassin would do.

And the rumour spread through all the country that Nicolette was lost. Some said she had fled, and others said that Count Garin had put her to death. If any man was pleased with the news, Aucassin was not that man. His father, Count Garin, took him from the prison, and called out the knights of the land and the young ladies, and held a right splendid feast, thinking to comfort his son, Aucassin, thereby. But when the feasting was at its height, there was Aucassin leaning against the balcony, all sorrowful and downcast. Amid all the merry-making, Aucassin had no wish for it: since he saw there nothing of the one thing he loved. A knight looked at him for a while, and came up to him and spoke.

" Aucassin," said he, " in my time I have been ill of the same malady that troubles you. If you will trust me, I will give you some good advice."

" Sir," said Aucassin, " I thank you. Good advice is a thing I hold dear."

" Mount on a horse," said the knight, " and ride along the forest side to refresh yourself. You will see the flowers and the plants and hear the little birds sing. And by chance, you may also hear some words that will make you better."

" Sir," said Aucassin, " much thanks! I will do it."

He stole out of the hall and went down the stairs, and came to the stable where his war-horse was. He had him saddled and bridled, and putting his foot in the stirrup, he mounted and rode from the castle, and went on until he came to the forest. And riding still farther, he came to the spring, and found the herd-boys at the point of none. They had spread a cloak on the grass, and were eating their bread and making a great merriment.

Jolly herd-boys, every one!
Martin, Emery, and John,
Aubrey, Fruelin, and Bob,
Round the spring did they hob-nob!
"Mates, a toast!" cried Fruelin,
"Here's to handsome Aucassin!
God bless him! And the shapely lass,
With her blue eyes and shining face,
Young and yellow-haired and bonny—
She who gave us all this money,
Enough to buy us cake and fruit,
Hunting-horn and pipe and flute,
Cudgel and a long, sheathed knife—
God guard her life!"

When Aucassin heard the boys, he thought of Nicolette, his sweetest darling whom he loved so much: and he believed she must have been there. And pricking the horse with the spurs, he came to the herd-boys.

"Fair children, God help you!"

"God bless you," said the lad who was readier of speech than the others.

"Good boys," said Aucassin, "sing that song again that you were singing just now."

"We will not sing it," said the one with the ready speech. "God's curse on him who sings that song for you, fair sir!"

"Good boys," said Aucassin, "do you not know me?"

"Yes, we know you quite well. You are Aucassin, our young lord. But we are not your men: we are the Count's men!"

"Good boys, you will sing that song, I beg you!"

"By gog's heart, just listen to him!" said the herd-boy. "Why should I sing for you, if I do not want to? There is no man so powerful in this country, saving only Count Garin himself, who, if he found my oxen or cows or sheep in his meadows or wheatfields, would be daring enough to drive them out. For I would blind him for it! And why should I sing for you, if it does not suit me?"

"So help me God, sweet children, you will do what I want. Here are ten shillings that I have in my purse."

"Sir, we will take your money; but I will not sing you that song, for I have sworn I would not. But I will tell you a tale if you like."

" In God's name," said Aucassin, " I had rather listen to a tale than hear nothing."

" Sir, we were sitting just here, between prime and tierce, and eating our bread at this spring, as we are doing now. And a maid came here, the loveliest thing in the world, so that we fancied she was a fairy woman, and she lightened up all this wood. And she gave us money, and we made a bargain with her that if you came here we would tell you that you must go hunting through this forest. There is a beast there that, if you took it, you would not sell one of its limbs for five hundred pounds of silver, or for any wealth. For the beast has such a medicine that, if you can take it, you will be cured of all your troubles. Within three days must you capture it, and if you do not take it by then, you will never see it again. Now hunt it if you like, or leave it if you like ; for well have I carried out my part of the bargain ! "

" Fair boys," said Aucassin, " you have said enough, and God grant that I find it ! "

Hearing from the maid he loved,
Aucassin was deeply moved ;
Her words so touched him to the heart,
Quick from the boys did he depart,
Galloping into the deep wood,
And singing in a lightsome mood :
" Track of boar and slot of deer,
Neither do I follow here.
Nicolette it is I chase
Down the winding, woodland ways.
Your white body, your blue eyes,
Lovely laughter, low replies,
Wound me to the heart, my sweet !
But now we two again shall meet,
Please God ! my griefs draw to an end,
Sister and friend ! "

Aucassin ranged the forest from path to path, and his war-horse carried him at a quick gallop. But do not think that the briars and thorns spared him. Not at all ! They tore his clothes so that it would have been hard work to patch them together, and the blood ran from his arms, sides, and legs in thirty or forty places ; so that the lad could have been tracked by the blood that fell on the grass. But he thought so much on Nicolette, his sweet love, that he felt no hurt or pain, and all day long he rode in this way through the forest without hearing news of her. And when he saw that evening was drawing on, he began to weep because he had not found her.

While he was riding along an old grass-grown way, he looked ahead and saw a lad such as I will describe. He was tall and astonishing, and ugly and hideous. He had a great shock-head as black as coal, and his two eyes were more than a full palm breadth apart; and he had large cheeks, and an immense flat nose, and great wide nostrils, thick lips redder than roast-meat, and big, ugly yellow teeth. He had leggings and shoes of ox-hide, laced with bast above the knee; and wrapped in a rough cloak, he leaned on a great club. Aucassin sprang to meet him, and was terrified when he looked at him.

"Fair brother, God aid you!"

"God bless you!" said he.

"So help you God, what are you doing there?"

"What does it matter to you?"

"Nothing," said Aucassin. "I do not ask you for any ill cause."

"But why are you weeping," said he, "and making such sorrow? Faith! were I as rich a man as you are, nothing in all the world would make me weep."

"Bah, do you know me?" said Aucassin.

"Aye, I know very well that you are Aucassin, the Count's son, and if you will tell me why you weep, I will tell you what I am doing here."

"Faith!" said Aucassin, "right willingly will I tell you. I came this morning to hunt in the forest with a white greyhound, the finest of the age, and I have lost it, and it makes me weep."

"Hear him!" said he. "By the heart that the Lord had in His belly! You wept for a stinking dog! God curse him who thinks anything of you! Why, there is no rich man in this land but, if your father wanted ten or fifteen or twenty dogs, he would send them only too willingly, and be glad to get rid of them. I am the one who should weep and make sorrow."

"And why you, brother?"

"Sir, I will tell you. I was hired man to a rich farmer, and did his ploughing. I had four oxen, and three days ago a great misfortune happened to me. I lost my best ox, Roget—the finest of my team—and I have been looking for the beast ever since. I have had neither food nor drink for the last three days; and I dare not go into the town. For they would put me in prison, as I have not the money to pay for it. I have nothing in the world except what you see on my body. I have a poor, unhappy mother who had nothing of any value but a mattress, and they have dragged that from under her back, and left her to lie on the bare straw. I am more troubled for her than for myself. For money comes and goes. I have lost now, but I shall gain another time, and I shall pay for my ox when I can. Nor will I weep for it. And you wept for a dunghill dog! God's curse on him who thinks much of you again!"

"Faith, you are a good comforter, fair brother! Bless you for it! What was your ox worth?"

"Sir, twenty shillings is what they ask for it. I cannot beat them down a single farthing."

"Here are twenty shillings in my purse," said Aucassin, "take them and pay for your lost ox."

"Sir," said the ploughman, "great thanks. May God help you to find the thing you are looking for!"

He went away, and Aucassin rode on. The night was fine and still, and he wandered onward till he came to the place where the seven paths branched out, and saw before him the bower that Nicolette had made, lined within and without with flowers, and so lovely it could not be lovelier. When Aucassin saw it he reined up suddenly, and the light of the moon struck into the bower.

"Ah, God!" said Aucassin, "here Nicolette, my sweet love, has been, and she has made this with her fair hands. For the sweetness of her, and for her love, I shall alight now, and rest here for the night."

He put his foot from the stirrup to dismount, and his horse was big and high. He thought so much on Nicolette, his sweetest darling, that he fell hard upon a stone, and his shoulder shot out of place. He felt badly hurt, but struggled on as well as he could, and with his good hand he tied his horse to a hawthorn, and then, turning over on his side, he drew himself on his back into the bower. And looking through a hole in the leaves and the flowers he saw the stars of the sky; and seeing one brighter than the others, he began to sing:

"Little star, I see thee there,
Thou that the moon draws unto her!
My love with her golden head
Now is with thee. God has need
Of her loveliness on high,
To light up the evening sky;
And it is her yellow hair
Shining on the darkness there!
Oh, my love, were mine the bliss
To climb to you and take a kiss,
I would not regret the pain,
When I fell to earth again!

I would hold a kiss thus won,
Were I now a great king's son,
Worth life, dear one ! "

When Nicolette heard Aucassin she came to him, for she was not far off. Entering the bower, she threw her arms round his neck, and kissed him and embraced him.

" Fair, sweet friend, you are well met ! "

" And you, fair sweet love, you are well met ! "

And they kissed each other, and held each other fast, and their joy was lovely to see.

" Ha, sweetheart ! " said Aucassin, " just now I was sorely hurt in my shoulder, but since I found you I feel no sorrow or pain ! "

Nicolette searched for his hurt, and found that he had shot his shoulder. She handled it so with her white hands and so pulled it that—by the grace of God, who loves all lovers—it settled back in its place. Then she gathered flowers, fresh grass, and green leaves, and bound them on with a strip of her smock, and he was quite healed.

" Aucassin," said she, " fair, sweet friend, let us consider what is to be done. If your father has a search made through this forest to-morrow, and his men find me—whatever may happen to you—I shall be killed ! "

" Faith, my sweet and lovely love, I should be mightily grieved at that. But they shall never take you, if I can prevent it."

He mounted his horse and took his love in front of him, kissing and embracing her, and they rode out into the open fields.

Aucassin, the loving lad,
Tall and comely, brave and glad,
Rode from the wood, and his arms met
Round the body of Nicolette,
Sitting upon his saddle bow,
In front of him. Her eyes, her brow,
Her mouth, her chin, he kissed ; and then
He drew her back, and kissed again,
Till she asked him, anxiously,
" Aucassin, sweetheart, tell me
Through whose lands shall we now go ? "
" Dearest love, I do not know.
Little I reck what road we take,
Roundabout or through the brake,
So that you are with me still ! "
Down the valley and over the hill,
By castle and town they rode away ;
Reached the sea at break of day,
And alighted on the sand,
Down by the strand.

Aucassin and his love alighted as you have heard. Taking his horse by the bridle and his love by the hand, he began to walk along the shore; and as they were walking together, Aucassin saw some merchants sailing in a ship close to the land. He beckoned to them, and they landed, and he gave them some money, and they took him and his lady and his horse on their ship. And when they were on the high sea a great and marvellous storm arose which drove them from land to land, until they arrived in a strange country and entered the port of the Castle of Torelore. Then they asked what country it was, and they were told it was the land of the King of Torelore.

"What sort of man is he?" said Aucassin. "And is he engaged in any war?"

"Yes, a great war," said the men of the country.

Aucassin took leave of the merchants, and they commended him to God. Girding his sword about him, he mounted his horse, and set his love in front of him, and rode on till he came to the castle He asked where the King was, and he was told that he lay in child-bed.

"Where then is his wife?"

And they told him that she was with the army, and had taken all the people of the land with her on a great war.

And when Aucassin heard it he was struck with great astonishment, and alighting at the palace, he gave his horse to Nicolette to hold, and entered with his sword, and wandered about until he came to the room where the King lay.

Aucassin, the fair, young lord,
Entered the chamber with drawn sword;
Angrily strode up to the bed
On which the King was laid; and said,
"Fool! Why do you do this thing?"
"I have borne a son," said the King.
"When my month is gone at length,
And I come to health and strength,
Then shall I hear mass once more,
As my fathers did before;
And a great war undertake,
Till mine enemies I break,
And prisoners make."

When Aucassin heard the King speak in this way, he pulled all the sheets from the bed, and flung them down on the floor. He saw behind him a stick. He took it, and turned round, and beat the King so much that he was like to have killed him.

"Ha, fair sir!" said the King, "what is it that you want

of me? Have you lost your wits, you who beat me in my own house?"

"By the heart of God!" said Aucassin, "you shameless whoreson! I will kill you unless you give me your word that never another man in your land shall lie in child-bed."

The King plighted his word, and when this was done:

"Sir," said Aucassin, "now lead me to the place where your wife is with the army."

"Sir, willingly," said the King.

He mounted a horse and Aucassin mounted his, and Nicolette remained in the Queen's chamber. And the King and Aucassin rode till they came to the battlefield where the Queen was. And they found it was a battle of roasted crab apples from the wood, and eggs and fresh cheeses. And Aucassin began to stare and wonder greatly at the sight.

Aucassin, the gallant knight,
From his saddle watched the fight;
Saw the warriors trudge afar,
With their muniments of war.
In great stacks the cheeses stood,
And roast apples from the wood;
Mushrooms from the field they brought,
And with these they fiercely fought.
He who muddied most the ford
Was acclaimed the great war-lord.
But louder than the shouting after
Was Aucassin's laughter!

When Aucassin saw this strange thing, he went and spoke to the King.

"Sir," said Aucassin, "are those men there your enemies?'

"Yes, sir," said the King.

"And is it your wish that I should take vengeance on them for you?"

"Yes," he said, "certainly."

Aucassin took his sword in his hand, and sprang in the middle of them, and began to strike to the right and the left, and killed many of them. And when the King saw that the men were slain, he seized Aucassin's bridle:

"Ha, fair sir!" he said, "do not kill them in that way!"

"How," said Aucassin. "Do you not want me to revenge your wrongs?"

"Sir," said the King, "you have done it too well. It is not our custom to kill one another."

The enemy turned and fled, and the King and Aucassin went back to the Castle of Torelore. And the people of the country bade their King drive Aucassin out of the land, and keep Nicolette for his son, as she seemed to be a lady of noble race. And Nicolette heard of it, and she was not pleased, and she said:

"Though your people, my good King,
Deem me but a foolish thing;—
When in my love's arms I lie,
And he knows how sweet am I,
Then I am of such a mind
That I can no pleasure find
In dance and song and music born
Of fiddle and harp and flute and horn.
All other joys upon this earth
Seem nothing worth!"

Aucassin lived at the Castle of Torelore in great ease and in great delight, for he had with him Nicolette, his sweet darling whom he loved so much. And while he was living in such ease and such delight, a fleet of Saracens came over the sea, and attacked the castle, and took it by storm. They took its wealth, and led the people away to be sold as slaves. They took Nicolette and Aucassin, and bound Aucassin hand and foot, and threw him in one ship, and Nicolette in another, and a storm broke over the sea and drove the two ships apart. The ship in which Aucassin was cast drifted over the waters till it arrived at the Castle of Beaucaire; and the people of the country ran down to gut the wreck, and found Aucassin and recognised him. When the men of Beaucaire saw their young lord, they made great joy over him. For Aucassin had been living for more than three years at the Castle of Torelore, and his father and mother were dead. They led him to the Castle of Beaucaire, and they all became his liege men, and he held his land in peace.

To his city of Beaucaire
Did Count Aucassin repair,
Holding all his dignities
And his land and men in peace.
But by the might of God, he swore
To lose his lady pained him more
Than to find his kinsfolk gone,
Dead and buried every one!
"My sweet love, I do not know
Where in quest of you to go!
There is no land made by God,
Where ship has sailed or man has trod,
But I would search it through and through,
To light on you!"

Now we will leave Aucassin, and tell of Nicolette. The ship into which she was cast belonged to the King of Carthage, and he was her father, and she had twelve brothers, all Kings or Princes. When they saw how lovely was Nicolette, they treated her with high honour and rejoiced over her; and much they questioned her who she was, for she looked a very noble lady and of high degree. But she could not tell them who she was, for she had been carried off when she was a little child. They rowed on, till they came beneath the city of Carthage. And when Nicolette saw the walls of the castle and the country, she knew that it was there she had been brought up and carried off when she was a little child. But she was not so small a child but that she could not recollect that she had been daughter to the King of Carthage and bred in the city.

Brave was Nicolette and bright,
Till the shore came full in sight:
But when she descried the walls
Wharves and palaces and halls,
Sadly she began to cry:
"For my unhappiness was I
Born of the noblest lineage here,
Kinswoman to the great Amir,
And princess of fair Carthagen,
Where now, a slave, I land again!
Aucassin, fair, noble youth,
Soul of honour and of truth!
Your sweet love still drives me on,
Works in me, and will not be gone!
Spirit of God! grant me the grace,
To lie once more in your embrace,
Kissed on my mouth, my eyes, my face,
My love, my lord!"

When the King of Carthage heard Nicolette speak thus, he threw his arms round her neck:

"Sweet lovely darling," he said, "tell me who you are? Do not be afraid of me."

"Sir," said she, "I am daughter to the King of Carthage, and was carried off as a little child, full fifteen years ago."

When they heard her speak thus, they knew right well that she spoke truly, and they rejoiced greatly over her, and led her into the palace in great honour as the King's daughter. There she lived for three or four years, till one day they wished her to wed a great pagan King; but she had no liking for that marriage. She thought out some device by which she could go in search of Aucassin. She sought for a viol, and learnt to play it. Then she stole out at night, and came to the seaport, and lodged in the house of a poor woman by the shore. And she took an herb, and with it she smeared her head and face, so that she was all dark and stained. And she had a coat made, and cloak, shirt, and breeches. And she dressed herself up in the manner of a minstrel, and took her viol, and called on a mariner, and paid him money so that he took her on his ship. They set their sail and voyaged over the high sea till they reached the land of Provence. And Nicolette left the ship, and went playing through the country till she came to the Castle of Beaucaire where Aucassin was.

Under the tower of Beaucaire town,
Aucassin in state sat down:
And around him gathered then
The great lords who were his men.
Seeing all the flowers of spring,
And hearing all the small birds sing,
He called to mind the happy days,
When he rode the woodland ways
With his sweetheart, Nicolette,
Till his eyes with tears were wet.
And look you! Nicolette was there,
Standing on the castle stair!
She took her viol and her bow,
And cried: " Fair Barons, listen now!
Yes, those beneath and those above,
Please listen to a tale of love,
Of Aucassin, a gallant knight,
And Nicolette, a lady bright!
Long their love endured, and he
Sought her beneath the greenwood tree:
But from the tower of Torelore
The pagans the two lovers bore.
Of Aucassin is nothing known.
Nicolette is in Carthage town,
Where her father reigns as King,
And loves her more than anything.
Fain is he to marry her
To Caliph, Sultan, or Emir:
But she takes no thought of this.
All her love and all her bliss
Are set upon a Christian lad—
Aucassin was the name he had!
And in the Name of God she vows
Never a lord will she espouse,
Save one she now knows nothing of—
Her own true love!"

When Aucassin heard Nicolette sing, he was full of joy, and drew her on one side to speak to her:

" Fair, sweet brother," said Aucassin, " do you know anything of this Nicolette of whom you have sung ? "

" Sir, yes ! I know her as the noblest creature and the gentlest and wisest that ever was born. She is daughter to the King of Carthage, who captured her when Aucassin was taken, and carried her to his city as soon as he knew right well that she was his daughter, and made great rejoicing over her, and every day he wished to give her in marriage to one of the high Kings of Spain. But she would rather let herself be hanged or burnt than take any of them for husband, no matter how great they were."

" Ha ! fair, sweet brother ! " said Count Aucassin, " if you would go back to that land and tell her to come and speak to me, I would give you as much of my wealth as you dare ask or take. Do you know that for the love of her I will have no wife, no matter how high her birth ? So I wait for her, and I will not marry unless I have her. And had I known where I could find her, I should not have to seek her now."

" Sir," she said, " if you will do all you say, I will go to seek her for your sake and for hers, for I love her."

Aucassin pledged his word and then he ordered twenty pounds to be given to her. She turned away, and he fell weeping for the sweetness of Nicolette. And when she saw him weep :

" Sir," said she, " do not be afraid. In a little while I will bring her to you in this town, so that you shall see her."

And when Aucassin heard it, he was very joyful. And she left him and went into the town to the house of the Viscountess, for the Viscount, her godfather, was dead. She lodged there and spoke to the dame and revealed her secret, and the Viscountess recognised her, and knew right well it was Nicolette whom she had brought up. And she had her washed and bathed and made her stay eight full days with her. And Nicolette took a herb that is called the celandine, and anointed herself with it, and was as lovely as she had been at any time. She dressed herself in splendid cloths of silk, of which the dame had plenty, and she sat down in the chamber on a coverlet of cloth of silk, and called the dame, and told her to go for Aucassin her friend. And she did so. And when the dame came to the palace she found Aucassin weeping and lamenting for Nicolette his love, because she tarried so long. And the dame said :

" Aucassin, grieve no more ! But come with me, and I will show you the thing in the world that you love most. For it is Nicolette, your sweet darling, who has come to seek you from far-off lands."

And Aucassin was glad.

Now, when Aucassin was told
Of his love with the hair of gold,
That she would in Beaucaire arrive,
He was the happiest soul alive!
With the dame away went he
To her house, right hastily,
Into the chamber, all aflame,
Where his love, Nicolette, sat, he came!
And when she saw her love appear,
Her joy was more than she could bear.
She leaped to him, and stretching out
His arms, he folded her about.
Tender and long was his embrace:
He kissed her eyes and mouth and face:
So the night sped. Then Nicolette
And Aucassin at the altar met:
And she, the bride beyond compare,
Became the Lady of Beaucaire.
Long was their wedded life and sweet,
And great the joy they had in it.
Thus has Nicolette her bliss,
And her Aucassin has his.
Our song-story now o'er.
I know no more!

MEDIAEVAL ITALIAN
13TH CENTURY

KING PHILIP AND HIS GREEK SLAVE

IN a certain part of Greece there lived a King of great sway, of the name of Philip. This King, for some alleged crime or other, had imprisoned a Greek, a man of great learning, whose wisdom mounted to the skies. It happened one day that this monarch received from the King of Spain a present of a noble horse, of great size and of a beautiful form. The King sent for his farrier to learn his opinion of the horse, but he was told that he had better apply to the learned Greek. He therefore ordered the horse to be led into the field, and then commanded the Greek to be brought from his prison, and addressing him, said: "Master, let me have your opinion of this horse, for I have heard a great report of your wisdom."

The Greek inspected the horse, and replied: "Sire, this horse is indeed a beautiful courser, but in my opinion he has been nurtured on asses' milk."

The King sent to Spain to inquire how the horse had been brought up, and found that the dam had died, and that the foal, as the Greek had asserted, had been reared on asses' milk. This circumstance astonished the King not a little, and as a reward, he ordered half a loaf of bread a day to be given to the Greek at the expense of the court. It fell out on another occasion, that as the King was inspecting his jewels, he sent again for the Greek, and said to him: "Master, tell me, I pray you, which of these stones seems to you the most valuable."

The Greek replied: "Sire, which of them do you yourself consider as the most precious one?"

The King then took up one of the most beautiful amongst them and said: "This one, master, seems to me the most beautiful, and one of the highest value."

The Greek examined it, and straining it closely in the palm of his hand, and placing it to his ear, said: "This stone, sire, appears to me to have a living worm in it."

The King sent for his lapidary, and ordered him to break the stone, and to their surprise the animal was found within. The King now looked upon the Greek as a man of surprising wisdom, and ordered a whole loaf of bread to be given him daily at the expense of the court. It happened not many days after this that the King, entertaining some suspicions of his own legitimacy, again sent for the Greek, and taking him into his closet, said: " Master, I hold you for a man of great penetration, which indeed has been manifested in your answers to the questions I have proposed to you. I wish you now to inform me whose son I am."

The Greek then replied: " Sire, how strange a request! You well know that you are the son of your honoured predecessor."

But the King, dissatisfied, said: " Do not evade my question, but tell me the truth implicitly; for if you hesitate, you shall instantly die the death of a traitor." " Then, sire," answered the Greek, " I must inform you that you are the son of a baker."

Upon this, the King being anxious to know the real truth, sent for the Queen-Mother, and by threats compelled her to confess that the words of the Greek were true. The King then shut himself up in his chamber with the Greek, and said: " Master mine, I have received singular proofs of your wisdom, and I now entreat you to tell me how you have obtained a knowledge of these things."

Then the Greek replied: " Sire, I will inform you. With respect to the horse, I knew that he had been nourished with asses' milk from his hanging his ears, which is not natural to a horse. And that there was a live worm in the stone I knew from the fact that stones are naturally cold, but this one I found to be warm, and it was therefore evident that the heat could only proceed from a living animal within."

" And how," said the King, " did you discover that I was the son of a baker? "

The Greek then replied: " Because when I told you of the wonderful circumstances of the horse, you ordered me a gift of half a loaf a day; and when I told you of the stone with the living worm in it, you ordered me a whole loaf. I then felt assured whose son you were; for if you had really been a king's son, you would have presented me with a city, as my merits deserved; whereas your origin then betrayed itself, and your natural disposition was satisfied in giving me a loaf, as your father the baker would have done."

The King was then sensible of his own meanness, and immediately liberated the Greek from prison, and loaded him with gifts of value.

THE HERMIT AND THE TREASURE

Mediaeval Italian

A GENTLE hermit one day proceeding on his way through a vast forest, chanced to discover a large cave nearly hidden under ground. Being greatly fatigued, he entered to repose himself a while, and observing something shine brightly in the distance, he approached, and found it was a heap of gold. At the sight of the glittering bait he turned away, and hastening through the forest again as fast as possible, he had the farther misfortune to fall into the hands of three fierce robbers, always on the watch to despoil the unwary travellers who might pass that way. But, though inmates of the forest, they had never yet discovered the treasure from which the hermit now fled. The thieves on first perceiving him thus strangely flying, without any one in pursuit, were seized with a sort of unaccountable dread, though, at the same time, they ventured forward to ascertain the cause. On approaching to inquire, the hermit, without relaxing his pace, answered, " I flee from death, who is urging me sorely behind."

The robbers, unable to perceive any one, cried out, " Show us where he is, or take us to the place instantly."

The hermit therefore replied, in a hurried voice, " Follow me, then," and proceeded towards the grotto. He there pointed out to them the fatal place, beseeching them, at the same time, to abstain from even looking at it, as they had far better do as he had done, and avoid it. But the thieves, resolving to know what strange thing it was which had alarmed him, only bade him lead the way: which, being in terror of his life, the hermit quickly did; and showing them the heap of gold, " Here," he said, " is the death which was in pursuit of me "; and the thieves, suddenly seizing upon the treasure, began to rejoice exceedingly.

They afterwards permitted the good man to proceed upon his way, amusing themselves when he was gone with ridiculing his absurd conduct. The three robbers, guarding the gold in their possession, began to consider in what way they should employ it. One of them observed, " Since Heaven has bestowed such good fortune upon us, we ought by no means to leave the place for a moment without bearing the whole of it along with us."

" No," replied another, " it appears to me we had better not do so ; but let one of us take a small portion, and set out to buy wine and viands at the city, besides many other things he may think we are in want of " ; and to this the other two consented.

Now the great demon, who is very ingenious and busy on these occasions to effect as much mischief as possible, directly began to deal with the one fixed upon to furnish provisions from the city. " As soon," whispered the devil to him, " as I shall have reached the city, I will eat and drink of the best of everything, as much as I please, and then purchase what I want. Afterwards, I will mix with the food I intend for my companions something which I trust will settle their account, thus becoming sole master of the whole of the treasure, which will make me one of the richest men in this part of the world " ; and as he purposed to do, so he did.

He carried the poisoned food to his companions, who, on their part, while he had been away, had come to the conclusion of killing him on his return, in order that they might divide the booty between themselves, saying, " Let us fall upon him the moment he comes, and afterwards eat what he has brought, and divide the money between us in much larger shares than before."

The robber who had been at the city now returned with the articles he had bought, when the other two instantly pierced his body with their lances, and despatched him with their knives. They then began to feast upon the provisions prepared for them, and upon satiating their appetite, both soon after were seized with violent pangs, and fell dead upon the ground. In this manner all three fell victims to each other's avarice and cruelty, without obtaining their ill-gotten wealth, a striking proof of the judgment of Heaven upon traitors ; for, attempting to compass the death of others, they justly incurred their own. The poor hermit thus wisely fled from the gold, which remained without a single claimant.

TALES FROM THE GESTA ROMANORUM

THE HUSBAND OF AGLAES

IN Rome some time dwelt a mighty Emperor, named Philominus, who had one only daughter, who was fair and gracious in the sight of every man, who had to name Aglaes. There was also in the Emperor's palace a gentle knight that loved dearly this lady.

It befell after on a day, that this knight talked with this lady, and secretly uttered his desire to her. Then she said courteously, " Seeing you have uttered to me the secrets of your heart, I will likewise for your love utter to you the secrets of my heart, and truly I say, that above all other I love you best."

Then said the knight, " I purpose to visit the Holy Land, and therefore give me your troth, that this seven years you shall take no other man, but only for my love to tarry for me so long, and if I come not again by this day seven years, then take what man you like best. And likewise I promise you that within this seven years I will take no wife."

Then said she, " This covenant pleaseth me well."

When this was said, each of them was betrothed to other, and then this knight took his leave of the lady, and went to the Holy Land.

Shortly after the Emperor treated with the King of Hungary for the marriage of his daughter. Then came the King of Hungary to the Emperor's palace, to see his daughter, and when he had seen her, he liked marvellous well her beauty and her behaviour, so that the Emperor and the King were accorded in all things as touching the marriage, upon the condition that the damsel would consent.

Then called the Emperor the young lady to him, and said, " O my fair daughter, I have provided for thee, that a king shall be thy husband, if thou list consent, therefore tell me what answer thou wilt give to this."

Then said she to her father, " It pleaseth me well : but one thing, dear father, I intreat of you, if it might please you to grant me : I have vowed to keep my virginity and not to marry these seven years ; therefore, dear father, I beseech you for all the love that is between your gracious fatherhood and me, that you name no man to be my husband till these seven years be ended, and then I shall be ready in all things to fulfil your will."

Then said the Emperor, "Sith it is so that thou hast thus vowed, I will not break thy vow, but when these seven years be expired, thou shalt have the King of Hungary to thy husband."

Then the Emperor sent forth his letters to the King of Hungary, praying him if it might please him to stay seven years for the love of his daughter, and then he should speed without fail. Herewith the King was pleased and content to stay the prefixed day.

And when the seven years were ended, save a day, the young lady stood in her chamber window, and wept sore, saying, "Woe and alas, as to-morrow my love promised to be with me again from the Holy Land, and also the King of Hungary to-morrow will be here to marry me, according to my father's promise ; and if my love comes not at a certain hour, then am I utterly deceived of the inward love I bear to him."

When the day came, the King hasted toward the Emperor, to marry his daughter, and was royally arrayed in purple. And while the King was riding on his way, there came a knight riding on his way, who said,

"I am of the empire of Rome, and now am lately come from the Holy Land, and I am ready to do you the best service I can."

And as they rode talking by the way, it began to rain so fast, that all the King's apparel was sore wet.

Then said the knight, "My lord, ye have done foolishly, for as much as ye brought not with you your house."

Then said the King, "Why speakest thou so ? My house is large and broad, and made of stones, and mortar. How should I bring then with me my house ? Thou speakest like a fool."

When this was said, they rode on till they came to a great deep water, and the King smote his horse with his spurs, and leapt into the water, so that he was almost drowned. When the knight saw this, and was over on the other side of the water without peril, he said to the King, "Ye were in peril, and therefore ye did foolishly, because you brought not with you your bridge."

Then said the King, "Thou speakest strangely. My bridge is made of lime and stone, and containeth in quality more than half a mile. How should I then bear with me my bridge ? Therefore thou speakest foolishly."

"Well," said the knight, "my foolishness may turn thee to wisdom."

When the King had ridden a little farther, he asked the knight what time of day it was.

Then said the knight, " If any man hath list to eat, it is time of the day to eat. Wherefore, my lord, pray take a *modicum* with me, for that is no dishonour to you, but great honour to me before the states of this empire."

Then said the King, " I will gladly eat with thee."

They sat both down in a fair vine garden, and there dined together, both the King and the knight. And when dinner was done, and that the King had washed, the knight said unto the King, " My lord, ye have done foolishly, for that ye brought not with you your father and mother."

Then said the King, " What sayest thou ? My father is dead, and my mother is old, and may not travel. How should I then bring them with me ? Therefore, to say the truth, a foolisher man than thou art did I never hear."

Then said the knight, " Every work is praised at the end."

When the knight had ridden a little farther, and nigh to the Emperor's palace, he asked leave to go from him, for he knew a nearer way to the palace, to the young lady, that he might come first, and carry her away with him.

Then said the King, " I pray thee, tell me by what place thou purposeth to ride ? "

Then said the knight, " I shall tell you the truth : this day seven years I left a net in a place, and now I purpose to visit it, and draw it to me, and if it be whole, then will I take it to me, and keep it as a precious jewel ; if it be broken, then will I leave it." And when he had thus said, he took his leave of the King, and rode forth, but the King kept the broad highway.

When the Emperor heard of the King's coming, he went towards him with a great company, and royally received him, causing him to shift his wet clothes, and to put on fresh apparel. And when the Emperor and the King were set at meat, the Emperor welcomed him with all the cheer and solace that he could. And when he had eaten, the Emperor asked tidings of the King.

" My lord," said he, " I shall tell you what I have heard this day by the way : there came a knight to me, and reverently saluted me ; and anon after there fell a great rain, and greatly spoiled my apparel. And anon the knight said, ' Sir, ye have done foolishly, for that ye brought not with you your house.' "

Then said the Emperor, " What clothing had the knight on ? "

" A cloak," quoth the king.

Then said the Emperor, " Sure, that was a wise man, for the house whereof he spake was a cloak, and therefore he said to you, that you did foolishly because you came without your cloak, then your clothes had not been spoiled with rain."

Then said the King, " When we had ridden a little farther, we came to a deep water, and I smote my horse with my spurs, and I was almost drowned, but he rode through the water without any peril : then said he to me, ' You did foolishly, for that you brought not with you your bridge.' "

" Verily," said the Emperor, " he saith truth, for he called the squires the bridge, that should have ridden before you, and assayed the deepness of the water."

Then said the King, " We rode farther, and at the last he prayed me to dine with him. And when he had dined, he said I did unwisely, because I brought not with me my father and mother."

" Truly," said the Emperor, " he was a wise man, and saith [wisely], for he called your father and mother, bread and wine, and other victual."

Then said the King, " We rode farther, and anon after he asked me leave to go from me, and I asked earnestly whither he went : and he answered again, and said, ' This day seven years, I left a net in a private place, and now I will ride to see it ; and if it be broken and torn, then will I leave it, but if it be as I left it then shall it be unto me right precious.' "

When the Emperor heard this, he cried with a loud voice, and said, " O ye my knights and servants, come ye with me speedily unto my daughter's chamber, for surely that is the net of which he spake."

And forthwith his knights and servants went unto his daughter's chamber, and found her not, for the aforesaid knight had taken her with him. And thus the King was deceived of the damsel, and he went home again to his own country ashamed.

THEODOSIUS OF ROME

Gesta Romanorum

THEODOSIUS reigned, a wise Emperor, in the city of Rome, and mighty he was of power; the which Emperor had three daughters. So it liked to this Emperor to know which of his daughters loved him best.

And then he said to the eldest daughter, " How much lovest thou me ? "

" Forsooth," quoth she, " more than I do myself."

" Therefore," quoth he, " thou shalt be highly advanced," and married her to a rich and mighty king.

Then he came to the second, and said to her, " Daughter, how much lovest thou me ? "

" As much, forsooth," said she, " as I do myself."

So the Emperor married her to a duke.

And then he said to the third daughter, " How much lovest thou me ? "

" Forsooth," quoth she, " as much as ye be worthy, and no more."

Then said the Emperor, " Daughter, sith thou lovest me no more, thou shalt not be married so richly as thy sisters be."

And then he married her to an earl.

After this it happened that the Emperor held battle against the King of Egypt. And the King drove the Emperor out of the empire, in so much that the Emperor had no place to abide in. So he wrote letters, ensealed with his ring, to his first daughter, that said that she loved him more than herself, for to pray her of succouring in that great need, because he was put out of his empire.

And when the daughter had read these letters, she told it to the King, her husband. Then, quoth the King, " It is good that we succour him in this need. I shall," quoth he, " gather an host and help him in all that I can or may, and that will not be done without great costage."

" Yea," quoth she, " it were sufficient if that we would grant him five knights to be in fellowship with him, while he is out of his empire."

And so it was done indeed. And the daughter wrote again to the father, that other help might he not have but five knights of the King to be in his fellowship, at the cost of the King her husband. And when the Emperor heard this, he was heavy in his heart, and said, " Alas! alas! all my trust was in her, for she said she loved me more than herself, and therefore I advanced her so high."

Then he wrote to the second that said she loved him as much as herself, and when she had read his letters, she showed his errand to her husband, and gave him in counsel that he should find him meat and drink and clothing honestly, as for the state of such a lord during time of his need.

And when this was granted, she wrote letters again to her father. The Emperor was heavy with this answer, and said, " Sith my two daughters have thus treated me, soothly I shall prove the third."

And so he wrote to the third, that said she loved him as much as he was worthy, and prayed her of succour in his need, and told her the answer of her two sisters.

So the third daughter, when she had considered the mischief of her father, she told her husband in this form: " My worshipful lord, do succour me now in this great need. My father is put out of his empire and his heritage."

Then spake he, " What were thy will I do thereto ? "

" That ye gather a great host," quoth she, " and help him to fight against his enemies."

" I shall fulfil thy will," said the Earl; and gathered a great host, and went with the Emperor at his own costage to the battle, and had the victory, and set the Emperor again in his heritage.

And then said the Emperor, " Blessed be the hour I gat my youngest daughter: I loved her less than any of the other, and now in my need she hath succoured me, and the other have failed me; and therefore after my death she shall have mine empire."

And so it was done indeed; for after the death of the Emperor the youngest daughter reigned in his stead, and ended peaceably.

THE THREE CASKETS

Gesta Romanorum

SOME time dwelt in Rome a mighty Emperor, named Anselm, who had married the King's daughter of Jerusalem, a fair lady, and gracious in the sight of every man, but she was long time with the Emperor ere she bare him any child; wherefore the nobles of the empire were very sorrowful, because their lord had no heir of his own body begotten: till at last it befell that this Anselm walked after supper, in an evening, into his garden, and bethought himself that he had no heir, and how the King of Ampluy warred on him continually, for so much as he had no son to make defence in his absence; therefore he was sorrowful, and went to his chamber and slept.

Then he thought he saw a vision in his sleep, that the morning was more clear than it was wont to be, and that the moon was much paler on the one side than on the other. And after he saw a bird of two colours, and by that bird stood two beasts, which fed that little bird with their heat. And after that came more beasts, and bowing their breasts towards the bird, went their way: then came there divers birds that sung sweetly and pleasantly. With that the Emperor awaked.

In the morning early this Anselm remembered his vision, and wondered much what it might signify; wherefore he called to him his philosophers, and all the states of the empire, and told them his dream, charging them to tell him the signification thereof on pain of death, and if they told him the true interpretation thereof, he promised them good reward.

Then said they, " Dear lord, tell us your dream, and we shall declare to you what it betokens."

Then the Emperor told them from the beginning to the ending, as is aforesaid. When the philosophers heard this, with glad cheer they answered and said:

" Sir, the vision that you saw betokeneth good, for the empire shall be clearer than it is.

" The moon that is more pale on the one side than on the other, betokeneth the Empress, that hath lost part of her colour, through the conception of a son that she hath conceived. The little bird betokeneth the son that she shall bear. The two beasts that fed this bird betokeneth the wise and rich men of the empire which shall obey the son. These other beasts that bowed their breasts to the bird betoken many other nations that shall do him homage. The bird that sang so sweetly to this little bird betokeneth the Romans, who shall rejoice and sing because of his birth. This is the very interpretation of your dream."

When the Emperor heard this, he was right joyful. Soon after that, the Empress travailed in childbirth, and was delivered of a fair son, at whose birth there was great and wonderful joy made.

When the King of Ampluy heard this, he thought in himself thus: "Lo, I have warred against the Emperor all the days of my life, and now he hath a son, who, when he cometh to full age, will avenge the wrong I have done against his father; therefore it is better that I send to the Emperor, and beseech him of truce and peace, that the son may have nothing against me, when he cometh to manhood." When he had thus said to himself, he wrote to the Emperor, beseeching him to have peace.

When the Emperor saw that the King of Ampluy wrote to him more for fear than for love, he wrote again to him, that if he would find good and sufficient sureties to keep the peace, and bind himself all the days of his life to do him service and homage, he would receive him to peace.

When the King had read the tenor of the Emperor's letter, he called his council, praying them to give him counsel how he best might do as touching this matter.

Then said they: "It is good that ye obey the Emperor's will and commandment in all things. For first, in that he desired of you surety for the peace; to this we answer thus: 'Ye have but one daughter, and the Emperor one son, wherefore let a marriage be made between them, and that may be a perpetual covenant of peace.' Also he asketh homage and tribute, which it is good to fulfil."

Then the King sent his messengers to the Emperor, saying that he would fulfil his desire in all things, if it might please His Highness, that his son and the King's daughter might be married together. All this well pleased the Emperor, yet he sent again, saying, "If his daughter were a clean virgin from her birth unto that day, he would consent to that marriage."

Then was the King right glad, for his daughter was a clean virgin.

Therefore, when the letters of covenant and compact were sealed, the King furnished a fair ship, wherein he might send his daughter, with many noble knights, ladies, and great riches, unto the Emperor, for to have his son in marriage.

And when they were sailing in the sea, towards Rome, a storm arose so extremely and so horribly that the ship brake against a rock, and they were all drowned save only the young lady, which fixed her hope and heart so greatly on God that she was saved; and about three of the clock the tempest ceased, and the lady drove forth over the waves in that broken ship, which was cast up again. But a huge whale followed after, ready to devour both the ship and her.

Wherefore this young lady, when night came, smote fire with a stone, wherewith the ship was greatly lightened, and then the whale durst not adventure toward the ship for fear of that light. At the cock crowing, this young lady was so weary of the great tempest and trouble of sea that she slept, and within a little while after the fire ceased, and the whale came and devoured the virgin.

And when she awoke and found herself swallowed up in the whale's belly, she smote fire, and with a knife wounded the whale in many places, and when the whale felt himself wounded, according to his nature he began to swim to land.

There was dwelling at that time, in a country near by, a noble earl named Pirris, who, for his recreation walking on the sea-shore, saw the whale coming towards the land; wherefore he turned home again, and gathered a great many of men and women, and came thither again, and fought with the whale, and wounded him very sore, and as they smote, the maiden that was in his belly cried with a high voice, and said:

"O gentle friends, have mercy and compassion on me, for I am a king's daughter, and a true virgin from the hour of my birth unto this day."

When the Earl heard this, he wondered greatly, and opened the side of the whale, and found the young lady, and took her out; and when she was thus delivered, she told him forthwith whose daughter she was, and how she had lost all her goods in the sea, and how she should have been married unto the Emperor's son.

And when the Earl heard this he was very glad, and comforted her the more, and kept her with him till she was well refreshed. And in the meantime he sent messengers to the Emperor, letting him to know how the King's daughter was saved.

Then was the Emperor right glad of her safety, and, coming, had great compassion on her, saying, "Ah, good maiden, for the love of my son thou hast suffered much woe ; nevertheless, if thou be worthy to be his wife soon shall I prove."

And when he had thus said, he caused three vessels to be brought forth : the first was made of pure gold, well beset with precious stones without, and within full of dead men's bones, and thereupon was engraven this posy: WHOSO CHUSETH ME SHALL FIND THAT HE DESERVETH.

The second vessel was made of fine silver, filled with earth and worms ; the superscription was thus : WHOSO CHUSETH ME SHALL FIND THAT HIS NATURE DESIRETH.

The third vessel was made of lead, full within of precious stones, and thereupon was insculpt this posy : WHOSO CHUSETH ME SHALL FIND THAT GOD HATH DISPOSED FOR HIM.

These three vessels the Emperor showed the maiden, and said : " Lo, here, daughter, these be rich vessels ; if thou chuse one of these wherein is profit to thee and to others, then shalt thou have my son. And if thou chuse that wherein is no profit to thee, nor to any other, soothly thou shalt not marry him."

When the maiden heard this, she lifted up her hands to God, and said : " Thou, Lord, that knowest all things, grant me grace this hour so to chuse that I may receive the Emperor's son."

And with that she beheld the first vessel of gold, which was engraven royally, and read the superscription : *Whoso chuseth me shall find that he deserveth* ; saying thus : " Though this vessel be full precious and made of pure gold, nevertheless I know not what is within ; therefore, my dear lord, this vessel will I not chuse."

And then she beheld the second vessel, that was of pure silver, and read the superscription, *Whoso chuseth me shall find that his nature desireth* : Thinking thus within herself, if I chuse this vessel, what is within I know not, but well I know, there shall I find that nature desireth, and my nature desireth the lust of the flesh, and therefore this vessel will I not chuse.

When she had seen these two vessels, and had given an answer as touching them, she beheld the third vessel of lead, and read the superscription, *Whoso chuseth me shall find that God hath disposed* : Thinking within herself, this vessel is not very rich, nor outwardly precious, yet the superscription saith, *Whoso chuseth me shall find that God hath disposed* : and without doubt God never disposeth any harm, therefore, by the leave of God, this vessel will I chuse.

When the Emperor heard this, he said: "O fair maiden, open thy vessel, for it is full of precious stones, and see if thou hast well chosen or no."

And when this young lady had opened it, she found it full of fine gold and precious stones, as the Emperor had told her before.

Then said the Emperor: "Daughter, because thou hast well chosen thou shalt marry my son."

And then he appointed the wedding day; and they were married with great solemnity, and with much honour continued to their lives' end.

THE HUMBLING OF JOVINIAN

Gesta Romanorum

WHEN Jovinian was Emperor, he possessed very great power; and as he lay in bed reflecting upon the extent of his dominions, his heart was elated to an extraordinary degree. "Is there," he impiously asked, "is there any other god than I?" Amid such thoughts he fell asleep.

In the morning he reviewed his troops, and said, "My friends, after breakfast we will hunt." Preparations being made accordingly, he set out with a large retinue. During the chase, the Emperor felt such extreme oppression from the heat that he believed his very existence depended upon a cold bath. As he anxiously looked around, he discovered a sheet of water at no great distance.

"Remain here," said he to his guard, "until I have refreshed myself in yonder stream." Then, spurring his steed, he rode hastily to the edge of the water. Alighting, he divested himself of his apparel, and experienced the greatest pleasure from its invigorating freshness and coolness. But whilst he was thus employed, a person similar to him in every respect—in countenance and gesture—arrayed himself unperceived in the Emperor's dress, and then, mounting his horse, rode off to the attendants. The resemblance to the sovereign was such that no doubt was entertained of the reality; and when the sport was over command was issued for their return to the palace.

Jovinian, however, having quitted the water, sought in every possible direction for his horse and clothes, and to his utter astonishment could find neither. Vexed beyond measure at the circumstance (for he was completely naked, and saw no one near to assist him), he began to reflect upon what course he should pursue.

"Miserable man that I am," said he, "to what a strait am I reduced! There is, I remember, a knight residing close by, whom I have promoted to a military post; I will go to him and command his attendance and service. I will then ride on to the palace and strictly investigate the cause of this extraordinary occurrence."

Jovinian proceeded, naked and ashamed, to the castle of the aforesaid knight, and beat loudly at the gate. The porter inquired the cause of the knocking.

"Open the gate," said the enraged Emperor, "and you will see who I am."

The gate was opened; and the porter, struck with the strange appearance he exhibited, replied, "In the name of all that is marvellous, what are you?"

"I am," said he, "Jovinian, your Emperor; go to your lord, and command him from me to supply the wants of his sovereign. I have lost both horse and clothes."

"Thou liest, infamous ribald!" shouted the porter; "just before thy approach the Emperor Jovinian, accompanied by the officers of his household, entered the palace. My lord both went and returned with him; and but even now sat with him at meat. But because thou hast called thyself the Emperor, my lord shall know of thy presumption."

The porter entered, and related what had passed. Jovinian was introduced, but the knight retained not the slightest recollection of his master, although the Emperor remembered him.

"Who are you?" said the former, "and what is your name?"

"I am the Emperor Jovinian," rejoined he; "canst thou have forgotten me? At such a time I promoted thee to a military command."

"Why, thou most audacious scoundrel," said the knight, "darest thou call thyself the Emperor? I rode with him myself to the palace, from whence I am this moment returned. But thy impudence shall not go without its reward. Flog him," said he, turning to his servants, "flog him soundly, and drive him away."

This sentence was immediately executed, and the poor Emperor, bursting into a convulsion of tears, exclaimed, "Oh, my God, is it possible that one whom I have so much honoured and exalted should do this? Not content with pretending ignorance of my person, he orders these merciless villains to abuse me!"

He next thought within himself, "There is a certain duke, one of my privy councillors, to whom I will make known my calamity. At least, he will enable me to return decently to the palace."

To him, therefore, Jovinian proceeded, and the gate was opened at his knock. But the porter, beholding a naked man, exclaimed in the greatest amaze, "Friend, who are you, and why come you here in such a guise?"

He replied, "I am your Emperor; I have accidentally lost my clothes and my horse, and I have come for succour to your lord. I beg you, therefore, to do me this errand to the Duke."

The porter, more and more astonished, entered the hall, and communicated the strange intelligence which he had received.

"Bring him in," said the Duke. He was brought in, but neither did he recognise the person of the Emperor.

"What art thou?" he asked.

"I am the Emperor," replied Jovinian, "and I have promoted thee to riches and honour, since I made thee a duke and one of my councillors."

"Poor mad wretch!" said the Duke; "a short time since I returned from the palace, where I left the very Emperor thou assumest to be. But since thou hast claimed such rank, thou shalt not escape unpunished. Carry him to prison, and feed him with bread and water."

The command was no sooner delivered than obeyed; and the following day his naked body was submitted to the lash, and he was again cast into the dungeon.

Thus afflicted, he gave himself up to the wretchedness of his untoward condition. In the agony of his heart, he said, "What shall I do? Oh, what will be my destiny? I am loaded with the coarsest contumely, and exposed to the malicious observation of my people. It were better to hasten immediately to my palace, and there discover myself—my servants will know me; and even if they do not, my wife will know me!"

Escaping, therefore, from his confinement, he approached the palace and beat upon the gate.

"Who art thou?" said the porter.

"It is strange," replied the aggrieved Emperor, "it is strange that thou shouldest not know me; thou, who has served me so long!"

"Served *thee*!" returned the porter indignantly, "thou liest abominably. I have served none but the Emperor."

"Why," said the other, "thou knowest that I am he. Yet, though you disregard my words, go, I implore you, to the Empress; communicate what I will tell thee, and by these signs bid her send the imperial robes, of which some rogue has deprived me. The signs I tell thee of are known to none but to ourselves."

"In verity," said the porter, "thou art mad: at this very moment my lord sits at table with the Empress herself. Nevertheless, out of regard for thy singular merits, I will intimate thy declaration within; and rest assured, thou wilt presently find thyself most royally beaten."

The porter went accordingly, and related what he had heard. But the Empress became very sorrowful, and said, "Oh, my lord, what am I to think? The most hidden passages of our lives are revealed by an obscene fellow at the gate, and repeated to me by the porter, on the strength of which he declares himself the Emperor and my espoused lord!"

When the fictitious monarch was apprised of this, he commanded him to be brought in. He had no sooner entered than a large dog, which couched upon the hearth, and had been much cherished by him, flew at his throat, and, but for timely prevention, would have killed him. A falcon, also, seated upon her perch, no sooner beheld him than she broke her jesses and flew out of the hall. Then the pretended Emperor, addressing those who stood about him, said, "My friends, hear what I will ask of yon ribald. Who are you? and what do you want?"

"These questions," said the suffering man, "are very strange. You know I am the Emperor and master of this place."

The other, turning to the nobles who sat or stood at the table, continued, "Tell me, on your allegiance, which of us two is your lord and master?"

"Your Majesty asks us an easy thing," replied they, "and need not to remind us of our allegiance. That obscene wretch we have never before seen. You alone are he whom we have known from childhood; and we entreat that this fellow may be severely punished, as a warning to others how they give scope to their mad presumption."

Then turning to the Empress, the usurper said, "Tell me, my lady, on the faith you have sworn, do you know this man who calls himself thy lord and Emperor?"

She answered, "My lord, how can you ask such a question? Have I not known thee more than thirty years, and borne thee many children? Yet, at one thing I do marvel. How can this fellow have acquired so intimate a knowledge of what has passed between us?"

The pretended Emperor made no reply, but, addressing the real one, said, "Friend, how darest thou to call thyself Emperor? We sentence thee, for this unexampled impudence, to be drawn, without loss of time, at the tail of a horse. And if thou utterest the same words again, thou shalt be doomed to an ignominious death."

He then commanded his guards to see the sentence put in force, but to preserve his life. The unfortunate Emperor was now almost distracted; and, urged by his despair, wished vehemently for death.

"Why was I born?" he exclaimed. "My friends shun me; and my wife and children will not acknowledge me. But there is my confessor, still. To him will I go; perhaps he will recollect me, because he has often received my confessions."

He went accordingly, and knocked at the window of his cell.

"Who is there?" said the confessor.

"The Emperor Jovinian," was the reply; "open the window, and I will speak to thee."

The window was opened; but no sooner had the confessor looked out than he closed it again in great haste.

"Depart from me," said he, "accursed thing: thou art not the Emperor, but the devil incarnate."

This completed the miseries of the persecuted man; and he tore his hair, and plucked up his beard by the roots.

"Woe is me!" he cried, "for what strange doom am I reserved?" At this crisis, the impious words which, in the arrogance of his heart, he had uttered, crossed his recollection. Immediately he beat again at the window of the confessor's cell, and exclaimed, "For the love of Him who was suspended from the cross, hear my confession with the window closed."

The recluse said, "I will do this with pleasure"; and then Jovinian acquainted him with every particular of his past life; and principally how he had lifted himself up against his Maker, saying that he believed there was no other god but himself.

The confession made, and absolution given, the recluse opened the window, and directly knew him. "Blessed be the most high God," said he, "now do I know thee. I have here a few garments: clothe thyself, and go to the palace. I trust that they also will recognise thee."

The Emperor did as the confessor directed. The porter opened the gate, and made a low obeisance to him. "Dost thou know me?" said he.

"Very well, my lord!" replied the menial; "but I marvel that I did not observe you go out."

Entering the hall of his mansion, Jovinian was received by all with a profound reverence. The strange Emperor was at that time in another apartment with the Queen; and a certain knight came out of the chamber, looked narrowly at Jovinian, and returning to the supposed Emperor, said, " My lord, there is one in the hall to whom everybody bends ; he so much resembles you that we know not which is the Emperor."

Hearing this, the usurper said to the Empress, " Go and see if you know him."

She went, and returned greatly surprised at what sne saw. " Oh, my lord," said she, " I declare to you that I know not whom to trust."

" Then," returned he, " I will go and determine you." When he had entered the hall, he took Jovinian by the hand and placed him near him. Addressing the assembly, he said, " By the oaths you have taken, declare which of us is your Emperor."

The Empress answered, " It is incumbent on me to speak first ; but Heaven is my witness that I am unable to determine which is he."

And so said all. Then the feigned Emperor spoke thus : " My friends, hearken ! That man is your King and your Lord. He exalted himself to the disparagement of his Maker ; and God therefore scourged and hid him from your knowledge. I am the angel that watches over his soul, and I have guarded his kingdom while he was undergoing his penance. But his repentance removes the rod ; he has now made ample satisfaction ; and again let your obedience wait upon him. Commend yourselves to the protection of Heaven."

So saying, he disappeared. The Emperor gave thanks to God, and lived happily, and finished his days in peace.

Application

My beloved, the Emperor represents any one whom the pride and vanity of life wholly engross. The knight to whom Jovinian first applied is Reason ; which ever disclaims the pomps and fooleries of life. The duke is conscience ; the savage dog is the flesh, which alarms the falcon, that is, divine grace. The wife is the human soul ; the clothes in which the Emperor was at last arrayed are the virtues that befit the true sovereign, that is, the good Christian.

THE THREE MAXIMS

Gesta Romanorum

DOMITIAN was a very wise and just prince, and suffered no offender to escape. It happened that as he once sat at table, a certain merchant knocked at the gate. The porter opened it, and asked what he pleased to want.

" I have brought some useful things for sale," answered the merchant. The porter introduced him; and he very humbly made obeisance to the Emperor.

" My friend," said the latter, " what merchandise have you to dispose of ? "

" Three maxims of especial wisdom and excellence, my lord."

" And how much will you take for your maxims ? "

" A thousand florins."

" And so," said the Emperor, " if they are of no use to me, I lose my money ? "

" My lord," answered the merchant, " if the maxims do not stand you in stead, I will return the money."

" Very well," said the Emperor; " let us hear your maxims."

" The first, my lord, is this—' Whatever you do, do wisely, and think of the consequences.' The second is—' Never leave the *highway* for a *byway*.' And, thirdly, ' Never stay all night as a guest in that house where you find the master an old man, and his wife a young woman.' These three maxims, if you attend to them, will be extremely serviceable."

The Emperor, being of the same opinion, ordered him to be paid a thousand florins; and so pleased was he with the first, that he commanded it to be inscribed in his court, in his bed-chamber, and in every place where he was accustomed to walk; and even upon the tablecloths of the palace. Now, the rigid justice of the Emperor occasioned a conspiracy among a number of his subjects; and finding the means of accomplishing their purposes somewhat difficult, they engaged a barber, by large promises, to cut his throat as he shaved him. When the Emperor, therefore, was to be shaved, the barber lathered his beard, and began to operate upon it ; but casting his eyes over the towel which he had fastened round the royal neck, he perceived woven thereon—" Whatever you do, do wisely, and think of the consequences."

The inscription startled the tonsor, and he said to himself : " I am to-day hired to destroy this man ; if I do it, my end will be ignominious ; I shall be condemned to the most shameful death. Therefore, whatsoever I do, it is good to consider the end, as the writing testifies."

These cogitations disturbed the worthy tonsor so much that his hand trembled, and the razor fell to the ground. The Emperor seeing this, inquired the cause.

" Oh, my lord," said the barber, " have mercy upon me : I was hired this day to destroy you ; but accidentally, or rather by the will of God, I read the inscription on the towel, ' Whatever you do, do wisely, and think of the consequences.' Whereby, considering that, of a surety, the consequence would be my own destruction, my hand trembled so much, that I lost all command over it."

" Well," thought the Emperor, " this first maxim hath assuredly saved my life : in a good hour was it purchased. My friend," said he to the tonsor, " on condition that you be faithful hereafter, I pardon you."

The noblemen, who had conspired against the Emperor finding that their project had failed, consulted with one another what they were to do next.

" On such a day," said one, " he journeys to a particular city ; we will hide ourselves in a bypath, through which he will pass, and so kill him."

The counsel was approved. The Emperor, as had been expected, prepared to set out ; and riding on till he came to the bypath, his knights said :

" My lord, it will be better for you to go this way, than to pass along the broad road ; it is considerably nearer."

The Emperor pondered the matter within himself. " The second maxim," thought he, " admonishes me never to forsake the highway for a byway. I will adhere to that maxim."

Then, turning to his soldiers, " I shall not quit the public road ; but you, if it please ye, may proceed by that path, and prepare for my approach."

Accordingly a number of them went ; and the ambush, imagining that the Emperor rode in their company, fell upon them and put the greater part to the sword. When the news reached the Emperor, he secretly exclaimed, " My second maxim hath also saved my life."

Now the conspirators again took counsel, and said among themselves:

" On a certain day he will lodge in a particular house, where all the nobles lodge, because there is no other fit for his reception. Let us then agree with the master of that house and his wife, for a sum of money, then to kill the Emperor as he lies in bed."

This was agreed to. But when the Emperor had come into the house, he commanded his host to be called into his presence. Observing that he was an old man, the Emperor said, " Have you not a wife ? "

" Yes, my lord."

" I wish to see her."

The lady came; and when it appeared that she was very young, the Emperor said hastily to his chamberlain: " Away, prepare me a bed in another house. I will remain here no longer."

" My lord," replied he, " be it as you please. But they have made everything ready for you: were it not better to lie where you are, for in the whole city there is not so commodious a place? "

" I tell you," answered the Emperor, " I will sleep elsewhere."

The chamberlain, therefore, removed; and the Emperor went privately to another residence, saying to the soldiers about him:

" Remain here, if you like; but join me early in the morning."

Now, while they slept, the old man and his wife arose, being bribed to kill the Emperor in his sleep, and put to death all the soldiers who had remained. In the morning the Emperor found his soldiers slain. " Oh," cried he, " if I had continued here, I should have been destroyed. So the third maxim hath also preserved me."

But the old man and his wife, with the whole of their family, were crucified. The Emperor retained the three maxims in memory during life, and ended his days in peace.

Application

My beloved, the Emperor is any good Christian; the porter is free will. The merchant represents our Lord Jesus Christ. The florins are virtues, and the maxims received for them are the grace and favour of God. The highway is the ten commandments; the byway, a bad life; those who lay in ambush are heretics. The old man is the world, and his wife is vanity. The conspirators are devils.

THE KNIGHTS OF EGYPT AND BALDAC

Gesta Romanorum

PETRUS ALPHONSUS relates a story of two knights, of whom one dwelt in Egypt and the other in Baldac (Bagdad). Messengers often passed between them; and whatever there was curious in the land of Egypt, the knight of that country sent to his friend, and he, in like manner, sent back an equivalent. Thus much kindness was manifested on both sides. But neither had ever seen the other.

As the knight of Baldac once lay upon his bed, he held the following soliloquy:

"My correspondent in Egypt has discovered much friendship for me; but I have never yet seen him: I will go and pay him a visit."

Accordingly, he hired a ship and went into Egypt; and his friend, hearing of his arrival, met him by the way, and received him with much pleasure. Now, the knight had a very beautiful girl in his house, with whom the knight of Baldac was so smitten, that he fell sick and pined away.

"My friend," said the other, "what is the matter with you?"

"My heart," returned his comrade, "has fixed itself upon one of the women of your household, and unless I may espouse her I shall die."

Upon this, all the household, save the individual in question, were summoned before him; and having surveyed them, he exclaimed, "I care little or nothing for these. But there is one other whom I have not seen; and her my soul loveth."

At last this girl was shown to him. He protested that it was to her alone that he must owe his life.

"Sir," said his friend, "I brought this girl up with the intention of making her my wife; and I shall obtain much wealth with her. Nevertheless, so strong is my affection for you, that I give her to you with all the riches which should have fallen to my share."

The sick knight, overjoyed at his good fortune, received the lady and the money, and returned with her to Baldac.

After a while the knight of Egypt became so extremely indigent that he possessed no habitation. "I had better," thought he, "go to my friend of Baldac, to him whom I enriched, and inform him of my wants."

He did so; and reached Baldac a while after sunset. "It is night," said he to himself; "if I go now to my friend's house, he will not know me, for I am so poorly dressed. I, who once used to have a large household about me, am now desolate and destitute. To-night, therefore, I will rest, and on the morrow will go to his mansion."

Happening to look toward a burial-ground, he observed the gates of a church thrown open, and here he determined to remain for the night. But while he was endeavouring to compose himself to sleep, in a court of that place there entered two men, who engaged in battle; and one was slain. The murderer instantly fled to the burial-ground, and escaped on the other side. By and by an extraordinary clamour penetrated through the whole city.

"Where is the murderer? Where is the traitor?" was the general cry.

"I am he," said our knight; "take me to crucifixion."

They laid hands on him and led him away to prison. Early the next morning the city bell rang, and the judge sentenced him to be crucified. Amongst those who followed to witness his execution was the knight whom he had befriended; and the former, seeing him led towards the cross, knew him at once.

"What!" cried he, "shall he be crucified, and I alive?"

Shouting, therefore, with a loud voice, he said, "My friends! destroy not an innocent man. I am the murderer, and not he."

Satisfied with his declaration, they immediately seized him and brought both to the cross. When they were near the place of execution, the real murderer, who happened to be present, thought thus:

"I will not permit innocent blood to be shed: the vengeance of God will sooner or later overtake me, and it is better to suffer a short pain in this world than subject myself to everlasting torments in the next."

Then, lifting up his voice: "My friends! for God's sake, slay not the guiltless. The dead man was killed without premeditation, and without the knowledge of either of these men. I only am the murderer; let these men go."

The crowd, hearing what he said, instantly apprehended and brought him with no little amazement to the judge. The judge, seeing the reputed criminals along with them, asked with surprise why they had returned. They related what had occurred; and the judge, addressing the first knight, said, " Friend, why did you confess yourself the murderer ? "

" My lord," answered he, " I will tell you without deceit. In my own land I was rich ; and everything that I desired I had. But I lost all this ; and possessing neither house nor home, I was ashamed, and sought in this confession to obtain a remedy. I am willing to die ; and for Heaven's love command me to be put to death."

The judge then, turning to the knight of Baldac—" And you, my friend ! why did you avow yourself the murderer ? "

" My lord," replied he, " this knight bestowed upon me a wife, whom he had previously educated for himself, with an infinite store of wealth. When, therefore, I perceived my old and valued friend reduced to such an extremity, and saw him led rudely to the cross, I proclaimed myself the murderer. For his love I would willingly perish."

" Now then," said the judge to the real homicide, " what have you to say for yourself ! "

" I have told the truth," answered he. " It would have been a heavy crime, indeed, had I permitted two innocent men to perish by my fault, and I therefore prefer to undergo the penalty here, than to be punished at some other time, or perhaps in hell."

" Well," returned the judge, " since you have declared the truth and saved the lives of the innocent, study to amend your future life ; for this time I pardon you—go in peace."

The people unanimously applauded the decision of the judge in acquitting the guilty person, whose magnanimity had rescued two innocent persons from death.

Application

My beloved, the Judge is God ; the two knights, Christ and our first parent. The beautiful girl is the soul. The dead man is the spirit destroyed by the flesh.

THE FAITHFUL KNIGHT
OR GUIDO AND TYRIUS

Gesta Romanorum

IN the reign of a certain King of England, there were two knights, one of whom was called Guido, and the other Tyrius. The former engaged in many wars, and always triumphed. He was enamoured of a beautiful girl of noble family, but whom he could not prevail upon to marry him, until he had encountered many enemies for her sake. At last, at the conclusion of a particular exploit, he gained her consent, and married her with great splendour. On the third night succeeding their nuptials, about cock-crowing, he arose from his bed to look upon the sky; and amongst the most lustrous stars he clearly distinguished our Lord Jesus Christ, who said, "Guido, Guido! you have fought much and valiantly for the love of a woman; it is now time that you should encounter My enemies with equal resolution."

Having so said, our Lord vanished. Guido, therefore, perceiving that it was His pleasure to send him to the Holy Land, to avenge Him upon the infidels, returned to his wife. "I go to the Holy Land; should Providence bless us with a child, attend carefully to its education until my return."

The lady, startled at these words, sprung up from the bed as one distracted, and catching a dagger, which was placed at the head of the couch, cried out: "Oh, my lord, I have always loved you, and looked forward with anxiety to our marriage, even when you were in battle, and spreading your fame over all the world; and will you now leave me? First will I stab myself with this dagger."

Guido arose, and took away the weapon. "My beloved," said he, "your words alarm me. I have vowed to God that I will visit the Holy Land. The best opportunity is the present, before old age come upon me. Be not disturbed; I will soon return."

Somewhat comforted with this assurance, she presented to him a ring. "Take this ring, and as often as you look upon it in your pilgrimage, think of me. I will await with patience your return."

The knight bade her farewell, and departed in company with Tyrius. As for the lady, she gave herself up to her sorrows for many days, and would not be consoled. In due time she brought forth a son of extreme beauty, and tenderly watched over his infant years.

Guido and Tyrius, in the meanwhile, passed through many countries, and heard at last that the kingdom of Dacia had been subdued by the infidels. "My friend," said Guido to his associate, "do you enter this kingdom; and since the King of it is a Christian, assist him with all your power. I will proceed to the Holy Land; and when I have combated against the foes of Christ, I will return to you, and we will joyfully retrace our steps to England."

"Whatever pleases you," replied his friend, "shall please me. I will enter this kingdom; and if you live, come to me. We will return together to our country."

Guido promised; and exchanging kisses, they separated with much regret. The one proceeded to the Holy Land, and the other to Dacia. Guido fought many battles against the Saracens, and was victorious in all; so that his fame flew to the ends of the earth. Tyrius, in like manner, proved fortunate in war, and drove the infidels from the Dacian territory. The King loved and honoured him above all others, and conferred on him great riches. But there was at that time a savage nobleman, called Plebeus, in whose heart the prosperity of Tyrius excited an inordinate degree of hate and envy. He accused him to the King of treason, and malevolently insinuated that he designed to make himself master of the kingdom. The King credited the assertion, and ungratefully robbed Tyrius of all the honours which his bounty had conferred. Tyrius, therefore, was reduced to extreme want, and had scarcely the common sustenance of life. Thus desolate, he gave free course to his griefs; and exclaimed in great tribulation, "Wretch that I am! what will become of me?"

While he was taking a solitary walk in sorrow, Guido, journeying alone in the habit of a pilgrim, met him by the way, and knew him, but was not recognised by his friend. He, however, presently remembered Tyrius, and retaining his disguise, approached him, and said, "My friend, from whence are you?"

"From foreign parts," answered Tyrius, "but I have now been many years in this country. I had once a companion in arms, who proceeded to the Holy Land; but if he be alive or dead I know not, nor what have been his fortunes."

"For the love of thy companion, then," said Guido, "suffer me to rest my head upon your lap, and sleep a little, for I am very weary."

He assented, and Guido fell asleep.

Now, while he slept, his mouth stood open; and as Tyrius looked, he discovered a white weasel pass out of it, and run toward a neighbouring mountain, which it entered. After remaining there a short space, it returned, and again ran down the sleeper's throat. Guido straightway awoke, and said, "My friend, I have had a wonderful dream! I thought a weasel went out of my mouth, and entered yon mountain, and after that returned."

"Sir," answered Tyrius, "what you have seen in a dream I beheld with my own eyes. But what that weasel did in the mountain, I am altogether ignorant."

"Let us go and look," observed the other; "perhaps we may find something useful."

Accordingly, they entered the place which the weasel had been seen to enter, and found there a dead dragon filled with gold. There was a sword also, of peculiar polish, and inscribed as follows: "BY MEANS OF THIS SWORD, GUIDO SHALL OVERCOME THE ADVERSARY OF TYRIUS."

Rejoiced at the discovery, the disguised pilgrim said, "My friend, the treasure is thine, but the sword I will take into my own possession."

"My lord," he answered, "I do not deserve so much gold; why should you bestow it upon me?"

"Raise your eyes," said Guido. "I am your friend!"

Hearing this, he looked at him more narrowly; and when he recollected his heroic associate, he fell upon the earth for joy, and wept exceedingly. "It is enough; I have lived enough, now that I have seen you."

"Rise," returned Guido, "rise quickly; you ought to rejoice rather than weep at my coming. I will combat your enemy, and we will proceed honourably to England. But tell no one who I am."

Tyrius arose, fell upon his neck, and kissed him. He then collected the gold, and hastened to his home; but Guido knocked at the gate of the King's palace. The porter inquired the cause, and he informed him that he was a pilgrim newly arrived from the Holy Land. He was immediately admitted, and presented to the King, at whose side sat the invidious nobleman who had deprived Tyrius of his honours and wealth. "Is the Holy Land at peace?" inquired the monarch.

" Peace is now firmly established," replied Guido, " and many have been converted to Christianity."

King. Did you see an English knight there, called Guido, who has fought so many battles ?

Guido. I have seen him often, my lord, and have eaten with him.

King. Is any mention made of the Christian Kings ?

Guido. Yes, my lord ; and of you also. It is said that the Saracens and other infidels had taken possession of your kingdom, and that from their thraldom you were delivered by the valour of a noble knight, named Tyrius, afterwards promoted to great honour and riches. It is likewise said that you unjustly deprived this same Tyrius of what you had conferred, at the malevolent instigation of a knight called Plebeus.

Plebeus. False pilgrim ! since thou presumest to utter these lies, hast thou courage enough to defend them ? If so, I offer thee battle. That very Tyrius would have dethroned the King. He was a traitor, and therefore lost his honours.

Guido (to the King). My lord, since he has been pleased to say that I am a false pilgrim, and that Tyrius is a traitor, I demand the combat. I will prove upon his body that he lies.

King. I am well pleased with your determination ; nay, I entreat you not to desist.

Guido. Furnish me with arms, then, my lord.

King. Whatever you want shall be got ready for you.

The King then appointed a day of battle ; and fearing lest the pilgrim Guido should in the meantime fall by treachery, he called to him his daughter, a virgin, and said, " As you love the life of that pilgrim, watch over him, and let him want for nothing."

In compliance, therefore, with her father's wish, she brought him into her own chamber, bathed him, and supplied him with every requisite. On the day of battle Plebeus armed himself, and standing at the gate, exclaimed, " Where is that false pilgrim ? Why does he tarry ? "

Guido, hearing what was said, put on his armour, and hastened to the lists. They fought so fiercely, that Plebeus would have died had he not drunk. Addressing his antagonist, he said, " Good pilgrim, let me have one draught of water."

" I consent," answered Guido, " provided you faithfully promise to use the same courtesy to me, should I require it."

" I promise," replied the other. Having quenched his thirst, he rushed on Guido, and they continued the battle with redoubled animosity. By and by, however, Guido himself thirsted, and required the same courtesy to be shown him as he had exhibited.

" I vow to Heaven," answered his enemy, " that you shall taste nothing, except by the strong hand."

At this ungrateful return, Guido, defending himself as well as he could, approached the water, leaped in, and drank as much as he wished. Then springing out, he rushed upon the treacherous Plebeus like a raging lion, who at last sought refuge in flight. The King, observing what passed, caused them to be separated, and to rest for that night, that in the morning they might be ready to renew the contest. The pilgrim then re-entered his chamber, and received from the King's daughter all the kindness it was in her power to display. She bound up his wounds, prepared supper, and placed him upon a strong wooden pallet. Wearied with the exertions of the day, he fell asleep.

Now, Plebeus had seven sons, all strong men. He sent for them, and spoke thus: " My dear children, I give you to understand that, unless this pilgrim be destroyed to-night, I may reckon myself among the dead to-morrow. I never looked upon a braver man."

" My dear father," said one, " we will presently get rid of him."

About midnight, therefore, they entered the girl's chamber, where the pilgrim slept, and beneath which the sea flowed. They said to one another, " If we destroy him in bed, we are no better than dead men; let us toss him, bed and all, into the sea. It will be thought that he has fled."

This scheme was approved; and accordingly they took up the sleeping warrior, and hurled him into the waves. He slept on, however, without perceiving what had happened. The same night a fisherman, following his occupation, heard the fall of the bed, and by the light of the moon saw him floating upon the water. Much surprised, he called out, " In the name of God, who are you? Speak, that I may render assistance, before the waves swallow you up."

Guido, awoke by the clamour, arose, and perceiving the sky and stars above, and the ocean beneath, wondered where he was. " Good friend," said he to the fisherman, " assist me, and I will amply reward you. I am the pilgrim who fought in the lists; but how I got hither, I have no conception."

The man, hearing this, took him into his vessel, and conveyed him to his house, where he rested till the morning.

The sons of Plebeus, in the meanwhile, related what they thought the end of the pilgrim, and bade their parent discard his fear. The latter, much exhilarated, arose, and armed himself; and going to the gate of the palace, called out, "Bring forth that pilgrim, that I may complete my revenge."

The King commanded his daughter to awake and prepare him for battle. Accordingly, she went into his room, but he was not to be found. She wept bitterly, exclaiming that some one had conveyed away her treasure; and the surprise occasioned by the intelligence was not less when it became known that his bed was also missing Some said that he had fled; others, that he was murdered. Plebeus, however, continued his clamour at the gate. "Bring out your pilgrim; to-day I will present his head to the King."

Now, while all was bustle and inquiry in the palace, the fisherman made his way to the royal seat, and said, "Grieve not, my lord, for the loss of the pilgrim. Fishing last night in the sea, I observed him floating upon a bed. I took him on board my vessel, and he is now asleep at my house."

This news greatly cheered the King, and he immediately sent to him to prepare for a renewal of the contest. But Plebeus, terrified, and apprehensive of the consequence, besought a truce. This was denied, even for a single hour. Both, therefore, re-entered the lists, and each struck twice; but at the third blow Guido cut off his opponent's arm, and afterwards his head. He presented it to the King, who evinced himself well satisfied with the event; and hearing that the sons of Plebeus were instruments in the meditated treachery, he caused them to be crucified. The pilgrim was loaded with honours, and offered immense wealth if he would remain with the King, which he resolutely declined. Through him Tyrius was reinstated in his former dignity, and recompensed for his past suffering. He then bade the King farewell.

"Good friend," returned the monarch, "for the love of Heaven, leave me not ignorant of your name."

"My lord," answered he, "I am that Guido of whom you have often heard."

Overjoyed at this happy discovery, the King fell upon his neck, and promised him a large part of his dominions if he would remain. But he could not prevail; and the warrior, after returning his friendly salutation, departed.

Guido embarked for England, and hastened to his own castle. He found a great number of paupers standing about his gate ; and amongst them, habited as a pilgrim, sat the Countess, his wife. Every day did she thus minister to the poor, bestowing a penny upon each, with a request that he would pray for the safety of her husband Guido, that once more, before death, she might rejoice in his presence. It happened, on the very day of his return, that his son, now seven years of age, sat with his mother among the mendicants, sumptuously apparelled. When he heard his mother address the person who experienced her bounty in the manner mentioned above, " Mother," said he, " is it not my father whom you recommend to the prayers of these poor people ? "

" It is, my son," replied she, " the third night following our marriage he left me, and I have never seen him since."

Now, as the lady walked among her dependents, who were ranged in order, she approached her own husband Guido, and gave him alms—but she knew not who he was. He bowed his head in acknowledgment, fearful lest his voice should discover him. As the Countess walked, her son followed ; and Guido raising his eyes and seeing his offspring, whom he had not before seen, he could not contain himself. He caught him in his arms, and kissed him. " My darling child," said he, " may the Lord give thee grace to do that which is pleasing in His eyes."

The damsels of the lady, observing the emotion and action of the pilgrim, called to him and bade him stand there no longer. He approached his wife's presence, and without making himself known, entreated of her permission to occupy some retired place in the neighbouring forest ; and she, supposing that he was the pilgrim he appeared to be, for the love of God and of her husband built him a hermitage, and there he remained a long time. But being on the point of death, he called his attendant, and said, " Go quickly to the countess ; give her that ring, and say that if she wishes to see me, she must come hither with all speed."

The messenger went accordingly, and delivered the ring. As soon as she had seen it, she exclaimed, " It is my lord's ring ! " and with a fleet foot hurried into the forest.

But Guido was dead. She fell upon the corpse, and with a loud voice cried, " Woe is me ! my hope is extinct ! " and then with sighs and lamentations continued, " Where are now the alms I distributed in behalf of my lord ? I beheld my husband receive my gifts with his own hands, and knew him not. And as for thee " (apostrophizing the dead body), " thou sawest thy child, and touchedst him. Thou didst kiss him, and yet revealedst not thyself to me ! What hast thou done ? Oh, Guido ! Guido ! never shall I see thee more ! "

She sumptuously interred his body; and bewailed his decease for many days.

Application

My beloved, the knight represents Christ ; the wife is the soul, and Tyrius is man in general. The weasel typifies John and the other prophets, who predicted the coming of Christ. The mountain is the world. The dead dragon is the old law, and the treasure within it is the ten commandments. The sword is authority ; the King's daughter, the Virgin Mary. The seven sons of Plebeus are seven mortal sins ; the fisherman is the Holy Ghost.

SWEDISH
14TH CENTURY

THE WEREWOLF

THERE was once a King, who ruled over a large kingdom. He was married to a beautiful Queen, by whom he had only one child, a daughter. Hence it naturally followed that the little one was to her parents as the apple of their eye, and was dear to them beyond all other things, so that they thought of nothing with such delight as of the pleasure they should have in her when she grew up. But much falls out contrary to expectation; for before the Princess was out of her childhood, the Queen, her mother, fell sick and died.

Now, it is easy to imagine that there was sadness not only in the royal court, but over the whole kingdom, for the Queen was greatly beloved by all. The King himself was so deeply afflicted that he resolved never to marry again, but placed all his comfort and joy in the little Princess.

In this manner a considerable time passed on; the young Princess grew from day to day taller and fairer, and everything she at any time desired was by her father immediately granted her; many attendants being placed about her, for the sole purpose of being at hand to execute all her commands. Among these there was a woman who had been previously married, and had two daughters. She was of an agreeable person, and had a persuasive tongue, so that she well knew how to put her words together; added to all which she was as soft and pliant as silk; but her heart was full of artifices and all kinds of falsehood.

No sooner was the Queen dead than she began to devise plans how she might become consort to the King, and her daughters be honoured as King's daughters. With this object she began by winning the affection of the young Princess, praised beyond measure all that she said or did, and all her talk ended in declaring how happy they would be if the King would take to himself a new wife. On this subject the conversation oftenest turned both early and late, till at length the Princess could not believe otherwise than that all the woman said was true. She therefore asked her what description of wife it were most desirable that the King should select. The woman, in many words, all sweet as honey, answered:

"Ill would it become me to give an opinion in such a case, hoping only he may choose for his Queen one who will be kind to my little Princess. But this I know, that were I so fortunate as to be the object of his choice, I should think only of what might please the Princess; and if she wished to wash her hands, one of my daughters should hold the basin, and the other hand her the towel."

This and much more she said to the Princess, who believed her, as children readily believe all that is told them is true.

Not a day now passed in which the King was free from the solicitations of his daughter, who incessantly besought him to marry the handsome waiting-woman; but he would not. Nevertheless, the Princess would not desist from her entreaties, but spoke incessantly precisely as she had been taught by the false waiting-woman. One day, when she was talking in the same strain, the King broke forth:

"I see very well that it must at length be as you have resolved, greatly as it is against my wish; but it shall be only on one condition."

"What is the condition?" asked the Princess, overjoyed.

"It is," said the King, "that, as it is for your sake if I marry again, you shall promise me that if at any future time you shall be discontented with your stepmother or your stepsisters, I shall not be troubled with your complaints and grievances."

The Princess made the promise, and it was settled that the King should marry the waiting-woman, and make her Queen over all his realm.

As time passed on the King's daughter grew up to be the fairest maid in all the land; while the Queen's daughters were as ugly in person as in disposition, so that no one had a good word for them. There could not, therefore, fail of being a number of young princes and knights, from both east and west, coming to demand the young Princess; while not one vouchsafed to woo either of the Queen's daughters. At this the stepmother was sorely vexed at heart, however she might conceal her feelings, being, to all outward appearance, as smooth and humble as before. Among the suitors there was a king's son from a distant country, who was both young and valorous, and as he passionately loved the Princess, she listened to his addresses, and plighted her faith to him in return.

The Queen observed all this with a jaundiced eye; for she would fain have had the Prince marry one of her own daughters and therefore resolved that the young couple should never be united with each other. From that moment her thoughts were solely bent on the destruction both of them and their love.

An opportunity soon offered itself to her ; for just at that time intelligence was received that an enemy had invaded the country, so that the King was obliged to take the field. The Princess was now soon made to learn what kind of a stepmother she had got ; for hardly had the King departed before the Queen began to show her true disposition, so that she now was as cruel and malignant as she had previously appeared to be friendly and obliging. Not a day passed on which the Princess did not hear maledictions and hard words ; nor did the Queen's daughters yield to their mother in wickedness.

But a lot still more cruel awaited the young Prince, the lover of the Princess. While engaged in the chase he had lost his way, and got separated from his companions. Availing herself of the opportunity, the Queen practised on him her wicked arts, and transformed him into A WEREWOLF, so that for the remainder of his days he should be a prowler of the forest. When evening drew on, and the Prince did not appear, his men returned home ; and the sorrow may be easily imagined with which the Princess was overwhelmed when she was informed how the chase had terminated. She wept and mourned day and night, and would not be comforted. But the Queen laughed at her affliction, and rejoiced in her false heart that everything had turned out so agreeably to her wishes.

As the Princess was one day sitting alone in her maiden-bower, it entered her mind that she would visit the forest in which the young Prince had disappeared. She went, therefore, to her stepmother, and asked permission to go to the wood, that she might for a little while forget her heavy affliction. To her request the Queen would hardly give her consent, as she was always more inclined to say no than yes ; but the Princess besought her so earnestly that at last her stepmother could no longer withhold her permission, only ordering one of her daughters to accompany and keep watch over her.

A long dispute now arose between mother and daughters, neither of the stepsisters being willing to go with her, but excusing themselves, and asking what pleasure they could have in following her who did nothing but weep. The matter ended by the Queen insisting that one of her daughters should go with the Princess, however much it might be against her will. The maidens then strolled away from the palace and reached the forest, where the Princess amused herself with wandering among the trees, and listening to the song of the little birds, and thinking on the friend she loved so dearly, and whom she now had lost; the Queen's daughter following all the while, with a heart full of rancorous feeling for the Princess and her grief.

After having wandered about for some time they came to a small cottage that stood far in the dark forest. At the same moment the Princess was seized with a burning thirst, and entreated her stepsister to accompany her to the cottage, that she might get a draught of water. At this the Queen's daughter became only more ill-humoured, and said:

"Is it not enough that I follow you up and down in the wild wood? Now, because you are a Princess, you require me to go into such a filthy nest. No, my foot shall never enter it. If you will go, go alone."

The Princess took no long time to consider, but did as her stepsister said, and entered the cabin. In the little apartment she saw an aged woman sitting on a bench, who appeared so stricken with years that her head shook. The Princess saluted her, as was her wont, in a friendly tone, with "Good evening, good mother! may I ask you for a little drink of water?"

"Yes, and right welcome," answered the old woman. "Who are you that come under my humble roof with so kind a greeting?"

The Princess told her that she was the King's daughter, and had come out to divert herself, with the hope, in some degree, of forgetting her heavy affliction.

"What affliction have you, then?" asked the old woman.

"Well may I grieve," answered the Princess, "and never more feel joyful. I have lost my only friend, and God alone knows whether we shall ever meet again."

She then related to the old woman all that had taken place, while the tears flowed from her eyes in such torrents that no one could have refrained from pitying her.

When she had concluded, the old woman said: "It is well that you have made your grief known to me; I have experienced much, and can, perhaps, give you some advice. When you go from hence you will see a lily growing in the field. This lily is not like other lilies, but has many wonderful properties. Hasten, therefore, to pluck it. If you can do so, all will be well; for then there will come one who will tell you what you are to do."

They then parted; the Princess, having thanked her, continued her walk, and the old woman remained sitting on her bench and shaking her head. But the Queen's daughter had been standing during the whole time outside the door, murmuring and fretting that the Princess stayed so long.

When she came out she had to hear much chiding from her stepsister, as was to be expected; but to this she gave very little heed, thinking only how she should find the flower of which the old woman had spoken. She therefore proceeded farther into the forest, and in the selfsame moment her eye fell on a spot where there stood a beautiful white lily in full bloom before her. On seeing it she was so glad, so glad, and instantly ran to gather it, but it vanished on a sudden and appeared again at some distance.

The Princess was now eager beyond measure, and no longer gave heed to the voice of her stepsister, but continued running; though every time she put forth her hand to take the flower it was already away, and immediately afterwards reappeared at a short distance farther off. Thus it continued for a considerable time, and the Princess penetrated farther and farther into the dense forest, the lily all the while appearing and vanishing, and again showing itself, and every time looking taller and more beautiful than before. In this manner the Princess at length came to a high mountain, when, on casting her eyes up to the summit, there stood the flower on the very edge, as brilliant and fair as the brightest star. She now began to climb up the mountain, caring for neither the stocks nor the stones that lay in the way, so great was her ardour. When she at length had gained the mountain's top, lo! the lily no longer moved, but continued stationary. The Princess then stooped and plucked it, and placed it in her bosom, and was so overjoyed that she forgot both stepsister and everything in the world besides.

For a long time the Princess could not sufficiently feast her eyes with the sight of the beautiful flower. It then on a sudden entered her mind what her stepmother would say, when she returned home, for having stayed out so long. She looked about her before returning to the palace, but on casting a glance behind her she saw that the sun had gone down, and that only a strip of day yet tarried on the mountain's summit; while down before her the forest appeared so dark and gloomy that she did not trust herself to find the way through it.

She was now exceedingly weary and exhausted, and saw no alternative but that she must remain for the night where she was. Sitting then down on the rock, she placed her hand under her cheek and wept, and thought on her wicked stepmother and stepsisters, and all the bitter words she must hear when she returned home, and on the King, her father, who was absent, and on the beloved of her heart, whom she should never see again ; but abundantly as her tears flowed she noticed them not, so absorbing was her affliction. Night now drew on, all was shrouded in darkness, the stars rose and set, but the Princess still continued sitting on the same spot, weeping without intermission. While thus sitting, lost in thought, she heard a voice greeting her with " Good evening, fair maiden ! Why do you sit here so lonely and sorrowful ? "

She started, and was greatly surprised, as may easily be imagined ; and on looking back there stood a little, little old man, who nodded and looked so truly benevolent. She answered :

" I may well be sorrowful, and never more be glad. I have lost my best beloved, and have, moreover, missed my path in the forest, so that I am fearful of being devoured by the wild beasts."

" Oh," said the old man, " don't be disheartened for that. If you will obey me in all that I say, I will help you."

To this the Princess readily assented, seeing herself forsaken by the whole world besides. The old man then drew forth a flint and steel, and said: " Fair maiden ! now, in the first place, you shall kindle a fire."

The King's daughter did as she was desired, gathered moss, twigs, and dry wood, and kindled a fire on the mountain's brow. When she had done this the old man said to her: " Go now farther on the mountain, and you will find a pot full of tar : bring it hither."

The Princess did so. The old man continued : " Now set the pot on the fire."

The Princess did so. " When, now, the tar begins to boil," said the old man, " cast your white lily into the pot."

This seemed to the Princess a very hard command, and she prayed earnestly that she might retain her lily ; but the old man said : " Have you not promised to obey me in all that I desire ? Do as I tell you ; you will not repent."

The Princess then, with eyes averted, cast the lily into the boiling pot, although it grieved her to the heart ; so dear to her was the beautiful flower.

At the same instant a hollow roaring was heard from the forest, like the cry of a wild beast, which came nearer and nearer, and passed into a hideous howl, so that the mountain re-echoed on every side. At the same time was heard a crackling and rustling among the trees, the bushes gave way, and the Princess beheld a huge grey wolf come rushing out of the forest just opposite to the spot where they were sitting.

In her terror she would gladly have fled from it ; but the old man said : " Make haste, run to the brow of the mountain, and the moment the wolf comes before you, empty the tar-pot over him."

The Princess, although so terrified that she was hardly conscious of what she did, nevertheless followed the old man's direction, and poured the tar over the wolf, just as he came running towards her. But now a wonderful event took place, for scarcely had she done so when the wolf changed his covering, the great grey skin started off from him, and, instead of a ravenous wild beast, there stood a comely youth with eyes directed towards the brow of the mountain ; and when the Princess had so far recovered from her fright that she could look on him, whom did she behold before her but her own best beloved, who had been transformed into a werewolf !

Now let any one, who can, imagine what the feelings of the Princess were at this moment. She stretched out her arms towards him, but could neither speak nor answer, so great were her surprise and joy. But the Prince ran up the mountain and embraced her with all the ardour of the truest affection, and thanked her for having restored him. Nor did he forget the little old man, but thanked him in many kind words for his powerful aid. They then sat down on the mountain-top and conversed lovingly with each other.

The Prince related how he had been changed into a wolf, and all the privations he had suffered while he had to range about the forest ; and the Princess recounted to him her sorrow and all the tears she had shed during his absence. Thus they sat throughout the night, heedless of the passing hour, until the stars began gradually to retire before the daylight, so that the surrounding objects were visible. When the sun had risen they perceived that a wide road ran from the foot of the hill quite up to the royal palace. Then said the old man : " Fair maiden, turn about. Do you see anything yonder ? "

" Yes," answered the Princess, " I see a horseman on a foaming horse ; he rides along the road at full speed."

" That," said the old man, " is a messenger from the King, your father. He will follow forthwith with his whole army."

Now was the Princess glad beyond measure, and wished instantly to descend to meet her father ; but the old man held her back, saying, " Wait : it is yet too soon. Let us first see how things will turn out."

After some time the sun shone bright, so that its rays fell on the palace down before them. Then said the old man : " Fair maiden, turn about. Do you see anything yonder ? "

" Yes," answered the Princess, " I see many persons coming out of my father's palace, some of whom proceed along the road, while others hasten towards the forest."

The old man said : " They are your stepmother's servants. She has sent one party to meet the King and bid him welcome ; but the other is going to the forest in search of you."

At hearing this the Princess was troubled, and was with difficulty induced to remain, but wished to go down to the Queen's people : but the old man held her back, saying, " Wait yet a little while : we will first see how things turn out."

For some time the Princess continued with her looks directed towards the road by which the King was to come. Then said the old man again : " Fair maiden, turn about. Do you observe anything yonder ? "

" Yes," answered the Princess, " there is a great stir in my father's palace ; and see ! now they are busy in hanging the whole palace with black."

The old man said : " That is your stepmother and her servants. They wish to make your father believe that you are dead."

At this the Princess was filled with anxiety, and prayed fervently, saying, " Let me go, let me go, that I may spare my father so great an affliction."

But the old man detained her, saying, " No, wait. It is still too soon. We will first see how things turn out."

Again another interval passed, the sun rose high in the heaven, and the air breathed warm over field and forest ; but the royal children and the little old man continued sitting on the mountain where we left them. They now observed a small cloud slowly rising in the horizon, which grew larger and larger, and came nearer and nearer along the road ; and as it moved they saw that it glittered with weapons, and perceived helmets nodding and banners waving, heard the clanking of swords and the neighing of horses, and at length recognised the royal standard. Now it is easy to imagine that the joy of the Princess exceeded all bounds, and that she only longed to go and greet her father. But the old man held her back, saying, " Turn about, fair maiden, do you see nothing at the King's palace ? "

" Yes," answered the Princess, " I see my stepmother and my stepsisters coming out clad in deep mourning, and holding white handkerchiefs to their faces, and weeping bitterly."

The old man said, " They are now pretending to mourn for your death ; but wait awhile, we have yet to see how things will turn out."

Some time after, the old man asked again, " Fair maiden, turn about. Do you observe anything yonder ? "

" Yes," answered the Princess, " I see them come bearing a black coffin. Now my father orders it to be opened. And see ! the Queen and her daughters fall on their knees, and my father threatens them with his sword."

The old man said, " The King desired to see your corpse, and so your wicked stepmother has been forced to confess the truth."

On hearing this, the Princess entreated fervently : " Let me go, let me go, that I may console my father in his great affliction."

But the old man still detained her, saying, " Attend to my counsel, and stay here a little while. We have not yet seen how everything will terminate."

Another interval passed, and the Princess, and the Prince, and the little old man still continued sitting on the mountain. Then said the old man, " Turn about, fair maiden. Do you observe anything yonder ? "

" Yes," answered the Princess, " I see my father, and my stepmother, and my stepsisters coming this way with all their attendants."

The old man continued, " They have now set out in search of you. Go down now, and bring the wolfskin which is lying below."

The King's daughter did so, and the old man then said, " Place yourself on the brink of the mountain."

The Princess did so, and at the same moment perceived the Queen and her daughters coming along the road just beneath the mountain where they were sitting.

" Now," said the old man, " cast the wolfskin straight down." The Princess obeyed, and cast the wolfskin as the old man had directed. It fell exactly over the wicked Queen and her two daughters. But now a wonderful event took place, for hardly had the skin touched the three women than they changed their guise, gave a hideous howl, and were transformed into three fierce werewolves, which at full speed rushed into the wild forest.

Scarcely had this taken place before the King himself with all his men came to the foot of the mountain. When he looked up and beheld the Princess, he could not at first believe his eyes, but stood immovable, thinking it was a spectre. The old man then cried, " Fair maiden, hasten now down and gladden the heart of your father."

The Princess did not wait to be told a second time, but, taking her lover by the hand, was in an instant at the mountain's foot. When they reached the spot where the King was standing, the Princess fell on her father's breast and wept for joy ; the young Prince also wept ; even the King himself shed tears, and to every one present their meeting was a delightful spectacle. Great joy was there and many embracings, and the Princess related all she had suffered from her stepmother and stepsisters, and all about her beloved Prince, and the little old man who had so kindly assisted them. But when the King turned to thank him he had already vanished, and no one could ever say either who he was or whither he went.

The King and all his suite now returned to the palace, on their way towards which much was said both about the little old man and what the Princess had undergone. On reaching home the King ordered a sumptuous banquet to be prepared, to which he invited all the most distinguished and exalted persons of his kingdom, and bestowed his daughter on the young Prince ; and their nuptials were celebrated with games and rejoicings for many days. And I, too, was at the feastings ; and as I rode through the forest I was met by a wolf with two young ones ; they were ravenous, and seemed to suffer much. I have since learned that they were no other than the wicked stepmother and her two daughters.

ICELANDIC
14TH CENTURY

THE STORY OF FRITHIOF THE BOLD

I

Of King Beli and Thorstein Vikingson and their Children

THUS beginneth the tale, telling how that King Beli ruled over Sogn-land; three children had he, whereof Helgi was his first son, and Halfdan his second, but Ingibiorg his daughter. Ingibiorg was fair of face and wise of mind, and she was ever accounted the foremost of the King's children.

Now a certain strand went west of the firth, and a great stead was thereon, which was called Baldur's Meads; a Place of Peace was there, and a great temple, and round about it a great garth of pales; many gods were there, but amidst them all was Baldur held of most account. So jealous were the heathen men of this stead, that they would have no hurt done therein to man nor beast, nor might any man have dealings with a woman there.

Snowstrand was the name of that stead whereat the King dwelt; but on the other side the firth was an abode named Foreness, where dwelt a man called Thorstein, the son of Viking; and his stead was over against the King's dwelling.

Thorstein had a son by his wife called Frithiof; he was the tallest and strongest of men, and more furnished of all prowess than any other man, even from his youth up. Frithiof the Bold was he called, and so well beloved was he, that all prayed for good things for him.

Now the King's children were but young when their mother died; but a goodman of Sogn, named Hilding, prayed to have the King's daughter to foster; so there was she reared well and heedfully; and she was called Ingibiorg the Fair. Frithiof also was fostered of goodman Hilding, wherefore was he foster-brother to the King's daughter, and they two were peerless among children.

Now King Beli's chattels began to ebb fast away from his hands, for he was grown old.

Thorstein had rule over the third part of the realm, and in him lay the King's greatest strength.

Every third year Thorstein feasted the King at exceeding great cost, and the King feasted Thorstein the two years between.

Helgi, Beli's son, from his youth up turned much to blood-offering; neither were those brethren well-beloved.

Thorstein had a ship called *Ellidi*, which pulled fifteen oars on either board; it ran up high stem and stern, and was strong-built like an ocean-going ship, and its bulwarks were clamped with iron.

So strong was Frithiof that he pulled the two bow oars of *Ellidi*; but either oar was thirteen ells long, and two men pulled every oar otherwhere.

Frithiof was deemed peerless amid the young men of that time, and the King's sons envied him, whereas he was more praised than they.

Now King Beli fell sick; and when the sickness lay heavy on him he called his sons to him and said to them: " This sickness will bring me to mine end, therefore will I bid you this, that ye hold fast to those old friends that I have had; for meseems in all things ye fall short of that father and son, Thorstein and Frithiof, yea, both, in good counsel and in hardihood. A mound ye shall raise over me."

So with that Beli died.

Thereafter Thorstein fell sick; so he spake to Frithiof: " Kinsman," says he, " I will crave this of thee, that thou bow thy will before the King's sons, for their dignity's sake; yet doth my heart speak goodly things to me concerning thy fortune. Now would I be laid in my mound over against King Beli's mound, down by the sea on this side the firth, whereas it may be easiest for us to cry out each to each of tidings drawing nigh."

A little after this Thorstein departed, and was laid in mound even as he had bidden; but Frithiof took the land and chattels after him. Biorn and Asmund were Frithiof's foster-brethren; they were big and strong men both.

II

Frithiof wooeth Ingibiorg of those Brethren

So Frithiof became the most famed of men, and the bravest in all things that may try a man.

Biorn, his foster-brother, he held in most account of all, but Asmund served the twain of them.

The ship *Ellidi*, he gat, the best of good things, of his father's heritage, and another possession therewith—a gold ring; no dearer was in Norway.

So bounteous a man was Frithiof withal, that it was the talk of most that he was a man of no less honour than those brethren, but it were for the name of king; and for this cause they held Frithiof in hate and enmity, and it was a heavy thing to them that he was called greater than they; furthermore they thought they could see that Ingibiorg, their sister, and Frithiof were of one mind together.

It befell hereon that the kings had to go to a feast to Frithiof's house at Foreness; and there it happened according to wont that he gave to all men beyond that they were worthy of. Now Ingibiorg was there, and she and Frithiof talked long together; and the King's daughter said to him: "A goodly gold ring hast thou."

"Yea, in good sooth," said he.

Thereafter went those brethren to their own home, and greater grew their enmity of Frithiof.

A little after grew Frithiof heavy of mood, and Biorn, his foster-brother, asked him why he fared so.

He said he had it in his mind to woo Ingibiorg. "For though I be named by a lesser name than those brethren, yet am I not fashioned lesser."

"Even so let us do then," quoth Biorn. So Frithiof fared with certain men unto those brethren; and the kings were sitting on their father's mound when Frithiof greeted them well, and then set forth his wooing, and prayed for their sister Ingibiorg, the daughter of Beli.

The kings said: "Not overwise is this thine asking, whereas thou wouldst have us give her to one who lacketh dignity; wherefore we gainsay thee this utterly."

Said Frithiof: "Then is mine errand soon sped; but in return never will I give help to you henceforward, nay, though ye need it never so much."

They said they heeded it nought; so Frithiof went home, and was joyous once more.

III

Of King Ring and those Brethren

There was a king named Ring, who ruled over Ringrealm, which also was in Norway; a mighty folk-king he was, and a great man, but come by now unto his latter days.

Now he spake to his men : " Lo, I have heard that the sons of King Beli have brought to nought their friendship with Frithiof, who is the noblest of men ; wherefore will I send men to these kings, and bid them choose whether they will submit them to me and pay me tribute, or else that I bring war on them ; and all things shall then lie ready to my hand to take, for they have neither might nor wisdom to withstand me ; yet great fame were it to my old age to overcome them."

After that fared the messengers of King Ring, and found those brethren, Helgi and Halfdan, in Sogn, and spake to them thus : " King Ring sends bidding to you to send him tribute or else will he war against your realm."

They answered and said that they would not learn in the days of their youth what they would be loth to know in their old age, even how to serve King Ring with shame. " Nay, now shall we draw together all the folk that we may."

Even so they did ; but now, when they beheld their force that it was but little, they sent Hilding their fosterer to Frithiof to bid him come help them against King Ring. Now Frithiof sat at the knave-play when Hilding came thither, who spake thus : " Our kings send thee greeting, Frithiof, and would have thy help in battle against King Ring, who cometh against their realm with violence and wrong."

Frithiof answered him nought, but said to Biorn, with whom he was playing : " A bare place in thy board, foster-brother, and nowise mayst thou amend it ; nay, for my part I shall beset thy red piece there, and wot whether it be safe."

Then Hilding spake again :

" King Helgi bade me say thus much, Frithiof, that thou shouldst go on this journey with them, or else look for ill at their hands when they at the last come back."

" A double game, foster-brother," said Biorn ; " and two ways to meet thy play."

Frithiof said : " Thy play is to fall first on the knave, yet the double game is sure to be."

No other outcome of his errand had Hilding ; he went back speedily to the kings, and told them Frithiof's answer.

They asked Hilding what he made out of those words. He said :

" Whereas he spake of the bare place he will have been thinking of the lack in this journey of yours ; but when he said he would beset the red piece, that will mean Ingibiorg, your sister ; so give ye all the heed ye may to her. But whereas I threatened him with ill from you, Biorn deemed the game a double one; but Frithiof said that the knave must be set on first, speaking thereby of King Ring."

So then the brethren arrayed them for departing; but ere they went, they let bring Ingibiorg and eight women with her to Baldur's Meads, saying that Frithiof would not be so mad rash as to go see her thither, since there was none who durst make riot there.

Then fared those brethren south to Jadar, and met King Ring in the Sogn-Sound.

Now, herewith was King Ring most of all wroth that the brothers had said that they accounted it a shame to fight with a man so old that he might not get a-horseback unholpen.

IV

Frithiof goes to Baldur's Meads

Straightway whenas the kings were gone away Frithiof took his raiment of state and set the goodly gold ring on his arm; then went the foster-brethren down to the sea and launched *Ellidi*. Then said Biorn: "Whither away, foster-brother?"

"To Baldur's Meads," said Frithiof, "to be glad with Ingibiorg."

Biorn said: "A thing unmeet to do, to make the gods wroth with us."

"Well, it shall be risked this time," said Frithiof; "and withal, more to me is Ingibiorg's grace than Baldur's grame."

Therewith they rowed over the firth, and went up to Baldur's Meads and to Ingibiorg's bower, and there she sat with eight maidens, and the newcomers were eight also.

But when they came there, lo, all the place was hung with cloth of pall and precious webs.

Then Ingibiorg arose and said:

"Why art thou so overbold, Frithiof, that thou art come here without the leave of my brethren to make the gods angry with thee?"

Frithiof says: "Howsoever that may be, I hold thy love of more account than the gods' hate."

Ingibiorg answered: "Welcome art thou here, thou and thy men!"

Then she made place for him to sit beside her, and drank to him in the best of wine; and thus they sat and were merry together.

Then beheld Ingibiorg the goodly ring on his arm, and asked him if that precious thing were his own. Frithiof said Yea, and she praised the ring much. Then Frithiof said:

" I will give thee the ring if thou wilt promise to give it to no one, but to send it to me when thou no longer shalt have will to keep it; and hereon shall we plight troth each to other."

So with this troth-plighting they exchanged rings.

Frithiof was oft at Baldur's Meads a-night time, and every day between whiles would he go thither to be glad with Ingibiorg.

V

Those Brethren come Home again

Now tells the tale of those brethren, that they met King Ring, and he had more folk than they; then went men betwixt them, and sought to make peace, so that no battle should be; thereto King Ring assented on such terms that the brethren should submit them to him, and give him in marriage Ingibiorg their sister, with the third part of all their possessions.

The kings said Yea thereto, for they saw that they had to do with overwhelming might; so the peace was fast bound by oaths, and the wedding was to be at Sogn whenas King Ring should go see his betrothed.

So those brethren fare home with their folk, right ill content with things. But Frithiof, when he deemed that the brethren might be looked for home again, spake to the King's daughter:

" Sweetly and well have ye done to us, neither has goodman Baldur been wroth with us; but now as soon as ye wot of the kings' coming home, spread the sheets of your beds abroad on the Hall of the Goddesses, for that is the highest of all the garth, and we may see it from our stead."

The King's daughter said: " Thou dost not after the like of any other; but certes, we welcome dear friends whenas ye come to us." So Frithiof went home; and the next morning he went out early, and when he came in then he spake and sang:

" Now must I tell
To our good men
That over and done
Are our fair journeys;
No more a-shipboard
Shall we be going,
For there are the sheets
Spread out a-bleaching."

Then they went out, and saw that the Hall of the Goddesses was all thatched with white linen. Biorn spake and said: "Now are the kings come home, and but a little while have we to sit in peace, and good were it, meseems, to gather folk together."

So did they, and men came flocking thither.

Now the brethren soon heard of the ways of Frithiof and Ingibiorg, and of the gathering of men. So King Helgi spake:

"A wondrous thing how Baldur will bear what shame soever Frithiof and she will lay on him! Now will I send men to him, and wot what atonement he will offer us, or else will I drive him from the land, for our strength seemeth to me not enough that we should fight with him as now."

So Hilding, their fosterer, bare the King's errand to Frithiof and his friends, and spake in such wise: "This atonement the kings will have of thee, Frithiof, that thou go gather the tribute of the Orkneys, which has not been paid since Beli died, for they need money, whereas they are giving Ingibiorg their sister in marriage, and much of wealth with her."

Frithiof said: "This thing only somewhat urges us to peace, the goodwill of our kin departed; but no trustiness will those brethren show herein. But this condition I make, that our lands be in good peace while we are away." So this was promised and all bound by oaths.

Then Frithiof arrays him for departing, and is captain of men brave and of good help, eighteen in company.

Now his men asked him if he would not go to King Helgi and make peace with him, and pray himself free from Baldur's wrath.

But he answered: "Hereby I swear that I will never pray Helgi for peace."

Then he went aboard *Ellidi*, and they sailed out along the Sognfirth.

But when Frithiof was gone from home, King Halfdan spake to Helgi his brother: "Better lordship and more had we if Frithiof had payment for his masterful deed; now therefore let us burn his stead, and bring on him and his men such a storm on the sea as shall make an end of them."

Helgi said it was a thing meet to be done.

So then they burned up clean all the stead at Foreness and robbed it of all goods; and after that sent for two witch-wives, Heidi and Hamglom, and gave them money to raise against Frithiof and his men so mighty a storm that they should all be lost at sea. So they sped the witch-song, and went up on the witch-mount with spells and sorcery.

VI

Frithiof sails for the Orkneys

So when Frithiof and his men were come out of the Sognfirth there fell on them great wind and storm, and an exceeding heavy sea: but the ship drave on swiftly, for sharp-built she was, and the best to breast the sea.

So Frithiof now sang:

" Oft let I swim from Sogn
My tarred ship sooty-sided,
When maids sat o'er the mead-horn
Amidst of Baldur's Meadows:
Now while the storm is wailing
Farewell I bid you maidens,
Still shall ye love us, sweet ones,
Though *Ellidi* the sea fill."

Said Biorn: " Thou mightest well find other work to do than singing songs over the maids of Baldur's Meadows."

" Of such work shall I not speedily run dry, though," said Frithiof.

Then they bore up north to the sounds nigh those isles that are called Solundir, and therewith was the gale at its hardest.

Then sang Frithiof:

" Now is the sea a-swelling,
And sweepeth the rack onward;
Spells of old days cast o'er us
Make ocean all unquiet;
No more shall we be striving
'Mid storm with wash of billows,
But Solundir shall shelter
Our ship with ice-beat rock-walls."

So they lay to under the lee of the isles hight Solundir, and were minded to abide there; but straightway thereon the wind fell: then they turned away from under the lee of the islands, and now their voyage seemed hopeful to them, because the wind was fair awhile: but soon it began to freshen again.

Then sang Frithiof:

" In days foredone
From Foreness strand
I rowed to meet
Maid Ingibiorg:

But now I sail
Through chilly storm
And wide away
My long-worm driveth."

And now when they were come far out into the main, once more the sea waxed wondrous troubled, and a storm arose with so great drift of snow, that none might see the stem from the stern ; and they shipped seas, so that they must be ever a-baling. So Frithiof sang :

" The salt waves see we nought
As seaward drive we ever
Before the witch-wrought weather,
We well-famed kings'-defenders :
Here are we all a-standing,
With all Solundir hull-down,
Eighteen brave lads a-baling
Black *Ellidi* to bring home."

Said Biorn : " Needs must he who fareth far fall in with diverse hap."

" Yea, certes, foster-brother," said Frithiof. And he sang withal :

" Helgi it is that helpeth
The white-head billows' waxing ;
Cold time unlike the kissing
In the close of Baldur's Meadow !
So is the hate of Helgi
To that heart's love she giveth.
O would that here I held her,
Gift high above all giving ! "

" Maybe," said Biorn, " she is looking higher than thou now art ; what matter when all is said ? "

" Well," says Frithiof, " now is the time to show ourselves to be men of avail, though blither tide it was at Baldur's Meadows."

So they turned to in manly wise, for there were the bravest of men come together in the best ship of the Northlands. But Frithiof sang a stave :

" So come in the West-sea
Nought see I the billows,
The sea-water seemeth
As sweeping of wild-fire.
Topple the rollers,
Toss the hills swan-white,
Ellidi wallows
O'er steep of the wave-hills."

Then they shipped a huge sea, so that all stood a-baling. But Frithiof sang :

" With love-moved mouth the maiden
Me pledgeth though I founder.
Ah ! bright sheets lay a-bleaching,
East there on brents the swan loves."

Biorn said : " Art thou of mind belike that the maids of Sogn will weep many tears over thee ? "

Said Frithiof : " Surely that was in my mind."

Therewith so great a sea broke over the bows, that the water came in like the in-falling of a river ; but it availed them much that the ship was so good, and the crew aboard her so hardy.

Now sang Biorn :

" No widow, methinks,
To thee or me drinks :
No ring-bearer fair
Biddeth draw near ;
Salt are our eyne
Soaked in the brine ;
Strong our arms are no more,
And our eyelids smart sore."

Quoth Asmund : " Small harm though your arms be tried somewhat, for no pity we had from you when we rubbed our eyes whenas ye must needs rise early a-mornings to go to Baldur's Meadows."

" Well," said Frithiof, " why singest thou not, Asmund ? "

" Not I," said Asmund ; yet sang a ditty straightway :

" Sharp work about the sail was
When o'er the ship seas tumbled,
And there was I a-working
Within-board 'gainst eight balers ;
Better it was to bower,
Bringing the women breakfast,
Than here to be 'mid billows
Black *Ellidi* a-baling."

" Thou accountest thy help of no less worth than it is ? " said Frithiof, laughing therewith ; " but sure it showeth the thrall's blood in thee that thou wouldst fain be awaiting at table."

Now it blew harder and harder yet, so that to those who were aboard liker to huge peaks and mountains than to waves seemed the sea-breakers that crashed on all sides against the ship

Then Frithiof sang :

" On bolster I sat
In Baldur's Mead erst,
And all songs that I could
To the king's daughter sang ;

Now on Ran's bed belike
Must I soon be a-lying,
And another shall be
By Ingibiorg's side."

Biorn said: " Great fear lieth ahead of us, foster-brother, and now dread hath crept into thy words, which is ill with such a good man as thou."

Says Frithiof: " Neither fear nor fainting is it, though I sing now of those our merry journeys; yet perchance more hath been said of them than need was: but most men would think death surer than life, if they were so bested as we be."

" Yet shall I answer thee somewhat," said Biorn, and sang:

" Yet one gain have I gotten
Thou gatst not 'mid thy fortune,
For meet play did I make me
With Ingibiorg's eight maidens:
Red rings we laid together
Aright in Baldur's Meadow,
When far off was the warder
Of the wide land of Halfdan."

" Well," said he, " we must be content with things as they are, foster-brother."

Therewith so great a sea smote them, that the bulwark was broken and both the sheets and four men were washed overboard and all lost.

Then Frithiof sang:

" Both sheets are bursten
Amid the great billows,
Four swains are sunk
In the fathomless sea."

" Now, meseems," said Frithiof, " it may well be that some of us will go to the house of Ran, nor shall we deem us well sped if we come not thither in glorious array; wherefore it seems good to me that each man of us here should have somewhat of gold on him."

Then he smote asunder the ring, Ingibiorg's gift, and shared it between all his men, and sang a stave withal:

" The red ring here I hew me
Once owned of Halfdan's father,
The wealthy lord of erewhile,
Or the sea waves undo us,
So on the guests shall gold be,
If we have need of guesting;
Meet so for mighty men-folk
Amid Ran's hall to hold them."

"Not all so sure is it that we come there," said Biorn; "and yet it may well be so."

Now Frithiof and his folk found that the ship had great way on her, and they knew not what lay ahead, for all was mirk on either board, so that none might see the stem or stern from amidships; and therewith was there great drift of spray amid the furious wind, and frost, and snow, and deadly cold.

Now Frithiof went up to the masthead, and when he came down he said to his fellows: "A sight exceeding wondrous have I seen, for a great whale went in a ring about the ship, and I misdoubt me that we come nigh to some land, and that he is keeping the shore against us; for certes King Helgi has dealt with us in no friendly wise, neither will this his messenger be friendly. Moreover, I saw two women on the back of the whale, and they it be who will have brought this great storm on us with the worst of spells and witchcraft; but now we shall try which may prevail, my fortune or their devilry, so steer ye at your straightest, and I will smite these evil things with beams."

Therewith he sang a stave:

> "See I troll women
> Twain on the billows,
> E'en they whom Helgi
> Hither has sent.
> *Ellidi* now
> Or ever her way stop
> Shall smite the backs
> Of these asunder."

So tells the tale that this wonder went with the good ship *Ellidi*, that she knew the speech of man.

But Biorn said: "Now may we see the treason of those brethren against us." Therewith he took the tiller, but Frithiof caught up a forked beam, and ran into the prow, and sang a stave:

> "*Ellidi*, hail!
> Leap high o'er the billows!
> Break of the troll wives
> Brow or teeth now!
> Break cheek or jaw
> Of the cursed woman,
> One foot or twain
> Of the ogress filthy."

Therewith he drave his fork at one of the skin-changers, and the beak of *Ellidi* smote the other on the back, and the backs of both were broken; but the whale took the deep, and gat him gone, and they never saw him after.

Then the wind fell, but the ship lay waterlogged; so Frithiof called out to his men, and bade bale out the ship, but Biorn said:

"No need to work now, verily!"

"Be thou not afeard, foster-brother," said Frithiof, "ever was it the wont of good men of old time to be helpful while they might, whatsoever should come after."

And therewith he sang a stave:

"No need, fair fellows,
To fear the death-day;
Rather be glad,
Good men of mine:
For if dreams wot aught
All nights they say
I yet shall have
My Ingibiorg."

Then they baled out the ship; and they were now come nigh unto land; but there was yet a flaw of wind in their teeth. So then did Frithiof take the two bow oars again, and rowed full mightily. Therewith the weather brightened, and they saw that they were come out to Effia Sound, and so there they made land.

The crew were exceeding weary; but so stout a man was Frithiof that he bore eight men a-land over the fore-shore, but Biorn bore two, and Asmund one. Then sang Frithiof:

"Fast bare I up
To the fire-lit hou.
My men all dazed
With the drift of the storm:
And the sail moreover
To the sand I carried;
With the might of the sea
Is there no more to do."

VII

Frithiof at the Orkneys

Now Earl Angantyr was at Effia whenas Frithiof and his folk came a-land there. But his way it was, when he was sitting at the drink, that one of his men should sit at the watch-window, looking weatherward from the drinking-hall, and keep watch there. From a great horn drank he ever: and still as one was emptied another was filled for him

And he who held the watch when Frithiof came a-land was called Hallward; and now he saw where Frithiof and his men went, and sang a stave:

> " Men see I a-baling
> Amid the storm's might;
> Six bale on *Ellidi*
> Seven are a-rowing;
> Like is he in the stem,
> Straining hard at the oars,
> To Frithiof the bold,
> The brisk in the battle."

So when he had drunk out the horn, he cast it in through the window, and spake to the woman who gave him drink:

> " Take up from the floor,
> O fair-going woman,
> The horn cast adown
> Drunk out to the end!
> I behold men at sea
> Who, storm-beaten, shall need
> Help at our hands
> Ere the haven they make."

Now the Earl heard what Hallward sang; so he asked for tidings, and Hallward said: " Men are come a-land here, much forwearied, yet brave lads belike: but one of them is so hardy that he beareth the others ashore."

Then said the Earl, " Go ye, and meet them, and welcome them in seemly wise: if this be Frithiof, the son of Hersir Thorstein, my friend, he is a man famed far and wide for all prowess."

Then there took up the word a man named Atli, a great viking, and he spake: " Now shall that be proven which is told of, that Frithiof hath sworn never to be first in the craving of peace."

There were ten men in company with him, all evil and outrageous, who often wrought berserksgang.

So when they met Frithiof they took to their weapons. But Atli said:

" Good to turn hither, Frithiof! Clutching ernes should claw; and we no less, Frithiof! Yea, and now may'st thou hold to thy word, and not crave first for peace."

So Frithiof turned to meet them, and sang a stave:

> " Nay, nay, in nought
> Now shall ye cow us.
> Blenching hearts,
> Isle-abiders!

Alone with you ten
The fight will I try
Rather than pray
For peace at your hands."

Then came Hallward thereto, and spake:

"The Earl wills that ye all be made welcome here: neither shall any set on you."

Frithiof said he would take that with a good heart; howsoever he was ready for either peace or war.

So thereon they went to the Earl, and he made Frithiof and all his men right welcome, and they abode with him, in great honour holden, through the wintertide, and oft would the Earl ask of their voyage: so Biorn sang:

"There baled we, wight fellows,
Washed over and over
On both boards
By billows;
For ten days we baled there,
And eight thereunto."

The Earl said: "Well-nigh did the King undo you; it is ill seen of such-like kings as are meet for nought but to overcome men by wizardry. But now I wot," says Angantyr, "of thine errand hither, Frithiof, that thou art sent after the scat: whereto I give thee a speedy answer, that never shall King Helgi get scat of me, but to thee will I give money, even as much as thou wilt; and thou mayest call it scat if thou hast a mind to, or whatso else thou wilt."

So Frithiof said that he would take the money.

VIII

King Ring weddeth Ingibiorg

Now shall it be told of what came to pass in Norway the while Frithiof was away; for those brethren let burn up all the stead at Foreness. Moreover, while the weird sisters were at their spells they tumbled down from off their high witch-mount, and brake both their backs.

That autumn came King Ring north to Sogn to his wedding, and there at a noble feast drank his bridal with Ingibiorg.

"Whence came that goodly ring which thou hast on thine arm?" said King Ring to Ingibiorg.

She said her father had owned it, but he answered and said:

"Nay, for Frithiof's gift it is: so take it off thine arm straightway; for no gold shalt thou lack whenas thou comest to Elfhome."

So she gave the ring to King Helgi's wife, and bade her give it to Frithiof when he came back.

Then King Ring wended home with his wife, and loved her with exceeding great love.

IX

Frithiof brings the Tribute to the Kings

The spring after these things Frithiof departed from the Orkneys and Earl Angantyr in all good liking; and Hallward went with Frithiof.

But when they came to Norway they heard tell of the burning of Frithiof's stead.

So when he was gotten to Foreness, Frithiof said: "Black is my house waxen now; no friends have been at work here." And he sang withal:

"Frank and free,
With my father dead,
In Foreness old
We drank aforetime.
Now my abode
Behold I burned;
For many ill deeds
The kings must I pay."

Then he sought rede of his men what was to be done; but they bade him look to it: then he said that the scat must first be paid out of hand. So they rowed over the firth to Snowstrand; and there they heard that the kings were gone to Baldur's Meads to sacrifice to the gods; so Frithiof and Biorn went up thither, and bade Hallward and Asmund break up meanwhile all ships, both great and small, that were anigh; and they did so. Then went Frithiof and his fellow to the door of Baldur's Meads, and Frithiof would go in. Biorn bade him fare warily, since he must needs go in alone; but Frithiof charged him to abide without, and keep watch; and he sang a stave:

"All alone go I
Unto the stead;
No folk I need
For the finding of kings;
But cast ye the fire
O'er the kings' dwelling,
If I come not again
In the cool of the even."

"Ah," said Biorn, "a goodly singing!"

Then went Frithiof in, and saw but few folk in the Hall of the Goddesses; there were the kings at their blood-offering, sitting a-drinking; a fire was there on the floor, and the wives of the kings sat thereby, a-warming the gods, while others anointed them, and wiped them with napkins.

So Frithiof went up to King Helgi and said: "Have here thy scat!"

And therewith he heaved up the purse wherein was the silver, and drave it on to the face of the King; whereby were two of his teeth knocked out, and he fell down stunned in his high seat; but Halfdan got hold of him, so that he fell not into the fire. Then sang Frithiof:

"Have here thy scat,
High Lord of the warriors!
Heed that and thy teeth,
Lest all tumble about thee!
Lo the silver abideth
At the bight of this bag here,
That Biorn and I
Betwixt us have borne thee."

Now there were but few folk in the chamber, because the drinking was in another place; so Frithiof went out straightway along the floor, and beheld therewith that goodly ring of his on the arm of Helgi's wife as she warmed Baldur at the fire; so he took hold of the ring, but it was fast to her arm and he dragged her by it over the pavement towards the door, and Baldur fell from her into the fire; then Halfdan's wife caught hastily at Baldur, whereby the god she was warming fell likewise into the fire; and the fire caught both the gods, for they were anointed, and ran up thence into the roof, so that the house was all ablaze: but Frithiof got the ring to him ere he came out.

So then Biorn asked him what had come of his going in there; but Frithiof held up the ring and sang a stave:

"The heavy purse smote Helgi
Hard 'midst his scoundrel's visage:
Lowly bowed Halfdan's brother,
Fell bundling 'mid high seat;
There Baldur fell a-burning,
But first my bright ring gat I.
Fast from the roaring fire
I dragged the best crone forward."

Men say that Frithiof cast a firebrand up on to the roof, so that the hall was all ablaze, and therewith sang a stave:

" Down stride we toward the sea-strand,
And strong deeds set a-going,
For now the blue flame bickers
Amidst of Baldur's Meadow."

And therewith they went down to the sea.

X

Frithiof made an Outlaw

But as soon as King Helgi had come to himself he bade follow after Frithiof speedily, and slay them all, him and his fellows : " A man of forfeit life, who spareth no Place of Peace ! "

So they blew the gathering for the kings' men, and when they came out to the hall they saw that it was afire ; so King Halfdan went thereto with some of the folk, but King Helgi followed after Frithiof and his men, who were by then gotten a-shipboard and were lying on their oars.

Now King Helgi and his men find that all the ships are scuttled, and they have to turn back to shore, and have lost some men : then waxed King Helgi so wroth that he grew mad, and he bent his bow, and laid an arrow on the string, and drew at Frithiof so mightily that the bow brake asunder in the midst.

But when Frithiof saw that, then he gat him to the two bow oars of *Ellidi,* and laid so hard on them that they both brake, and with that he sang a stave :

" Young Ingibiorg
Kissed I aforetime,
Kissed Beli's daughter
In Baldur's Meadow
So shall the oars
Of *Ellidi*
Break both together
As Helgi's bow breaks."

Then the land-wind ran down the firth and they hoisted sail and sailed ; but Frithiof bade them look to it that they might have no long abiding there. And so withal they sailed out of the Sognfirth, and Frithiof sang :

" Sail we away from Sogn,
E'en as we sailed aforetime,
When flared the fire all over
The house that was my fathers'.
Now is the bale a-burning
Amidst of Baldur's Meadow :
But wend I as a wild-wolf,
Well wot I they have sworn it."

" What shall we turn to now, foster-brother ? " said Biorn.

" I may not abide here in Norway," said Frithiof : " I will learn the ways of warriors, and sail a-warring."

So they searched the isles and out-skerries the summer long, and gathered thereby riches and renown ; but in autumn-tide they made for the Orkneys, and Angantyr gave them good welcome, and they abode there through the winter-tide.

But when Frithiof was gone from Norway the kings held a Thing, whereat was Frithiof made an outlaw throughout their realm ; they took his lands to them, moreover, and King Halfdan took up his abode at Foreness, and built up again all Baldur's Meadow, though it was long ere the fire was slaked there. This misliked King Helgi most, that the gods were all burned up, and great was the cost or ever Baldur's Meadow was built anew fully equal to its first estate.

So King Helgi abode still at Snowstrand.

XI

Frithiof fareth to see King Ring and Ingibiorg

Frithiof waxed ever in riches and renown whithersoever he went : evil men he slew, and grimly strong-thieves, but husbandmen and chapmen he let abide in peace ; and now was he called anew Frithiof the Bold ; he had gotten to him by now a great company well arrayed, and was become exceedingly wealthy of chattels.

But when Frithiof had been three winters a-warring he sailed west, and made the Wick ; then he said that he would go a-land : " But ye shall fare a-warring without me this winter ; for I begin to weary of warfare, and would fain go to the Uplands, and get speech of King Ring ; but hither shall ye come to meet me in the summer, and I will be here the first day of summer."

Biorn said : " This counsel is naught wise, though thou must needs rule ; rather would I that we fare north to Sogn, and slay both those kings, Helgi and Halfdan."

" It is all naught," said Frithiof ; " I must needs go to see King Ring and Ingibiorg."

Says Biorn : " Loth am I hereto that thou shouldst risk thyself alone in his hands ; for this Ring is a wise man and of great kin, though he be somewhat old."

But Frithiof said he would have his own way: " And thou, Biorn, shalt be captain of our company meanwhile."

So they did as he bade, and Frithiof fared to the Uplands in the autumn, for he desired sore to look upon the love of King Ring and Ingibiorg. But or ever he came there he did on him, over his clothes, a great cloak all shaggy; two staves he had in his hand, and a mask over his face, and he made as if he were exceeding old.

So he met certain herdsmen, and, going heavily, he asked them: " Whence are ye? "

They answered and said: " We are of Streitaland, whereas the King dwelleth."

Quoth the carle: " Is King Ring a mighty king then? "

They answered: " Thou lookest to us old enough to have cunning to know what manner of man is King Ring in all wise."

The carle said that he had heeded salt-boiling more than the ways of kings; and therewith he goes up to the King's house.

So when the day was well worn he came into the hall, blinking about as a dotard, and took an outward place, pulling his hood over him to hide his visage.

Then spake King Ring to Ingibiorg: " There is come into the hall a man far bigger than other men."

The Queen answered: " That is no such great tidings here."

But the King spake to a serving-man who stood before the board, and said: " Go thou, and ask yon cowled man who he is, whence he cometh, and of what kin he is."

So the lad ran down the hall to the new-comer and said: " What art thou called, thou man? Where wert thou last night? Of what kin art thou? "

Said the cowled man: " Quick come thy questions, good fellow! but hast thou skill to understand if I shall tell thee hereof? "

" Yea, certes," said the lad.

" Well," said the cowl-bearer, " Thief is my name, with Wolf was I last night, and in Grief-ham was I reared."

Then ran the lad back to the King, and told him the answer of the new-comer.

" Well told, lad," said the King; ' but for that land of Grief-ham, I know it well; it may well be that the man is of no light heart, and yet a wise man shall he be, and of great worth I account him."

Said the Queen: " A marvellous fashion of thine, that thou must needs talk so freely with every carle that cometh hither! Yea, what is the worth of him, then?"

"That wottest thou no clearer than I," said the King; "but I see that he thinketh more than he talketh, and is peering all about him."

Therewith the King sent a man after him, and so the cowl-bearer went up before the King, going somewhat bent, and greeted him in a low voice.

Then said the King: "What art thou called, thou big man?"

And the cowl-bearer answered and sang:

"PEACE-THIEF they called me
On the prow with the Vikings:
But WAR-THIEF whenas
I set widows a-weeping;
SPEAR-THIEF when I
Sent forth the barbed shafts;
BATTLE-THIEF when I
Burst forth on the King;
HEL-THIEF when I
Tossed up the small babies:
ISLE-THIEF when I
In the outer isles harried;
SLAINS-THIEF when I
Sat aloft over men:
Yet since have I drifted
With salt-boiling carles,
Needy of help
Ere hither I came."

Said the King: "Thou hast gotten thy name of Thief from many a matter, then; but where wert thou last night, and what is thy home?"

The cowl-bearer said: "In Grief-ham I grew up; but heart drave me hither, and home have I nowhere."

The King said: "Maybe indeed that thou hast been nourished in Grief-ham a certain while; yet also maybe that thou wert born in a place of peace. But in the wild wood must thou have lain last night, for no good-man dwelleth anigh named Wolf; but whereas thou sayest thou hast no home, so is it, that thou belike deemest thy home naught, because of thy heart that drave thee hither."

Then spake Ingibiorg: "Go, Thief, get thee to some other harbour, or in to the guest-hall."

"Nay," said the King, "I am old enow to know how to marshal guests; so do off thy cowl, new-comer, and sit down on my other hand."

"Yea, old, and over old," said the Queen, "when thou settest staff-carles by thy side."

"Nay, lord, it beseemeth not," said Thief; "better it were as the Queen sayeth. I have been more used to boiling salt than sitting beside lords."

"Do thou my will," said the King, "for I will rule this time."

So Thief cast his cowl from him, and was clad thereunder in a dark blue kirtle; on his arm, moreover, was the goodly gold ring, and a thick silver belt was round about him, with a great purse on it, and therein silver pennies glittering; a sword was girt to his side, and he had a great fur hood on his head, for his eyes were bleared, and his face all wrinkled.

"Ah! now we fare better, say I," quoth the King; "but do thou, Queen, give him a goodly mantle, well shapen for him."

"Thou shalt rule, my lord," said the Queen, "but in small account do I hold this Thief of thine."

So then he gat a good mantle over him, and sat down in the high-seat beside the King.

The Queen waxed red as blood when she saw the goodly ring, yet would she give him never a word; but the King was exceedingly blithe with him and said: "A goodly ring hast thou on thine arm there; thou must have boiled salt long enough to get it."

Says he: "That is all the heritage of my father."

"Ah!" says the King, "maybe thou hast more than that; well, few salt-boiling carles are thy peers, I deem, unless eld is deep in mine eyes now."

So Thief was there through the winter amid good entertainment, and well accounted of by all men; he was bounteous of his wealth, and joyous with all men: the Queen held but little converse with him; but the King and he were ever blithe together.

XII

Frithiof saves the King and Queen on the Ice

The tale tells that on a time King Ring and the Queen, and a great company, would go to a feast. So the King spake to Thief: "Wilt thou fare with us, or abide at home?"

He said he had liefer go; and the King said: "Then am I the more content."

So they went on their ways, and had to cross a certain frozen water.

Then said Thief: " I deem this ice untrustworthy; meseemeth ye fare unwarily."

Quoth the King: " It is often shown how heedful in thine heart thou wilt be to us."

So a little after the ice broke in beneath them, and Thief ran thereto, and dragged the wain to him, with all that was therein; and the King and the Queen both sat in the same: so Thief drew it all up on to the ice, with the horses that were yoked to the wain.

Then spake King Ring: " Right well drawn, Thief! Frithiof the Bold himself would have drawn no stronger had he been here; doughty followers are such as thou!"

So they came to the feast, and there is naught to tell thereof, and the King went back again with seemly gifts.

XIII

The King sleeps before Frithiof

Now weareth away the mid-winter, and when spring cometh, the weather groweth fair, the wood bloometh, the grass groweth, and ships may glide betwixt land and land. So on a day the King says to his folk: " I will that ye come with us for our disport out into the woods, that we may look upon the fairness of the earth."

So did they, and went flock-meal with the King into the woods; but so it befell, that the King and Frithiof were gotten alone together afar from other men, and the King said he was heavy, and would fain sleep. Then said Thief: " Get thee home, then, lord, for it better beseemeth men of high estate to lie at home than abroad."

" Nay," said the King, " so will I not do." And he laid him down therewith, and slept fast, snoring loud.

Thief sat close by him, and presently drew his sword from his sheath and cast it far away from him.

A little while after the King woke up, and said: " Was it not so, FRITHIOF, that a many things came into thy mind e'en now? But well hast thou dealt with them, and great honour shalt thou have of me. Lo, now, I knew thee straightway the first evening thou camest into our hall: now nowise speedily shalt thou depart from us; and somewhat great abideth thee."

Said Frithiof: " Lord King, thou hast done to me well, and in friendly wise ; but yet must I get me gone soon, because my company cometh speedily to meet me, as I have given them charge to do."

So then they rode home from the wood, and the King's folk came flocking to him, and home they fared to the hall and drank joyously ; and it was made known to all folk that Frithiof the Bold had been abiding there through the winter-tide.

XIV

King Ring's Gift to Frithiof

Early of a morning-tide one smote on the door of that hall, wherein slept the King and Queen, and many others : then the King asked who it was that called at the hall door ; and so he who was without said : " Here am I, Frithiof ; and I am arrayed for my departure."

Then was the door opened, and Frithiof came in, and sung a stave :

" Have great thanks for the guesting
Thou gavest with all bounty ;
Dight fully for wayfaring
Is the feeder of the eagle ;
But, Ingibiorg, I mind thee
While yet on earth we tarry ;
Live gloriously ! I give thee
This gift for many kisses."

And therewith he cast the goodly ring towards Ingibiorg, and bade her take it.

The King smiled at this stave of his, and said : " Yea, forsooth, she hath more thanks for thy winter quarters than I ; yet hath she not been more friendly to thee than I."

Then sent the King his serving-folk to fetch victuals and drink, and saith that they must eat and drink before Frithiof departed. " So arise, Queen, and be joyful ! " But she said she was loth to fall a-feasting so early.

" Nay, we will eat all together," said King Ring, and they did so.

But when they had drunk a while King Ring spake : " I would that thou abide here, Frithiof ; for my sons are but children and I am old, and unmeet for the warding of my realm, if any should bring war against it."

Frithiof said : " Speedily must I be gone, lord." And he sang :

" Oh, live, King Ring,
Both long and hale !
The highest King
Neath heaven's skirt :

Ward well, O King,
Thy wife and land,
For Ingibiorg now
Nevermore shall I meet."

Then quoth King Ring:

" Fare not away,
O Frithiof, thus,
With downward heart,
O dearest of chieftains!
For now will I give thee
For all thy good gifts,
Far better things
Than thou wottest thyself."

And again he sang:

" To Frithiof the famous
My fair wife I give,
And all things therewith
That are unto me."

Then Frithiof took up the word and sang:

" Nay, how from thine hands
These gifts may I have,
But if thou hast fared
By the last way of fate!"

The King said: " I would not give thee this, but that I deem it will soon be so, for I sicken now. But of all men I would that thou shouldst have the joy of this; for thou art the crown of all Norway. The name of King will I give thee also; and all this, because Ingibiorg's brethren would begrudge thee any honour; and would be slower in getting thee a wife than I am."

Said Frithiof: " Have all thanks, lord, for thy goodwill beyond that I looked for! but I will have no higher dignity than to be called Earl."

Then King Ring gave Frithiof rule over all his realm in due wise, and the name of Earl therewith; and Frithiof was to rule it until such time as the sons of King Ring were of age to rule their own realm. So King Ring lay sick a little while, and then died; and great mourning was made for him; then was there a mound cast over him, and much wealth laid therein, according to his bidding.

Thereafter Frithiof made a noble feast, whereunto his folk came; and thereat was drunken at one and the same time the heritage feast after King Ring, and the bridal of Frithiof and Ingibiorg.

After these things Frithiof abode in his realm, and was deemed therein a most noble man; he and Ingibiorg had many children.

XV

Frithiof King in Sogn

Now those kings of Sogn, the brethren of Ingibiorg, heard these tidings, how that Frithiof had gotten a King's rule in Ringrealm, and had wedded Ingibiorg their sister. Then says Helgi to Halfdan, his brother, that unheard of it was, and a deed over-bold, that a mere Hersir's son should have her to wife; and so thereat they gather together a mighty army, and go their ways therewith to Ringrealm, with the mind to slay Frithiof, and lay all his realm under them.

But when Frithiof was ware of this, he gathered folk, and spake to the Queen moreover: "New war is come upon our realm; and now, in whatso wise the dealings go, fain am I that thy ways to me grow no colder."

She said: "In such wise have matters gone that I must needs let thee be the highest."

Now was Biorn come from the east to help Frithiof; so they fared to the fight, and it befell, as ever erst, that Frithiof was the foremost in the peril: King Helgi and he came to handy-blows, and there he slew King Helgi.

Then bade Frithiof raise up the Shield of Peace, and the battle was stayed; and therewith he cried to King Halfdan: "Two choices are in thine hands now, either that thou give up all to my will, or else gettest thou thy bane like thy brother; for now may men see that mine is the better part."

So Halfdan chose to lay himself and his realm under Frithiof's sway; and so now Frithiof became ruler over Sogn-folk, and Halfdan was to be Hersir in Sogn and pay Frithiof tribute, while Frithiof ruled Ringrealm. So Frithiof had the name of King of Sogn-folk from the time that he gave up Ringrealm to the sons of King Ring, and thereafter he won Hordaland also. He and Ingibiorg had two sons, called Gunnthiof and Hunthiof, men of might, both of them.

AND SO HERE ENDETH THE STORY OF FRITHIOF THE BOLD.

DANISH
14TH CENTURY

THE NESS KING

ABOUT four miles from Fredericia, where the village of Egeskov now is, there once stood a castle of the same name. Its last owner was Lars Brokhuus ; but before the castle fell into his hands it belonged to a knight named Börre, who dwelt there with his daughter Mette. The knight being far from wealthy, was desirous of seeing his child provided for before his death, and therefore determined upon making a " Brudeskue " (bride-show).

This, in former times, was a fête at which all the nobles, knights, and esquires assembled, tilted with each other, rode at the ring, and, lastly, paid their court to the fair daughter of the house with costly presents. In consequence of Mette's great beauty and amiable character, many were the knights assembled at the fête. For several days previous to the festivities every room at Egeskov was occupied by the guests, while fresh ones still continued to arrive, so that Börre at length knew not where to find room for all the strangers.

The last day, just before the running at the ring commenced, a young knight with a numerous retinue arrived at Egeskov. He was splendidly armed, and bore himself so proudly and arrogantly, that he looked with scorn on all those who were riding to the castle at the same time. Among these was an esquire, named Ebbe, from a manor which lay a little westward of the creek of Veile-fiord, which on the other side of Rosenvold runs in between Veilby and the parish of Gaarslev. The poverty of this esquire was become proverbial among the people of that time ; they had made a lampoon on him, in which it was said :

> Ebbe from Nebbe, with all his men good,
> Has neither food nor fire-wood.

He was mounted on a horse, which in its younger days had been a noble animal, but was now old and worn-out. His armour was riven and mended in many places, as were also his kirtle and mantle. When Ebbe and Sir Olaf (such was the name of the haughty knight) met, the latter immediately began to jeer and taunt the other ; and when they both arrived at the castle-gate, Ebbe fell back while Olaf with all his retinue pressed forward, in order to enter first. Ebbe, however, took but little heed of Sir Olaf's jeers: "Ride on," cried he to the knight, "when the lord enters his castle the lowest servants are always accustomed to go first to prepare the way."

They rode immediately up to the racecourse, where the eyes of all the dames and damsels were directed to Olaf, on account of his handsome figure and costly equipment. Ebbe, on the contrary, excited no notice, and remained a little behind the others; as if he were too bashful to come forward and expose his poverty. But when it came to the running at the ring he was the foremost of all, and Sir Olaf, let him strive and manage his horse as he might, was unable to carry off more than one ring on his spear, while Ebbe bore away three. When all the assembled knights had ridden at the ring, they began to try their skill at tilting.

At this game Ebbe was for a long time the most successful candidate, and challenged Olaf, who had already unhorsed many knights; but he at length began to tire, and his worn-out horse tottered under him. Olaf, on the contrary, rode a noble steed, and had, moreover, changed his horse after riding at the ring. Ebbe, nevertheless, ventured to encounter him, and fought bravely as long as he was able; but in a short time Olaf overpowered him. Ebbe fell, and left the tilting-ground, and as there were no other competitors, Olaf was declared victor, and received the prize from the hand of Mette.

In the evening all the guests assembled in the knights' hall, where the different suitors entered, according to their rank and condition, bringing with them presents to Mette. The greater number brought costly gifts; but herein also, Olaf surpassed all the others. Besides the costly present which he brought for Mette, he gave to the knight Börre two small castles of embossed gold, saying: "These two castles, of which you here see a representation, belong to me, and I will share them with your daughter, if you will bestow her on me."

Last of all came Ebbe. The knights smiled on seeing him, poor and meanly clad, without a gift, appear before Börre. Ebbe was not unconscious of their contempt, but without deigning to notice them, he bent his knee before Mette, and said in a loud and audible voice: "I approach you last, as is befitting a poor man, who is so far beneath the other suitors in condition and wealth. I here lay at your feet the most precious thing I own"; with these words he placed his sword on the ground before Mette.

"That's no great thing to give away," observed Olaf contemptuously, "seeing you have been so recently overpowered, while you bore this sword in your hand."

"God grant, Sir Olaf," answered Ebbe, "that Mette may receive my poor gift as surely as thou shouldst have suffered a mischance under this sword, had our conditions been more equally matched."

Several of the guests here interfered between the speakers, in order to make peace, and the two rivals separated. It was now agreed among those assembled that Mette should be allowed a month for consideration before she fixed her choice.

The following day there was a great hunt at Egeskov. From early dawn the huntsman's horn resounded through the forest, and here, as at the tilting, every one was eager to show his skill. The ladies, according to the fashion of the times, partook in the amusement of the chase, and followed the deer with all the ardour of the bolder sex. Most of them gathered round Mette, but foremost rode Sir Olaf, and to judge from the friendly looks with which the lady regarded him, it seemed as if he would be the object of her choice. Ebbe was last of all. His horse had not yet recovered from the fatigues of the preceding day. He would not, therefore, force it on, as he cared but little at being left far behind the others. Thus passed the greater part of the forenoon, and the hunt took its course farther and farther down towards Trelde, when Ebbe, just as he was turning his horse into a cross path, saw Mette returning and coming towards him. After riding together a short way, Mette said:

"I am tired of the pursuit after hares and deer, and will accompany you among these green trees. Why are you so far behind the others? Are you not fond of hunting?"

"Yes, undoubtedly I am," replied Ebbe, "but my poor horse is old and tired, and I must spare him."

"I think," said Mette, "it would be better to part with him, than always to be the last in jousts and other manly games."

"That I would not do willingly," answered Ebbe; "this horse is all my father had to leave me; many years it carried him, and has done good service in its better days; in reward for which, I will cherish him out of my slender means, now that he is old."

"Do you know what I am thinking of, Ebbe?" said Mette. "I will make an exchange with you. Give me your horse, and you shall have mine instead; it is young and strong, and then you need no longer remain in the background, when there is a striving who shall be foremost."

" That bargain," replied Ebbe, " you would hardly stand to, and my horse must be where I am ; he is my greatest treasure."

" Then," said Mette, " your words yesterday were but empty sounds, when you told me you gave me the most valuable thing you owned."

Before Ebbe had time to answer, Mette urged on her horse, and rode from him into the wood. The following day all the knights took their departure from Egeskov, and were invited to return when a month had elapsed, in order that they might know whose gift Mette preferred, and, consequently, whom she chose for her husband. Mette stood on the balcony, and courteously greeted them as they passed ; but when Ebbe, the last of all, rode through the gate, she turned her head away and would not greet him. Dejected at the unlucky result of his visit, he took the road back to Nebbegaard. When he reached that part of the wood where the shepherd from Egeskov was sitting tending his flock, he called to him and said :

" Go and greet the lady Mette from Ebbe, and tell her that when she offered to exchange horses with him yesterday, he refused, because he would not barter his steed ; but that she may know he spoke only the truth, when he said he offered her the dearest thing of all that he possessed, relate what thou hast seen him do."

Ebbe caressed his horse, and when the animal bent down his head on his master's shoulder and neighed with joy, he exclaimed : " I offer thee to Mette's beauty."

At the same moment he drew his sword and killed the horse. Thus closed the " Brudeskue " at Egeskov.

Almost all the knights that had been present felt convinced that Olaf would be the fortunate suitor with Mette and her father, on account of his youth, beauty, and manly accomplishments, and also because he was related to a man of whom Börre would not willingly make an enemy.

On the point of Trelde, surrounded and concealed by a thick forest, there was at that time a castle belonging to a rich and powerful Ness king (or sea-king), named Trolle. His reputation was so great and widespread, that there was not a tract of land in the whole country where he was not known, at least by name. From the beginning of spring until late in the winter he sailed along the coasts of Jutland, Fyen, and Seeland, with his well-manned vessels (Snekker), in order to plunder all the merchantmen he found ; and not unfrequently landed on the coasts, wherever he saw there was an opportunity of carrying off any booty.

Trolle was a man of such extraordinary strength and courage, that he had no need to rely on the number of his companions. He had frequently engaged single-handed against four, and always come off victorious. Although the Danish kings, even at that early period, sought to check these lawless men, who disturbed the peaceable inhabitants of the kingdom, and destroyed all confidence in commerce ; yet there was no one bold enough to encounter Trolle. He laughed at the King's laws, and cared but little for being proclaimed an outlaw. On the ocean he was master wherever his vessels appeared, and his castle at the Ness of Trelde was so well fortified and guarded that he never needed to fear a surprise.

The knight Börre, who was Trolle's nearest neighbour, was not well pleased with the proximity, especially as it often happened that he was aggrieved by the many wanton annoyances he was compelled to submit to during the winter months, at which time the Ness King remained at his castle of Trelde. After enduring many vexations, he resolved on forming a plan to rid himself of his adversary, and just before Christmas sent a secret message to all his neighbours. They came, and it was settled among them that each should quietly assemble as many of his followers as possible, and attack Trolle on the following New Year's eve. When this was arranged, as well as the best method they could adopt for making the attack, they separated, and each returned home.

But the evening after, when all the confederates were assembled at a Yule festivity in the neighbourhood, the Ness King and his men suddenly burst into the apartment, extinguished the lights, made prisoners of five of the knights, and bore them off to Trelde, where they were kept in durance, until they had paid a very large ransom. No one could imagine how Trolle became acquainted with their plan ; but certain it is, that from that time none of his neighbours thought any more of attacking him, considering it more prudent to bear patiently with the annoyances to which he subjected them.

Ebbe's father had been one of the confederates, and his poverty was partly in consequence of the heavy ransom he had been obliged to pay for the recovery of his liberty. One day, just before the festivities took place at Egeskov, Börre went out to hunt, and returned towards evening loaded with game. On coming to the boundary between Egeskov and Trelde, he met Trolle, who also had been out hunting on that day.

"Thanks for the past, Sir Börre," said Trolle with a scornful laugh. "You ride about here killing game in our woods, so that at last I must put a stop to it."

"I have not been hunting on your domain, Trolle," answered Börre; "and the right of hunting here belongs to me."

"It matters little to whom the right of hunting belongs," answered Trolle; "for when you have destroyed all the game in your own woods, the deer will go from mine over to yours; but I think I shall be able to find a remedy for that, when I am so inclined. 'Those who stretch out farthest can embrace the most,' says an old proverb; but this time I will not be so particular, as I hear that Olaf looks with a favourable eye on your daughter."

With these words the Ness King rode back to Trelde. Olaf was the son of the Ness King.

To resume our story. After slaying his horse, Ebbe returned home to Nebbegaard.

A week after this event, his servant came early one morning to tell him that a beautiful horse, ready saddled, stood fastened at the castle-gate, and no one knew to whom it belonged. Greatly surprised, Ebbe went out to look at the horse, which stood proudly and impatiently stamping on the ground. The rein was of crimson silk, on which was embroidered the old proverb:

A straightforward difference is easiest settled.

No sooner had Ebbe read these words than he understood their meaning, and felt pleased and happy in the thought that the horse came from Mette, and in the hope that her present raised in him. He led the horse into the castle, and passed the remainder of the time that Mette had required in riding and exercising it.

At the expiration of the month, the knights again assembled at Egeskov to learn their fate. They were received with equal kindness by Börre and his daughter; and after their repast, the old knight conducted them into the great hall, where all the presents which they had brought on their former visits were displayed on a table. Mette walked at her father's side into the apartment. To the surprise of all, she took up the sword of the poor esquire, kissed the hilt, and said:

"As Ebbe has given me all that he owned, I will return gift for gift, and call him my husband."

No one present expected this. Ebbe fell on his knee before Mette, kissed her hand, and said : " May heaven bless you, Mette, and grant that you may never repent those words, or of the happiness you bestow on so poor a man."

Olaf could hardly control his anger at finding himself supplanted and eclipsed by an obscure esquire. Börre then came forward, and said to Mette : " My daughter, as thou hast chosen him thou thinkest best of, I will now say a word which shall be carried into effect. The last time we were all assembled here, Ebbe had but little luck either in the tournament or the chase ; to-morrow, therefore, at break of day, we will meet in the forest, and afford him an opportunity of proving his manhood."

" 'Tis well," said Ebbe, " be it as you say ; and when the chase is over, I will challenge each of Mette's knightly suitors to single combat with sharp or blunt lances, or with any weapon they may choose."

" That challenge I accept," answered Olaf angrily. " To-morrow we shall hunt, but the day after you shall do battle with me for life or death ; and I will advise the lady Mette, while we are away, to pray that heaven may grant her betrothed better luck than he had the last time our swords met."

" Good luck will come when I stand in need of it," answered Ebbe, " and Mette can spare her prayers until she knows which of us two most requires them."

The next morning at sunrise, all the knights rode out into the forest, to strive which could bring home the largest quantity of game. This time Mette and the other ladies at the castle did not join in the hunt. Towards evening they came back, one after another, and showed Börre the result of their day's sport. They had all assembled, with the exception of Olaf and Ebbe. Mette began to be very uneasy ; she wished most anxiously that Ebbe might bring the greatest share, and could not imagine what detained him so long. At length she began to fear that he and Olaf had met each other in the forest, and had fought together ; but her father calmed her by saying, that before they left in the morning for the chase, each had pledged his word that they would not engage in combat at the hunt.

At length, just as it was growing late, Olaf returned, and that day, as on the former occasion, his success had been greater than that of the others, and every one was now anxious to see what Ebbe would bring home with him. But hour passed after hour, and there were no tidings of him, and Börre gave the signal for the guests to go to table. At the same moment the watchman's horn was heard, and Ebbe came riding into the castle-yard, and greeted the company.

" Well, Sir Ebbe," cried Olaf, in a sarcastic tone, " where is your booty ? It appears you have been as fortunate this time as you were at the last hunt."

" Much game I certainly do not bring," answered Ebbe, coolly, " and what I have was hardly worth the trouble of bringing home ; but at the chase, things go by chance, and one must take what one can get."

" Well ! but, let us see what you bring," cried Börre, impatiently.

" Here it is," said Ebbe, throwing aside his cloak, and casting a human head across the table to Olaf. " Do you know that head ? The crows in the forest are feeding on the carcase."

A cry of surprise was uttered by all the knights present, for in the distorted features each recognised the formidable sea-robber, the Ness King Trolle, Olaf's father. Before the knights had recovered from their astonishment, Ebbe continued : " I have slain that lawless man, Sir Börre, in order to rid you of a troublesome neighbour, and in retribution for the wrong he did to my father. To-morrow I will defend my deed against the knight Olaf, in whatever way he chooses."

But no combat took place between Ebbe and Olaf ; for with the father's death, the son's courage departed, and he thought it not advisable to meet an adversary who had prevailed over the far-dreaded Ness King.

Olaf immediately departed from Egeskov and returned to Trelde. The following day he, together with all Trolle's men, left their castle, and from that time were never seen or heard of more. Some said that Olaf had gone more northward, and settled in Sallingland with his followers, while others thought he had quitted Denmark altogether.

Ebbe's valour gained him great consideration in Börre's family ; he and Mette lived happily together for many years.

GLOB AND ALGER

Danish

BEFORE Jutland was united under one sovereign there were many petty kings there, each of whom had his portion of land to rule over, who were almost always engaged in quarrels and warfare with one another. One of these kings was named Alger ; he ruled over Sallingland. His neighbour was Glob of Fuur, an isle also in the Limfiord, about a mile from Salling. Glob had come from Thy with a great army, and warred with the King of Fuurland, until he at length slew him, drove away his son, and made himself King over the people of Fuur. Alger was thus King in Salling, and Glob in Fuur.

The fugitive prince fled from place to place, without having any fixed abode ; for Glob had declared him an outlaw, and set a price upon his head. At the time these events took place, he lived in a small dwelling in the neighbourhood of Alger's castle at Salling. When Glob had gained a firm footing in Fuurland he resolved on extending his power, and trying whether he could not also become King over Salling. For this purpose he assembled a large army and crossed the fiord ; but his attempt ended by his being driven back with great loss, and it subsequently appeared that he had given up all hostile designs against Alger.

In the meantime Alger, placing but little reliance on Glob's pacific policy, entered into a secret alliance with some of his neighbours, by which they bound themselves to come to his aid with all the force they could bring, as soon as Alger should light the beacons outside his castle, as a sign that the enemy was in the neighbourhood.

When Glob made his attack on Salling, it happened that one of his courtiers, named Birke, saw Alger's daughter Helvig, and became enamoured of her. When the two Kings had settled their quarrel, Birke crossed over to Salling and visited Alger. Glob saw this with pleasure, because, when he asked permission of the King to go, he promised to avail himself of the opportunity to spy out all he could. Alger, on his part, was also glad to see Birke, knowing how high he stood in Glob's favour, and that no one could give better information of the King's intentions and feelings than he.

But it was impossible for Birke to preserve the favour of both princes. When he had been for some time at Alger's, and had nearly obtained the promise of Helvig's hand, his love triumphed, and made him a traitor to Glob, so that he revealed to Alger all the King's plans, informing him that he only waited for an opportunity to make an attack on Salling. This soon reached the ear of Glob, who was bitterly enraged at the conduct of his emissary.

He immediately sent a messenger over to Alger, demanding that he should give up the traitor Birke, also the fugitive Prince Eiler, who had found shelter in his land. Alger refused to comply with either of these demands, and laughed at the threats uttered by the King's messenger.

With regard to Alger's daughter Helvig, her beauty had already called forth a host of suitors who, to gain her favour, vied with each other in knightly games and song, long before Glob came to Fuurland. But Helvig was indifferent to them all; she had secretly engaged herself to the fugitive Eiler, who lived in the neighbourhood of Alger's castle, and was their daily guest. At first she only viewed with pity the unfortunate prince; but this feeling soon turned to fervent love, and Helvig called Heaven to witness that she would rather sink into the grave than choose any other for her husband.

Alger was attached to Eiler, but his interest bade him favour Birke; he therefore commanded Helvig to give her promise to Birke and forget Eiler. But the maiden was not to be persuaded.

Two years had nearly passed, and Glob had taken no hostile steps against Alger. The latter had sent many spies over to Fuur, in order to find out whether Glob had any warlike intentions against him; but the King seemed occupied only in chivalrous games and the chase. He even once sent a messenger over to Sallingland to invite Alger to visit him. Birke advised the King not to go, adding that he knew Glob too well not to feel certain that it was only a stratagem to get him into his power. Alger followed his counsel and remained at home.

It was in the winter, just before Yule, that this invitation was sent from Fuurland to the King. A few days after, Alger had a great banquet, and drank Yule-ale with his guests. Birke in the meanwhile was growing impatient at the long procrastination of his wishes, and obtained Alger's promise that he should have his daughter's consent before the New Year's festivities were over.

In the evening, when all the guests were assembled at the castle, and just as the mirth was at its height, the watchman's horn sounded from the tower. At the same moment a retainer rushed into the hall, announcing that he had seen a number of boats from Fuurland coming in the direction of Salling. Immediately after, another messenger arrived, who related that King Glob had landed with his men, and was burning and destroying everything as he advanced. The guests were paralysed at these unlooked-for tidings. Alger alone retained his self-possession.

"I thought rightly enough," said he, "that Glob would invite himself to our festivity, since I refused to go over to him. It concerns all when the wolf is at the door. Our business is now to receive him in a fitting manner, and that that may take place, I beseech you, my friends, to lend me your aid."

The guests were silent and looked at each other: they had assembled at the castle to drink Yule-ale but not to fight, and Alger plainly saw that their silence signified no less than a refusal. His embarrassment was the greater, as, in consequence of the mildness of the winter, many of his men were gone to sea, to plunder along the coast of Norway.

Before Alger's guests had come to any determination, Helvig entered the hall, and thus addressed them:

"Be it known to all here assembled, that I am the betrothed of Eiler, the son of the late King of Fuurland, and that I would rather endure the greatest sufferings than break my word, were not my father's life and fortune now threatened; but as I see among his guests men who have been suitors for my hand, I say to them, that to him who is able to free us from this danger, I will give myself and be his dutiful wife, so may God help me, as I will keep my promise."

These words had a powerful effect on all. The young were inflamed to daring deeds in the hope of possessing the lovely Helvig, the older were moved by her devotion to her father; and thus they left the castle, firmly resolved to exert all their power to save Alger, and drive Glob from Salling.

The same night, some hours after the guests had departed, while Glob was making preparations to invest the castle on the following day, Helvig left her chamber, and, accompanied by an attendant, glided silently through a secret passage that led into a copse, at the opposite side of which Eiler abode. He was greatly surprised at seeing them enter his dwelling.

"Rise, Eiler," said Helvig, "it is not fitting that thou shouldst sleep when Alger's enemies are awake."

She now related to the Prince the promise that, urged by necessity, she had been obliged to make to her father's guests, and prayed of him to devise some means of anticipating the others. "Take thy sword," added she, "for to-night thy part will be to save thyself, my father, and our youthful love."

She then took leave of him, and the two females returned home.

But Eiler remained motionless and mute long after Helvig's departure. He felt how much depended on immediate action, he wished so heartily to save Alger; but he seemed destitute of all the means necessary for that object. After reflecting some time, he rose, threw a dark cloak over his weapons, and stole into the thicket, towards the spot where Glob had pitched his camp.

There all was life and activity; for the King had resolved upon attempting a storm as soon as daylight appeared, fearing, if he delayed longer, he should be attacked by Alger's friends.

Eiler crept as near as he could to the camp, so that he heard the enemy's men conversing together; but he was concealed from their sight by the rushes on the bank of a deep ditch, which conveyed the water from the Limfiord into the fosses surrounding Alger's castle. Towards morning, Glob had completed his preparations. He had caused a small hut to be raised for himself of turf and hides, in which he hoped to take some rest before the dawn gave the signal for the attack.

All was quiet in the camp.

When the men had lain down to sleep where they best could, Eiler approached softly, and crept along the edge of the ditch, concealed among the rushes, until he had passed the watch. He then walked fearlessly forward. The camp-fires were nearly burnt out, and the darkness veiled his features, so that those of the enemy who were not yet asleep took him for one of their comrades, and let him pass where he pleased.

When he came to the spot where Glob slept, he gently raised the hide which hung before the entrance, and crept into the hut.

The King lay on a bench, wrapped in his scarlet cloak. A torch was burning on a sod, which threw a red glare over the sleeper's countenance. Eiler drew a dagger from his belt, held his breath, and glided noiselessly as a snake towards the bench.

He thought of his father, whom Glob had dethroned and slain ; he thought of the injury he had himself suffered, how his youth had been passed amid dangers and want, during the many years Glob had hunted him as an outlaw from place to place ; he thought also that Glob's death would free Alger from a dangerous foe, and gain for him Helvig, the dear object of all his thoughts ; but yet he hesitated to plunge the dagger in Glob's breast.

The King lay still and motionless in a deep sleep, his hands folded, as if he had fallen asleep while repeating his evening prayer. The longer Eiler looked on him, the more incapable he became of killing the unarmed. He fixed the dagger into the couch close to the King's head ; then left the hut, and stole softly out of the camp, as unobserved and silently as he had entered it.

When he had reached the copse, he continued along the secret path that led up to Alger's castle. He went to the King, informed him of what he had overheard in the enemy's camp, and what he had done. Alger praised Eiler's daring, and, although he might have been freed from a dangerous enemy, who threatened him with destruction, he could not withhold his admiration of the youth's exploit, and would rather live and die with honour than owe his deliverance to treachery and crime. Eiler remained in the castle, resolved to meet his death with the rest of the warriors.

As the morning sun rose over the wood, the horns were sounded in Glob's camp, and the King moved forwards towards the castle with all his men, and the strife began. All went as Alger had predicted ; his force was too weak and small to prevent his enemy from ascending the ramparts, and when the bells over in Fuur sounded for matins, Glob was master of the castle. Alger ordered his men to lay down their arms, and no longer fight against such overwhelming numbers. He then descended into the courtyard, took the royal crown from his head, and laid it at the feet of Glob.

" God's peace, and a kindly greeting to you, my brother," cried Fuurland's King to him, at the same time smilingly lifting off his helmet and wiping his forehead. " You see how anxious I am to enjoy your company by coming to invite you myself ; although you refused to be my guest. But why take off your crown ; I think such a greeting too lowly."

" I give you my crown," answered Alger, " that you may take it as you have taken my castle and my kingdom."

" Take back your crown, brother," replied Glob, " it is shaped to your head, and is much better there than at my feet. And know that I am come to-day with the intention of giving, not of taking."

In saying these words he drew from his belt the dagger which Eiler the previous night had stuck in his couch.

" Look here," said he, " I bring you a knife which one of your people, whoever he may be, left behind him in my tent last night; and we have been obliged to creep over the wall to get in, as you had barred your gates against us. Let me now have a few words with the man who owns this knife."

" The knife is mine," said Eiler, advancing towards the King. " God delivered thy life into my hands, and I spared it, although I have suffered wrongs and bitter misery from thee."

" And was my life really in thy hand, Eiler ? " answered Glob. " Then, as thou hast spared me, I will reward thee in the best way I can; and if I have not enough to give, Alger shall help me. What thinkest thou, my brother ? If thou wilt give Eiler thy daughter, I will give them their outfit. I think that my kingdom of Fuurland will suffice for them. I am an old and childless man, and if Eiler will take reparation for blood, he and Helvig shall be my children."

Alger could hardly believe what he heard, so great was his surprise. He shed tears for joy, as he threw his arms round Glob and pressed him to his breast; and as the horn in the morning sounded for battle, so did the music in the evening resound to the dance; for that same night the marriage of Helvig and Eiler was celebrated.

All Helvig's suitors, who had promised to help Alger against his enemy, arrived at the castle just in time to be present at the wedding.

ARABIAN NIGHTS
1400–1500 A.D.

THE FISHERMAN AND THE GENIE

THERE was formerly an aged fisherman, so poor that he could barely obtain food for himself, his wife, and his three children. He went out early every morning to his employment ; and he had imposed a rule upon himself never to cast his nets above four times a day.

On one occasion he set out before the morn had disappeared. When he reached the seashore, he undressed himself, and cast his nets. In drawing them to land three times in succession, he felt sure from their resistance and weight that he had secured an excellent draught of fish. Instead of which, he only found on the first haul the carcase of an ass ; on the second, a large pannier filled with sand and mud ; and on the third, a large quantity of heavy stones, shells, and filth. It is impossible to describe his disappointment and despair. The day now began to break, and having, like a good Mussulman, finished his prayer, he threw his nets for the fourth time. Again he supposed he had caught a great quantity of fish, as he drew them with as much difficulty as before. He nevertheless found none ; but discovered a heavy vase of yellow copper, shut up and fastened with lead, on which there was the impression of a seal. " I will sell this to a founder," said he with joy, " and with the money I shall get for it I will purchase a measure of corn."

He examined the vase on all sides ; he shook it, but could hear nothing ; and this, together with the impression of the seal on the lead, made him think it was filled with something valuable. In order to find this out, he took his knife and got it open. He directly turned the top downward, and was much surprised to find nothing come out ; he then set it down before him, and while he was attentively observing it there issued from it so thick a smoke that he was obliged to step back a few paces. This smoke, by degrees, rose almost to the clouds, and spread itself over both the water and the shore, appearing like a thick fog. The fisherman, as may easily be imagined, was a good deal surprised at this sight. When the smoke had all come out from the vase, it again collected itself, and became a solid body, and then took the shape of a genie of a gigantic size. The genie, looking at the fisherman, exclaimed, " Humble thyself before me, or I will kill thee."

" And for what reason, pray, will you kill me ? " answered the fisherman ; " have you already forgotten that I have set you at liberty ? "

" I remember it very well," returned he ; " but that shall not prevent my destroying thee, and I will only grant thee one favour."

" And pray what is that ? " said the fisherman.

" It is," replied the genie, " to permit thee to choose the manner of thy death. I can treat thee no otherwise," said the genie ; " and to convince thee of it, hear my history :

" I am one of those spirits who rebelled against the sovereignty of God. Solomon, the son of David, the prophet of God, commanded me to acknowledge his authority, and submit to his laws. I haughtily refused. In order, therefore, to punish me, he enclosed me in this copper vase ; and, to prevent me forcing my way out, he put upon the leaden cover the impression of his seal, on which the great name of God is engraven. This done, he gave the vase to one of those genies who obeyed him, and ordered him to cast me into the sea.

" During the first century of my captivity, I swore that if any one delivered me before the first hundred years were passed, I would make him rich. During the second century, I swore that if any released me, I would discover to him all the treasures of the earth. During the third, I promised to make my deliverer a most powerful monarch, and to grant him every day any three requests he chose. These centuries passed away without any deliverance. Enraged, at last, to be so long a prisoner, I swore that I would, without mercy, kill whoever should in future release me, and that the only favour I would grant him should be, to choose what manner of death he pleased. Since, therefore, thou hast come here to-day, and hast delivered me, fix upon whatever kind of death thou wilt."

The fisherman was in great distress at finding him thus resolved on his death, not so much on his own account as for his three children, whose means of subsistence would be greatly reduced by his death. " Alas ! " he cried, " have pity on me, remember what I have done for thee."

" Let us lose no time," cried the genie ; " your arguments avail not. Make haste, tell me how you wish to die."

Necessity is the mother of invention ; and the fisherman thought of a stratagem. " Since, then," said he, " I cannot escape death, I submit to the will of God ; but before I choose the sort of death, I conjure you, by the great name of God, which is graven upon the seal of the prophet Solomon, the son of David, answer me truly to a question I am going to put to you." The genie trembled at this adjuration, and said to the fisherman, " Ask what thou wilt, and make haste."

" Dare you, then, to swear by the great name of God that you really were in that vase ? This vase cannot contain one of your feet ; how, then, can it hold your whole body ? "

" I swear to thee, notwithstanding," replied he, " that I was there just as thou seest me. Wilt thou not believe me after the solemn oath I have taken ? "

" No, truly," added the fisherman, " I shall not believe you unless I were to see it."

Immediately the form of the genie began to change into smoke, and extended itself, as before, over both the shore and the sea ; and then, collecting itself, began to enter the vase, and continued to do so, in a slow and equal manner, till nothing remained without. The fisherman immediately took the leaden cover, and put it on the vase.

" Genie," he cried, " it is now your turn to ask pardon. I shall throw you again into the sea, and I will build, opposite the very spot where you are cast, a house upon the shore, in which I will live, to warn all fishermen that shall come and throw their nets, not to fish up so evil a genie as thou art, who makest an oath to kill the man who shall set thee at liberty."

The genie tried every argument to move the fisherman's pity, but in vain. " You are too treacherous for me to trust you," returned the fisherman ; " I should deserve to lose my life if I put myself in your power a second time."

THE STORY OF THE ONE-EYED CALENDER[1]

ARABIAN NIGHTS

TO show by what strange accident I became blind of the right eye, I must give you the account of my life. I was yet a youth, when the Sultan, my father (for you must know I am a prince by birth), perceived that I was endowed with good natural ability, and spared nothing proper for improving it. No sooner was I able to read and write, but I learned the Koran from beginning to end by heart, all the traditions collected from the mouth of our prophet, and the works of poets. I applied myself to geography, chronology, and to speak the Arabian language in its purity; not forgetting in the meantime all such exercises as were proper for a prince to understand. But one thing which I was fond of, and succeeded in, was penmanship: wherein I surpassed all the celebrated scribes of our kingdom.

The fame of my learning reached the Emperor of Hindostan, who sent an embassy with rich presents to my father and invited me to his court. I returned with the ambassador.

We had been about a month on our journey, when we saw in the distance an immense cloud of dust, and soon after we discovered fifty fierce horsemen, sons of the desert, well armed.

Not being able to repel force by force, we told them we were the ambassadors of the Sultan of India; but the sons of the desert insolently answered, "Why do you wish us to respect the Sultan, your master? We are not his subjects, nor even within his realm."

They attacked us on all sides. I defended myself as long as I could, but finding that I was wounded, and that the ambassador and all our attendants were overthrown, I took advantage of the remaining strength of my horse, and escaped. My horse was wounded and suddenly fell dead under me. Alone, wounded, and a stranger, I bound up my own wound and walked on the rest of the day, and arrived at the foot of a mountain, where I perceived, as the sun set, a cave; I went

[1] A Calender was a privileged beggar or mendicant pilgrim among the Mohammedans.

in, and stayed there that night, after I had eaten some fruits that I gathered by the way. I continued my journey for several successive days without finding any place of abode; but after a month's time I came to a large town, well inhabited—it was surrounded by several streams, so that it seemed to enjoy perpetual spring.

My face, hands, and feet were black and sunburnt; and by my long journey, my boots were quite worn out, so that I was forced to walk barefooted; and my clothes were all in rags. I entered the town to inform myself where I was, and addressed myself to a tailor that was at work in his shop; who made me sit down by him, and asked me who I was, from whence I came, and what had brought me thither. I did not conceal anything that had befallen me, nor made I any scruple to reveal to him my rank. The tailor listened to me with attention; and brought me something to eat, and offered me an apartment at his house, which I accepted.

Some days after my arrival, the tailor asked me if I knew anything by which I could acquire a livelihood. I told him that I was well versed in the science of laws, both human and divine; that I was a grammarian, a poet, and, above all, that I wrote remarkably well. "None of these things will avail you here. If you will follow my advice," he added, "you will procure a short jacket, and as you are strong and in good health, you may go into the neighbouring forest, and cut wood for fuel. You may then go and expose it for sale in the market. By these means, you will be enabled to wait till the cloud which hangs over you, and obliges you to conceal your birth, shall have blown over. I will furnish you with a cord and hatchet."

The next day the tailor brought me a rope, a hatchet, and a short jacket, and recommended me to some poor people who gained their bread after the same manner, that they might take me into their company. They conducted me to the wood, and the first day I brought in as much upon my head as procured me half a piece of gold of the money of that country; for though the wood was not far distant from the town, yet it was very scarce, by reason that few would be at the trouble of fetching it for themselves. I gained a good sum of money in a short time, and repaid my tailor what he had lent me.

I continued this way of living for a whole year. One day, having by chance penetrated farther into the wood than usual, I happened to light on a pleasant spot, where I began to cut; and in pulling up the root of a tree I espied an iron ring, fastened to a trap-door of the same metal. I took away the earth that covered it, and having lifted it up, discovered a flight of stairs, which I descended with my axe in my hand.

When I reached the bottom, I found myself in a palace, which was as well lighted as if it had been above ground in the open air. I went forward along a gallery supported by pillars of jasper, the base and capitals being of massy gold: when I saw a lady of a noble and graceful air, and extremely beautiful, coming toward me. I hastened to meet her; and as I was making a low obeisance, she asked me, "Are you a man, or a genie?"

"A man, madam," said I.

"By what adventure," said she (fetching a deep sigh), "are you come hither? I have lived here twenty-five years, and you are the first man I have beheld in that time."

Her great beauty, and the sweetness and civility wherewith she received me, emboldened me to say, "Madam, before I satisfy your curiosity, give me leave to say that I am infinitely gratified with this unexpected meeting, which offers me an occasion of consolation in the midst of my affliction; and perhaps it may give me an opportunity of making you also more happy than you are."

I then related my story to her from beginning to end.

"Alas! Prince," she replied, sighing, "the most enchanting spots cannot afford delight when we are there against our wills. But hear now my history. I am a princess, the daughter of a sultan, the King of the Ebony Island, to which the precious wood found in it has given its name.

"The King, my father, had chosen for my husband a prince, who was my cousin; but on the very night of the bridal festivities, in the midst of the rejoicings of the court, a genie took me away. I fainted with alarm, and when I recovered I found myself in this place. I was long inconsolable; but time and necessity have reconciled me to see the genie. Twenty-five years I have passed in this place, in which I have everything necessary for life and splendour.

"Every ten days," continued the Princess, "the genie visits me. In the meantime, if I have any occasion for him, I have only to touch a talisman, and he appears. It is now four days since he was here, and I have therefore to wait six days more before he again makes his appearance. You, therefore, may remain five with me, if it be agreeable to you, in order to keep me company; and I will endeavour to regale and entertain you equal to your merit and dignity."

The Princess then conducted me to a bath, the most commodious and the most sumptuous imaginable ; and when I came forth, instead of my own clothes I found another costly robe, which I did not esteem so much for its richness, as because it made me appear worthy to be in her company. We sat down on a sofa covered with rich tapestry, with cushions of the rarest Indian brocade ; and some time after she covered a table with several dishes of delicate meats. We ate, and passed the remaining part of the day, as also the evening, together very pleasantly.

The next day I said to her, " Fair Princess, you have been too long buried alive in this subterranean palace ; pray rise—follow me and enjoy the light of day, of which you have been deprived so many years."

" Prince," replied she, with a smile, " if you out of ten days will grant me nine, and resign the tenth to the genie, the light of day would be nothing to me."

" Princess," said I, " the fear of the genie makes you speak thus ; for my part I regard him so little, that I will break in pieces his talisman, with the spell that is written about it. Let him come ; and how brave or powerful he be, I will defy him."

On saying this I gave the talisman a kick with my foot, and broke it in pieces.

The talisman was no sooner broken than the whole palace shook as if ready to fall to atoms, and the walls opened to afford a passage to the genie. I had no sooner felt the shock than, at the earnest request of the Princess, I took to flight. Having hastily put on my own robe, I ascended the stairs leading to the forest, and reached the town in safety. My landlord, the tailor, was very glad to see me. I had, however, in my haste, left my hatchet and cord in the Princess's chamber. Shortly after my return, while brooding over this loss, and lamenting the cruel treatment to which the Princess would be exposed, the tailor came in and said, " An old man, whom I do not know, brings your hatchet and cord, and wishes to speak to you, for he will deliver them to none but yourself."

At these words I changed colour, and fell a-trembling. While the tailor was asking me the reason, my chamber door opened, and the old man, having no patience to stay, appeared with my hatchet and cord " I am a genie," said he, speaking to me, " a grandson of Eblis, prince of genies. Is not this your hatchet and is not this your cord ? "

After the genie had put these questions to me he gave me no time to answer. He grasped me by the middle, dragged me out of the chamber, and mounting into the air carried me up to the skies with extraordinary swiftness. He descended again in like manner to the earth, which on a sudden he caused to open with a stroke of his foot, when I found myself in the enchanted palace, before the fair Princess of the Isle of Ebony. But, alas! what a spectacle was there! I saw what pierced me to the heart; this poor Princess was weltering in her blood, and lay upon the ground, more like one dead than alive, with her cheeks bathed in tears.

The genie having loaded us both with many insults and reproaches, drew his scimitar and declared that he would give life and liberty to either of us who would with his scimitar cut off the head of the other. We both resolutely declined to purchase freedom at such a price, and asserted our choice to be to die rather in the presence of each other.

"I see," said the genie, "that you both outbrave me, but both of you shall know by my treatment of you of what I am capable."

At these words the monster took up the scimitar and cut off one of her hands, which left her only so much life as to give me a token with the other that she bade me for ever adieu; and then she died. I fainted at the sight. When I was come to myself again, I cried, "Strike, for I am ready to die, and await death as the greatest favour you can show me."

But instead of killing me, he said, "Behold how genies revenge themselves on those who offend them. Thou art the least to blame and I will content myself with transforming thee into a dog, ape, lion, or bird; take thy choice of any of these, I will leave it to thyself."

These words gave me some hope of being able to appease him.

"O genie," said I, "restrain your rage, and since you will not take away my life, pardon me freely, as a good dervish pardoned one who envied him."

"And how was that?" said he.

Whereupon I told the story to the genie, employing all my eloquence to persuade him to imitate so good an example, and to grant me pardon; but it was impossible to move his compassion.

"All that I can do for thee," said he, "is to grant thee thy life, but I must place thee under enchantments." So saying, he seized me violently, and carried me through the arched roof of the subterraneous palace, which opened to give him passage. He ascended with me into the air to such a height that the earth appeared like a little white cloud. He then descended again like lightning, and alighted upon the summit of a mountain.

Here he took up a handful of earth, and, muttering some words which I did not understand, threw it upon me. "Quit," said he, "the form of a man and take that of an ape." He instantly disappeared, and left me alone, transformed into an ape, and overwhelmed with sorrow, in a strange country, not knowing whether I was near or far from my father's dominions.

I descended the mountain, and entered a plain, level country, which took me a month to travel over, and then I came to the seaside. It happened at the time to be perfectly calm, and I espied a vessel about half a league from the shore. Unwilling to lose so good an opportunity I broke off a large branch from a tree, carried it into the sea, and placed myself astride upon it, with a stick in each hand, to serve me for oars.

I launched out on this frail bark, and rowed toward the ship. When I had approached sufficiently near to be seen, the seamen and passengers on the deck regarded me with astonishment. In the meantime I got on board, and laying hold of a rope, jumped upon the deck, but having lost my speech, I found myself in great perplexity; and indeed the risk I ran was not less than when I was at the mercy of the genie.

The merchants, being both superstitious and scrupulous, thought if they received me on board I should be the occasion of some misfortune to them during their voyage. On this account they said, "Let us throw him into the sea." Some one of them would not have failed to carry this threat into execution, had I not gone to the captain, thrown myself at his feet, and taken hold of his skirt in a supplicating posture. This action, together with the tears which he saw gush from my eyes, moved his compassion. He took me under his protection, and loaded me with a thousand caresses. On my part, though I had not power to speak, I showed by my gestures every mark of gratitude in my power.

The wind that succeeded the calm continued to blow in the same direction for fifty days, and brought us safe to the port of a city, well peopled, and of great trade, where we cast anchor.

Our vessel was instantly surrounded with multitudes of boats full of people. Among the rest, some officers of the Sultan came on board, and said, "Our master rejoices in your safe arrival, and he beseeches each of you to write a few lines upon this roll. The Grand Vizier, who, besides possessing great abilities for the management of public affairs could write in the highest perfection, died a few days since, and the Sultan has made a solemn vow not to give the place to any one who cannot write equally well. No one in the empire has been judged worthy to supply the Vizier's place."

Those of the merchants who thought they could write well enough to aspire to this high dignity wrote one after another what they thought fit. After they had done, I advanced, and took the roll, but all the people cried out that I would tear it or throw it into the sea, till they saw how properly I held the roll, and made a sign that I would write in my turn. Their apprehensions then changed into wonder. However, as they had never seen an ape that could write, and could not be persuaded that I was more ingenious than others of my kind, they wished to take the roll out of my hand; but the captain took my part once more. "Let him alone," said he; "allow him to write." Perceiving that no one opposed my design, I took the pen, and wrote six sorts of hands used among the Arabians, and each specimen contained an extemporary distich or quatrain (a stanza of four lines) in praise of the Sultan. When I had done, the officers took the roll, and carried it to the Sultan.

The Sultan took little notice of any of the writings except mine, which pleased him so much that he said to the officers, "Take the finest horse in my stable, with the richest trappings, and a robe of the most sumptuous brocade to put on the person who wrote the six hands, and bring him hither."

At this command the officers could not forbear laughing. The Sultan was incensed at their rudeness, and would have punished them, had they not explained. "Sir," said they, "we humbly beg your Majesty's pardon. These hands were not written by a man, but by an ape."

"What do you say?" exclaimed the Sultan. "Those admirable characters, are they not written by the hands of a man?"

"No, sir," replied the officers; "we assure your Majesty that it was an ape, who wrote them in our presence."

The Sultan was too much surprised at this account not to desire a sight of me, and therefore said, "Do what I command you, and bring me speedily that wonderful ape."

The officers returned to the vessel, and showed the captain their order, who answered, "The Sultan's command must be obeyed." Whereupon they clothed me with the rich brocade robe, and carried me ashore, where they set me on horseback, while the Sultan waited for me at his palace with a great number of courtiers.

The procession commenced; the harbour, the streets, the public places, windows, terraces, palaces, and houses were filled with an infinite number of people of all ranks, who flocked from every part of the city to see me; for the rumour was spread in a moment that the Sultan had chosen an ape to be his Grand Vizier; and after having served for a spectacle to the people, who could not forbear to express their surprise by redoubling their shouts and cries, I arrived at the Sultan's palace.

I found the Prince on his throne in the midst of the grandees; I made my obeisance three times very low, and at last kneeled and kissed the ground before him, and afterward took my seat in the posture of an ape. The whole assembly viewed me with admiration, and could not comprehend how it was possible that an ape should so well understand how to pay the Sultan his due respect; and he himself was more astonished than any. In short, the usual ceremony of the audience would have been complete, could I have added speech to my behaviour.

The Sultan dismissed his courtiers, and none remained by him but the chief of the attendants of the palace, a little young slave, and myself. He went from his chamber of audience into his own apartment, where he ordered dinner to be brought. As he sat at table, he made me a sign to approach and eat with them; to show my obedience, I kissed the ground, arose, and placed myself at the table, and ate.

Before the table was cleared, I espied a standish, which I made a sign to have brought me; having got it, I wrote upon a large peach some verses expressive of my acknowledgment to the Sultan; who, having read them, after I had presented the peach to him, was still more astonished. When the things were removed, they brought him a particular liquor, of which he caused them to give me a glass. I drank, and wrote upon the glass some new verses, which explained the state of happiness I was now in, after many sufferings. The Sultan read these likewise, and said, "A man that was capable of composing such poetry would rank among the greatest of men."

The Sultan caused to be brought to him a chess-board, and asked me by a sign if I understood that game, and would play with him. I kissed the ground; and laying my hand upon my head, signified that I was ready to receive that honour. He won the first game; but I won the second and third; and perceiving he was somewhat displeased at my success, I made a stanza to pacify him, in which I told him that two potent armies had been fighting furiously all day, but that they concluded a peace toward the evening, and passed the remaining part of the night very amicably together upon the field of battle.

So many circumstances appearing to the Sultan beyond what had ever either been seen or known of apes, he determined not to be the only witness of these prodigies himself, but having a daughter, called the Lady of Beauty, sent for her, that she should share his pleasure.

The Princess, who had her face unveiled, no sooner came into the room than she put on her veil, and said to the Sultan, " Sir, I am surprised that you have sent for me to appear before men. That seeming ape is a young Prince, son of a powerful Sultan, and has been metamorphosed into an ape by enchantment. When I was just out of the nursery, an old lady who waited on me was a most expert magician, and taught me seventy rules of magic. By this science I know all enchanted persons at first sight: I know who they are, and by whom they have been enchanted; therefore do not be surprised if I should forthwith restore this Prince, in spite of the enchantments, to his own form."

" Do so, then," interrupted the Sultan, " for you cannot give me greater pleasure, as I wish to have him for my Grand Vizier, and bestow you upon him for a wife."

" I am ready, sire," answered the Princess, " to obey you in all things you please to command."

The Princess, the Lady of Beauty, went into her apartment, and brought thence a knife, which had some Hebrew words engraven on the blade: she made the Sultan, the little slave, and myself, descend into a private court of the palace, and there left us under a gallery that went round it. She placed herself in the middle of the court, where she made a great circle, and within it she wrote several words in ancient Arabian characters.

When she had finished and prepared the circle, she placed herself in the centre of it, where she began incantations, and repeated verses of the Koran. The air grew insensibly dark, as if it had been night; we found ourselves struck with consternation, and our fear increased when we saw the genie appear suddenly in the shape of a lion of gigantic size.

" Thou shalt pay dearly," said the lion, " for the trouble thou hast given me in coming here." In saying this, he opened his horrible jaws, and advanced forward to devour her ; but she, being on her guard, jumped back, and had just time to pluck out a hair ; and pronouncing two or three words, she changed it into a sharp scythe, with which she immediately cut the lion in two pieces, through the middle.

The two parts of the lion directly disappeared, and the head changed into a large scorpion. The Princess then took the form of a serpent, and fought the scorpion, which, finding itself defeated, changed into an eagle, and flew away. But the serpent then became another eagle, black, and very large, and went in pursuit of it. We now lost sight of them for some time.

Shortly after they had disappeared, the earth opened before us, and a black and white cat appeared, the hairs of which stood quite on end, and which made a most horrible mewing. A black wolf directly followed after her, and gave her no time to rest. The cat, being thus hard pressed, changed into a worm, and hid itself in a pomegranate which lay by accident on the ground ; but the pomegranate swelled immediately, and became as big as a gourd, which, lifting itself up to the roof of the gallery, rolled there for some time backward and forward ; it then fell down again into the court, and broke into several pieces.

The wolf had in the meanwhile transformed itself into a cock, and now fell to picking up the seeds of the pomegranate one after another ; but finding no more, he came toward us with his wings spread, making a great noise, as if he would ask us whether there were any more seed. There was one lying on the brink of the canal, which the cock perceiving as he went back, ran speedily thither ; but just as he was going to pick it up the seed rolled into a fountain and turned into a little fish.

The cock, flying toward the fountain, turned into a pike, and pursued the small fish ; they continued both under water above two hours, and we knew not what was become of them ; but suddenly we heard terrible cries, which made us tremble, and a little while after we saw the genie and Princess all in flames. They threw flashes of fire out of their mouths at each other, till they came to close combat ; then the two fires increased, with a thick, burning smoke, which mounted so high that we had reason to apprehend it would set the palace on fire.

But we very soon had a more pressing occasion of fear, for the genie having got loose from the Princess, came to the gallery where we stood, and blew flames of fire upon us. We must all have perished had not the Princess, running to our assistance, forced him to retire, and defend himself against her; yet, notwithstanding all her exertions, she could not hinder the Sultan's beard from being burned, and his face scorched, and a spark from entering my right eye, and making it blind. The Sultan and I expected nothing but death, when we heard a cry of "Victory, victory!" and instantly the Princess appeared in her natural shape; but the genie was reduced to a heap of ashes.

The Princess approached us and hastily called for a cupful of water, which the young slave, who had received no hurt, brought her. She took it, and after pronouncing some words over it, threw it upon me saying, "If thou art become an ape by enchantment, change thy shape, and take that of a man, which thou hadst before." These words were hardly uttered, when I again became a man in every respect as I was before my transformation, excepting the loss of my eye.

I was preparing to return the Princess my thanks, but she prevented me by addressing herself to her father: "Sire, I have gained the victory over the genie; but it is a victory that costs me dear. I have but a few minutes to live; the fire has pierced me during the terrible combat, and I find it is gradually consuming me. This would not have happened, had I perceived the last of the pomegranate seeds, and swallowed it, as I did the others when I was changed into a cock; the genie had fled thither as to his last intrenchment, and upon that the success of the combat depended. This oversight obliged me to have recourse to fire, and to fight with those mighty arms as I did, between heaven and earth, in your presence; for in spite of all, I made the genie know that I understood more than he; I have conquered and reduced him to ashes, but I cannot escape death, which is approaching."

Suddenly the Princess exclaimed, "I burn, I burn!" She found that the fire had at last seized upon her vital parts, which made her still cry, "I burn"; until death had put an end to her intolerable pains. The effect of that fire was so extraordinary, that in a few moments she was wholly reduced to ashes, as the genie had been.

I cannot tell you how much I was grieved at so dismal a spectacle; I had rather all my life have continued an ape or a dog, than to have seen my benefactress thus miserably perish. The Sultan cried piteously, and beat himself on his head and breast, until, being quite overcome with grief, he fainted away. In the meantime, the attendants and officers came running at the Sultan's lamentations, and with much difficulty brought him to himself.

When the knowledge of the death of the Princess had spread through the palace and the city, all the people greatly bewailed. Public mourning was observed for seven days, and many ceremonies were performed. The ashes of the genie were thrown into the air ; but those of the Princess were collected into a precious urn, to be preserved ; and the urn was deposited in a superb mausoleum constructed for that purpose on the spot where the Princess had been consumed.

The grief of the Sultan for the loss of his daughter confined him to his chamber for a whole month. Before he had fully recovered his strength, he sent for me and said, " You are the cause of all these misfortunes ; depart hence therefore in peace, without further delay, and take care never to appear again in my dominions on penalty of thy life."

I was obliged to quit the palace, again cast down to a low estate, and an outcast from the world. Before I left the city, I went into a bagnio, where I caused my beard and eyebrows to be shaved, and put on a calender's robe. I passed through many countries without making myself known ; at last I resolved to visit Bagdad, in hope of meeting with the Commander of the Faithful, to move his compassion by relating to him my unfortunate adventures.

ALI BABA AND THE FORTY THIEVES

Arabian Nights

THERE once lived in a town of Persia two brothers, one named Cassim and the other Ali Baba. Their father divided a small inheritance equally between them. Cassim married a very rich wife, and became a wealthy merchant. Ali Baba married a woman as poor as himself, and lived by cutting wood, and bringing it upon three asses into the town to sell.

One day, when Ali Baba was in the forest, and had just cut wood enough to load his asses, he saw at a distance a great cloud of dust, which seemed to approach him. He observed it with attention, and distinguished soon after a body of horsemen, who he suspected might be robbers. He determined to leave his asses to save himself. He climbed up a large tree, planted on a high rock, whose branches were thick enough to conceal him, and yet enabled him to see all that passed without being discovered.

The troop, who were to the number of forty, all well mounted and armed, came to the foot of the rock on which the tree stood, and there dismounted. Every man unbridled his horse, tied him to some shrub, and hung about his neck a bag of corn which they brought behind them. Then each of them took off his saddle-bag, which seemed to Ali Baba to be full of gold and silver from its weight. One, whom he took to be their captain, came under the tree in which Ali Baba was concealed; and making his way through some shrubs, pronounced these words: "Open, Sesame!"[1] As soon as the captain of the robbers had thus spoken, a door opened in the rock; and after he had made all his troop enter before him, he followed them, when the door shut again of itself.

The robbers stayed some time within the rock, during which Ali Baba, fearful of being caught, remained in the tree.

At last the door opened again, and as the captain went in last, so he came out first, and stood to see them all pass by him, when Ali Baba heard him make the door close by pronouncing these words,

[1] "Sesame" is a small grain.

" Shut, Sesame ! " Every man at once went and bridled his horse, fastened his wallet, and mounted again. When the captain saw them all ready, he put himself at their head, and they returned the way they had come.

Ali Baba followed them with his eyes as far as he could see them ; and afterward stayed a considerable time before he descended. Remembering the words the captain of the robbers used to cause the door to open and shut, he had the curiosity to try if his pronouncing them would have the same effect. Accordingly, he went among the shrubs, and perceiving the door concealed behind them, stood before it, and said, " Open, Sesame ! " The door instantly flew wide open.

Ali Baba, who expected a dark, dismal cavern, was surprised to see a well-lighted and spacious chamber, which received the light from an opening at the top of the rock, and in which were all sorts of provisions, rich bales of silk, stuff, brocade, and valuable carpeting, piled upon one another ; gold and silver ingots in great heaps, and money in bags. The sight of all these riches made him suppose that this cave must have been occupied for ages by robbers, who had succeeded one another.

Ali Baba went boldly into the cave, and collected as much of the gold coin, which was in bags, as he thought his three asses could carry. When he had loaded them with the bags, he laid wood over them in such a manner that they could not be seen. When he had passed in and out as often as he wished, he stood before the door, and pronouncing the words, " Shut, Sesame ! " the door closed of itself. He then made the best of his way to town.

When Ali Baba got home, he drove his asses into a little yard, shut the gates very carefully, threw off the wood that covered the panniers, carried the bags into his house, and ranged them in order before his wife. He then emptied the bags, which raised such a great heap of gold as dazzled his wife's eyes, and then he told her the whole adventure from beginning to end, and, above all, recommended her to keep it secret.

The wife rejoiced greatly at their good fortune, and would count all the gold piece by piece. " Wife," replied Ali Baba, " you do not know what you undertake, when you pretend to count the money ; you will never have done. I will dig a hole, and bury it. There is no time to be lost."

" You are in the right, husband," replied she, " but let us know, as nigh as possible, how much we have. I will borrow a small measure, and measure it, while you dig the hole."

Away the wife ran to her brother-in-law Cassim, who lived just by, and addressing herself to his wife, desired her to lend her a measure for a little while. Her sister-in-law asked her whether she would have a great or a small one. The other asked for a small one. She bade her stay a little, and she would readily fetch one.

The sister-in-law did so, but as she knew Ali Baba's poverty, she was curious to know what sort of grain his wife wanted to measure, and artfully putting some suet at the bottom of the measure, brought it to her, with an excuse that she was sorry that she had made her stay so long, but that she could not find it sooner.

Ali Baba's wife went home, set the measure upon the heap of gold, filled it, and emptied it often upon the sofa, till she had done, when she was very well satisfied to find the number of measures amounted to so many as they did, and went to tell her husband, who had almost finished digging the hole. While Ali Baba was burying the gold, his wife, to show her exactness and diligence to her sister-in-law, carried the measure back again, but without taking notice that a piece of gold had stuck to the bottom. " Sister," said she, giving it to her again, " you see that I have not kept your measure long. I am obliged to you for it, and return it with thanks."

As soon as Ali Baba's wife was gone, Cassim's looked at the bottom of the measure, and was in inexpressible surprise to find a piece of gold sticking to it. Envy immediately possessed her breast. " What ! " said she, " has Ali Baba gold so plentiful as to measure it ? Whence has he all this wealth ? "

Cassim, her husband, was at his counting-house. When he came home, his wife said to him, " Cassim, I know you think yourself rich, but Ali Baba is infinitely richer than you. He does not count his money, but measures it." Cassim desired her to explain the riddle, which she did, by telling him the stratagem she had used to make the discovery, and showed him the piece of money, which was so old that they could not tell in what prince's reign it was coined.

Cassim, after he had married the rich widow, had never treated Ali Baba as a brother, but neglected him ; and now, instead of being pleased, he conceived a base envy at his brother's prosperity. He could not sleep all that night, and went to him in the morning before sunrise. " Ali Baba," said he, " I am surprised at you ; you pretend to be miserably poor, and yet you measure gold. My wife found this at the bottom of the measure you borrowed yesterday."

By this discourse, Ali Baba perceived that Cassim and his wife, through his own wife's folly, knew what they had so much reason to conceal; but what was done could not be undone. Therefore, without showing the least surprise or trouble, he confessed all, and offered his brother part of his treasure to keep the secret.

"I expect as much," replied Cassim haughtily; "but I must know exactly where this treasure is, and how I may visit it myself when I choose; otherwise, I will go and inform against you, and then you will not only get no more, but will lose all you have, and I shall have a share for my information."

Ali Baba told him all he desired, even to the very words he was to use to gain admission into the cave.

Cassim rose the next morning long before the sun, and set out for the forest with ten mules bearing great chests, which he designed to fill, and followed the road which Ali Baba had pointed out to him. He was not long before he reached the rock, and found out the place, by the tree and other marks which his brother had given him. When he reached the entrance of the cavern, he pronounced the words, "Open, Sesame!"

The door immediately opened, and, when he was in, closed upon him. In examining the cave, he was in great admiration to find much more riches than he had expected from Ali Baba's relation. He quickly laid as many bags of gold as he could carry at the door of the cavern; but his thoughts were so full of the great riches he should possess, that he could not think of the necessary word to make it open, but instead of "Sesame," said, "Open, Barley!" and was much amazed to find that the door remained fast shut. He named several sorts of grain, but still the door would not open.

Cassim had never expected such an incident, and was so alarmed at the danger he was in, that the more he endeavoured to remember the word "Sesame," the more his memory was confounded, and he had as much forgotten it as if he had never heard it mentioned. He threw down the bags he had loaded himself with, and walked distractedly up and down the cave, without having the least regard to the riches that were round him.

About noon the robbers visited their cave. At some distance they saw Cassim's mules straggling about the rock, with great chests on their backs. Alarmed at this, they galloped at full speed to the cave. They drove away the mules, who strayed through the forest so far that they were soon out of sight, and went directly, with their naked sabres in their hands, to the door, which, on their captain pronouncing the proper words, immediately opened.

Cassim, who heard the noise of the horses' feet, at once guessed the arrival of the robbers, and resolved to make one effort for his life. He rushed to the door, and no sooner saw the door open than he ran out and threw the leader down, but could not escape the other robbers, who with their scimitars soon deprived him of life.

The first care of the robbers after this was to examine the cave. They found all the bags which Cassim had brought to the door, to be ready to load his mules, and carried them again to their places, but they did not miss what Ali Baba had taken away before. Then holding a council, and deliberating upon this occurrence, they guessed that Cassim, when he was in, could not get out again, but could not imagine how he had learned the secret words by which alone he could enter. They could not deny the fact of his being there; and to terrify any person or accomplice, who should attempt the same thing, they agreed to cut Cassim's body into four quarters—to hang two on one side and two on the other, within the door of the cave.

They had no sooner taken this resolution than they put it in execution; and when they had nothing more to detain them, left the place of their hoards well closed. They mounted their horses, went to beat the roads again, and to attack the caravans they might meet.

In the meantime, Cassim's wife was very uneasy when night came and her husband was not returned. She ran to Ali Baba in great alarm, and said: "I believe, brother-in-law, that you know Cassim is gone to the forest, and upon what account; it is now night, and he has not returned; I am afraid some misfortune has happened to him." Ali Baba told her that she need not frighten herself, for that certainly Cassim would not think it proper to come into the town till the night should be pretty far advanced.

Cassim's wife, considering how much it concerned her husband to keep the business secret, was the more easily persuaded to believe her brother-in-law. She went home again, and waited patiently till midnight. Then her fear redoubled, and her grief was the more sensible because she was forced to keep it to herself. She repented of her foolish curiosity, and cursed her desire of prying into the affairs of her brother- and sister-in-law. She spent all the night in weeping; and as soon as it was day went to them, telling them, by her tears, the cause of her coming.

Ali Baba did not wait for his sister-in-law to desire him to go to see what was become of Cassim, but departed immediately with his three asses, begging of her first to moderate her affliction. He went to the forest, and when he came near the rock, having seen neither his brother nor the mules in his way, was seriously alarmed at finding some blood spilt near the door, which he took for an ill omen; but when he had pronounced the word, and the door had opened, he was struck with horror at the dismal sight of his brother's body.

He was not long in determining how he should pay the last dues to his brother; but without adverting to the little fraternal affection he had shown for him, went into the cave, to find something to enshroud his remains; and having loaded one of his asses with them, covered them over with wood. The other two asses he loaded with bags of gold, covering them with wood also as before; and then bidding the door shut, came away; but was so cautious as to stop some time at the end of the forest, that he might not go into the town before night. When he came home, he drove the asses loaded with gold into his little yard, and left the care of unloading them to his wife, while he led the other to his sister-in-law's house.

Ali Baba knocked at the door, which was opened by Morgiana, a clever, intelligent slave, who was fruitful in inventions to meet the most difficult circumstances. When he came into the court, he unloaded the ass, and taking Morgiana aside, said to her: "You must observe an inviolable secrecy. Your master's body is contained in these two panniers. We must bury him as if he had died a natural death. Go now and tell your mistress. I leave the matter to your wit and skilful devices."

Ali Baba helped to place the body in Cassim's house, again recommended to Morgiana to act her part well, and then returned with his ass.

Morgiana went out early the next morning to a druggist, and asked for a sort of lozenge which was considered efficacious in the most dangerous disorders. The apothecary inquired who was ill. She replied, with a sigh: "Her good master, Cassim himself: and that he could neither eat nor speak."

In the evening Morgiana went to the same druggist's again, and with tears in her eyes asked for an essence which they used to give to sick people only when at the last extremity. " Alas ! " said she, taking it from the apothecary, " I am afraid that this remedy will have no better effect than the lozenges ; and that I shall lose my good master."

On the other hand, as Ali Baba and his wife were often seen to go between Cassim's and their own house all that day, and to seem melancholy, nobody was surprised in the evening to hear the lamentable shrieks and cries of Cassim's wife and Morgiana, who gave out everywhere that her master was dead. The next morning, at daybreak, Morgiana went to an old cobbler whom she knew to be always early at his stall, and, bidding him good-morrow, put a piece of gold into his hand, saying, " Baba Mustapha, you must bring with you your sewing tackle, and come with me ; but I must tell you, I shall blindfold you when you come to such a place."

Baba Mustapha seemed to hesitate a little at these words. " Oh ! oh ! " replied he, " you would have me do something against my conscience, or against my honour ? "

" God forbid," said Morgiana, putting another piece of gold into his hand, " that I should ask anything that is contrary to your honour ! only come along with me and fear nothing."

Baba Mustapha went with Morgiana, who, after she had bound his eyes with a handkerchief at the place she had mentioned, conveyed him to her deceased master's house, and never unloosed his eyes till he had entered the room where she had put the corpse together. " Baba Mustapha," said she, " you must make haste and sew the parts of this body together ; and when you have done I will give you another piece of gold."

After Baba Mustapha had finished his task, she blindfolded him again, gave him the third piece of gold as she had promised, and recommending secrecy to him carried him back to the place where she first bound his eyes, pulled off the bandage, and let him go home, but watched him that he returned toward his stall till he was quite out of sight, for fear he should have the curiosity to return and dodge her ; she then went home.

Morgiana, on her return, warmed some water to wash the body, and at the same time Ali Baba perfumed it with incense, and wrapped it in the burying clothes with the accustomed ceremonies. Not long after the proper officer brought the bier, and when the attendants of the mosque, whose business it was to wash the dead, offered to perform their duty, she told them that it was done already.

Shortly after this, the imaum and the other ministers of the mosque arrived. Four neighbours carried the corpse to the burying-ground, following the imaum, who recited some prayers. Ali Baba came after with some neighbours, who often relieved the others in carrying the bier to the burying-ground. Morgiana, a slave to the deceased, followed in the procession, weeping, beating her breast, and tearing her hair. Cassim's wife stayed at home mourning, uttering lamentable cries with the women of the neighbourhood, who came, according to custom, during the funeral, and, joining their lamentations with hers, filled the quarter far and near with sounds of sorrow.

In this manner Cassim's melancholy death was concealed and hushed up between Ali Baba, his widow, and Morgiana, his slave, with so much contrivance that nobody in the city had the least knowledge or suspicion of the cause of it. Three or four days after the funeral, Ali Baba removed his few goods openly to his sister-in-law's house, in which it was agreed that he should in future live ; but the money he had taken from the robbers he conveyed thither by night. As for Cassim's warehouse, he entrusted it entirely to the management of his eldest son.

While these things were being done, the forty robbers again visited their retreat in the forest. Great, then, was their surprise to find Cassim's body taken away, with some of their bags of gold. " We are certainly discovered," said the captain. " The removal of the body, and the loss of some of our money, plainly shows that the man whom we killed had an accomplice : and for our own lives' sake we must try and find him. What say you, my lads ? "

All the robbers unanimously approved of the captain's proposal.

" Well," said the captain, " one of you, the boldest and most skilful among you, must go into the town, disguised as a traveller and a stranger, to try if he can hear any talk of the man whom we have killed, and endeavour to find out who he was and where he lived. This is a matter of the first importance, and for fear of any treachery I propose that whoever undertakes this business without success, even though the failure arises only from an error of judgment, shall suffer death."

Without waiting for the sentiments of his companions, one of the robbers started up, and said : " I submit to this condition, and think it an honour to expose my life to serve the troop."

After this robber had received great commendations from the captain and his comrades, he disguised himself so that nobody would take him for what he was ; and taking his leave of the troop that night, went into the town just at daybreak ; and walked up and down, till accidentally he came to Baba Mustapha's stall, which was always open before any of the shops.

Baba Mustapha was seated with an awl in his hand, just going to work. The robber saluted him, bidding him good-morrow ; and perceiving that he was old, said : " Honest man, you begin to work very early ; is it possible that one of your age can see so well ? I question, even if it were somewhat lighter, whether you could see to stitch."

" You do not know me," replied Baba Mustapha ; " for old as I am, I have extraordinarily good eyes ; and you will not doubt it when I tell you that I sewed the body of a dead man together in a place where I had not so much light as I have now."

" A dead body ! " exclaimed the robber, with affected amazement.

" Yes, yes," answered Baba Mustapha, " I see you want to have me speak out, but you shall know no more."

The robber felt sure that he had discovered what he sought. He pulled out a piece of gold, and putting it into Baba Mustapha's hand, said to him : " I do not want to learn your secret, though I can assure you you might safely trust me with it. The only thing I desire of you is to show me the house where you stitched up the dead body."

" If I were disposed to do you that favour," replied Baba Mustapha, " I assure you I cannot. I was taken to a certain place, whence I was led blindfold to the house, and afterward brought back again in the same manner ; you see, therefore, the impossibility of my doing what you desire."

" Well," replied the robber, " you may, however, remember a little of the way that you were led blindfold. Come, let me blind your eyes at the same place. We will walk together ; perhaps you may recognise some part ; and as everybody ought to be paid for their trouble, there is another piece of gold for you ; gratify me in what I ask you." So saying, he put another piece of gold into his hand.

The two pieces of gold were great temptations to Baba Mustapha. He looked at them a long time in his hand, without saying a word, but at last he pulled out his purse and put them in. " I cannot promise," said he to the robber, " that I can remember the way exactly ; but since you desire, I will try what I can do." At these words Baba Mustapha rose up, to the great joy of the robber, and led him to the place where Morgiana had bound his eyes. "It was here," said Baba Mustapha, "I was blindfolded; and I turned this way."

The robber tied his handkerchief over his eyes, and walked by him till he stopped directly at Cassim's house, where Ali Baba then lived. The thief, before he pulled off the band, marked the door with a piece of chalk, which he had ready in his hand, and then asked him if he knew whose house that was; to which Baba Mustapha replied, that as he did not live in that neighbourhood, he could not tell.

The robber, finding he could discover no more from Baba Mustapha, thanked him for the trouble he had taken, and left him to go back to his stall, while he returned to the forest, persuaded that he should be very well received.

A little after the robber and Baba Mustapha had parted, Morgiana went out of Ali Baba's house upon some errand, and upon her return, seeing the mark the robber had made, stopped to observe it. "What can be the meaning of this mark?" said she to herself; "somebody intends my master no good: however, with whatever intention it was done, it is advisable to guard against the worst." Accordingly, she fetched a piece of chalk, and marked two or three doors on each side, in the same manner, without saying a word to her master or mistress.

In the meantime, the robber rejoined his troop in the forest, and recounted to them his success; expatiating upon his good fortune, in meeting so soon with the only person who could inform him of what he wanted to know. All the robbers listened to him with the utmost satisfaction; when the captain, after commending his diligence, addressing himself to them all, said: "Comrades, we have no time to lose: let us set off well armed, without its appearing who we are; but that we may not excite any suspicion, let only one or two go into the town together, and join at our rendezvous, which shall be the great square. In the meantime, our comrade who brought us the good news and I will go and find out the house, that we may consult what had best be done."

This speech and plan was approved of by all, and they were soon ready. They filed off in parties of two each, after some interval of time, and got into the town without being in the least suspected. The captain, and he who had visited the town in the morning as spy, came in the last. He led the captain into the street where he had marked Ali Baba's residence; and when they came to the first of the houses which Morgiana had marked, he pointed it out. But the captain observed that the next door was chalked in the same manner, and in the same place; and showing it to his guide, asked him which house it was—that, or the first.

The guide was so confounded, that he knew not what answer to make; but still more puzzled, when he and the captain saw five or six houses similarly marked. He assured the captain, with an oath, that he had marked but one, and could not tell who had chalked the rest, so that he could not distinguish the house which the cobbler had stopped at.

The captain, finding that their design had proved abortive, went directly to the place of rendezvous, and told his troop that they had lost their labour, and must return to their cave. He himself set them the example, and they all returned as they had come.

When the troop was all got together, the captain told them the reason of their returning; and presently the conductor was declared by all worthy of death. He condemned himself, acknowledging that he ought to have taken better precaution, and prepared to receive the stroke from him who was appointed to cut off his head.

But as the safety of the troop required the discovery of the second intruder into the cave, another of the gang, who promised himself that he should succeed better, presented himself, and his offer being accepted, he went and corrupted Baba Mustapha, as the other had done; and being shown the house, marked it in a place more remote from sight, with red chalk.

Not long after, Morgiana, whose eyes nothing could escape, went out, and seeing the red chalk, and arguing with herself as she had done before, marked the other neighbours' houses in the same place and manner.

The robber, on his return to his company, prided himself much on the precaution he had taken, which he looked upon as an infallible way of distinguishing Ali Baba's house from the others; and the captain and all of them thought it must succeed. They conveyed themselves into the town with the same precaution as before; but when the robber and his captain came to the street, they found the same difficulty; at which the captain was enraged, and the robber in as great confusion as his predecessor.

Thus the captain and his troop were forced to retire a second time, and much more dissatisfied; while the robber who had been the author of the mistake underwent the same punishment, which he willingly submitted to.

The captain, having lost two brave fellows of his troop, was afraid of diminishing it too much by pursuing this plan to get information of the residence of their plunderer. He found by their example that their heads were not so good as their hands on such occasions; and therefore resolved to take upon himself the important commission.

Accordingly, he went and addressed himself to Baba Mustapha, who did him the same service he had done to the other robbers. He did not set any particular mark on the house, but examined and observed it so carefully, by passing often by it, that it was impossible for him to mistake it.

The captain, well satisfied with his attempt, and informed of what he wanted to know, returned to the forest; and when he came into the cave, where the troop waited for him, said: "Now, comrades, nothing can prevent our full revenge, as I am certain of the house; and in my way hither I have thought how to put it into execution, but if any one can form a better expedient, let him communicate it."

He then told them his contrivance; and as they approved of it, ordered them to go into the villages about, and buy nineteen mules, with thirty-eight large leather jars, one full of oil, and the others empty.

In two or three days' time the robbers had purchased the mules and jars, and as the mouths of the jars were rather too narrow for his purpose, the captain caused them to be widened, and after having put one of his men into each, with the weapons which he thought fit, leaving open the seam which had been undone to leave them room to breathe, he rubbed the jars on the outside with oil from the full vessel.

Things being thus prepared, when the nineteen mules were loaded with thirty-seven robbers in jars, and the jar of oil, the captain, as their driver, set out with them, and reached the town by the dusk of the evening, as he had intended. He led them through the streets, till he came to Ali Baba's, at whose door he designed to have knocked; but was prevented by his sitting there after supper to take a little fresh air. He stopped his mules, addressed himself to him, and said: "I have brought some oil a great way, to sell at to-morrow's market; and it is now so late that I do not know where to lodge. If I should not be troublesome to you, do me the favour to let me pass the night with you, and I shall be very much obliged by your hospitality."

Though Ali Baba had seen the captain of the robbers in the forest, and had heard him speak, it was impossible to know him in the disguise of an oil merchant. He told him he should be welcome, and immediately opened his gates for the mules to go into the yard. At the same time he called to a slave, and ordered him, when the mules were unloaded, to put them into the stable, and to feed them; and then went to Morgiana, to bid her get a good supper for his guest. After they had finished supper, Ali Baba, charging Morgiana afresh to take care of his guest, said to her: "To-morrow morning I design to go to the bath before day; take care my bathing linen be ready, give it to Abdalla (which was the slave's name), and make me some good broth against I return." After this he went to bed.

In the meantime the captain of the robbers went into the yard, and took off the lid of each jar, and gave his people orders what to do. Beginning at the first jar, and so on to the last, he said to each man: "As soon as I throw some stones out of the chamber window where I lie, do not fail to come out, and I will immediately join you." After this he returned into the house, when Morgiana, taking up a light, conducted him to his chamber, where she left him; and he, to avoid any suspicion, put the light out soon after, and laid himself down in his clothes, that he might be the more ready to rise.

Morgiana, remembering Ali Baba's orders, got his bathing linen ready, and ordered Abdalla to set on the pot for the broth; but while she was preparing it the lamp went out, and there was no more oil in the house, nor any candles. What to do she did not know, for the broth must be made. Abdalla, seeing her very uneasy, said: "Do not fret and tease yourself, but go into the yard, and take some oil out of one of the jars."

Morgiana thanked Abdalla for his advice, took the oil-pot, and went into the yard; when, as she came nigh the first jar, the robber within said softly, "Is it time?"

Though naturally much surprised at finding a man in the jar instead of the oil she wanted, she immediately felt the importance of keeping silence, as Ali Baba, his family, and herself were in great danger; and collecting herself, without showing the least emotion, she answered, "Not yet, but presently." She went quietly in this manner to all the jars, giving the same answer, till she came to the jar of oil.

By this means Morgiana found that her master Ali Baba had admitted thirty-eight robbers into his house, and that this pretended oil merchant was their captain. She made what haste she could to fill her oil-pot, and returned into her kitchen, where, as soon as she had lighted her lamp, she took a great kettle, went again to the oil-jar, filled the kettle, set it on a large wood fire, and as soon as it boiled, went and poured enough into every jar to stifle and destroy the robber within.

When this action, worthy of the courage of Morgiana, was executed without any noise, as she had projected, she returned into the kitchen with the empty kettle; and having put out the great fire she had made to boil the oil, and leaving just enough to make the broth, put out the lamp also, and remained silent, resolving not to go to rest till she had observed what might follow through a window of the kitchen, which opened into the yard.

She had not waited long before the captain of the robbers got up, opened the window, and finding no light, and hearing no noise, or any one stirring in the house, gave the appointed signal, by throwing little stones, several of which hit the jars, as he doubted not by the sound they gave. He then listened, but not hearing or perceiving anything whereby he could judge that his companions stirred, he began to grow very uneasy, threw stones again a second and also a third time, and could not comprehend the reason that none of them should answer his signal.

Much alarmed, he went softly down into the yard, and going to the first jar, while asking the robber, whom he thought alive, if he was in readiness, smelt the hot boiled oil, which sent forth a steam out of the jar. Hence he suspected that his plot to murder Ali Baba, and plunder his house, was discovered. Examining all the jars, one after another, he found that all his gang were dead; and, enraged to despair at having failed in his design, he forced the lock of a door that led from the yard to the garden, and climbing over the walls made his escape.

When Morgiana saw him depart, she went to bed, satisfied and pleased to have succceeded so well in saving her master and family.

Ali Baba rose before day, and, followed by his slave, went to the baths, entirely ignorant of the important event which had happened at home.

When he returned from the baths, he was very much surprised to see the oil-jars, and that the merchant was not gone with the mules. He asked Morgiana, who opened the door, the reason of it. "My good master," answered she, "God preserve you and all your family.

You will be better informed of what you wish to know when you have seen what I have to show you, if you will follow me."

As soon as Morgiana had shut the door, Ali Baba followed her, when she requested him to look into the first jar, and see if there was any oil. Ali Baba did so, and seeing a man, started back in alarm, and cried out.

" Do not be afraid," said Morgiana, " the man you see there can do neither you nor anybody else any harm. He is dead."

" Ah, Morgiana," said Ali Baba, " what is it you show me ? Explain yourself."

" I will," replied Morgiana. " Moderate your astonishment, and do not excite the curiosity of your neighbours ; for it is of great importance to keep this affair secret. Look into all the other jars."

Ali Baba examined all the other jars, one after another ; and when he came to that which had the oil in, found it prodigiously sunk, and stood for some time motionless, sometimes looking at the jars, and sometimes at Morgiana, without saying a word, so great was his surprise. At last, when he had recovered himself, he said, " And what is become of the merchant ? "

" Merchant ! " answered she ; " he is as much one as I am. I will tell you who he is, and what is become of him ; but you had better hear the story in your own chamber ; for it is time for your health that you had your broth after your bathing."

Morgiana then told him all she had done, from the first observing the mark upon the house, to the destruction of the robbers, and the flight of their captain.

On hearing of these brave deeds from the lips of Morgiana, Ali Baba said to her, " God, by your means, has delivered me from the snares these robbers laid for my destruction. I owe, therefore, my life to you ; and, for the first token of my acknowledgment, give you your liberty from this moment, till I can complete your recompense as I intend."

Ali Baba's garden was very long, and shaded at the farther end by a great number of large trees. Near these he and the slave Abdalla dug a trench, long and wide enough to hold the bodies of the robbers ; and as the earth was light, they were not long in doing it. When this was done, Ali Baba hid the jars and weapons ; and as he had no occasion for the mules, he sent them at different times to be sold in the market by his slave.

While Ali Baba took these measures, the captain of the forty robbers returned to the forest with inconceivable mortification. He did not stay long ; the loneliness of the gloomy cavern became frightful to him. He determined, however, to avenge the fate of his companions, and to accomplish the death of Ali Baba. For this purpose he returned to the town, and took a lodging in a khan, and disguised himself as a merchant in silks. Under this assumed character he gradually conveyed a great many sorts of rich stuffs and fine linen to his lodging from the cavern, but with all the necessary precautions to conceal the place whence he brought them. In order to dispose of the merchandise, when he had thus amassed them together, he took a warehouse, which happened to be opposite to Cassim's, which Ali Baba's son had occupied since the death of his uncle.

He took the name of Cogia Houssain, and, as a new-comer, was, according to custom, extremely civil and complaisant to all the merchants his neighbours. Ali Baba's son was, from his vicinity, one of the first to converse with Cogia Houssain, who strove to cultivate his friendship more particularly. Two or three days after he was settled Ali Baba came to see his son, and the captain of the robbers recognised him at once, and soon learned from his son who he was. After this he increased his assiduities, caressed him in the most engaging manner, made him some small presents, and often asked him to dine and sup with him, when he treated him very handsomely.

Ali Baba's son did not choose to lie under such obligation to Cogia Houssain ; but was so much straitened for want of room in his house, that he could not entertain him. He therefore acquainted his father, Ali Baba, with his wish to invite him in return.

Ali Baba with great pleasure took the treat upon himself. " Son," said he, " to-morrow being Friday, which is a day that the shops of such great merchants as Cogia Houssain and yourself are shut, get him to accompany you, and as you pass by my door, call in. I will go and order Morgiana to provide a supper."

The next day Ali Baba's son and Cogia Houssain met by appointment, took their walk, and as they returned, Ali Baba's son led Cogia Houssain through the street where his father lived, and when they came to the house, stopped and knocked at the door. " This, sir," said he, " is my father's house, who, from the account I have given him of your friendship, charged me to procure him the honour of your acquaintance ; and I desire you to add this pleasure to those for which I am already indebted to you."

Though it was the sole aim of Cogia Houssain to introduce himself into Ali Baba's house, that he might kill him, without hazarding his own life or making any noise, yet he excused himself, and offered to take his leave; but a slave having opened the door, Ali Baba's son took him obligingly by the hand, and, in a manner, forced him in.

Ali Baba received Cogia Houssain with a smiling countenance, and in the most obliging manner he could wish. He thanked him for all the favours he had done his son; adding withal, the obligation was the greater as he was a young man, not much acquainted with the world, and that he might contribute to his information.

Cogia Houssain returned the compliment by assuring Ali Baba, that though his son might not have acquired the experience of older men, he had good sense equal to the experience of many others. After a little more conversation on different subjects, he offered again to take his leave, when Ali Baba, stopping him, said, "Where are you going, sir, in so much haste? I beg you would do me the honour to sup with me, though my entertainment may not be worthy your acceptance; such as it is, I heartily offer it."

"Sir," replied Cogia Houssain, "I am thoroughly persuaded of your good-will; but the truth is, I can eat no victuals that have any salt in them; therefore judge how I should feel at your table."

"If that is the only reason," said Ali Baba, "it ought not to deprive me of the honour of your company; for, in the first place, there is no salt ever put into my bread, and as to the meat we shall have to-night, I promise you there shall be none in that. Therefore you must do me the favour to stay. I will return immediately."

Ali Baba went into the kitchen, and ordered Morgiana to put no salt to the meat that was to be dressed that night; and to make quickly two or three ragouts besides what he had ordered, but be sure to put no salt in them.

Morgiana, who was always ready to obey her master, could not help being surprised at his strange order. "Who is this strange man," said she, "who eats no salt with his meat? Your supper will be spoiled, if I keep it back so long."

"Do not be angry, Morgiana," replied Ali Baba; "he is an honest man, therefore do as I bid you."

Morgiana obeyed, though with no little reluctance, and had a curiosity to see this man who ate no salt. To this end, when she had finished what she had to do in the kitchen, she helped Abdalla to carry up the dishes ; and looking at Cogia Houssain, knew him at first sight, notwithstanding his disguise, to be the captain of the robbers, and examining him very carefully, perceived that he had a dagger under his garment. "I am not in the least amazed," said she to herself, "that this wicked man, who is my master's greatest enemy, would eat no salt with him, since he intends to assassinate him ; but I will prevent him."

Morgiana, while they were at supper, determined in her own mind to execute one of the boldest acts ever meditated. When Abdalla came for the dessert of fruit, and had put it with the wine and glasses before Ali Baba, Morgiana retired, dressed herself neatly, with a suitable head-dress like a dancer, girded her waist with a silver-gilt girdle, from which there hung a poniard with a hilt and guard of the same metal, and put a handsome mask on her face. When she had thus disguised herself, she said to Abdalla, "Take your tabor, and let us go and divert our master and his son's friend, as we do sometimes when he is alone."

Abdalla took his tabor and played all the way into the hall before Morgiana, who, when she came to the door, made a low obeisance by way of asking leave to exhibit her skill, while Abdalla left off playing. "Come in, Morgiana," said Ali Baba, "and let Cogia Houssain see what you can do, that he may tell us what he thinks of your performance."

Cogia Houssain, who did not expect this diversion after supper, began to fear he should not be able to take advantage of the opportunity he thought he had found ; but hoped, if he now missed his aim, to secure it another time, by keeping up a friendly correspondence with the father and son ; therefore, though he could have wished Ali Baba would have declined the dance, he pretended to be obliged to him for it, and had the complaisance to express his satisfaction at what he saw, which pleased his host.

As soon as Abdalla saw that Ali Baba and Cogia Houssain had done talking, he began to play on the tabor, and accompanied it with an air, to which Morgiana, who was an excellent performer, danced in such a manner as would have created admiration in any company.

After she had danced several dances with much grace, she drew the poniard, and holding it in her hand, began a dance, in which she outdid herself by the many different figures, light movements, and the surprising leaps and wonderful exertions with which she accompanied it. Sometimes she presented the poniard to one breast, sometimes to another, and oftentimes seemed to strike her own. At last, she snatched the tabor from Abdalla with her left hand, and holding the dagger in her right presented the other side of the tabor, after the manner of those who get a livelihood by dancing, and solicit the liberality of the spectators.

Ali Baba put a piece of gold into the tabor, as did also his son; and Cogia Houssain seeing that she was coming to him, had pulled his purse out of his bosom to make her a present; but while he was putting his hand into it, Morgiana, with a courage and resolution worthy of herself, plunged the poniard into his heart.

Ali Baba and his son, shocked at this action, cried out aloud. "Unhappy woman!" exclaimed Ali Baba, "what have you done to ruin me and my family?"

"It was to preserve, not to ruin you," answered Morgiana; "for see here," continued she, opening the pretended Cogia Houssain's garment, and showing the dagger, "what an enemy you had entertained? Look well at him, and you will find him to be both the fictitious oil merchant and the captain of the gang of forty robbers. Remember, too, that he would eat no salt with you; and what would you have more to persuade you of his wicked design? Before I saw him, I suspected him as soon as you told me you had such a guest. I knew him, and you now find that my suspicion was not groundless."

Ali Baba, who immediately felt the new obligation he had to Morgiana for saving his life a second time, embraced her: "Morgiana," said he, "I gave you your liberty, and then promised you that my gratitude should not stop there, but that I would soon give you higher proofs of its sincerity, which I now do by making you my daughter-in-law."

Then addressing himself to his son, he said, "I believe you, son, to be so dutiful a child, that you will not refuse Morgiana for your wife. You see that Cogia Houssain sought your friendship with a treacherous design to take away my life; and if he had succeeded, there is no doubt that he would have sacrificed you also to his revenge. Consider, that by marrying Morgiana you marry the preserver of my family and your own."

The son, far from showing any dislike, readily consented to the marriage; not only because he would not disobey his father, but also because it was agreeable to his inclination. After this they thought of burying the captain of the robbers with his comrades, and did it so privately that nobody discovered their bones till many years after, when no one had any concern in the publication of this remarkable history.

A few days afterward, Ali Baba celebrated the nuptials of his son and Morgiana with great solemnity, a sumptuous feast, and the usual dancing and spectacles ; and had the satisfaction to see that his friends and neighbours, whom he invited, had no knowledge of the true motives of the marriage ; but that those who were not unacquainted with Morgiana's good qualities commended his generosity and goodness of heart. Ali Baba did not visit the robbers' cave for a whole year, as he supposed the other two, whom he could get no account of, might be alive.

At the year's end, when he found they had not made any attempt to disturb him, he had the curiosity to make another journey. He mounted his horse, and when he came to the cave he alighted, tied his horse to a tree, and, approaching the entrance, pronounced the words, ' Open, Sesame ! " whereupon the door opened.

He entered the cavern, and by the condition he found things in, judged that nobody had been there since the captain had fetched the goods for his shop. From this time he believed he was the only person in the world who had the secret of opening the cave, and that all the treasure was at his sole disposal. He put as much gold into his saddle-bag as his horse would carry, and returned to town. Some years later he carried his son to the cave and taught him the secret, which he handed down to his posterity, who, using their good fortune with moderation, lived in great honour and splendour.

THE STORY OF THE LITTLE HUNCHBACK

Arabian Nights

THERE was in former times at Kashgar, on the extreme boundaries of Tartary, a tailor, who was married to a wife to whom he was tenderly attached. One day while he was at work, a little hunchback seated himself at the shop door, and began to sing and play upon a tabor. The tailor was pleased with his performance, and resolved to take him to his house to entertain his wife. Immediately after their arrival, the tailor's wife placed before them a dish of fish ; but as the little man was eating, he unluckily swallowed a bone, which, notwithstanding all that the tailor and his wife could do, choked him. This accident greatly alarmed them both, lest they should be punished as murderers. Now, it so happened that a doctor, a Jew, lived close by, and the tailor and his wife devised a scheme for placing the body of the dwarf in his house. On their knocking at the door, the servant-maid came down without any light, and asked what they wanted.

" Go and tell your master," said the tailor, putting a piece of money in her hand, " we have brought him a man who is ill, and want his advice."

While the servant was gone up to inform her master, the tailor and his wife hastily conveyed the body of the hunchback, supposed to be dead, to the head of the stairs, and leaving it there, hurried away.

In the meantime the doctor, transported with joy at being paid beforehand, hastily ran toward the head of the stairs without waiting for a light, and came against the body of the hunchback with so much violence, that he precipitated it to the bottom.

' Bring me a light ! " cried he to the maid ; " quick, quick ! "

At last she brought a light, and he went downstairs with her ; but when he saw what he had done, " Unhappy man that I am ! " said he, " why did I attempt to come without a light ? I have killed the poor fellow who was brought to me to be cured ; and unless Esdra's ass come to assist me, the authorities will be here, and drag me out of my house for a murderer."

The doctor then called his wife, and consulted with her how to dispose of the dead body during the night. The doctor racked his brain in vain; he could not think of any stratagem to relieve his embarrassment; but his wife, who was more fertile in invention, said: "A thought has just come into my head; carry the dead body to the terrace of our house, and let it down the chimney of our Mussulman neighbour."

This Mussulman was one of the Sultan's purveyors for furnishing oil, butter, and articles of a similar nature, and had a magazine in his house, where the rats and mice made prodigious havoc.

The Jewish doctor approving the proposed expedient, his wife and he took the little dwarf up to the roof of the house, and, placing ropes under his arm-pits, let him down the chimney into the purveyor's chamber so dexterously that he stood upright against the wall, as if he had been alive. They were scarcely got back into their own chamber, when the purveyor, who had returned late from a wedding feast, went into his room, with a lantern in his hand. He was not a little surprised to discover a human figure standing in his chimney; but being a stout fellow, and apprehending him to be a thief, he took up a stick, and, "Ah," said he, "I thought the rats and mice ate my butter and tallow; but it is you who come down the chimney to rob me? However, I think you will have no wish to come here again." Upon this he attacked the hunchback, and struck him several times with his stick.

The body fell down flat on the ground, and the purveyor redoubled his blows. But observing that the body did not move, he stood a little time to regard it; and then, fear succeeding his anger, "Wretched man that I am!" said he, "what have I done! I have killed a man! alas, I have carried my revenge too far."

He stood pale and thunderstruck, and could not tell what resolution to take, when on a sudden he took up the body supposed to be dead, and carried it to the end of the street, where he placed it in an upright posture against a shop; and then returned without once looking behind him.

A few minutes before daybreak, a wealthy Christian merchant, coming home from a night's festivity, passed by the spot where the Sultan's purveyor had put the dead body, which, being jostled by him, tumbled upon the merchant's back. The merchant, thinking he was attacked by a robber, knocked it down. and after redoubling his blows, cried out, " Thieves ! "

The outcry alarmed the watch, who came up immediately, and finding a Christian beating a Mussulman, " What reason have you," said he, " to abuse a Mussulman in this manner ? "

" He would have robbed me," replied the merchant, " and jumped upon my back in order to take me by the throat."

" If he did," said the watch, " you have revenged yourself sufficiently ; come, get off him." At the same time perceiving the little man to be dead, he said : " Is it thus that a Christian dares to assassinate a Mussulman ? " So saying, he laid hold of the Christian and carried him to the house of the cadi. In the meantime, the Christian merchant, reflecting upon his adventure, could not conceive how such slight blows of his fist could have killed the man.

The judge having heard the report of the watch, and viewed the body, which they had brought to his house, interrogated the Christian merchant, who could not deny the death, though he had not caused it. But the judge, considering that the little dwarf belonged to the Sultan, for he was one of his buffoons, would not put the Christian to death till he knew the Sultan's pleasure. For this end he went to the palace, and acquainted the Sultan with what had happened ; and received this answer : " I have no mercy to show to a Christian who kills a Mussulman." Upon this the cadi ordered a stake to be prepared, and sent criers all over the city to proclaim that they were about to impale a Christian for killing a Mussulman.

At length the merchant was brought to the place of execution ; and the executioner was about to fasten him to the stake, when the Sultan's purveyor pushed through the crowd, calling to him to stop, for that the Christian had not committed the murder, but he himself had done it, and related how he had attacked him, under the impression that he was a thief.

" Let the Christian go," said the cadi to the executioner, " and impale this man in his stead, since it appears by his own confession that he is guilty."

Thereupon the executioner released the merchant, and seized the purveyor ; but just as he was going to impale him, he heard the voice of the Jewish doctor, earnestly entreating him to suspend the execution, and make room for him to approach, as he was the real criminal, and stating how he had, by his hasty imprudence, caused his death.

The chief-justice, being now persuaded that the Jewish doctor was the murderer, gave orders to the executioner to seize him and release the purveyor. Accordingly the doctor was just going to be impaled, when the tailor appeared crying, in his turn, to the executioner to hold his hand, and make room for him, that he might come and make his confession to the cadi, as, after all, he was the person really answerable for the death of the hunchback, and he could not bear that an innocent man should suffer for his crime.

The cadi being now fairly perplexed to decide who was the real culprit amongst so many self-accusing criminals, determined to refer the matter to the Sultan himself, and proceeded to the palace, accompanied by the tailor, the Jewish doctor, the Sultan's purveyor, and the Christian merchant, while four of his men carried on a bier the body of the dwarf, supposed to be dead.

When they appeared in the Sultan's presence, the cadi prostrated himself at his feet; and on rising, gave him a faithful relation of all he knew of the story of the dwarf, and of the men who, one after the other, accused themselves of his involuntary murder. The story appeared so extraordinary to the Sultan that he ordered his own historian to write it down with all its circumstances.

THE PILGRIM AND THE ROBBERS

A MAN of the name of Shems, with two other inhabitants of Nishapúr, joined a caravan of pilgrims going to Mecca. After journeying some days they entered a desert. One evening, when the sun had covered himself with the mantle of concealment, and the night had begun to display her dusky ringlets, these three men, who had never travelled before and were ignorant of the customs of caravans, felt tired and sleepy; they lost the reins of endurance from their hands, and agreed to repose for a short time to recover their strength, confident that they should afterwards overtake the caravan. They went to sleep, but were so intoxicated with the goblet of unconsciousness that they did not awake before the night had passed, and the sailor of destiny had again propelled the golden boat of the sun into the midst of the azure ocean of the firmament. When they awoke they threw their arrows of vision in all directions, and sent the couriers of their glances to the right and left, but were unable to discover any trace of the caravan. They arose under great apprehensions and hastened forward; but although they did their utmost, they merely retraced their steps to the same place, in spite of themselves, like a boat in an eddy. They despaired of joining the caravan, and being in deadly fear, did not know what plaster would heal the dreadful wound which they had inflicted upon themselves by their carelessness, or by what means they might come out from the well of their misfortune.

The three pilgrims continued to roam through the desert till the afternoon of next day, although they were hungry and thirsty. At last they perceived on the horizon something moving, which put them into still greater fright; it was an Arab, one of the robbers of the desert, who was sufficiently alert to jump from the lasso of swiftness to the top of the firmament, and to rob the sun and moon of their splendour, and by the twinkling of his eye to separate the meanings from words; in valour and strength he accounted Rustam (the Persian Hercules) as an old woman compared with himself. He had long stuck to the desert like the disease of cancer, and made it his employment to deprive of life and property whom he could. As soon as he had reached the three wanderers, he tied them to his horse and dragged them after him till he arrived at a spring of water, where he drew forth his sword and killed two of the men. Then laying his sword on the ground, he proceeded to rifle his victims, and while thus occupied, Shems, who was yet alive, suddenly burst his bonds, snatched up the sword and pierced with it one side of the robber, so that it came out at the other side, and the owl of his accursed soul flew to the ruinous habitation of non-existence. When Shems had thrown this thorn of life out of the way of the bare-footed travellers on that road, he thanked Allah, took from the corpse the money of his companions, and mounted the robber's horse. As he knew not in what direction to proceed, he considered that the horse must needs be able to find some inhabited place, so he threw the reins on its neck, and the steed ran with the velocity of lightning till it reached an encampment, the black tents of which were scattered on the surface of the desert like the moles on the cheeks of Laylá.[1]

This was the place where the slain robber dwelt, and from which he used to sally forth. A week had elapsed since he had left, and his tribesmen were astonished at his absence. They all came out to meet him, but soon discovered that it was another man mounted on his horse; so, taking the bridle, they led him into the camp, and small and great commenced to attack him. Shems concluded that the robber he had slain must have belonged to this encampment, and that these were his relations who were abusing him. The colour of the flower of his life having been blown away from his cheek by the autumnal blast of the tempest of this accident, he reflected that he had escaped from the jaws of the wolf of destruction, but that destiny had again stretched the bow-string of an unfortunate coincidence, and that the breeze of fate had caused a strange flower to bloom, which required a strong arm, so that it would be almost impossible to be saved from this misfortune. He turned this over in his mind, and considering that all things depend upon prudent management, he thought that to gain time was the first step, so he said to the crowd: "The rose-bush of my life is so withered, from travelling on the road of accidents and exhaustion, that the breeze of no power could move it. If you have any food, bring some of it to me, that I may strengthen myself

[1] Laylá and Majnún are the typical lovers of the Mohammedans.

and relate the story of that young man." They brought him victuals, which he ate, and having arranged the arrow of stratagem in the bow of his mind, he thus spoke:

"Know, ye inhabitants of these tents, that I belong to the caravans of the pilgrims, which had stopped at a certain halting-place, when all of a sudden the Rustam-like warrior made his appearance on the verge of the desert. If his flashing scimitar had swept over the firmament, it would have cut it in twain; and if the whistling sound of his sword coming down with force in battle had reached the ear of the mountain Káf, it would have taken refuge under the wings of the Anka.[1] He attacked the caravan, killed some and wounded others. He was like an eagle falling on a flock of pigeons, or like a spark of fire in a ripe field which grows into a conflagration and burns up everything. As the caravan consisted of ten or twelve thousand men, some of them attacked him, and, after having slain a number of them, he was made prisoner. They purposed extinguishing the lamp of his life with the tempest of enmity; but the leader of the caravan and some influential men thought it would be a pity to sever the tree of life of so valiant a youth with the saw of annihilation. So they said: 'We shall save your life if you pay the price of blood of those whom you have exterminated, and if you swear never in future to commit such a crime,' and they fixed his ransom at ten thousand dínars. Said the young warrior: 'I would give you even more than this sum, but I have not even a hundred dirhams with me. But my friends and family live in a camp not far hence, and there I possess much money and property. If you could get some person to mount my horse, to ride to the encampment, and to explain my condition, you would probably obtain gold and silver far beyond the amount you have named.' Everybody in his turn was invited to undertake the task, but all refused; and when the relatives of the slain men saw that they were disappointed in their expectation of blood-ransom, they were ready to put him to death. I was sorry that the granary of life of so brave a man should be trodden down by the foot of destruction, so I rose and said: 'It is a good tree which bears only the fruits of expectation of good deeds. I will undertake to carry the message; but I know neither the road nor the people.' He answered: 'My horse knows the way, and will carry you to the place. Tell my friends to send ten thousand dínars and not to grudge

[1] A mythical bird that dwells in Mount Káf and is supposed to bring good fortune to whomsoever it overshadows with its wings.

them, for they are the ransom of my life, and such a case is the opportunity to show their love for me.' "

When Shems had concluded his oration, the friends of the robber looked at each other in astonishment and said : " What impossible things do you relate to us ! That young man is tried and experienced in the arts of horsemanship and warfare. He does not engage in a conflict before he is convinced that he will come out of it victorious. And it is extremely improbable that such an accident should have happened to him. However, this is certainly his own steed, and there may be some truth in what you have said."

Shems replied : " What I have told you is in conformity with common sense. Do you think that I, who am weak and could in no wise cope with his strength and valour, would have been able to deprive him of his horse ? This is not a time for squabbling. You ought to make haste to show him your friendship in delivering him from the relatives of the men he has slain. I have obtained two days' respite, and if I do not return within that time, your kinsman will certainly be put to death and your repentance will come too late. I apprehend you will fare like the watchmen who were overreached by a cunning thief, and that you will gain nothing by scratching the breast of repentance and sorrow."

They asked him : " How was this ? " and Shems related the story of the watchmen outwitted by a thief.

On a certain night a thief, who was able to steal the five senses from the body, and himself possessed the senses of all bodies, broke into the house of a rich man and collected many valuables. When he wished to go away and had reached the door of the house, he met a number of watchmen, and considered with what snare he might entangle their feet. Seeing a broom, he commenced to sweep. The watchmen arrived and asked what occasion there was to sweep the house at midnight. The thief answered : " The master of the house died in the evening, and the passage is dirty, and as there will be plenty of other work to do in the morning, I am doing this now."

The watchmen asked : " How is it that we do not hear the voice of lamentation ? "

Quoth the thief : " To-morrow morning you will hear the sounds of distress."

Upon this the watchmen went away, and the thief took the articles which he had stolen. When it was morning the master of the house made a great outcry because of the robbery, and when the police heard of it they knew that the man was a thief and had swept the house by way of stratagem; they searched everywhere, but they reaped only the fruits of repentance.

"I have told you this story," continued Shems, "to show you that when the leading-string of an affair falls into our hands we must not regard it lightly, and that it is of no use whatever to gnaw the finger of indecision. The duties of friendship which you owe to your kinsman require that you should now despatch along with me some messengers with the ransom-money."

They agreed to this, and ten men were selected, each of whom carried a thousand dínars and other presents. The caravan being tracked from stage to stage till it was overtaken at a halting-place, Shems said to the Arabs: "Remain for awhile till I go forward and explain your business." He then advanced and informed the leader of the caravan of his adventure and of the death of his two companions, of the robber's friends, and of the ruse by which he had saved himself from them. The leader of the caravan praised him, and greatly approved of his cunning. Then the robber's friends were summoned and their presents accepted, after which the leader of the caravan explained to them the real facts of the case, and ordered them to be executed on the spot. But many of the pilgrims interceded, saying that the guilty man had fallen into the well of his own crime, and that these not being so blameable had not forfeited their lives. So they were dismissed, after pledging themselves to abstain in future from attacking travellers.

THE KAZI OF EMESSA

Persian

THERE lived once, in the same city, a wealthy Jew and a poor Mussulman. The latter fell at length into such distress that he went to the Jew, and begged a loan of a hundred dínars; saying that he had a favourable opportunity of trading with the money, and promising half the profits in return for the favour. The Jew, though a great miser, had long cast the eyes of affection on the Mussulman's wife, a woman of extraordinary beauty, but of strict chastity, and fondly attached to her husband. He hoped, however, that if he could involve the poor man in distress, and force her to intercede for him, he might gain his wicked purpose. With this motive, therefore, he spoke kindly, and said, "If you will give the pledge I shall require, you shall have the money without interest." The Mussulman, somewhat astonished at his liberality, asked what pledge he wanted, and the Jew replied: "Consent that, in case you do not pay the money by a given day, I shall cut off a pound of flesh from your body." But the poor man, fearing the dangers and delays which might befall him, refused. In a couple of months, however, being hard pressed by poverty and the hunger of his children, he came back and took the money; and the Jew had the precaution to call in several respectable men of the Mohammedan faith to witness the terms of their agreement.

So the Mussulman set off on his journey, which was prosperous; and sent the money in good time to his wife, that she might discharge the debt. But she, not knowing what pledge had been given, and being much perplexed by domestic difficulties, applied the money to her household purposes; and the penalty of the bond was incurred. It was some time after this that the Mussulman was joyfully returning, with large gains, and in the confident belief that he had escaped from the snares of the Jew, when he fell among thieves, who plundered him of all, and he came home as poor as he went out.

Presently the Jew called and politely asked after his health; and next day he returned to claim the fulfilment of his bond. The luckless merchant told him his story; the relentless Jew replied: "My money or the pledge." And thus they went on for some days in hot contention till the neighbours, interfering, advised them to refer the matter to the Kazi. To the Kazi accordingly they went; who, after a patient hearing of the case, decreed that the merchant had forfeited his pledge, and must submit to the penalty. But to this he would by no means consent; protesting against the legality of the decree, and claiming a right of appeal. Upon which the Jew desired him to name the judge with whose decision he would be content; and he selected the Kazi of Emessa, as a man of profound knowledge and strict justice. The Jew agreed to the appeal, on consideration that both parties should bind themselves to accept his judgment as final; and this point being settled, they both set out for the city of Emessa.

They had not gone far when they met a runaway mule, with his master in pursuit, who called to them to stop the animal or turn him back; and the merchant, after several vain efforts, flung a stone at the beast, which knocked out one of its eyes. Upon this the owner came up, and seizing the poor merchant, accused him of blinding his mule, and insisted on the full value. To this, however, the Jew objected, as he had a prior claim; but he told him that he might come with them if he liked, and hear what the Kazi might have to say in the matter. And so the muleteer joined them, and the three pursued their journey together.

At night they reached a village, and as it was dark, they went quietly to sleep on the flat roof of a house; but by and by there was an uproar in the village, and the merchant, unable to resist the pleasure of mixing in the tumult, jumped suddenly down from the roof, and fell on a man who was sleeping below and caused his death. The two sons of the deceased laid hands on the unfortunate man, and threatened to kill him in retaliation. But the Jew and the muleteer opposed this design, unless they would first satisfy their demands; and advised the young men to come along with them, and lay their complaint before the Kazi. To this the heirs of the deceased consented, and the five now travelled together.

Next day they overtook a poor man whose ass had stuck in the mud, and which, with all his efforts, he could not get out. He begged them to help him; and while the others took hold each of a corner of the load, and he seized the bridle, the unlucky merchant lugged at the tail, which came off in his hands. The peasant was enraged, and said he must pay for the beast, which was now useless; but the others told him to be quiet, and come along with them, and tell his story to the judge.

Shortly after this they came to Emessa, and were astonished at seeing a venerable man, with a large turban and a robe which came down to his heels, and riding on an ass ; but disgracefully drunk and vomiting. Upon inquiry they learned that he was the censor. A little while after, they reached the mosque, which they found full of people engaged in gambling. And passing on they met a man tossing about on a bier, whom the people were carrying forth to his burial ; and when he protested against the measure, appealing to the bystanders to say whether he was not alive, they assured him that he was certainly dead ; and the poor man was buried.

Next morning they presented themselves before the Kazi, and began all at once to make their complaints ; but the Kazi told them to stop their clamour, and to speak one at a time. So the Jew began : " My lord, this man owes me a hundred dínars, upon the pledge of a pound of his flesh ; command him to pay the money or surrender the pledge."

Now it happened that the Kazi and the merchant were old friends ; so when the Kazi asked him what he had to say, he frankly confessed that what the Jew had alleged was all true ; but he was utterly unable to pay the debt : hoping, no doubt, that the contract would be declared null. He was, therefore, astounded at hearing the Kazi declare that if he could not give the money he must pay the penalty ; and when the officers were commanded to prepare a sharp knife for the purpose, he trembled, and gave himself up for lost.

Then the Kazi, addressing the Jew, said : " Arise, take the knife, and cut off the pound of flesh from his body ; but so that there be not a grain more or less. Your just right is one pound exactly ; take either more or less, by ever so little, and I will make you over to the Governor, who will put you to death."

To which the Jew replied : " It is not possible to cut it exactly, but there must needs be a little more or less."

But the Kazi told him it must be a pound exactly, and that any other quantity, being unjustifiable, would involve him in guilt.

The Jew, being frightened at this interpretation of his right, renounced his claim, and said he would forgive the debt altogether.

" Very well," said the Kazi ; " but if you have brought the man so far, on a claim which you cannot maintain, it is but reasonable that you should pay him for his time, and the support of his family during his absence."

The matter was then referred to arbitration, and the damages being assessed at two hundred dínars, the Jew paid the money and departed.

Next came the muleteer, and told his story; and the Kazi asked him what the value of the mule was: the man said it was fully worth a thousand dirhams before it lost its eye. "This is a very simple case," said the Kazi. "Take a saw, cut the mule in two; give him the blind half, for which he must pay you five hundred dirhams, and keep the other side to yourself." To this the man very much objected, because, he said, the mule was still worth 750 dirhams, so he preferred putting up with his loss, and would give up the suit. The Kazi admitted that he was at liberty to do so, but he must make amends to the man for such a frivolous and vexatious suit; and the poor muleteer kept his blind mule, and had to pay a hundred dínars in the shape of compensation to the merchant.

The next party were called on to state their grievance; and the Kazi, on hearing how the man had been killed, asked the sons if they thought the roof of the college was about the height of the house that the merchant jumped from. They said they thought it was. Upon which he decreed that the merchant should go to sleep on the ground, and that they should get upon the roof and jump down on him; and that as the right of blood belonged to them equally, they must take care to jump both at once. They accordingly went to the roof; but when they looked below, they felt alarmed at the height, and so came down again, declaring that, if they had ten lives, they could not expect to escape. The Kazi said he could not help that: they had demanded retaliation, and retaliation they should have; but he could not alter the law to please them. So they too gave up their claim, and with much difficulty got off, upon paying the merchant two hundred dínars for the trouble they had given him.

Last of all came the owner of the ass, and told the story of the injury which his poor beast had suffered. "What! another case of retaliation?" said the Kazi. "Well, fetch my ass, and let the man pull off his tail." The beast was accordingly brought, and the man exerted all his strength to revenge the insult which had been put upon his favourite. But an ass which had carried the Kazi was not likely to put up with such an indignity, and soon testified his resentment by several hearty kicks, which made the man faint. When he recovered, he begged leave to decline any further satisfaction ; but the Kazi said it was a pity he should not have his revenge, and that he might take his own time. But the more he pulled, the harder the vicious creature kicked, till at last the poor man, all bruises and blood, declared that he had accused the merchant falsely, for his own donkey never had a tail. The Kazi protested, however, that it was contrary to practice to allow a man to deny what he had once alleged, and that he must therefore maintain his suit. Upon which the poor fellow said, he saw how it was ; he supposed he would have to pay as well as the rest ; and he begged to know how much it was. So, after the usual pretences and dissensions, he was let off for a hundred dínars.

When all the plaintiffs had left the court, the Kazi, collecting the different fines which he had imposed upon them, divided the whole amount into two equal shares, one of which he reserved for himself, and the other he gave to the merchant ; but observing that he sat still and seemed very thoughtful, he asked him if he was satisfied.

" Perfectly so, my lord," said he ; " and full of admiration of your wisdom and justice. But I have seen some strange sights since I came to this city, which perplex me ; and I should esteem it a kindness if you would explain them."

The Kazi promised to give him all the satisfaction in his power ; and having learnt what had perplexed him, thus replied :

" The vintners of this city are a very dishonest set of people, who adulterate the wine, mix water with it, or sell it of an inferior quality. So the censor, every now and then, goes round to examine it ; and if he should taste but even so little at each place where it is sold, it will at last get into his head ; and that is why he got so drunk yesterday. The mosque where you saw them gambling has no endowment, and was very much out of repair ; so it has been let for a gaming house, and the profit will serve to put it in order as a place of worship. And as for the man who excited your compassion, I can assure you he was really dead, as I will show you. Two months ago his wife came into court, and pleaded that her husband had died in a distant country, and claimed legal authority for marrying again. I required her to produce evidence of his death ; and she brought forward two credible witnesses, who deposed to the truth of what she had said. I therefore gave decree accordingly, and she was married. But the other day he came before me, complaining that his wife had taken another husband,

and requiring an order that she should return to him; and as I did not know who he was, I summoned the wife before me, and ordered her to account for her conduct. Upon which she said that he was the man whom she had two months ago proved to be dead; and that she had married another by my authority. I then told the man that his death had been clearly established on evidence which could not be refuted; that my decree could not be revoked; and that all the relief I could afford him was to give orders for his funeral."

The merchant expressed his admiration of the Kazi's acuteness and wisdom, and thanked him for his impartial judgment in his own behalf, as well as for his great condescension in explaining these singular circumstances. He then returned to his own city, where he passed the rest of his days in the frugal enjoyment of the wealth which he had gained at Emessa.

THE ENVIOUS VIZIER

Persian

IN ancient times there lived a king of Africa named Mulukara, who was much honoured by all. Notwithstanding the splendour of the star of his pomp and circumstance, he always kept the lamp of godliness burning near him, associated with pious dervishes, and took lessons from them in the laws of wisdom and experience. In the gates and streets of the city he posted servants, whom he instructed to bring into his presence any dervishes or pious men who came into his kingdom. It was his custom to pass the greater part of the day in dispensing justice to rich and poor, to his soldiers and his subjects, and to pass the remainder of the day in the society of men of knowledge and piety.

Once a Dervish passed through his capital, who had quaffed from the cup of travel by land and sea the liquor of experience and science, and the stature of whose accomplishments was adorned with external and internal perfections. He was introduced to the King, and as he possessed a ready knowledge of the position of every country, and was well acquainted with its customs and manners, the spread-table of his company became so palatable to the King that his Majesty's pleasure increased from day to day to such a degree that his presence at Court became almost indispensable. But as the weeds and rubbish of envy and hatred are always the offspring of the garden of royal consideration and favour, so it was also in this case.

The King had a Vizier who was unique in his kind for envy and covetousness, and far removed from the ways and habits of humanity and justice—nay, an entire stranger to them; so much so, that he wished neither the poor nor the rich, neither the small nor the great, should eat one morsel from the banquet of the King's table; nor that a thousand ants should be allowed to carry away a single grain of royal bounty and favour. The humane disposition of the King was unpleasing to the invidious wretch, and the flame of ill-will of his evil-omened mind having been fanned into a blaze, he ran the charger of his imagination into the hippodrome of stratagems, hurled the dice of falsehood about seeking for an opportunity to throw cold water on the amiable occupations of his Majesty, and to remove this Dervish from his sight. One day the Vizier found the King alone, and, intending to avail himself of this opportunity, he thus addressed him :

" It is long since your Majesty's humble servant has considered it his highest privilege to enjoy your intimacy, and he has never for a moment acted contrary to the laws of gratitude. But when those who have been so cherished in the royal service, and who observe the duties of fidelity, take notice of events endangering your Majesty's dignity, they feel compelled to bestir themselves in your behalf. Your servant has grave cause to trouble your Majesty at present. Having abandoned the affairs of the kingdom, your Majesty often associates intimately with useless beggars who enjoy no reputation or honour, and who, on account of their evil deeds, have strayed from the regions of felicity and perfection. It is a shame and a disgrace that persons of high descent, of dignity, and of power should soil their pure skirts of prosperity by mixing with the dregs of homeless vagabonds.

" Alas, that a royal pearl should not know its own value !
If it fall into jewellers' hands,
Everybody will highly esteem it :
Should it be in a hawker's box,
It will be mistaken for a bead.

It is the duty of potentates," added the Vizier, " to regulate the affairs of their armies and subjects, and to keep in order the manufactures which pertain to the maintenance either of peace or of war."

After the King had listened to this, he said : " Do you, who are expert, like Asaf, tell me, then, what neglect there has been in the administration of civil or military affairs, so that we may remedy any defect ; otherwise you have been talking nonsense. Those endowed with knowledge and wisdom, who are sitting on the carpet of good manners, have compared royal personages with rose-gardens, which are frequented by thousands of persons of all grades, and nothing is lost of their freshness or perfume. Thus all creatures are benefited by the rays of the world-illuming sun, yet its splendour is not diminished. Kings profit in various ways by the society of experienced and travelled men, and become thereby fortified in power. And I have many reasons for associating with such people."

During this conversation the Dervish made his appearance. The King inquired as to his welfare, and the Vizier took his leave, thinking that it was impossible to deprive the Dervish of the King's favour.

Nevertheless, he let fly the bird of envy into the space of intrigues; he drew the sword of hypocrisy over the whetstone of enmity; and spanned the bow of malevolence, in hopes that the arrow of falsehood and cunning might strike the target of his desires. One day meeting the Dervish, he began to flatter him, saying:

"O thou pillar of the righteous and quintessence of the diligent, although the breeze of your mind pervades the pleasure-garden of the society of royalty and of those who are powerful, yet do the weak and humble, like myself, hope to attract your attention, because the company of the enlightened bestows happiness upon all hearts.

> "The society of the wise confers polish on the mirror of the mind;
> The splendour of the sun lights the lamp of the moon.

Since abundant blessings and infinite advantages result from attending the service of the pious, I venture to hope that any day when your presence at Court is not required you will condescend to illuminate the poor dwelling of your devoted servant with the rays of the torch of your noble presence."

The Dervish was overcome by the flattery and smoothness of the Vizier, and consented. Shortly after this the King, being indisposed, did not quit his harem the whole day. The Dervish remembered the promise he had made to the Vizier, went to visit him, and was received with great apparent friendliness. Evening having set in, and the other guests gone to their respective homes, the Vizier said: "Since the enjoyment of the company of dervishes is one of the indications of prosperity and good luck, and as such happiness does not often fall to our lot, I have been seated long in the lair of expectation, waiting that such a gift might be transferred from the ledger of destiny to the horoscope of my name. I humbly hope that you will, like the full moon, condescend to abide in the mansion of your servant."

The Dervish stayed all night, and in the morning the Vizier said to him: "They have cooked a dish in the house, into which they have put a great deal of garlic," and placing it before the Dervish, continued: "Thou receptacle of sweet converse and chosen vessel of devotion, as it is customary to prepare dishes of this kind each morning during winter-time, I have brought you some of it; all its ingredients are lawful substances, and no harm will come to you from eating it."

The Dervish gladly accepted the food, but the Vizier excused himself from partaking of it, saying: "To-day is the 14th day of the month of Showal and the King's birthday, and it is my custom to fast on this day, in conformity with a vow which I made many years ago."

The Dervish ate heartily of the savoury dish, after which the Vizier said: "Although garlic is very palatable and in many respects profitable to health, it is strange that our King greatly dislikes it, and hates every man who smells of it." Presently information was brought that the King had come out of his private apartments; and the Vizier advised the Dervish to go to the bath in order to remove from his person the smell of garlic, while he proceeded on urgent business to the palace.

When the Vizier made his appearance, the King inquired of him: "Where is the Dervish?"

He answered: "Yesterday and to-day the Dervish was in my house; he purposed going to the bath, and probably is there now."

Said the King: "This Dervish has been in my service for some time, and I have greatly profited by intercourse with him, therefore I feel somewhat ashamed at not having yet given him a worthy present. You know it is in accordance with human nature to have desires and to expect gifts. As I have not hitherto rewarded the Dervish, I wish to know whether you have heard him utter anything like words of complaint about me."

The Vizier stretched out his neck and said, as if in hesitation: "Well." Then the King's curiosity was excited, and he ordered the Vizier to tell him the truth.

The Vizier, having thus found an opportunity, drove the courser of suspicion into the plain of enmity and self-interest, and writing with the pen of laudation on the page of flattery, thus began: "It is not hidden from your exalted Majesty's understanding that troops of such like men are wandering about everywhere, and that with whatever people they may chance to live, they observe their ways and customs as long as they are with them; but as soon as they leave them they will propagate a thousand erroneous notions about them in the next place where they sojourn. Persons of this kind have no fixed principles or religion; everything is lawful with them. Therefore, to associate with them is against the law of God and the Prophet; the wise have always shunned such unhallowed companions, and have never placed confidence in them."

The King replied: "Say, at least, what you have heard of the Dervish with reference to me."

Quoth the Vizier: "Since he is well aware that I am a devoted servant of your Majesty, he dare not say aught disparaging of you. He could not, however, altogether control his tongue, but once said that your Majesty had no fault excepting a foul breath, from which he suffered much whenever he sat near you. When the wretch made such an aspersion I was strongly disposed to reprove him, but refrained, lest I should give occasion to malignant reports."

The King was much astonished at this speech, but suspected that the Vizier was actuated by interested motives.

In the meanwhile the Dervish entered, and as he was conscious that the odour of garlic was still about his person, he seated himself in a much lower place than usual. The Vizier went out, and the King was as friendly to the Dervish as before, albeit the words of the Vizier still weighed on his mind. He called him to approach nearer, when he perceived where he had seated himself, but the Dervish begged his pardon and did not move from his place. Then the King himself arose and went near him; but as the Dervish had heard from the Vizier that the effluvium from garlic was extremely disagreeable to the King, he gradually drew back, and every time he addressed his Majesty he turned his face away from him. When the King perceived this, he said to himself: "Apparently the Vizier is quite right: this is the consequence of showing kindness to a mean fool. I must punish him, and in such a way that nobody shall become aware of it, nor I be accused of being of a changeable disposition and of discarding my favourites, lest any dervishes should in future be shy of my society."

The King had a country house at the distance of two farsangs from the city, where he kept several slaves whom he had commanded, whenever it should become necessary to put any person secretly to death, they should behead such as came to them with a letter in his own handwriting, even were they his own children. In this way he caused several criminals to be executed by them, without the knowledge of any but himself and these slaves. Designing to have the Dervish thus despatched, he said to him: "I know you must long to revisit your own country, and as I have not hitherto assisted you, here is an order for a thousand dínars, to defray the expenses of your journey, and you can have the money on presenting it at my country house."

The Dervish took his leave of the King and departed. Meeting the Vizier, he informed him of his dismissal and showed him the bill, at the same time saying he did not know where the King's country house was situated. The Vizier, concluding that if the Dervish did not receive the money he would again return to Court, said: " Friend Dervish, I will give you the money myself, and you can leave the bill with me." So the Dervish handed over the paper, received the money, and went his way. As the Vizier was entirely ignorant of the peculiar arrangement at the King's country house, after a few days he resolved to make a pleasure excursion thither. He set out, and having found the place, showed the paper to the servants, who immediately surrounded him, drew their swords and cut him to pieces.

The world is a place of retribution ;
It is like a mirror, it shows you your own image.

GIOVANNI BOCCACCIO
1313–1375

STORY OF THE THREE RINGS

SALADIN was so brave and great a man, that he had raised himself, from an inconsiderable station, to be Sultan of Babylon, and had gained many victories over both Turkish and Christian princes. This monarch, having in divers wars, and by many extraordinary expenses, run through all his treasure, some urgent occasion fell out that he wanted a large sum of money. Not knowing which way he might raise enough to answer his necessities, he at last called to mind a rich Jew of Alexandria, named Melchizedeck, who let out money at interest. Him he believed to have wherewithal to serve him ; but then he was so covetous, that he would never do it willingly, and Saladin was loath to force him. But as necessity has no law, after much thinking which way the matter might best be effected, he at last resolved to use force under some colour of reason. He therefore sent for the Jew, received him in a most gracious manner, and making him sit down, thus addressed him :

" Worthy man, I hear from divers persons that thou art very wise and knowing in religious matters ; wherefore I would gladly know from thee which religion thou judgest to be the true one, viz. the Jewish, the Mohammedan, or the Christian ? "

The Jew (truly a wise man) found that Saladin had a mind to trap him, and must gain his point should he exalt any one of the three religions above the others ; after considering, therefore, for a little how best to avoid the snare, his ingenuity at last supplied him with the following answer :

" The question which your Highness has proposed is very curious ; and, that I may give you my sentiments, I must beg leave to tell a short story. I remember often to have heard of a great and rich man, who among his most rare and precious jewels had a ring of exceeding beauty and value. Being proud of possessing a thing of such worth, and desirous that it should continue for ever in his family, he declared, by will, that to whichsoever of his sons he should give this ring, him he designed for his heir, and that he should be respected as the head of the family. That son to whom the ring was given, made the same law with respect to his descendants, and the ring passed from one to another in long succession, till it came to a person who had three sons, all virtuous and dutiful to their father, and all equally beloved by him. Now the young men, knowing what depended upon the ring, and ambitious of superiority, began to entreat their father, who was now grown old, every one for himself, that he would give the ring to him. The good man, equally fond of all, was at a loss which to prefer; and, as he had promised all, and wished to satisfy all, he privately got an artist to make two other rings, which were so like the first, that he himself scarcely knew the true one. When he found his end approaching, he secretly gave one ring to each of his sons; and they, after his death, all claimed the honour and estate, each disputing with his brothers, and producing his ring; and the rings were found so much alike, that the true one could not be distinguished. To law then they went, as to which should succeed, nor is that question yet decided. And thus it has happened, my Lord, with regard to the three laws given by God the Father, concerning which you proposed your question: every one believes he is the true heir of God, has his laws, and obeys his commandments; but which is in the right is uncertain, in like manner as with the rings."

Saladin perceived that the Jew had very cleverly escaped the net which was spread for him: he therefore resolved to discover his necessity to him, and see if he would lend him money, telling him at the same time what he had designed to do, had not that discreet answer prevented him. The Jew freely supplied the monarch with what he wanted; and Saladin afterwards paid him back in full, made him large presents, besides maintaining him nobly at his court, and was his friend as long as he lived.

GILLETTE OF NARBONNE

Boccaccio

THERE lived in France a gentleman named Isnard, Count de Roussillon, who, because he was in a bad state of health, always kept a physician in his house, called Master Gerard de Narbonne. Now the Count had an only son, whose name was Bertram, a fine youth, who had been brought up along with other children of his own age, amongst whom was a daughter to this physician, called Gillette, who had for him an infinite esteem and love, more than is common for one at such an age. His father's death, and his being left to the King's care, obliged him to go to Paris, which gave her the utmost concern. Shortly afterwards, her own father dying also, she would gladly, if she could have found a fit pretence, have gone thither to see Bertram; but such care was taken of her, because she was an heiress, that it was impossible. Being now of an age to marry, and being unable to forget her first love, though she had many suitors, on one of whom her guardians would willingly have bestowed her, she rejected them all, without assigning any reason.

In the meantime, her love growing more violent every day, being fed by the admirable reports she heard of Bertram, news was brought that the King of France had a dangerous ailment, which succeeded an ill-cured swelling in his breast, and gave him extreme anguish; nor could he meet with a physician, though he had tried many, who was able to heal it; on the contrary, they had made it worse, insomuch that he was determined to have no more advice. This was agreeable enough to the young lady, not only as it afforded a pretence for her going to Paris, but also as she had great hopes, if the disorder proved of the kind suspected, of getting Bertram for her husband. So, mixing up such drugs as her father was wont to use in cases of that nature, she hastened away to Paris.

The first thing she did, after she had obtained a sight of Bertram, was to wait upon the King, and desire he would acquaint her with his malady. His Majesty most graciously condescended to grant her request; when she was instantly convinced she was able to make a cure, and said, " Sir, if you will give me leave, I hope, without any pain or trouble, to restore your health in eight days."

The King could not help making a jest of this, saying to himself, " What ! shall a woman undertake to do that which has baffled all the best physicians in the world ? " He thanked her, therefore, for her good intention, and told her that he was resolved to try no more medicines.

" Sir," replied the lady, " you ridicule my art because I am young, and a woman ; but I must remind you that I do not pretend to this from my own knowledge ; but I rely upon the help of God, and the judgment of Master Gerard de Narbonne, who was a most eminent physician in his time, and my father."

The King, hearing this, said to himself, " Perhaps she is sent from God to my assistance ; why should I not, therefore, make trial of her, as she promises to cure me, without any trouble, in so short a time ? " Then, turning to her, " But suppose you should prove mistaken, what would you forfeit for making us break our resolution ? "

She replied, " If your Majesty pleases, you may set a guard upon me ; and if you are not cured in eight days, then burn me alive : but if I succeed, and you get well, what reward am I then to have ? "

" You are a maiden, it appears," said the King : " we will dispose of you in marriage to a person of great account."

" Sir," quoth she, " I accept your offer of a husband, but I will name the person, excepting all of your royal house."

He immediately promised, and she began to administer her medicines ; and before the limited time she had wrought a thorough cure. The King then said, " Fair maid, you have well earned a husband."

" Then, sir," she replied, " I have gained the Count de Roussillon, whom I have loved ever since I was a child."

The King thought her demand very great, but, as he had given his word, he would not depart from it. He sent for the Count, therefore, and said to him, " Bertram, you are now of age to take upon you the government of your own country ; it is our will that you return thither, and take a wife whom we shall recommend to you."

" And who is the lady, my liege ? " replied Bertram.

" It is she," said the King, " who has cured us with her medicines."

Bertram knew and liked her well enough, only that he thought her birth too low for his quality ; so he said, with some disdain, " And does your Majesty then mean to give me a doctress for my wife? Surely I may do much better for myself."

"Then," quoth the King, "would you have us be worse than our word? She requested to have you, and we promised, upon condition that we were made well."

"My liege," replied Bertram, "you may take away what I now possess, or you may add to it if you please; but this I assure your Majesty, that I will never consent to such a match."

"It is our pleasure to have it so," continued the King; "she is a prudent and beautiful lady, and you may be happier with her than if you were married to one of greater quality."

Bertram then held his peace; and the King ordered a magnificent entertainment in honour of the nuptials, and, when the day came, Bertram espoused Gillette, much against his will, in the King's presence, which being done, he took his leave of his Majesty, as if he were going to keep his wedding in his own country; but, instead of that, he went a quite different way, and came to Tuscany. Finding that the Florentines were at war with the Sienese, he willingly joined them, and, having a command given him, he continued some time in their service.

The bride, not at all pleased with his behaviour, went to Roussillon, in hope of gaining his affections by her prudent management, and was received by his people as their lady and mistress. Finding everything in disorder, on account of her husband's long minority, she used such care and diligence in restoring all to its wonted tranquillity, that she gained the favour and good-will of her subjects, who blamed the Count highly for his neglect of her. When that was done, she sent two knights to him, desiring to know if it was on her account he stayed away from home; and bidding them tell him that she was willing to go elsewhere to please him. But he answered roughly, that she might use her pleasure: "For," said he, "I will go to her only when she shall have this ring upon her finger, and a son, begotten by me, in her arms." Now he valued the ring at a high rate, and never parted with it from his finger, because of some secret virtue which he supposed it to have. The knights looked upon the condition as implying two impossibilities; and, perceiving that he was not to be moved from his resolution, they returned, and reported his answer.

The lady was much afflicted at this, and began to consider, if there were no way to effect these two points, and consequently regain her husband. Taking her measures then accordingly, she assembled all the principal people of the country, when she recounted to them, in a most tender and affectionate manner, all that she had done for the love of the Count, and what ensued thereupon ; and she let them know that it never was her intention, by staying amongst them, to keep him in perpetual banishment : therefore was she resolved to spend the remainder of her life in pilgrimage, for the good of her soul ; and her desire was, that they would take the government upon them, and inform the Count that she had quitted possession, and left the country with a design never more to return. As she was speaking these words, they all began to weep, and they entreated her much to change her resolution, but to no purpose. Taking her leave, then, and being attended only by a maid-servant and a relation, they set forward together like pilgrims, having provided themselves well with money and jewels ; and, without anybody's knowing whither they were gone, they made no stop till they came to Florence. There, by chance, they met with an inn that was kept by a widow, where she stayed, with a desire of learning some news concerning her lord.

The next day it happened that he passed by the house on horseback, along with his troops, when, though she knew him very well, yet she asked the landlady who he was ? " It is a gentleman, a stranger," answered she, " one of the best-natured men in the world, and much respected in this country, who is in love with a gentlewoman of small fortune in this neighbourhood : she bears a good character, but is yet unmarried, on account of her scanty circumstances, and lives with her mother."

The Countess, upon hearing this, began to consider more fully what she should do. Having learned the young lady's name, and where she lived, she went one day to the house, and, after the usual salutation, told the mother that she had a mind to speak to her : the other rose, and said with all her heart. They then went into a chamber by themselves, and, sitting down together, the Countess began in this manner : " Madam, you seem to be as little obliged to fortune as myself ; but perhaps it is now in your power to do us both a kindness."

The other replied, that she should be very willing, if it could be done honestly.

The Countess rejoined, " I put myself entirely into your hands ; if you deceive me, you frustrate the purposes of both."

" Speak out," said the lady ; " you shall find I never will deceive you."

The Countess then related her whole story, from beginning to end, part of which the old lady had heard from common report, and she added, " You now hear the two things which I am to compass to gain my husband, with regard to which there is no person in the world can serve me besides yourself, if it be true, as I am told, that he is violently in love with your daughter."

" Madam," quoth the lady, " there is some appearance of the Count's liking my daughter ; but whether there be anything real, that I cannot pretend to say. But what has this to do with your affair ? "

" That," answered she, " I shall soon tell you. But you must first hear what I intend to do in consideration of this service of yours. I understand that you have a daughter, of age to marry, whom you are forced to keep at home with you, for want of a fortune to give her : now my design is, to advance such a sum of money as you yourself shall think sufficient to marry her reputably."

The lady liked the offer very well, but yet, having the spirit of a gentlewoman, she replied, " Tell me what you want to have done, and if it appear fair and honest, I will do it most willingly, and leave the reward to you."

The Countess then said, " You must give the Count to understand, by some person whom you can trust, that your daughter is ready to oblige him, as soon as she can be assured that he has that real love for her which he pretends, and which she knows not how to credit, unless he sends her the ring that he usually wears, and which, she hears, he sets such a value upon. This ring you must give to me, and then you may let him know that your daughter is at his service, and that he may come privately hither as soon as he pleases, when you must put me to bed to him instead of your daughter. Perhaps, by God's grace, I may prove with child ; so that, by having his ring on my finger, and a son of his in my arms, which were the two conditions required, I may live with him afterwards as my husband, and you be the happy instrument of it."

The lady hesitated at first, fearing some scandal might befall her daughter ; but considering afterwards how fit it was that the good lady should have her husband, she not only promised her assistance, but in a few days obtained the ring, much against the Count's will, and afterwards put the lady to bed to him, instead of her daughter. Accordingly it happened that she became with child of two sons, as the event made manifest. Nor was it once only that the lady afforded the Countess the enjoyment of her husband's embraces, but many times, taking her measures so secretly that the Count never knew a word of it, but always thought he was with his mistress, not with his wife.

At last, when the Countess found herself pregnant, not wishing to give the lady more trouble, she said to her, " Madam, my end is now answered; I have nothing more to do but to satisfy you for your trouble."

She replied, " If you are contented, it is well ; I did it out of no expectation of reward, but only as it appeared to me quite a right thing."

" Madam," continued the Countess, " I am entirely pleased, and I intend to make you a recompense suitable to your great merit." She then, moved by her necessity, desired, but with the utmost modesty, a hundred pounds for her daughter's portion ; whilst the other, knowing her great worth, and hearing her humble demand, gave her five hundred, and jewels to the amount of as much more, for which she was very thankful ; and, to take away all pretence of the Count's coming any more to her house, the lady removed with her daughter to her friends in the country.

After some time, Bertram, hearing that his Countess had departed out of his territories, went thither, at the request of his subjects, whilst she stayed at Florence till her time of labour came, when she was brought to bed of two sons, very like their father. She took care to have them well nursed, and, in due time, without being discovered by any person, she came to Montpelier, where she made some stay to rest herself, and to make inquiry concerning her husband. Hearing, at last, that he was to make a great feast at Roussillon, on the day of All Saints, she went thither in the same pilgrim's dress as she first set out in ; and, just as the guests were going to sit down at table, she pressed forwards, through the midst of the crowd of gentlemen and ladies, with her two children in her arms, till, coming where the Count was, she threw herself at his feet, saying, with tears :

" My lord, I am your unhappy wife, who have undertaken a long pilgrimage in order that you might return to your own house. I conjure you, in the presence of God, that you abide by the two conditions enjoined me by the two knights whom I sent to you. Behold, not one son only of yours in my arms, but two ; and, see, here is the ring."

The Count was confounded with admiration, recognising the ring, and the children too, they were so like him, and said : " How can this have happened ? "

The Countess then related the whole story before all the company ; whilst he, knowing her to speak the truth, perceiving also her constancy and good management, and beholding two such pretty children, was moved to fulfil his promise, as well as to oblige the whole company, who requested him to take her as his wife : upon all these considerations, I say, he laid his inveterate hatred aside, raised her up, and saluted her, acknowledging her for his lawful Countess and the two babies for his children : he ordered also suitable apparel to be brought for them, to the great joy of the whole court ; whilst the feasting continued not that day only, but many others : and from that time he showed her all due respect, and they continued happy together as long as they lived.

TANCRED, PRINCE OF SALERNO

Boccaccio

TANCRED, Prince of Salerno, was a most humane and generous lord, had he not in his old age defiled his hands in a lover's blood. Through the whole course of his life he had only one daughter; and happy had he been not to have possessed her. No child could be more dear to a parent than she was, and so loath was he to part with her, that she had been many years of marriageable age before he could bring himself to bestow her on a son of the Duke of Capoa. But she was soon left a widow, and came home again to her father. She was a lady of great beauty and understanding, and continuing thus in the court of her father, who took no care to marry her again, and it seeming not so modest in her to ask it, she resolved at last to have a lover privately. Accordingly she made choice of a person of low parentage, but noble qualities, whose name was Guiscard, with whom she became violently in love, as he did with her. Such being their secret feelings, the lady who desired nothing so much as to be with Guiscard, and did not dare to trust any person with the affair, contrived a new stratagem in order to apprise him of the means. She wrote a letter, wherein she mentioned what she would have him do the next day for her; this she put into a hollow cane, and giving it to him one day, she said, pleasantly, " You may make a pair of bellows of this, for your servant to blow the fire with this evening."

He took the cane, supposing very justly that she had some covert meaning, and, opening it at home he found the letter, which filled him with the utmost joy; and he immediately took measures to meet her in the manner she had directed him.

On one side of the palace, and under a mountain, was a grotto, which had been made time out of mind, and into which no light could come but through a little opening dug in the mountain, and which, as the grotto had been long in disuse, was grown over with briars and thorns. Into this grotto was a passage, by a private staircase, out of one of the rooms of the palace, which belonged to the lady's apartment and was secured by a very strong door. This passage was so far out of every one's thoughts, having been disused for so long a time, that nobody remembered anything about it: but love, whose notice nothing can escape, brought it fresh into the mind of the enamoured lady. To keep this thing entirely private she laboured all alone some days before she could get the door open; when, having gone down into the cave, and observed the opening, and how high it might be from the bottom, she acquainted Guiscard with these details. He then provided a ladder of cords; and casing himself well with leather, to defend him from the thorns, he fixed one end of the ladder to the stump of a tree which was near, and slid down by the help of it to the bottom, where he stayed, expecting the lady.

The following day, therefore, having sent her maids out of the way, under pretence that she was going to lie down, and locking herself up alone in her chamber, she opened the door and descended into the grotto, where she met her paramour to their intense mutual satisfaction. Thence she showed him the way to her chamber, where they were together the greatest part of the day, and, after they had taken proper measures for the time to come, he went away through the cave, and she returned to her maids. He did the same the next night; and he followed this course for a considerable time, till fortune, as if she envied them their happiness, thought fit to change their mirth into mourning.

Tancred used sometimes to come into his daughter's chamber, to pass away a little time with her. Going thither, quite unperceived, one day after dinner, whilst Ghismond (this was the lady's name) was with her maids in the garden; and, not yet wishing to take her from her diversion, finding also the windows shut, and the curtains drawn to the feet of the bed, he threw himself down in a great chair, which stood in a corner of the room, leaned his head upon the bed, drew the curtain before him, as if he concealed himself on purpose, and fell asleep.

In the meantime, Ghismond, having made an appointment with her lover, left the maids in the garden, and came into her chamber, which she secured, not thinking of any person being there. Then she went to meet Guiscard, who was in the cave waiting for her, and brought him into her chamber; when her father awoke, and was a witness to all that passed between them. This was the utmost affliction to him, and he was about to cry out, but upon second thoughts he resolved to keep the matter private if possible, that he might be able to do more securely, and with less disgrace, what he had resolved upon. The lovers stayed together their usual time, without perceiving anything of Tancred, who, after they were departed, got out of the window into the garden, old as he was, and went, without being seen by any one, very sorrowful to his chamber.

The next night, according to his orders, Guiscard was seized by two men as he was coming out of the cave, and carried by them in his leathern doublet to Tancred, who, as soon as he saw him, said, with tears in his eyes, " Guiscard, you have ill requited my kindness towards you, by this outrage and shame which you have brought upon me, and of which this very day I have been an eye-witness."

Guiscard made no other answer but this: " Sir, love has greater power than either you or I."

Tancred then ordered that he should be kept in secret custody.

The next day he went to his daughter's apartment as usual (she knowing nothing of what had happened), and, after locking the door, said to her, weeping, " Daughter, I had such an opinion of your modesty and virtue, that I could never have believed, had I not seen it with my own eyes, that you would have violated either, even so much as in thought. The recollection of this will make the pittance of life that is left very grievous to me. As you were determined to act in that manner, would to Heaven you had made choice of a person more suitable to your own quality; but this Guiscard is one of the very meanest persons about my court. This gives me such concern, that I scarcely know what to do. As for him, he was secured by my order last night, and his fate is determined. But with regard to yourself, I am influenced by two different motives: on one side, the tenderest regard that a father can have for a child; and on the other, the justest vengeance for the great folly you have committed. One pleads strongly in your behalf; and the other would excite me to do an act contrary to my nature. But, before I come to a resolution, I would hear what you have to say for yourself."

And when he said this, he hung down his head, and wept like a child.

She, hearing this from her father, and perceiving that their amour was not only discovered, but her lover in prison, with difficulty refrained from breaking out into loud and grievous lamentations, as is the way of women in distress; but she conquered this weakness, and putting on a settled countenance, resolved firmly in her own mind not to outlive her Guiscard, who she supposed was already dead. With the utmost composure, therefore, she spoke to this effect:

"Father, it is not my purpose either to deny or to entreat; for as the one can avail me nothing, so I intend the other shall be of little service. I will by no means bespeak your love and tenderness towards me; but shall first, by an open confession, endeavour to vindicate myself, and then do what the greatness of my soul prompts me to. It is most true that I have loved, and do still love, Guiscard; and whilst I live, which will not be long, shall continue to love him; and, if such a thing as love be after death, I shall never cease to love him. To this I was induced, not so much by female frailty, as by his superior worth, and the little care you took to marry me again. It ought to have been plain to you that, as you are made of flesh and blood, your daughter was not stone or iron, and you should have remembered, though now you are old, what is the nature and force of youthful passions; and as your best years have been spent in part in the toils of wars, you should the better have known what are the effects of ease and indulgence, not alone on the young, but even on the old. I am then a creature of flesh and blood; I am still young; and for both reasons possessed with desires which have become the more intense because having been married I have known the pleasure derived from gratifying them. Unable, then, to resist their force, I determined to obey their impulse; and, with all the power of my soul, I resolved, that so far as in me lay, no shame should befall you or me from that to which a natural weakness impelled me. In this I was favoured by Love and Fortune, who showed me a very secret way by which, unperceived by any one, I attained my wishes; and this, whoever disclosed it to you, or however you came to know it, I do not deny. I did not take up with Guiscard by accident, as many do, but I chose him deliberately before all others, admitted him to my chamber with settled forethought, and with resolute perseverance on his part and mine, I long enjoyed my desires. It appears from what you say, that you would have been less incensed if I had made choice of a nobleman, and you bitterly reproach me for having condescended to a man of low condition. In this you speak according to vulgar prejudice, and not according to truth; nor do you perceive that the fault you blame is not mine, but fortune's, who often exalts the unworthy, and leaves the worthiest in low estate. But, not to dwell on such considerations, look a little into first principles, and you will see that we are all formed of the same materials, and by the same hand. The first difference amongst mankind, who are all born equal, was made by virtue; they who were virtuous were deemed noble, and the rest were all accounted otherwise. Though this law, therefore, may have been obscured by contrary custom, yet is it discarded neither by nature nor good manners. If then you regard only the worth and virtue of your courtiers, and consider that of Guiscard, you will find him the only noble person, and the others a set of poltroons. With regard to his worth and valour, I appeal to yourself. Who ever commended man more for every thing that was praiseworthy than you have commended him? and deservedly, in my judgment; but if I was deceived, it was by following your opinion. If you say, then, that I have had an affair with a person base and ignoble, I deny it; if with a poor one, it is to your shame to let such merit go unrewarded. Now, concerning your last doubt, namely, how you are to deal with me; use your pleasure. If you are disposed to commit an act of cruelty, I shall say nothing to prevent such a resolution. But this I must apprise you of, that unless you do the same to me, which you either have done, or mean to do to Guiscard, my own hands shall do it for you. Leave tears then to women; and if you mean to act with severity, cut us off both together, if it appear to you that we have deserved it."

The Prince knew full well the greatness of his daughter's soul; yet he could by no means persuade himself, that she would have resolution enough to do what her words seemed to threaten. Dismissing, then, all thoughts of doing her hurt in person, and intending to wean her affection from her lover by taking him off, he gave orders to the two men, who guarded Guiscard, to strangle him privately in the night, and to take his heart out of his body, and bring it to him. They executed his commands, and the next day Tancred called for a golden cup, and putting the heart into it, he had it conveyed by a trusty servant to his daughter, with this message: "Your father sends this present to comfort you with what was most dear to you; even as he was comforted by you in what was most dear to him."

She had remained unshaken in her resolution since her father left her, and therefore had prepared the juices of some poisonous plants, which she had mixed with water, to be at hand if what she feared should come to pass. When the servant had delivered the present and the message, she took the cup, without changing countenance, and seeing the heart therein, and knowing by the servant's words that it must be Guiscard's, she looked steadfastly at the man, and said, "My father hath done very wisely; such a heart as this requires no worse a sepulchre than one of gold."

Then she lifted it to her mouth and kissed it, saying: "All my life long, even to this last period of it, have I found my father's love most abundant towards me; but now more than ever: therefore return him in my name the last thanks that I shall ever be able to give him for such a present." Looking then towards the cup, which she held fast in her hand, she said: "Alas! dearest end and centre of all my wishes! Cursed be the cruelty of him, by whom these eyes now see you; although my soul hath long viewed and known you. You have finished your course; such a one indeed as fortune has thought fit to allot you; you are arrived at the goal to which we all tend; you have left the miseries of this world far behind, and have obtained such a sepulchre from your very enemy as your merit required. Nothing remained to make your obsequies complete but the tears of her who was so dear to you whilst you were living; and which, that you should not now want, Heaven put it into the mind of my relentless father to send you to me. And you shall have them, though I had purposed to die unmoved and without shedding a tear; and when I have done, I will instantly join my soul to yours; for in what other company can I go better and safer to those unknown regions, where, I doubt not, your soul is now expecting mine?"

When she had done speaking, she shed a flood of tears, kissing the heart a thousand times; whilst the damsels who were about her knew neither what heart it was, nor what her words imported; but being moved with pity they joined with her, begging to know the cause of her grief, and endeavouring all they could to comfort her.

After she had lamented as long as she thought fit, she raised up her head, and wiping her eyes, said, "Thou heart most dearly beloved! All my duty is now performed towards thee; nothing more remains, but for my soul to accompany thine."

Upon this she bade them reach the vessel of water, which she had prepared the day before, and pouring it into the cup with the heart, which she had sufficiently washed with her tears, she drank it all off without the least dread or apprehension, and threw herself upon the bed with the cup in her hand; composing her body as decently as she could, and pressing her lover's heart to hers, she lay without uttering a word more, expecting death.

The maids, when they saw this, though they knew not what it was she had drunk, sent to acquaint Tancred, who, fearing what had really happened, came into the room soon after she had laid herself down, and finding it was too late, began to lament most grievously.

"Sir," she said to him, "save those tears against worse fortune that may happen, for I want them not. Who but yourself would mourn for a thing of your own doing? But if any part of that love now remain in you which you once had for me, the last request I shall make is that since you would not suffer us to be happy together whilst living, our two bodies (wherever you have disposed of his) may be publicly interred together when dead."

Extreme grief would not suffer the Prince to reply.

Presently, finding herself near her end, she strained the heart strongly to her breast, saying, "Receive us, Heaven, I die!" Then closing her eyes, all sense forsook her, and she departed this miserable life.

Such an end had the amours of Guiscard and Ghismond, as you have now heard; and the Prince, repenting of his cruelty when it was too late, had them buried in one grave in the most public manner, amid the general grief of all the people of Salerno.

CYMON AND IPHIGENIA

Boccaccio

According to the ancient histories of Cyprus, there lived sometime in that island, one of great rank and distinction, called Aristippus, who was the wealthiest person in all the country. If he was unhappy in any one respect, it was in having, amongst his other children, a son, who, though he exceeded most young people of his age in stature and comeliness, yet was a perfect idiot; his name was Galeso, but as neither the labour nor skill of his master nor the correction of his father was ever able to beat one letter into his head, or the least instruction of any kind, and as his voice and manner of speaking were strangely harsh and uncouth, he was, by way of disdain, called only Cymon; which, in their language, signified *beast*. The father had long beheld him with infinite vexation, and as all hopes were vanished concerning him, to remove out of his sight an object which afforded constant matter of grief, he ordered him away to his country-house, to be there with his slaves.

This was extremely agreeable to Cymon, because people of that sort had always been most to his mind. Residing there and doing all sorts of drudgery pertaining to that kind of life, it happened one day, as he was going, about noon-tide, with his staff upon his shoulder, from one farm to another, that he passed through a pleasant grove, which, as it was then the month of May, was all in bloom. Thence, as his stars led him, he came into a meadow surrounded with high trees, in one corner of which was a crystal spring, and by the side of it, upon the grass, lay a most beautiful damsel asleep, clothed with a mantle so exceedingly fine and delicate as scarcely to conceal the exquisite whiteness of her skin; only from her waist downwards she wore a white silken quilt, and at her feet were sleeping two women and a man-servant.

As soon as Cymon cast his eyes upon her, he stood leaning upon his staff, as if he had never seen the face of a woman before, and began to gaze with the utmost astonishment without speaking a word. Presently, in his rude uncivilised breast, which had hitherto been incapable of receiving the least sense of good-breeding whatever, a sudden thought arose, which seemed to intimate to his gross and shallow understanding that this was the most agreeable sight that ever was seen. Starting from that fixed point, he began to examine each part by itself, commending every limb and feature; and having now from being a mere idiot become a judge of beauty, he grew very desirous of seeing the fair sleeper's eyes, for which purpose he was going several times to wake her; but as she so far excelled all other women that he ever saw, he was in doubt whether she was a mortal creature. This made him wait to see if she would awake of her own accord; and though that expectation seemed tedious to him, yet so pleasing was the object that he had no power to leave it. After a long time she came to herself, and raising up her head, saw Cymon stand propped upon his stick before her, at which she was surprised, and said, " Cymon " (for he was known all over the country, as well for his own rusticity as his father's nobility and great wealth), " what are you looking for here at this time of day ? "

He made no answer, but stood with his eyes fixed upon hers, which seemed to dart a sweetness that filled him with a kind of joy to which he had hitherto been a stranger; whilst she, observing this, and not knowing to what his rudeness might prompt him, called up her women, and then said, " Cymon, go about your business."

He replied, " I will go along with you."

And though she was afraid, and would have avoided his company, yet he would not leave her till he had brought her to her own house; thence he went home to his father, and he declared that he would return no more into the country. This was very disagreeable to all his friends, yet they let him alone, waiting to see what this change of temper could be owing to.

Love having thus penetrated his heart, where no lesson of any kind could ever find admittance, in a little time his way of thinking and behaviour were so far changed that his father and friends were strangely surprised at it, as well as everybody that knew him. First of all then, he asked his father to let him have clothes and everything else like his brothers; to which the father very willingly consented. Conversing, too, with young gentlemen of character, and observing their ways and manner of behaving, in a very short time he not only got over the first rudiments of learning, but attained to some knowledge in philosophy. Afterwards (his love for Iphigenia being the sole cause) his rude and rustic speech was changed into a tone more agreeable and civilised:

he grew also a master of music: and with regard to the military art, as well by sea as land, he became as expert and gallant as the best. In short, not to run over all his excellences, before the expiration of the fourth year from his being first in love, he turned out the most accomplished young gentleman in every respect that ever Cyprus could boast of. What, then, most gracious ladies, shall we say of Cymon? Surely nothing less than this; that all the noble qualities, which had been infused by Heaven into his generous soul, were shut up as it were by invidious fortune, and bound fast with the strongest fetters in a small corner of his heart, till love broke the enchantment, and drove with all its might these virtues out of that cruel obscurity, to which they had been long doomed, to a clear and open day; plainly showing whence it draws those spirits that are its votaries, and whither its mighty influence conducts them.

Cymon might have his flights like other young people, with regard to his love for Iphigenia; yet, when Aristippus considered it was that which had made a man of him, he not only bore with it, but encouraged him in the pursuit of his pleasures. Cymon, nevertheless, who refused to be called Galeso, remembering that Iphigenia had styled him Cymon, being desirous of bringing that affair to a happy conclusion, had often requested her in marriage of her father, who replied that he had already promised her to one Pasimunda, a young nobleman of Rhodes, and that he intended not to break his word. The time then being come that was appointed for their nuptials, and the husband having sent in form to demand her, Cymon said to himself:

"O Iphigenia, the time is now come when I shall give proof how I love you! I am become a man on your account; and could I but obtain you, I should be as glorious and happy as the gods themselves; and have you I will, or else I will die."

Immediately he prevailed upon some young noblemen who were his friends, to assist him; and, fitting out a ship of war privately, they put to sea, in order to intercept the vessel that was to transport Iphigenia; who, after great respect and honour showed by her father to her husband's friends, embarked with them for Rhodes. Cymon, who had but little rest that night, overtook them on the following day, when he called out, "Stop, and strike your sails; or expect to go at once to the bottom of the sea."

They, on the other hand, had got all their arms on deck, and were prepared to make a vigorous defence. He therefore threw a grappling iron upon the other ship, which was making the best of its way, and drew it close to his own ; when, like a lion, without waiting for any one to second him, he jumped singly among his enemies, as if he cared not for them ; and love spurring him on with incredible force, he cut and drove them all like so many sheep before him, till they soon threw down their arms, acknowledging themselves his prisoners ; when he addressed them in the following manner :

" Gentlemen, it was not a desire of plunder, nor enmity to any of your company, that made me leave Cyprus to fall upon you here in this manner. What occasioned it is a matter, the success of which is of the utmost consequence to myself, and as easy for you to grant me quietly : it is Iphigenia, whom I love above all the world ; and as I could not have her from her father peaceably, and as a friend, my love constrains me to win her from you as an enemy by force of arms. Therefore I am resolved to be to her what your Pasimunda was to have been. Resign her then to me, and go away in God's name."

The people, more by force than any good will, gave her up, all in tears, to Cymon : who, seeing her lament in that manner, said, " Fair lady, be not discouraged ; I am your Cymon, who has a much better claim to your affection, on account of his long and constant love, than Pasimunda can have by virtue of a promise." Taking her then on board his ship, without meddling with anything that belonged to them, he suffered them to depart.

Cymon thus being the most overjoyed man that could be, after comforting the lady under her calamity, consulted with his friends what to do, who were of opinion that they should by no means return to Cyprus yet ; but that it were better to go directly to Crete where they all had relations and friends, but Cymon especially, on which account he might be more secure there along with Iphigenia ; and accordingly they directed their course that way.

But fortune, who had given the lady to Cymon by an easy conquest, soon changed his immoderate joy into most sad and bitter lamentation. In about four hours from his parting with the Rhodians, night came upon them, which was more welcome to Cymon than any of the rest, and with it a most violent tempest, which overspread the face of the heavens in such a manner that they could neither see what they did, nor whither they were carried ; nor were they able at all to steer the ship. You may easily suppose what was Cymon's grief on this occasion. He concluded that Heaven had crowned his desires only to make death more grievous to him, which before would have been but little regarded. His friends also were greatly affected, but especially Iphigenia, who trembled at every shock, still sharply upbraiding his ill-timed love, and declaring that this tempest was sent by Providence for no other reason than to disappoint his presumption in resolving to have her, contrary to the will and disposal of Heaven, and that, seeing her die first, he might die likewise in the same miserable manner. Amongst such complaints as these, they were carried at last, the wind growing continually more violent, near the island of Rhodes; and not knowing where they were, they endeavoured, for the safety of their lives, to get to land if possible.

In this they succeeded, and got into a little bay, where the Rhodian ship had arrived just before them; nor did they know they were at Rhodes till the next morning, when they saw, about a bow-shot from them, the same ship they had parted with the day before. Cymon was greatly concerned at this, and fearing what afterwards came to pass, he bade them put to sea if possible, and trust to fortune, for they could never be in a worse place. They used all possible means then to get out, but in vain; the wind was strongly against them, and drove them to shore in spite of all they could do to prevent it. They were soon known by the sailors of the other ship, who had now gained the shore, and who ran to a neighbouring town, to which the young gentlemen that had been on board the ship were just gone before, and informed them how Cymon and Iphigenia were, like themselves, driven thither by stress of weather. They, hearing this, brought a great number of people from the town to the sea-side, and captured Cymon and all his companions, who had got on shore, with a design of fleeing to a neighbouring wood, as also Iphigenia, and brought them all together to the town.

Pasimunda, upon hearing the news, went and made his complaints to the senate, who, accordingly, sent Lysimachus, the chief magistrate of that year, along with a guard of soldiers, to conduct them to prison. Thus the miserable and enamoured Cymon lost his mistress soon after he had gained her, and without having scarcely so much as a kiss for his pains.

In the meantime Iphigenia was handsomely received by many ladies of quality, and comforted for the trouble she had sustained in being made a captive, as well as in the storm at sea; and she remained with them till the day appointed for her nuptials. However, Cymon and his friends had their lives granted them (though Pasimunda used all his endeavours to the contrary) for the favour shown to the Rhodians the day before; but they were sentenced to perpetual imprisonment, where they remained sorrowfully enough, as they had no hope of obtaining their liberty.

Now, whilst Pasimunda was making preparation for his nuptials, Fortune, as if she had repented the injury done to Cymon, produced a new circumstance for his deliverance. Pasimunda had a brother, beneath him in years, but not in virtue, called Ormisda, who had been long talked of as about to marry a beautiful lady of that city, called Cassandra, whom Lysimachus was also in love with, and had for some time been prevented from marrying her, by divers unlucky accidents. Now, as Pasimunda was to celebrate his own nuptials with great state and feasting, he supposed it would save a great deal of expense and trouble if his brother were to marry at the same time. He consequently proposed the thing again to Cassandra's friends, and they soon brought it to a conclusion; when it was agreed by all parties that the same day that Pasimunda brought home Iphigenia, Ormisda should bring home Cassandra.

This was very grating to Lysimachus, who saw himself now deprived of the hope which he had hitherto entertained of marrying her himself; but he was wise enough to conceal it, contriving a way to prevent its taking effect if possible; none however appeared, but that of taking her away by force. This seemed easy enough on account of his office; still he thought it not so reputable as if he had borne no office at all at that time; but in fine, after a long debate with himself, honour gave way to love, and he resolved, happen what would, to bear away Cassandra. Thinking then what companions he should make choice of for this enterprise, as well as the means that were to be taken, he soon called Cymon to mind, whom he had in custody, as also his companions; and thinking he could have nobody better to assist him, nor one more trusty and faithful on that occasion than Cymon, the next night he had him privately into his chamber, where he spoke to him in this manner:

"Cymon, as the gods are the best and most liberal givers of all things to mankind, so are they also the ablest judges of our several virtues and merits; such then as they find to be firm and constant in every respect, them do they make worthy of the greatest things. Now concerning your worth and valour, they are willing to have more certain proof of both, than it was possible for you to show while your life actions were limited to the house of your father, whom I know to be a person of the greatest distinction ; for first, by the subtle force of love, as I am informed, have they, from a mere insensible creature, made a man of you ; and afterwards, by adverse fortune, and now, by a miserable imprisonment, are they willing to see if your soul be changed from what it was, when you appeared flushed so lately with the prize you had won. If that continues the same, I can propose nothing so agreeable to you as what I am now going to offer ; which, that you may resume your former might and valour, I shall immediately disclose. Pasimunda, overjoyed with your disappointment, and a zealous promoter, as far as in him lay, of your being put to death, is now about to celebrate his marriage with your Iphigenia, that he may enjoy that blessing, which Fortune, when she was favourable, first put into your power, and afterwards snatched away from you ; but how this must afflict you, I can easily suppose by myself, who am like to undergo the same injury, and at the same time, with regard to my mistress Cassandra, who is to be married to his brother Ormisda. Now I see no remedy for either of us, but what consists in our own resolution, and the strength of our arms : it will be necessary, therefore, to make our way with our swords, for each of us to gain his lady : if then you value—I will not say your liberty, because that, without her, would be of little weight with you ; but, I say, if you value—your mistress, you need only follow me, and Fortune has put her into your hands."

These words spoke comfort to the drooping soul of Cymon, who immediately replied : " Lysimachus, you could never have a more stout or a more trusty friend for such an enterprise than myself, if it be as you seem to promise : tell me then what you would have me do, and you shall see me put it nobly into execution."

Lysimachus made answer : " Three days hence the ladies are to be brought home to their espoused husbands, when you, with your friends and myself, and some people whom I can confide in, will go armed in the evening, and enter their house whilst they are in the midst of their mirth, where we will seize on the two brides, and carry them away to a ship which I have secretly provided, killing all that shall presume to oppose us."

This scheme was entirely to Cymon's liking, and he waited quietly till the time appointed. The wedding-day being now come, and every part of the house full of mirth and feasting, Lysimachus, after giving the necessary orders, at the time fixed, divided Cymon and his companions with his own friends into three parties, and putting arms under their several cloaks, and animating them boldly to pursue what they had undertaken, he sent one party to the haven to secure their escape, and went with the other two to Pasimunda's house; one party he stationed at the gate, to prevent any persons from shutting them up in the house; whilst he, along with Cymon, went upstairs with the remaining party. Coming then into the dining-room, where the two brides, with many other ladies, were seated at supper, they advanced to them, and throwing down all the tables, seized each his lady, and giving them into the arms of their followers, ordered them to carry them away to their ship. The brides, as well as the other ladies and servants, cried out so much, that immediately there was a great tumult.

In the meantime, Cymon and Lysimachus, with their followers, drew their swords, and came downstairs again without any opposition, till they met with Pasimunda, whom the noise had drawn thither, having in his hand a great club, when Cymon, at one stroke, laid him dead at his feet, and whilst Ormisda was running to his assistance, he was likewise killed by Cymon; and many others also of their friends, who came to their relief, were wounded and beaten back. Leaving the house then, all full of blood and confusion, they joined parties, and went directly to the ship with the booty, without the least hindrance whatever; when, putting the ladies on board, and they with all their friends following them, the shore was soon filled with crowds of people who came to rescue them, upon which they plied their oars, and sailed joyfully away for Crete. There they were cheerfully received by all their friends and relations, when they espoused their ladies, and were well pleased with their several prizes.

This occasioned great quarrels afterwards between the two islands of Cyprus and Rhodes. At length, by the interposition of friends, everything was amicably adjusted, and then Cymon returned along with Iphigenia to Cyprus, and Lysimachus, in like manner, carried Cassandra back to Rhodes, where they lived very happily to the end of their days.

ANASTASIO

Boccaccio

IN Ravenna, an ancient city of Romagna, dwelt formerly many persons of quality; amongst the rest was a young gentleman, named Anastasio de gli Onesti, who, by the deaths of his father and uncle, was left immensely rich; and, being a bachelor, fell in love with one of the daughters of Signor Paolo Traversaro (of a family much superior to his own), and was in hopes, by his assiduous courtship, to gain her affection. But though his endeavours were generous, noble, and praiseworthy, so far were they from succeeding, that, on the contrary, they rather turned out to his disadvantage; and so cruel, and even savage, was the beloved fair one (either her singular beauty or noble descent having made her thus haughty and scornful), that neither he, nor anything that he did, could ever please her.

This so afflicted Anastasio, that he was going to lay violent hands upon himself; but, thinking better of it, he frequently had a mind to leave her entirely; or else to hate her, if he could, as much as she had hated him. But this proved a vain design; for he constantly found that the less his hope, the greater always was his love.

The young man persevered then in his love and his extravagant way of life, till his friends all agreed that he was destroying his constitution, as well as wasting his substance; they therefore advised and entreated that he would leave the place, and go and live somewhere else; for, by that means, he might lessen both his love and expense. For some time he made light of this advice, till being very much importuned, and not knowing how to refuse them, he promised to do so; when, making extraordinary preparations, as if he was going a long journey, either into France or Spain, he mounted his horse, and left Ravenna, attended by many of his friends, and went to a place about three miles off, called Chiassi, where he ordered tents and pavilions to be brought, telling those who had accompanied him, that he meant to stay there, but that they might return to Ravenna. There he lived in the most splendid manner, inviting sometimes this company, and sometimes that, both to dine and sup, as he had used to do before.

Now it happened in the beginning of May, the season being extremely pleasant, that, thinking of his cruel mistress, he ordered all his attendants to retire, and leave him to his own thoughts ; and then he walked along, step by step, and lost in reflection, till he came to a forest of pines. It being then the fifth hour of the day, and he advanced more than half a mile into the grove, without thinking either of his dinner, or any thing else but his love ; on a sudden he seemed to hear a most grievous lamentation, with the loud shrieks of a woman. This put an end to his meditation, when looking round him, to know what the matter was, he saw come out of a thicket full of briars and thorns, and run towards the place where he was, a most beautiful lady, quite naked, with her flesh all scratched and rent by the bushes, crying terribly, and begging for mercy. In close pursuit of her were two fierce mastiffs, biting and tearing wherever they could lay hold, and behind, upon a black steed, rode a gloomy knight, with a dagger in his hand, loading her with the bitterest imprecations.

The sight struck him at once with wonder and consternation, as well as pity for the lady, whom he was desirous to rescue from such trouble and danger, if possible ; but finding himself without arms, he tore off a branch of a tree, and went forward with it, to oppose both the dogs and the knight.

The knight observing this, called out, afar off, " Anastasio, do not concern yourself ; but leave the dogs and me to do by this wicked woman as she has deserved."

At these words the dogs laid hold of her, and he coming up to them, dismounted from his horse. Anastasio then stepped up to him, and said, " I know not who you are, that are acquainted thus with me : but I must tell you, that it is a most villainous action for a man, armed as you are, to pursue a naked woman, and to set dogs upon her also, as if she were a wild beast ; be assured that I shall defend her to the utmost of my power."

The knight replied, " I was once your countryman, when you were but a child, and was called Guido de gli Anastagi, at which time I was more enamoured with this woman, than ever you were with Traversaro's daughter ; but she treated me so cruelly, and with so much insolence, that I killed myself with this dagger which you now see in my hand, for which I am doomed to eternal punishment. Soon afterwards she, who moreover was rejoiced at my death, died likewise, and for her cruelty, as also for the joy which she expressed at my misery, she is condemned as well as myself ; our sentences are for her to flee before me, and for me, who loved her so well, to pursue her as a mortal enemy ; and when I overtake her, with this dagger, with which I murdered myself, do I murder her ; then I rip her open to the spine, and take out that hard and cold heart, which neither love nor pity could pierce, with all her entrails, and throw them to the dogs ; and in a little time (so wills the justice and power of Heaven) she rises, as though she had never been dead, and renews her miserable flight, whilst we pursue her over again. Every Friday in the year, about this time, do I sacrifice her here, as you see, and on other days in other places, wherever she has thought or done anything against me : and thus being from a lover become her mortal enemy, I am to follow her for years as many as the months she was cruel to me. Let then divine justice take its course, nor offer to oppose what you are no way able to withstand."

Anastasio drew back at these words, terrified to death, and waited to see what the other was going to do. The knight, having made an end of speaking, ran at her with the utmost fury, as she was seized by the dogs, and pulled down upon her knees begging for mercy. Then with his dagger he pierced through her breast, and tore out her heart and her entrails, which they immediately devoured as if half famished. In a little time she rose again, as if nothing had happened, and fled towards the sea, the dogs biting and tearing her all the way ; the knight also being remounted, and taking his dagger, pursued her as before, till they soon got out of sight.

Upon seeing these things, Anastasio stood divided betwixt fear and pity, and at length it came into his mind that, as it happened always on a Friday, it might be of particular use. Returning then to his servants, he sent for some of his friends and relations, and said to them :

" You have often importuned me to leave off loving this my enemy, and to contract my expenses ; I am ready to do so, provided you grant me one favour, which is this, that next Friday, you engage Paolo Traversaro, his wife and daughter, with all their women friends and relations, to come and dine with me : the reason of my requiring this you will see at that time."

This seemed to them but a small matter, and returning to Ravenna they invited those whom he had desired, and though they found it difficult to prevail upon the young lady, yet the others carried her at last along with them. Anastasio had provided a magnificent entertainment under the pines where that spectacle had lately been; and having seated all his company, he contrived that the lady should sit directly opposite to the scene of action. The last course then was no sooner served up, than the lady's shrieks began to be heard. This surprised them all, and they began to inquire what it was, and, as nobody could inform them, they all rose: when immediately they saw the lady, the dogs, and the knight, who were soon amongst them. Great was consequently the clamour, both against the dogs and the knight, and many of them went to the lady's assistance. But the knight made the same harangue to them, that he had done to Anastasio, which terrified and filled them with wonder; then he acted the same part over again, whilst the ladies (there were many of them present who were related to both the knight and lady, and who remembered his love and unhappy death) all lamented as much as if it had happened to themselves.

This tragical affair being ended, and the lady and knight both gone away, they held various discourse together about it; but none seemed so much affected as Anastasio's mistress, who had heard and seen everything distinctly, and was sensible that it concerned her more than any other person, calling to mind her invariable cruelty towards him; so that already she seemed to flee before his wrathful spirit, with the mastiffs at her heels. Such was her terror at this thought, that, turning her hatred into love, she sent that very evening a trusty damsel privately to him, to entreat him in her name to come and see her, for she was ready to fulfil his desires.

Anastasio replied, that nothing could be more agreeable to him; but that he desired no favour from her but what was consistent with her honour. The lady, who was sensible that it had been always her own fault they were not married, answered, that she was willing; and going herself to her father and mother, she acquainted them with her intention. This gave them the utmost satisfaction; and the next Sunday the marriage was solemnised with all possible demonstrations of joy. And that spectacle was not attended with this good alone; but all the women of Ravenna were ever after so terrified with it, that they were more ready to listen to and oblige the men than ever they had been before.

FEDERIGO AND THE FALCON

Boccaccio

AT Florence there dwelt a young gentleman named Federigo, son of Filippo Alberighi, who, in feats of arms and gentility, surpassed all the youth in Tuscany. This gentleman was in love with a lady called Monna Giovanna, one of the most agreeable women in Florence, and to gain her affection, he was continually making tilts, balls, and such diversions; lavishing away his money in rich presents, and everything that was extravagant. But she, as pure in conduct as she was fair, made no account either of what he did for her sake, or of himself.

As Federigo continued to live in this manner, spending profusely, and acquiring nothing, his wealth soon began to waste, till at last he had nothing left but a very small farm, the income of which was a most slender maintenance, and a single hawk, one of the best in the world. Yet loving still more than ever, and finding he could subsist no longer in the city, in the manner he would choose to live, he retired to his farm, where he went out fowling, as often as the weather would permit, and bore his distress patiently, without ever making his necessity known to anybody.

Now it happened, after he was thus brought low, the lady's husband fell sick, and, being very rich, he made a will by which he left all his substance to an only son, who was almost grown up, and if he should die without issue, he then ordered that it should revert to his lady, whom he was extremely fond of; and when he had disposed thus of his fortune, he died. Monna Giovanna now, being left a widow, retired, as our ladies usually do during the summer season, to a house of hers in the country, near to that of Federigo: whence it happened that her son soon became acquainted with him, and they used to divert themselves together with dogs and hawks; and the boy, having often seen Federigo's hawk fly, and being strangely taken with it, was desirous of having it, though the other valued it to that degree that he knew not how to ask for it.

This being so, the boy soon fell sick, which gave his mother great concern, as he was her only child, and she ceased not to attend on and comfort him; often requesting, if there was any particular thing which he fancied, to let her know it, and promising to procure it for him if it was possible. The young gentleman, after many offers of this kind, at last said, "Madam, if you could contrive for me to have Federigo's hawk, I should soon be well."

She was in some perplexity at this, and began to consider how best to act. She knew that Federigo had long entertained a liking for her, without the least encouragement on her part; therefore she said to herself, "How can I send or go to ask for this hawk, which I hear is the very best of the kind, and which is all he has in the world to maintain him? Or how can I offer to take away from a gentleman all the pleasure that he has in life?"

Being in this perplexity, though she was very sure of having it for a word, she stood without making any reply; till at last the love of her son so far prevailed, that she resolved at all events to make him easy, and not send, but go herself. She then replied, "Set your heart at rest, my boy, and think only of your recovery; for I promise you that I will go to-morrow for it the first thing I do." This afforded him such joy, that he immediately showed signs of amendment.

The next morning she went, by way of a walk, with another lady in company, to Federigo's little cottage to enquire for him. At that time, as it was too early to go out upon his diversion, he was at work in his garden. Hearing, therefore, that his mistress enquired for him at the door, he ran thither, surprised and full of joy; whilst she with a great deal of complaisance went to meet him: and, after the usual compliments, she said, "Good morning to you, Sir; I am come to make you some amends for the losses you have sustained on my account; what I mean is, that I have brought a companion to take a neighbourly dinner with you to-day."

He replied, with a great deal of humility, "Madam, I do not remember ever to have suffered any loss by your means, but rather so much good, that if I was worth anything at any time it was due to your singular merit, and the love I had for you: and most assuredly this courteous visit is more welcome to me than if I had all that I have wasted returned to me to spend over again; but you are come to a very poor host."

With these words he showed her into his house, seeming much out of countenance, and thence they went into the garden, when, having no company for her, he said, " Madam, as I have nobody else, please to admit this honest woman, a labourer's wife, to be with you, whilst I set forth the table."

Although his poverty was extreme, never till now had he been so sensible of his past extravagance ; but finding nothing to entertain the lady with, for whose sake he had treated thousands, he was in the utmost perplexity, cursing his evil fortune, and running up and down like one out of his wits.

At length, having neither money nor anything he could pawn, and longing to give her something, at the same time that he would not make his case known, even so much as to his own labourer, he espied his hawk upon the perch, seized it, and finding it very fat, judged it might make a dish not unworthy of such a lady. Without further thought, then, he wrung its head off, and gave it to a girl to dress and roast carefully, whilst he laid the cloth, having a small quantity of linen yet left ; and then he returned, with a smile on his countenance, into the garden to tell Monna Giovanna that what little dinner he was able to provide was now ready. She and her friend, therefore, entered and sat down with him, he serving them all the time with great respect, when they ate the good hawk, not knowing what it was.

After dinner was over, and they had sat chatting a little while together, the lady thought it a fit time to tell her errand, and addressed him courteously in this manner :

" Sir, if you call to mind your past life, and my resolution, which perhaps you may call cruelty, I doubt not but you will wonder at my presumption, when you know what I am come for : but if you had children of your own, to know how strong our natural affection is towards them, I am very sure you would excuse me. Now, my having a son forces me, against my own inclination, and all reason whatsoever, to request a thing of you, which I know you value extremely, as you have no other comfort or diversion left you in your small circumstances ; I mean your hawk, which he has taken such a fancy to, that unless I bring it back with me, I very much fear that he will die of his disorder. Therefore I entreat you, not for any regard you have for me (for in that respect you are no way obliged to me), but for that generosity with which you have always distinguished yourself, that you would please to let me have it, so that I may be able to say that my child's life has been restored to me through your gift, and that he and I are under perpetual obligations to you."

Federigo, hearing the lady's request, and knowing it was out of his power to fulfil it, began to weep before he was able to make a word of reply. This she at first attributed to his reluctance to part with his favourite bird, and expected that he was going to give her a flat denial; but after she had waited a little for his answer, he said:

"Madam, ever since I have fixed my affections upon you, fortune has still been contrary to me in many things, and sorely I have felt them; but all the rest is nothing to what has now come to pass. You are here to visit me in this my poor dwelling, to which in my prosperity you would never deign to come; you also entreat a small present from me, which it is wholly out of my power to give, as I am going briefly to tell you. As soon as I was acquainted with the great favour you designed me, I thought it proper, considering your superior merit and excellency, to treat you, according to my ability, with something choicer than is usually given to other persons, when, calling to mind my hawk, which you now request, and his goodness, I judged him a fit repast for you, and you have had him roasted. Nor could I have thought him better bestowed, had you not now desired him in a different manner, which is such a grief to me, that I shall never be at peace as long as I live": and saying this, he produced the hawk's feathers, feet, and talons. The lady began now to blame him for killing such a bird to entertain any woman with, in her heart all the while extolling the greatness of his soul, which poverty had no power to abase.

Having now no further hopes of obtaining the hawk, she took leave of Federigo, and returned sadly to her son; who, either out of grief for the disappointment, or through the violence of his disorder, died in a few days.

She continued sorrowful for some time; but being left rich, and young, her brothers were very pressing with her to marry again. This went against her inclination, but finding them still importunate, and remembering Federigo's great worth, and the late instance of his generosity, in killing such a bird for her entertainment, she said, "I should rather choose to continue as I am; but since it is your desire that I take a husband, I will have none but Federigo de gli Alberighi."

They smiled contemptuously at this, and said, "You simple woman! what are you talking of? He is not worth one farthing in the world."

She replied, "I believe it, brothers, to be as you say; but know, *that I would sooner have a man that stands in need of riches, than riches without a man.*"

They hearing her resolution, and well knowing his generous temper, gave her to him with all her wealth ; and he, seeing himself possessed of a lady whom he had so dearly loved, and of such a vast fortune, lived in all true happiness with her, and was a better manager of his affairs than he had been before.

THE PATIENT GRISELDA

BOCCACCIO

IT is a long time ago, that, among the marquisses of Saluzzo, the principal or head of the family was a youth, called Gualtieri, who, as he was a bachelor, spent his whole time in hawking and hunting, without any thought of ever being encumbered with a wife and children ; in which respect, no doubt, he was very wise. But this being disagreeable to his subjects, they often pressed him to marry, to the end that he might neither die without an heir, nor they be left without a lord ; offering themselves to provide such a lady for him, and of such a family, that they should have great hopes from her, and he reason enough to be satisfied.

" Worthy friends," he replied, " you urge me to do a thing which I was fully resolved against, considering what a difficult matter it is to find a person of a suitable temper, with the great abundance everywhere of such as are otherwise, and how miserable also the man's life must be who is tied to a disagreeable woman. As to your getting at a woman's temper from her family, and so choosing one to please me, that seems quite a ridiculous fancy ; for, besides the uncertainty with regard to their true fathers, how many daughters do we see resembling neither father nor mother ? Nevertheless, as you are so fond of having me noosed, I will agree to be so. Therefore, that I may have nobody to blame but myself, should it happen amiss, I will make my own choice ; and I protest, let me marry whom I will, that, unless you show her the respect that is due to her as my lady, you shall know, to your cost, how grievous it is to me to have taken a wife at your request, contrary to my own inclination."

The honest men replied, that they were well satisfied, provided he would but make the trial.

Now the Marquis had taken a fancy, some time before, to the behaviour of a poor country girl, who lived in a village not far from his palace, and thinking that he might live comfortably enough with her, he determined, without seeking any farther, to marry her. Accordingly, he sent for her father, who was a very poor man, and acquainted him with it. Afterwards, he summoned all his subjects together, and said to them, " Gentlemen, it was and is your desire that I take a wife : I do it rather to please you than out of any liking I have to matrimony. You know that you promised me to be satisfied, and to pay her due honour, whoever she is that I shall make choice of. The time is now come when I shall fulfil my promise to you, and I expect you to do the like to me ; I have found a young woman in the neighbourhood after my own heart, whom I intend to espouse, and bring home in a very few days. Let it be your care, then, to do honour to my nuptials, and to respect her as your sovereign lady ; so that I may be satisfied with the performance of your promise, even as you are with that of mine."

The people all declared themselves pleased, and promised to regard her in all things as their mistress. Afterwards they made preparations for a most noble feast, and the like did the Prince, inviting all his relations, and the great lords in all parts and provinces about him : he had also most rich and costly robes made, shaped by a person that seemed to be of the same size with his intended spouse ; and provided a girdle, ring, and fine coronet, with everything requisite for a bride. And when the day appointed was come, about the third hour he mounted his horse, attended by all his friends and vassals ; and having everything in readiness, he said : " My lords and gentlemen, it is now time to go for my new spouse."

So on they rode to the village, and when he was come near the father's house, he saw her carrying some water from the well, in great haste, to go afterwards with some of her acquaintance to see the new Marchioness ; when he called her by her name, which was Griselda, and inquired where her father was. She modestly replied, " My gracious lord, he is in the house."

He then alighted from his horse, commanding them all to wait for him, and went alone into the cottage, where he found the father, who was called Giannucolo, and said to him, " Honest man, I am come to espouse thy daughter, but would first ask her some questions before thee." He then inquired whether she would make it her study to please him, and not be uneasy at any time, whatever he should do or say ; and whether she would always be obedient ; with more to that purpose. To which she answered, " Yes."

He then led her out by the hand, and made her strip before them all ; and ordering the rich apparel to be brought which he had provided, he had her clothed completely, and a coronet set upon her head, all disordered as her hair was ; after which, every one being in amaze, he said, " Behold, this is the person whom I intend for my wife, provided she will accept of me for her husband." Then, turning towards her, who stood quite abashed, " Will you," said he, " have me for your husband ? "

She replied, " Yes, if it so please your lordship."

" Well," he replied, " and I take you for my wife."

So he espoused her in that public manner, and mounting her on a palfrey, conducted her honourably to his palace, celebrating the nuptials with as much pomp and grandeur as though he had been married to the daughter of the King of France ; and the young bride showed apparently, that with her garments she had changed both her mind and behaviour.

She had a most agreeable person, and was so amiable, and so good-natured withal, that she seemed rather a lord's daughter than a poor shepherd's ; at which every one that knew her before was greatly surprised. She was so obedient also to her husband, and so obliging in all respects, that he thought himself the happiest man in the world ; and to her subjects likewise so gracious and condescending, that they all honoured and loved her as their own lives, praying for her health and prosperity, and declaring, contrary to their former opinion, that Gualtieri was the most prudent and sharp-sighted Prince in the whole world ; for that no one could have discerned such virtues under a mean habit, and a country disguise, but himself.

In a very short time her discreet behaviour and good works were the common subject of discourse, not in that country only, but everywhere else ; and what had been objected to the Prince, with regard to his marrying her, now took a contrary turn. They had not lived long together before she proved with child, and at length brought forth a daughter, for which he made great rejoicings.

But soon afterwards a new fancy came into his head, and that was, to make trial of her patience by long and intolerable sufferings : so he began with harsh words, and an appearance of great uneasiness ; telling her that his subjects were greatly displeased with her for her mean parentage, especially as they saw she bore children ; and that they did nothing but murmur at the daughter already born. Which, when she heard, without changing countenance, or her resolution, in any respect, she replied, " My lord, pray dispose of me as you think most for your honour and happiness : I shall entirely acquiesce, knowing myself to be meaner than the meanest of the people, and that I was altogether unworthy of that dignity to which your favour was pleased to advance me." This was very agreeable to the Prince, seeing that she was no way elevated with the honour he had conferred upon her.

Afterwards, having often told her, in general terms, that his subjects could not bear with the daughter that was born of her, he sent one of his servants, whom he had instructed what to do, who, with a very sorrowful countenance, said to her, " Madam, I must either lose my own life, or obey my lord's commands : now he has ordered me to take your daughter, and——" without saying anything more. She, hearing these words, and noting the fellow's looks, remembering also what she had heard before from her lord, concluded that he had orders to destroy the child. So she took it out of the cradle, kissed it, and gave it her blessing ; when, without changing countenance, though her heart throbbed with maternal affection, she tenderly laid it in the servant's arms, and said, " Take it, and do what thy lord and mine has commanded ; but, prithee, leave it not to be devoured by the fowls or wild beasts, unless that be his will." Taking the child, he acquainted the Prince with what she said, who was greatly surprised at her constancy ; and he sent the same person with it to a relation at Bologna, desiring her, without revealing whose child it was, to see it carefully brought up and educated. Afterwards the lady became with child a second time, and was delivered of a son, at which he was extremely pleased.

But, not satisfied with what he had already done, he began to grieve and persecute her still more ; saying one day to her, seemingly much out of temper, " Since thou hast brought me this son, I am able to live no longer with my people ; for they mutiny to that degree, that a poor shepherd's grandson is to succeed, and be their lord after me, that, unless I would run the risk of being driven out of my dominions, I must needs dispose of this child as I did the other ; and then send thee away, in order to take a wife more suitable to me."

She heard this with a great deal of resignation, making only this reply : " My lord, study only your own ease and happiness, without the least care for me ; for nothing is agreeable to me, but what is pleasing to yourself."

Not many days after, he sent for the son in the same manner as he had done for the daughter ; and, seeming also as if he had procured him to be destroyed, had him conveyed to Bologna, to be taken care of with the daughter. This she bore with the same resolution as before, at which the Prince wondered greatly, declaring to himself, that no other woman was capable of doing the like. And, were it not that he had observed her extremely fond of her children, whilst that was agreeable to him, he should have thought it want of affection in her; but he saw it was only her entire obedience and condescension. The people, imagining that the children were both put to death, blamed him to the last degree, thinking him the most cruel and worst of men, and showing great compassion for the lady; who, whenever she was in company with the ladies of her acquaintance, and they condoled with her for her loss, would only say, "It was not my will, but his who begot them."

But more years being now passed, and he resolving to make the last trial of her patience, declared, before many people, that he could no longer bear to keep Griselda as his wife, owning that he had done very foolishly, and like a young man, in marrying her, and that he meant to solicit the Pope for a dispensation to take another, and send her away: for which he was much blamed by many worthy persons; but he said nothing in return, only that it should be so. She, hearing this, and expecting to go home to her father's, and possibly tend the cattle as she had done before; whilst she saw some other lady possessed of him, whom she dearly loved and honoured, was perhaps secretly grieved; but as she had withstood other strokes of fortune, so she determined resolutely to do now.

Soon afterwards, Gualtieri had counterfeit letters come to him, as from Rome, acquainting all his people that his Holiness thereby dispensed with his marrying another and turning away Griselda. He then had her brought before them, and said, "Woman, by the Pope's leave I may dispose of thee, and take another wife. As my ancestors, then, have been all sovereign princes of this country, and thine only peasants, I intend to keep thee no longer, but to send thee back to thy father's cottage, with the same portion which thou broughtest me, and afterwards to make choice of one more suitable in quality to myself."

It was with the utmost difficulty she could now refrain from tears; and she replied, "My lord, I was always sensible that my servile condition would no way accord with your high rank and descent. For what I have been, I own myself indebted to Providence and you; I considered it as a favour lent me: you are now pleased to demand it back; I therefore willingly restore it. Behold the ring with which you espoused me ; I deliver it to you. You bid me take the dowry back which I brought you ; you will have no need for a teller to count it, nor I for a purse to put it in, much less a sumpter-horse to carry it away ; for I have not forgotten that you took me naked ; and if you think it decent to expose that body, which has borne you two children, in that manner, I am contented ; but I would entreat you, as a recompense for my virginity, which I brought you, and do not carry away, that you would please to let me have one shift over and above my dowry."

He, though ready to weep, yet put on a stern countenance, and said, " Thou shalt have one only then." And, notwithstanding the people all desired that she might have an old gown, to keep her body from shame, who had been his wife thirteen years and upwards, yet it was all in vain ; so she left his palace in that manner, and returned weeping to her father's, to the great grief of all who saw her.

The poor man, never supposing that the Prince would keep her long as his wife, and expecting this thing to happen every day, had safely laid up the garments of which she had been despoiled the day he espoused her. He now brought them to her, and she put them on, and went as usual about her father's little household affairs, bearing this fierce trial of adverse fortune with the greatest courage imaginable. The Prince then gave it out that he was to espouse a daughter of one of the counts of Panago ; and, seeming as if he made great preparations for his nuptials, he sent for Griselda to come to him, and said to her, " I am going to bring this lady home whom I have just married, and intend to show her all possible respect at her first coming : thou knowest that I have no women with me able to set out the rooms, and do many other things which are requisite on so solemn an occasion. As, therefore, thou art best acquainted with the state of the house, I would have thee make such provision as thou shalt judge proper, and invite what ladies thou wilt, even as though thou wert mistress of the house, and when the marriage is ended, get thee home to thy father's again."

Though these words pierced like daggers to the heart of Griselda, who was unable to part with her love for the Prince so easily as she had done her great fortune, yet she replied, " My lord, I am ready to fulfil all your commands." She then went in her coarse attire into the palace, whence she had but just before departed in her shift, and with her own hands did she begin to sweep, and set all the rooms to rights, cleaning the stools and benches in the hall like the meanest servant, and directing what was to be done in the kitchen, never giving over till everything was in order, and as it ought to be. After this was done, she invited, in the Prince's name, all the ladies in the country to come to the feast. And on the day appointed for the marriage, meanly clad as she was, she received them in the most genteel and cheerful manner imaginable.

Now Gualtieri, who had his children carefully brought up at Bologna (the girl being about twelve years old, and one of the prettiest creatures that ever were seen, and the boy six), had sent to his kinswoman there, to desire she would bring them, with an honourable retinue, to Saluzzo; giving it out all the way she came that she was bringing the young lady to be married to him, without letting any one know to the contrary. Accordingly they all three set forwards, attended by a goodly train of gentry, and, after some days' travelling, reached Saluzzo about dinner-time, when they found the whole country assembled, waiting to see their new lady. The young lady was most graciously received by all the women present, and being come into the hall where the tables were all covered, Griselda, meanly dressed as she was, went cheerfully to meet her, saying, "Your ladyship is most kindly welcome."

The ladies, who had greatly importuned the Prince, though to no purpose, to let Griselda be in a room by herself, or else that she might have some of her own clothes, and not appear before strangers in that manner, were now seated, and going to be served round, whilst the young lady was universally admired, and every one said that the Prince had made a good change; but Griselda, in particular, highly commended both her and her brother. The Marquis, now thinking that he had seen enough with regard to his wife's patience, and perceiving that in all her trials she was still the same, being persuaded, likewise, that this proceeded from no want of understanding in her, because he knew her to be singularly prudent, he thought it time to take her from that anguish which he supposed she might conceal under her firm and constant deportment. So, making her come before all the company, he said, with a smile, "What thinkest thou, Griselda, of my bride?"

"My lord," she replied, "I like her extremely well; and if she be as prudent as she is fair, you may be the happiest man in the world with her: but I most humbly beg that you would not take those heart-breaking measures with this lady as you did with your last wife, because she is young, and has been tenderly educated, whereas the other was inured to hardships from a child."

Gualtieri, perceiving that, though Griselda thought that person was to be his wife, she nevertheless answered him with great humility and sweetness of temper, made her sit down by him, and said, " Griselda, it is now time for you to reap the fruit of your long patience, and that they who have reputed me to be cruel, unjust, and a monster in nature, may know that what I have done has been all along with a view to teach you how to behave as a wife ; to show them how to choose and keep a wife ; and, lastly, to secure my own ease and quiet as long as we live together, which I was apprehensive might have been endangered by my marrying. Therefore I had a mind to prove you by harsh and injurious treatment ; and not being sensible that you have ever transgressed my will, either in word or deed, I now seem to have met with that happiness I desired. I intend, then, to restore in one hour what I had taken away from you in many, and to make you the sweetest recompense for the many bitter pangs I have caused you to suffer. Accept, therefore, this young lady, whom you thought my spouse, and her brother, as your children and mine. They are the same whom you and many others believed that I had been the means of cruelly murdering : and I am your husband, who love and value you above all things ; assuring myself that no person in the world can be happier in a wife than I am."

With this he embraced her most affectionately, when, rising up together (she weeping for joy), they went where their daughter was sitting, quite astonished with these things, and tenderly saluted both her and her brother, undeceiving them and the whole company. At this the women all arose, overjoyed, from the tables, and taking Griselda into the chamber, they clothed her with her own noble apparel, and as a marchioness, resembling such an one even in rags, and brought her into the hall. And being extremely rejoiced with her son and daughter, and every one expressing the utmost satisfaction at what had come to pass, the feasting was prolonged many days.

The Marquis was judged a very wise man, though abundantly too severe, and the trial of his lady most intolerable ; but as for Griselda, she was beyond compare. In a few days the Marquis took Giannuculo from his drudgery, and maintained him as his father-in-law, and so he lived very comfortably to a good old age. Gualtieri afterwards married his daughter to one of equal nobility, continuing the rest of his life with Griselda, and showing her all the respect and honour that was possible.

What can we say, then, but that divine spirits may descend from heaven into the meanest cottages; whilst royal palaces shall produce such as seem rather adapted to have the care of hogs, than the government of men? Who but Griselda could, not only without a tear, but even with seeming satisfaction, undergo the most rigid and unheard-of trials by her husband? Many women there are, who, if turned out of doors naked in that manner, would have procured themselves fine clothes, adorning at once their own persons and their husband's brows.

FRANCO SACCHETTI
1335–1400

MESSER BERNABO OF MILAN

MESSER BERNABO, lord of Milan, once bestowed a handsome reward upon a certain miller, for the somewhat singular reason of having received from the shrewd artificer some very witty and caustic replies. Our said governor, who bore a most cruel and implacable disposition towards all kind of offenders, nevertheless possessed the art of tempering his ferocity so as to give it an air of real justice.

The case he had here in hand was that of a wealthy abbot, who had been fined by the governor in four florins for his negligent care in the education of two mastiff whelps entrusted to his spiritual direction, but which had turned out somewhat too cruel and quarrelsome. The covetous father upon this cried out for mercy, to which the governor merely replied, that he must infallibly pay the fine, unless he had the wit to give a satisfactory explanation of four points he should propose to him ; which were these :

" What distance, father, do you apprehend it is from hence to heaven ? What quantity of water is there in the sea ? What do people do in the infernal regions ? And fourthly, What may be the value of my person ? "

The good father hung his head on one side in a reflecting attitude for some time, but at length only uttered a deep sigh, perfectly at a loss what to do. To gain time, however, he begged he might be allowed to return home, to consider these important questions somewhat more maturely. His Excellency would only grant him a single day, and, moreover, made him enter into good security for his speedy return. The priest, in a doleful mood, then measured his steps back again to his abbey, blowing like a broken-winded steed. On his arrival, the first person he met was the jolly miller, who, observing his melancholy air, inquired into the nature of his distress and the exhausted state of his breathing.

" I may well be out of breath," he exclaimed, " when his Excellency has set me no less than four knotty points to solve, which neither the wisdom of Solomon, nor that of the Stagyrite himself, would have been able to unriddle."

"Very likely," returned the miller; "but if you will trust to me, I will bring you through the scrape at once."

"The Lord grant you could," said the poor abbot, with a pious ejaculation.

"Yes, and the Lord and all the saints in heaven will, if you will only let them; that I think I may fairly say."

"If you were really in earnest, and could be as good as your word, Mr. Miller, you might afterwards count upon me in everything during the whole of your life."

"That is saying a good deal too," returned the miller, "but I will give it full credit for the sake of your cloth."

"To be sure," said the reverend father; "but how do you propose to get me off the horns of this dilemma? that is the question."

"How!" exclaimed the miller in a scornful tone; "why, I shall shave my beard, and take your hood and cloak, and present myself to-morrow morning in your place. Trust me, I will answer his Excellency's questions, whatever they may be; and he shall never find out the difference between us, except it be from the difference in our wits."

"The Lord bless thee for an impudent varlet!" cried the honest father. "As I hope for salvation, I verily believe thou wilt bring me through! Get thee gone, and rely upon thy impudence; it will appear a thousand years until I hear the result."

Having disguised himself in the good abbot's suit, our knight of the white hat accordingly set out for the city early the ensuing day, and soon arriving at his Excellency's palace, knocked pretty loudly at the door, telling the porter he had brought the requisite answers for his master, which he must deliver by word of mouth.

Hearing who he was, his Excellency ordered the abbot to be brought straightway into his presence, wondering how he had already prepared himself for his task. The false friar, with reverence due, accosted his Excellency with a sidling air, having admirably metamorphosed his physiognomy and imitating the abbot's voice to perfection. With very little ceremony he was required to repeat what he had learned in the way of explanation of the four points in dispute. Expressing his readiness, he was first requested to point out the exact distance between earth and heaven.

"Having considered the matter very maturely," said the miller, "I find there are just thirty-six millions eight hundred and fifty-four miles, seventy-two yards, and twenty-two feet."

"You must have measured it very exactly," exclaimed his Excellency; "but how will you prove it is correct?"

"How!" retorted the bold miller; "as such matters are always proved. Let your Excellency refer it to arbitration, and if it should not be found upon a second measurement exactly what I have stated, hang me up by the neck upon the next tree. It seems you want to know next how much water there is contained in the sea. Now this has cost me a good deal of trouble, for it would neither stand still while I measured it, nor stop from receiving its tributary streams. Yet I have nevertheless compassed the difficulty, and find there are just twenty-five thousand nine hundred and eighty-two millions of vats, seven barrels, seven bottles, and two glasses of water in the sea."

"But how have you learned that, Mr. Abbot?" inquired the governor.

"Why, if you do not like to believe me," retorted the other, "order the proper vessels to be prepared, and measure it again. If you do not find just as much as I have told you, quarter me alive without any mercy. The third question, I think, you want resolved, is how people contrive to employ themselves in the world below. To this I answer, they do much as we do here; they cut and hack one another until they are weary of such sport; they persecute and they hang one another."

"But what are your reasons for this opinion?"

"Do you ask me for reasons?" returned the miller. "Why, I spoke with the very man who returned from a tour there, the same from whom the divine Florentine received his account of the infernal government, and the whole of its civil and judicial polity; but the traveller, I believe, is now dead, and went back again. And if you are not satisfied with my word for the truth of it, I refer you to him, and would advise you to send and see. The fourth and last of your questions concerns the worth of your own respected person; and I tell you it amounts to neither more nor less than two shillings and five pence."

Upon hearing this, Messer Bernabo rose in a furious passion, crying, "Villain, I will make you eat your words. How, you rogue abbot, am I worth no more than an old rusty pan?"

The poor miller, beginning to quake in his shoes, entreated in a somewhat milder tone that his Excellency would but deign to hear his reasons, saying, " You are aware, my honoured lord, that our great Lord and Master, Jesus Christ, was sold for only thirty pence, and surely you will not be offended at being rated one mark lower."

The moment he heard this answer, the governor was convinced he had no longer the honest abbot to deal with, and eyeing him more narrowly, he perceived him to be of larger dimensions, both in body and mind, than his friend the honest abbot could boast.

" You say very true," he exclaimed, " but you are not the abbot, friend: at least I have you there."

The poor miller, fearing upon this that it was all over with him, fell piteously upon his knees, with uplifted hands, confessing it was true he was only the good father's grinder of corn. He then proceeded to explain the occasion of his appearance in this disguise, for the mere purpose of amusing all parties, but of giving offence to none.

" Then by all the saints in heaven," cried Messer Bernabo, " I swear, since he has made thee abbot, an abbot thou shalt remain. By this sword I confirm his decree, and henceforth he shall serve thee, abbot, as thine honest miller, and cheat thee of thy flour. The proceeds of the monastery are thine, those of the mill shall be his"; and this sentence he strictly enforced.

THE BLIND BEGGAR OF ORVIETO

FRANCO SACCHETTI

A BLIND man of Orvieto, of the name of Cola, hit upon a device to recover a hundred florins he had been cheated of, which showed he was possessed of all the eyes of Argus, though he had unluckily lost his own. And this he did without wasting a farthing either upon law or arbitration, by sheer dexterity ; for he had formerly been a barber, and accustomed to shave very close, having then all his eyes about him, which had been now closed for about thirty years. Alms seemed then the only resource to which he could betake himself, and such was the surprising progress he in a short time made in his new trade, that he counted a hundred florins in his purse, which he secretly carried about him until he could find a safer place. His gains far surpassed anything he had realised with his razor and scissors ; indeed, they increased so fast that he no longer knew where to bestow them ; until one morning happening to remain the last, as he believed, in the church, he thought of depositing his purse of a hundred florins under a loose tile in the floor behind the door, knowing the situation of the place perfectly well.

After listening for some time, without hearing a foot stirring, he very cautiously laid it in the spot ; but unluckily there remained a certain Juccio Pezzicheruolo, offering his adoration before an image of San Giovanni Boccadoro, who happened to see Cola busily engaged behind the door. He continued his adorations until he saw the blind man depart, when, not in the least suspecting the truth, he approached and searched the place. He soon found the identical tile, and on removing it with the help of his knife, he found the purse, which he very quietly put into his pocket, replacing the tiles just as they were ; and resolving to say nothing about it, he went home.

At the end of three days, the blind mendicant, desirous of inspecting his treasure, took a quiet time for visiting the place, and removing the tile, searched a long while in great perturbation, but all in vain, to find his beloved purse. At last, replacing things just as they were, he was compelled to return in no very enviable state of mind to his dwelling and there meditating over his loss, the harvest of the toil of so many days, by dint of intense thinking a bright thought struck him, as frequently happens by cogitating in the dark, how he had yet a kind of chance of redeeming his lost spoils.

Accordingly, in the morning he called his young guide, a lad about nine years old, saying, " My son, lead me to church " ; and before setting out he tutored him how he was to behave, seating himself at his side before the entrance, and particularly remarking every person who should enter into the church. " Now, if you happen to see any one who takes particular notice of me, and who either laughs or makes any sign, be sure you observe it and tell me."

The boy promised he would ; and they proceeded accordingly, and took their station before the church. There they remained the whole of the morning, till just as they were beginning to despair, Juccio made his appearance, and fixing his eyes upon the blind man, could not refrain from laughing. When the dinner-hour arrived the father and son prepared to leave the place, the former inquiring by the way whether his son had observed any one looking hard at him as he passed along. " That I did," answered the lad, " but only one, and he laughed as he went past us. I do not know his name, but he is strongly marked with the smallpox, and lives somewhere near the Frati Minori."

" Do you think, my dear lad," said his father, " you could take me to his shop, and tell me when you see him there ? "

" To be sure I could," said the lad.

" Then come, let us lose no time," replied his father, " and when we are there tell me, and while I speak to him you can step on one side and wait for me."

So the sharp little fellow led him along the way until he reached a cheesemonger's stall, when he acquainted his father, and brought him close to it. No sooner did the blind man hear him speaking with his customers, than he recognised him for the same Juccio with whom he had formerly been acquainted during his days of light. When the coast was a little clear, our blind hero entreated some moments' conversation, and Juccio, half suspecting the occasion, took him on one side into a little room, saying,

" Cola, friend, what good news ? "

" Why," said Cola, " I am come to consult you, in great hope you will be of use to me. You know it is a long time since I lost my sight, and being in a destitute condition, I was compelled to earn my subsistence by begging alms. Now, by the grace of God, and with the help of you and of other good people of Orvieto, I have saved a sum of two hundred florins, one of which I have deposited in a safe place, and the other is in the hands of my relations, which I expect to receive with interest in the course of a week. Now if you would consent to receive, and to employ for me to the best advantage, the whole sum of two hundred florins, it would be doing me a great kindness, for there is no one besides in all Orvieto in whom I dare to confide; nor do I like to be at the expense of paying a notary for doing business which we can as well transact ourselves. Only I wish you would say nothing about it, but receive the two hundred florins from me to employ as you think best. Say not a word about it, for there would be an end of my calling were it known I had received so large a sum in alms."

Here the blind mendicant stopped; and the sly Juccio imagining he might thus become master of the entire sum, said he should be very happy to serve him in every way he could, and would return an answer the next morning as to the best way of laying out the money. Cola then took his leave, while Juccio going directly for the purse, deposited it in its old place, being in full expectation of soon receiving it again with the addition of the other hundred, as it was clear that Cola had not yet missed the sum. The cunning old mendicant on his part expected that he would do no less, and trusting that his plot might have succeeded, he set out the very same day to the church, and had the delight, on removing the tile, to find his purse really there. Seizing upon it with the utmost eagerness, he concealed it under his clothes, and placing the tiles exactly in the same position, he hastened home whistling, troubling himself very little about his appointment of the next day.

The sly thief, Juccio, set out accordingly the next morning to see his friend Cola, and actually met him on the road. "Whither are you going?" inquired Juccio.

"I was going," said Cola, "to your house."

The former then, taking the blind man aside, said, "I am resolved to do what you ask; and since you are pleased to confide in me, I will tell you of a plan I have in hand of laying out your money to advantage. If you will put the two hundred into my possession, I will make a purchase in cheese and salt meat, a speculation which cannot fail to turn to good account."

"Thank you," said Cola; "I am going to-day for the other hundred, which I mean to bring, and when you have got them both, you can do with them what you think proper."

Juccio said, " Then let me have them soon, for I think I can secure this bargain ; and as the soldiers are come into the town, who are fond of these articles, I think it cannot fail to answer ; so go, and Heaven speed you." And Cola went ; but with very different intentions from those imagined by his friend—Cola being now clear-sighted, and Juccio truly blind.

The next day Cola called on his friend with very downcast and melancholy looks, and when Juccio bade him good day, he said, " I wish from my soul it were good, or even a middling day for me."

" Why, what is the matter ? "

" The matter ! " said Cola, " why it is all over with me ; some rascal has stolen a hundred florins from the place where they were hidden, and I cannot recover a penny from my relations, so that I may eat my fingers off for anything I have to expect."

Juccio replied, " This is like all the rest of my speculations. I have invariably lost where I expected to make a good hit. What I shall do I know not ; for if the person should choose to keep me to the agreement I made for you, I shall be in a pretty dilemma indeed."

" Yet," said Cola, " I think my condition is still worse than yours. I shall be sadly distressed, and shall have to amass a fresh capital, which will take me ever so long. And when I have got it, I will take care not to conceal it in a hole in the floor, or trust it, Juccio, into any friend's hands."

" But," said Juccio, " if we could contrive to recover what is owing by your relations, we might still make some pretty profit by it, I doubt not." For he thought, if he could only get hold of the hundred he had returned, it would still be something in his way.

" Why," said Cola, " to tell the truth, if I were to proceed against my relations, I believe I might get it ; but such a thing would ruin my business, my dear Juccio, for ever : the world would know I was worth money, and I should get no more money from the world ; so I fear I shall hardly be able to profit by your kindness, though I shall always consider myself as much obliged as if I had actually cleared a large sum. Moreover, I am going to teach another blind man my profession, and if we have luck you shall see me again, and we can venture a speculation together."

So far the wily mendicant ; to whom Juccio said, " Well, go and try to get money soon, and bring it ; you know where to find me, but look sharp about you, and the Lord speed you : farewell."

" Farewell," said Cola, " and I am well rid of thee," he whispered to himself ; and going upon his way, in a short time he doubled his capital ; but he no longer went near his friend Juccio to know how he should invest it. He had great diversion in telling the story to his companions during their feasts, always concluding, " By St. Lucia ! Juccio is the blinder man of the two : he thought it was a bold stroke to risk his hundred to double the amount."

It is impossible to describe Juccio's vexation on going to the church and finding the florins were gone. His regret was far greater than if he had actually lost a hundred of his own ; as is known to be the case with all inveterate rogues, half of whose pleasure consists in depriving others of their lawful property.

MICHELOZZO AND THE ASSES

Franco Sacchetti

IT happened that a certain Spanish cavalier of the name of Messer Giletto, just returned from the Holy Sepulchre, arrived at Milan, bringing with him a beautiful ass, one of the pleasantest animals ever seen; for he would rise upon his hind-feet like a French dancing-dog, and caper as long as his master pleased, and when requested to sing, he would utter notes far more loud and sonorous than any of his race; indeed, such was its compass, that it displayed much of the variety of the human voice. Nor was this the least of his great accomplishments which attracted notice; and when his master paid a visit on him to Messer Bernabo of Milan, such was the fame thereof, that after their first introduction he immediately inquired to whom the ass belonged.

The cavalier answered that the ass was his, and was one of the most amusing animals in the world. Being very richly caparisoned, after a close inspection, Messer Bernabo declared that he appeared worthy of his master's praises, and admired him greatly. So he seated the cavalier by his side, who ordered the ass to display his paces, requesting to know if his Lordship would like to witness one of his tricks. "If it be anything new, let me see it, I entreat you," said the other, which the cavalier immediately did, to their no small diversion; M. Michelozzo, a Florentine, at the same time being present.

Messer Giletto, observing his Lordship so amazingly diverted with his tricks, said, "You will do me great honour, sir, as I have nothing better to give, would you deign to accept him at my hands, not indeed for his value, which is little, but in order to afford some amusement to your Lordship's family."

Messer Bernabo, highly gratified with the offer, accepted it, and the very same day the donor received a noble charger with more than a hundred florins in return; and after receiving many other honours, he continued his journey.

Now our friend Michelozzo, having witnessed the whole of these proceedings, also took leave of his Lordship and returned to Florence, where a bright thought struck him, that if he were to present the governor with a pair of fine asses, it might be no bad speculation, and perhaps advance him greatly in his favour. So he sent his emissaries through the Roman territories, and they had the good fortune to meet with two of a superior size, which cost him forty florins. On their arrival in Florence, he had them both very exactly measured by a saddler, commissioned to purchase the requisite quantity of fine scarlet and cloth of gold, who decked them out in the most splendid style, not omitting even to adorn their comely ears. The arms of the Visconti were likewise emblazoned on the neck and crest ; those of the owner being placed lower down, approaching the feet. Two handsome pages, one on horseback and one on foot, with a groom to urge them from behind, were next ordered to convey these beautiful animals very carefully, to be presented on his part to the said lord.

Great was the admiration of the Florentines as the procession passed along the streets ; and what it was, and where it was going, was the general cry. " They are asses, cannot you see ? " replied the page, " a present from Michelozzo to Lord Bernabo."

Some thought it very fine, some made faces and shrugged up their shoulders, while others declared it was all a piece of folly, such as they should not easily see again ; with other commentaries, of which the mouth of the people is usually full.

Having reached the gate of San Gallo, their splendid accoutrements were removed and carefully packed up, until they were about to enter Bologna, when the asses were again equipped, in order to attract the admiration of the citizens ; among whom the same questions as before took place : except that they were here mistaken for chargers going to enter the lists. This favourable opinion one of the animals, however, destroyed by braying in a most discordant tone, which elicited a shrewd remark from an old citizen : " Faith, I believe they are only a pair of stupid asses."

" Yes, sir," said the page, " which a gentleman of Florence is going to present to my lord of Milan."

" But," rejoined the citizen, " he ought to have put them in a cage, as they sing so well."

On arriving at the inn of Felice Ammannati, the entertainment was doubly renewed, every one declaring it the greatest wonder that had ever been known. " But I trust," said the facetious host, " that though these carcases are really going to the governor, they will leave behind them what I value much more for the benefit of my fields, unless it is to be forwarded to your master in Florence."

After a hearty laugh, the beasts proceeded on their journey; and such was the impression their appearance everywhere made, that their fame travelling before them, several miracles were said to have happened as of old in Parma, Piacenza, and Lodi ere they reached their destination. When they at length arrived there, the groom knocked at the city gate, informing the porter they had brought a rich present to his lord Bernabo on the part of Michelozzo, a gentleman of Florence.

The castellan observing through the wicket two asses thus gorgeously arrayed in scarlet trappings, hastened to acquaint his master with the fact. The governor, in no little perplexity on hearing this, gave orders that they should be admitted, when the head page explained the nature of his embassy, presenting the asses on the part of Michelozzo to the lord of Milan. The latter immediately replied, " You will tell your master that I am sorry he should think of thus depriving himself of the company of his companions, leaving himself behind; and so I bid you good day."

He then sent for one of his officers, of the name of Bergamino da Crema, commanding him to take the scarlet cloth, and to get a dress made of it for himself, and another for one of his muleteers; and to place the emblazoned coats of arms, one in the front, and one on the back of each dress, with those of Michelozzo below, when they were to await his further orders. Bergamino then went, and disposing of the asses in a stable, took possession of their rich accoutrements, sending the same day for a tailor to measure and cut them up into dresses for himself and three other muleteers of the court. This done, they proceeded to load the asses, and going out of Milan, they soon returned with them, bringing corn, and attracting the attention of the people wherever they passed along. On inquiry into the occasion of these fine scarlet dresses, " Michelozzo," replied they, " a Florentine gentleman, presented them to us, and so we wear them out of regard to the donor."

Bergamino next ordered the clerk of the governor to return a suitable reply to Michelozzo, how they had received the asses adorned with scarlet robes, and speedily put them under a course of burdens, finding them exceedingly useful in the service of his master, while their drivers had arrayed themselves in the rich trappings they formerly wore, besides displaying his coat of arms below that of their master, with all which, in honour of the donor, they had that day made a solemn procession with their burdens through Milan, attributing the whole honour to himself. This letter was signed and sealed, and sent, bearing the signature in proper form of "Bergamino da Crema, Equipage-master and Mule-driver to his Excellency the Lord of Milan," etc. etc., directed "To my brother Michelozzo, or Bambozzo de' Bamboli, of Florence"; and delivered to the messenger, who, after lingering in vain for a pecuniary gratification, set out with his despatches for Florence.

On perusing the direction, Signor Michelozzo began to change colour, and proceeding to read, he grew worse and worse, till he arrived at the name of his correspondent, the master of the mules. Clasping his hands in a paroxysm of despair, he inquired of the messenger to whom he had delivered the letter. "To the governor," replied the man.

"And what answer did he give?"

"He said he was sorry you should deprive yourself of your companions for his sake."

"And who gave you this letter?"

"His servant," replied he, "for I could never get to see his master again."

"Heavens!" cried Michelozzo, "you have ruined me! What know I of Bergamino or Merdollino? Get out of my house, and never come near me again."

"I will go or stay, just as you please," said the man; "but I must tell you the truth: we have made fools of ourselves wherever we appeared; it is impossible to say how much you were laughed at; you would be quite astonished if you knew."

"Why, what could they say? Did no one ever make a present to a lord, think you, before?"

"Yes, sir, but never of asses, I believe," said the man.

"But," returned his master, "you were with me yourself when the Spanish cavalier made a present of his."

"True, sir, but that was mere accident; besides, his was a knowing beast, and yours are as stupid as asses need to be."

"I tell you, you lie," said his master; "one of their feet was worth the whole body of the other ass, equipped as they were: you have ruined me, I say; and get about your business," which the man was glad enough to do.

In a short time after, our hero grew melancholy and sickened from the vexation of his adventure; in which, as the present which he made was of a novel nature, he was in return treated in a manner perfectly novel and appropriate.

SER GIOVANNI
1378

THE LOVE TALE OF GALGANO AND MINOCCIA

THERE resided in Sienna a noble youth of the name of Galgano, who, besides his birth and riches, was extremely clever, valiant, and affable, qualities which won him the regard of all ranks of people in the place. But I am very sorry to add that, attracted by the beauty of a Siennese lady, no other, you must know, than the fair Minoccia, wedded to our noble cavalier, Messer Stricca (though I beg this may go no farther), our young friend unfortunately, and too late, fell passionately in love with her.

So violently enamoured did he shortly become, that he purloined her glove, which he wore with her favourite colours wherever he went, at tilts and tourneys, at rich feasts and festivals, all of which he was proud to hold in honour of his love: yet all these failed to render him agreeable to the lady, a circumstance that caused our poor friend Galgano no little pain and perplexity. A prey to the excessive cruelty and indifference of one dearer to him than his own life, who neither noticed nor listened to him, he still followed her like her shadow, contriving to be near her at every party, whether a bridal or a christening, a funeral or a play. Long and vainly, with love-messages after love-messages, and presents after presents, did he sue; but never would the noble lady deign to receive or listen to them for a moment, ever bearing herself more reserved and harshly as he more earnestly pressed the ardour of his suit.

It was thus his fate to remain subject to this very irksome and overwhelming passion, until, wearied out, at length he would break into words of grief and bitterness against his "bosom's lord." "Alas! dread master of my destiny," he would say, "O Love! can you behold me thus wasting my very soul away, ever loving but never beloved again? See to it, dread lord, that you are not, in so doing, offending against your own laws!" And so, unhappily dwelling upon the lady's cruelty, he seemed fast verging upon despair; then again humbly resigning himself to the yoke he bore, he resolved to await some interval of grace, watching, however vainly, for some occasion of rendering himself more pleasing to the object he adored.

Now it happened that Messer Stricca and his consort went to pass some days at their country seat near Sienna; and it was not long before the love-sick Galgano was observed to cross their route, to hang upon their skirts, and to pass along the same way, always with the hawk upon his hand, as if violently set upon bird-hunting. Often, indeed, he passed so close to the villa where the lady dwelt, that one day being seen by Messer Stricca, who recognised him, he was very familiarly entreated to afford them the pleasure of his company; "and I hope," added Messer Stricca, "that you will stay the evening with us." Thanking his friend very kindly for the invitation, Galgano, strange to say, at the same time begged to be held excused, pleading another appointment, which he believed—he was sorry—he was obliged to keep."

"Then," added Messer Stricca, "at least step in and take some little refreshment" · to which the only reply returned was, "A thousand thanks, and farewell, Messer Stricca, for I am in haste."

The moment the latter had turned his back, our poor lover began to upbraid himself bitterly for not availing himself of the invitation, exclaiming, "What a wretch am I not to accept such an offer as this! I should at least have seen her—her whom from my soul I cannot help loving beyond all else in the world."

As he thus went, meditating upon the same subject along his solitary way, it chanced that he sprang a large jay, on which he instantly gave his hawk the wing, which pursuing its quarry into Messer Stricca's gardens, and there striking true, the ensuing struggle took place. Hearing the hawk's cry, both he and his lady ran towards the garden balcony, in time to see, and were surprised at the skill and boldness of the bird in seizing and bringing down its game. Not in the least aware of the truth, the lady inquired of her husband to whom the bird belonged.

"Mark the hawk," replied Messer Stricca; "it does its work well; it resembles its master, who is one of the handsomest and most accomplished young men in Sienna, and a very excellent young fellow, too;—yes, it does well."

"And who may that be?" said his wife, with a careless air.

"Who," returned he, "but the noble Galgano—the same, love, who just now passed by. I wished he would have come in to sup with us, but he would not. He is certainly one of the finest and best-tempered men I ever saw." And so saying, he rose from the window, and they went to supper.

Galgano, in the meanwhile, having given his hawk the call, quietly pursued his way; but the praises lavished upon him by her husband made an impression upon the lady's mind such as the whole of his previous solicitations had failed to produce. However strange, she dwelt upon them long and tenderly. It happened that about this very time Messer Stricca was chosen ambassador from the Siennese to the people of Perugia, and setting out in all haste, he was compelled to take a sudden leave of his lady.

I am sorry to have to observe that the moment the cavalcade was gone by, recalling the idea of her noble lover, the lady likewise despatched an embassy to our young friend, entreating him, after the example of her husband, to favour her with his company in the evening. No longer venturing to refuse he sent a grateful answer back that he would very willingly attend. And having heard tidings of Messer Stricca's departure for Perugia, he set out at a favourable hour in the evening, and speedily arrived at the house of the lady to whom he had been so long and so vainly attached.

Checking his steed in full career, he threw himself off, and the next moment found himself in her presence, falling at her feet and saluting her with the most respectful and graceful carriage. She took him joyously by the hand, bidding him a thousand tender welcomes, and setting before him the choicest fruits and refreshments of the season. Then inviting him to be seated, he was served with the greatest variety and splendour; and more delicious than all, the bright lady herself presided there, no longer frowning and turning away when he began to breathe the story of his love and sufferings into her ear. Delighted and surprised beyond his proudest hopes, Galgano was profuse in his expressions of gratitude and regard, though he could not quite conceal his wonder at this happy and unexpected change; entreating, at length, as a particular favour, that she would deign to acquaint him with its blessed cause.

"That will I do soon," replied the glowing beauty; "I will tell you every word, and therefore did I send for you"; and she looked into his face with a serene and pure yet somewhat mournful countenance.

"Indeed," returned her lover, a little perplexed, "words can never tell half of what I felt, dear lady, when I heard you had this morning sent for me, after having desired and followed you for so long a time in vain."

"Listen to me, and I will tell you, Galgano; but first sit a little nearer to me, for, alas! I love you. A few days ago, you know, you passed near our house when hawking, and my husband told me that he saw you, and invited you in to supper, but you would not come. At that moment your hawk sprang and pursued its prey, when seeing the noble bird make such a gallant fight, I inquired to whom it belonged, and my husband replied, 'To whom should it belong but to the most excellent young man in Sienna'; and that it did well to resemble you, as he had never met a more pleasing and accomplished gentleman."

"Did he—did he say that?" interrupted her lover.

"He did indeed, and much more, praising you to me over and over; until hearing it, and knowing the tenderness you have long borne me, I could not resist the temptation of sending for you hither"; and, half blushes, half tears, she confessed that he was no longer indifferent to her, and that such was the occasion of it.

"Can the whole of this be true?" exclaimed Galgano.

"Alas! too true," she replied. "I know not how it is, but I wish he had not praised you so."

After struggling with himself a few moments, the unhappy lover withdrew his hand from hers, saying, "Now God forbid that I should do the least wrong to one who has so nobly expressed himself, and who has ever shown so much kindness and courtesy to me."

Then suddenly rising, as with an effort, from his seat, he took a gentle farewell of the lady, not without some tears shed on both sides; both loving yet respecting each other. Never afterwards did this noble youth allude to the affair in the slightest way, but always treated Messer Stricca with the utmost regard and reverence during his acquaintance with the family.

BUCCIOLO AND HIS TUTOR

SER GIOVANNI

THERE were once two very intimate friends, both of the family of Savelli, in Rome, the name of one of whom was Bucciolo, of the other Pietro Paolo, both of good birth and easy circumstances. Expressing a mutual wish to study for a while together at Bologna, they took leave of their relatives and set out. One of them attached himself to the study of the civil, the other to that of the canon law; and thus they continued to apply themselves for some length of time. But as you are aware that the subject of the Decretals takes a much narrower range than is embraced by the common law, so Bucciolo, who pursued the former, made greater progress than did Pietro Paolo, and having taken a licentiate's degree, he began to think of returning to Rome.

"You see, my dear fellow-student," he observed to his friend Paolo, "I am now a licentiate, and it is time for me to think of moving homewards."

"Nay, not so," replied his companion; "I have to entreat you will not think of leaving me here this winter; stay for me till spring, and we can then return together. In the meanwhile you may pursue some other science, so that you need not lose any time."

To this Bucciolo at length consented, promising to await his relation's own good time. Having thus resolved, he had immediate recourse to his former tutor, informing him of his determination to bear his friend company a little longer, and entreating to be employed in some pleasant study to beguile the period during which he had to remain. The professor begged him to suggest something he would like, as he should be very happy to assist him in its attainment.

"My worthy tutor," replied Bucciolo, "I think I should like to learn the way in which one falls in love, and the best manner to begin."

"Oh, very good," cried the tutor, laughing, "you could have hit upon nothing better, for you must know that, if that be your object, I am a complete adept in the art. To lose no time, in the first place, go next Sunday morning to the Church of the Frati Minori, where all the ladies will be clustered together, and pay proper attention during service, in order to discover if any one of them in particular happen to please you. When you have done this, keep your eye upon her after service, to see the way she takes to her residence, and then come back to me. And let this be the first lesson, first part, of that in which it is my intention to instruct you."

Bucciolo went accordingly, and taking his station the next Sunday in the church as he had been directed, his eyes, wandering in every direction except the proper one, were fixed upon all the pretty women in the place, and upon one in particular who pleased him above all the rest. She was far the most attractive and beautiful lady he could find; and on leaving the church Bucciolo took care to obey his master, and follow her until he had made himself acquainted with her residence. Nor was it long before the young lady began to perceive that the student was smitten with her; upon which, Bucciolo, returning to his master, acquainted him with what he had done:

"I have learned as much as you ordered me, and found somebody I like very well."

"So far good," cried the professor, not a little amused at the sort of science to which his pupil thus seriously devoted himself, "so far good; and now mind what I have next to say to you. Take care to walk two or three times a day very respectfully before her house, casting your eyes about you in such a way that no one catch you staring in her face; but look in a modest and becoming manner, so that she cannot fail to perceive and to be struck with it. And then return to me, and this, sir, will be the second lesson in this gay science."

So the scholar went, and promenaded with great discretion before the lady's door, who certainly observed that he appeared to be passing to and fro out of respect to one of the inhabitants. This attracted her attention, for which Bucciolo very discreetly expressed his gratitude both by looks and bows, which being as often returned, the scholar began to be aware that the lady liked him. Upon this he immediately went and informed the professor of all that had passed, who replied, "Come, you have done very well; I am hitherto quite satisfied. It is now time for you to find some way of speaking to her, which you may easily do by means of one of those gipsies who haunt the streets of Bologna crying ladies' veils, purses, and other rare articles to sell. Send word by her that you are the lady's most faithful, devoted servant, and that there is no one in the world you so much wish to please. In short, let her urge your suit, and take care to bring the answer to me as soon as you have received it ; I will then tell you how you are to proceed."

Departing in all haste, he soon found a little old pedlar woman, quite perfect in her trade, to whom he said he should take it as a particular favour if she would do one thing, for which he would reward her handsomely.

Upon this she declared her readiness to serve him in anything he pleased, " for you know," she continued, " it is my business to get money in every way I can."

Bucciolo gave her two florins, saying, " I wish you to go as far as the Via Maccarella for me to-day, where resides a young lady of the name of Giovanna, for whom I have the very highest regard. Pray tell her so, and recommend me to her most affectionately, so as to obtain for me her good graces by every means in your power. I entreat you to have my interest at heart, and to say such pretty things as she cannot refuse to hear."

" Oh," said the little old woman, " leave that to me, sir ; I will not fail to say a good word for you at the proper time."

" Delay not," said Bucciolo, " but go now, and I will wait for you here " ; and she set off immediately, taking a basket of her trinkets under her arm.

On approaching the place, she saw the lady before the door enjoying the open air, and curtseying to her very low, " Do I happen to have anything here you would fancy ? " she said, displaying her treasures. " Pray, take something, madam, whatever pleases you best."

Veils, stays, purses, and mirrors were now spread in the most tempting way before her eyes, as the old woman took her station at the lady's side. Out of all these, her attention appeared to be most attracted by a beautiful purse, which she observed, if she could afford, she should like to buy.

" Nay, madam, do not think anything about the price," exclaimed the little pedlar ; " take anything you please, for they are all paid for, I assure you."

Surprised at hearing this, and observing the very respectful manner of the speaker, the lady replied, " Do you know what you are saying ? what do you mean by that ? "

The old creature, pretending now to be much affected, said, " Well, madam, if it must be so I will tell you. It is very true that a young gentleman of the name of Bucciolo sent me hither, one who loves you better than all the world besides. There is nothing he would not do to please you, and indeed he appears so very wretched because he cannot speak to you, and he is so very good, that it is quite a pity. I think it will be the death of him ; and then he is such a fine, such an elegant young man ; the more is the pity."

On hearing this, the lady, blushing deeply, turned sharply round upon the little old hag, exclaiming, " Oh, you wicked little creature ! were it not for the sake of my own reputation, I would give you such a lesson that you should remember it to the latest day of your life. A pretty story to come before decent people with ! Are not you ashamed of yourself to let such words come out of your mouth ? "

Then, seizing an iron bar that lay across the doorway, " Ill betide you, little wretch," she cried, as she brandished it ; " if you ever return this way again, you may depend upon it you will never go back alive ! "

The trembling old creature, quickly bundling up her pack, ran off, in dread of feeling that cruel weapon on her shoulders ; nor did she once think of stopping till she had reached the place where Signor Bucciolo stood. Eagerly inquiring the news, and in what way she had prospered : " Oh, very badly, very badly," answered the little gipsy ; " I never was in such a fright in all my life. Why, she will neither see nor listen to you, and if I had not run away, I should have felt the weight of her hand upon my shoulders. For my own part, I shall go there no more," chinking the two florins ; " and I would advise you to look to yourself how you proceed in such affairs in future."

Poor Bucciolo now became quite disconsolate, and returned in all haste to acquaint the professor with this unlucky result. But the tutor, not a whit cast down, consoled him, saying, " Do not despair, Bucciolo ; a tree is not levelled at a single stroke, you know. I think you must have a repetition of your lesson to-night. So go and walk before her door as usual ; notice how she eyes you, and whether she appears angry or not ; and then come back again to me."

He proceeded without delay to the lady's house, who, the moment she perceived him, called her maid, giving her directions as follows : " Quick, quick ! hasten after that young man—that is he ; and tell him from me that he must come and speak to me this evening without fail ; yes, without fail."

The girl soon came up with Bucciolo : " My lady, sir, my lady

Giovanna would be glad of the pleasure of your company this evening; she would be very glad to speak to you."

Greatly surprised at this, Bucciolo replied, "Tell your lady I shall be most happy to wait upon her"; and turning round, he set off once more to the professor, and reported the progress of the case.

But this time his master looked a little more serious, for, from some trivial circumstances put together, he began to entertain suspicions, as it really turned out, that the lady was no other than his own wife. So he rather anxiously inquired of Bucciolo whether he intended to accept the invitation.

"To be sure I do," replied his pupil.

"Then promise," rejoined the professor, "that you will come here before you set off."

"Certainly," said Bucciolo, "I will"; and he took his leave.

Now, our hero was far from suspecting that the lady boasted so near a relationship to his beloved tutor, although the latter began to feel rather uneasy as to the result, feeling certain twinges of jealousy by no means pleasant. For he passed most of his winter evenings at the college, where he gave lectures, and not unfrequently remained there for the night. "I should be sorry," thought he, "that this young gentleman were learning these things at my expense; and I must therefore know the real state of the case."

In the evening his pupil called again, saying, "Worthy sir, I am now ready to go."

"Well, go," replied the professor; "but be wise, Signor Bucciolo, be wise: think more than once what you are about."

"Trust me for that," replied the scholar, a little piqued; "I shall go well provided, and not walk like a fool into the mouth of danger unarmed."

And away he went, furnished with a good cuirass, a rapier, and a stiletto in his belt. He was no sooner on his way than the professor slipped out quietly after him, following him close at his heels, and truly he saw him stop at his own door, which, on a pretty smart tap being given, was opened in a moment, and the pupil was admitted by the lady herself. When the professor saw that it was indeed his own wife, he was quite overwhelmed, saying in a faint voice to himself, "Alas! I fear this young fellow has learned more than he confesses at my expense"; and making a cruel vow to revenge himself, he ran back to the college, where, arming himself with sword and knife, he hastened back in a terrible passion, with the intention of wreaking his vengeance on poor Bucciolo without delay.

Arriving at his own door, he gave a pretty smart knock, which the lady, sitting before the fire with Bucciolo, instantly recognised for her husband's. So taking hold of Bucciolo, she concealed him in all haste under a heap of damp clothes lying on a table near the window ready for ironing; and this done, she ran to the door, and inquired who was there. "Open, quick," returned the professor; "you vile woman, you shall soon know who I am."

On opening the door, she beheld him with a drawn sword, and exclaimed, "Oh, my dearest life! what means this?"

"You know very well," said he, "what it means; the villain is now in the house."

"Good heaven, what is it you say?" cried his wife; "are you gone out of your wits? Come and search the house, and if you find anybody, I will give you leave to kill me on the spot. What! do you think I should now begin to misconduct myself as I never before did, as none of my family ever did before? Beware lest the evil one should be tempting you, and suddenly depriving you of your senses, drive you to perdition."

But the professor, calling out for candles, began to search the house, from the cellars upwards, among the tubs and casks, in every place but the right one, running his sword through the beds and under the beds, and into every inch of the bedding, leaving no corner or crevice of the whole house untouched. The lady accompanied him with a candle in her hand, frequently interrupting him with, "Say your beads, say your beads, good sir; it is certain that the evil one is dealing with you; for were I half so bad as you esteem me, I would kill myself with my own hands. But I entreat you not to give way to his evil suggestions; oppose the adversary while you can."

Hearing these virtuous asseverations of his wife, and not being able to meet with any one after the strictest search, the professor began to think that he must indeed be possessed, and in a short time, extinguishing the lights, returned to his rooms. The lady, shutting the door upon him, called out to Bucciolo to come from his hiding-place, and stirring the fire, began to prepare a fine capon for supper, with some delicious wines and fruits. And thus they regaled themselves, highly entertained with each other; nor was it their least satisfaction that the professor had just left them, apparently convinced that they had learned nothing at his expense.

Proceeding the next morning to college, Bucciolo, without the least suspicion of the truth, informed his master that he had something for his ear which he was sure would make him laugh. "How, how so!" exclaimed the professor.

"Why," returned his pupil, "you must know that last night, just at the very time I was in the lady's house, who should come in but her husband, and in such a rage! He searched the whole house from top to bottom without being able to find me. I lay under a heap of newly-washed clothes, which were not half dry. In short, the lady played her part so well, that the poor gentleman forthwith took his leave, and we afterwards ate a fine fat capon for supper, and drank such wines, and with such a zest! It was really one of the pleasantest evenings I ever spent in my life. But I think I will go and take a nap, for I promised to return again this evening about the same hour."

"Then be sure before you go," said the professor, trembling with suppressed rage, "be sure to tell me when you set off."

"Oh, certainly," replied Bucciolo, and away he went. Such was now the unhappy tutor's condition as to render him incapable of delivering a single lecture during the whole day; and such his extreme vexation and desire to behold the evening, that he spent the whole time in arming himself cruelly with rapier, sword, and cuirass, dwelling only upon deeds of blood. At the appointed hour came Bucciolo with the utmost innocence, saying, "My dear tutor, I am going now."

"Yes, go," replied the professor, "and come back again to-morrow morning, if you can, to tell me how you have fared."

"I intend to do so," said Bucciolo, and departed at a brisk pace for the house of the lady. Armed cap-à-pie, the professor ran out after him, keeping pretty close at his heels, with the intention of catching him just as he entered. But the lady being on the watch, opened the door so quickly for the pupil, that she shut it in the master's face, who began to knock and to call out with a furious noise. Extinguishing the candle in a moment, the lady placed Bucciolo behind the door, and throwing her arms round her husband's neck as he entered, motioned to her lover, while she thus held his enemy, to make his escape; and he, upon the husband rushing forwards, stepped out from behind the door unperceived.

She then began to scream as loud as she could, "Help, help! the professor is run mad! Will nobody help me?" for he was in an ungovernable rage, and she clung faster to him than before. The neighbours running to her assistance, and seeing the peaceable professor thus armed with all these deadly weapons, and his wife crying out, "Help, for the love of Heaven; too much study hath driven him mad!" they really believed such to be the fact.

"Come, good master," they said, "what is all this? Try to compose yourself; nay, do not struggle so hard, but let us help you to your couch."

"How can I rest, think you," he replied, "while this wicked woman harbours paramours in my house? I saw him come in with my own eyes."

"Wretch that I am," cried his wife, "inquire of all my friends and neighbours whether any one of them ever saw anything the least unbecoming in my conduct."

The whole party, with one voice, entreated the master to lay such thoughts aside, for that there was not a better lady breathing, nor one who set a higher value upon her reputation. "But how can that be," said the tutor, "when I saw him enter the house with my own eyes? and he is in it now."

In the meanwhile the lady's two brothers arrived, when she began to weep bitterly, exclaiming, "Oh, my dear brothers! my poor husband is gone mad, quite mad; and he even says there is a man in the house! I believe he would kill me if he could; but you know me too well to listen a moment to such a story"; and she continued to weep.

The brothers forthwith accosted the professor in no very gentle terms. "We are surprised, we are shocked, sir, to find that you dare bestow such epithets on our sister; what can have led you, after living so amicably together, to bring these charges against her now?"

"I can only tell you," replied the enraged professor, "that there is a man in the house; I saw him."

"Then come and let us find him; show him to us, for we will sift this matter to the bottom," retorted the incensed brothers. "Show us the man, and we will then punish her in such a way as will satisfy you!"

One of them taking his sister aside, said, "First tell me, have you really got any one hidden in the house? Tell the truth."

"Heavens!" cried his sister; "I tell you I would rather suffer death. Should I be the first to bring a scandal on our house? I wonder you are not ashamed to mention such a thing."

Rejoiced to hear this, the brothers, directed by the professor, immediately commenced a search. Half frantic, he led them directly to the great bundle of linen, which he pierced through and through with his sword, firmly believing he was killing Bucciolo all the while, taunting him at the same time at every blow.

"There! I told you," cried his wife, "he was quite mad; to think of destroying his own property thus! It is plain he did not help to get them up," she continued, whimpering; "all my best clothes."

Having now sought everywhere in vain, one of the brothers observed, "He is indeed mad"; to which the other agreed, while he again attacked the professor in the bitterest terms. "You have carried things too far, sir; your conduct to our sister is shameful. nothing but insanity can excuse it."

Vexed enough before, the professor upon this flew into a violent passion, and brandished his naked sword in such a way that the others were obliged to use their sticks, which they did so very effectually, that, after breaking them over his back, they chained him down like a madman upon the floor, declaring he had lost his wits by excessive study; and taking possession of his house, they remained with their sister the whole night. The next morning they sent for a physician, who ordered a couch to be placed as near as possible to the fire; that no one should be allowed to speak or reply to the patient; and that he should be strictly dieted until he recovered his wits; and this regimen was diligently enforced.

A report immediately spread throughout Bologna that the good professor had become insane, which caused very general regret, his friends observing to each other, "It is indeed a bad business, but I suspected yesterday how it was: he could scarcely get a word out as he was delivering his lecture; did you perceive?"

"Yes, I saw him change colour, poor fellow"; and everywhere, by everybody, it was decided that the professor was mad.

In this situation numbers of his scholars went to see him, and among the rest Bucciolo, knowing nothing of what had passed, agreed to accompany them to the college, desirous of acquainting his master with his last night's exploit. What was his surprise to learn that he had actually taken leave of his senses; and being directed, on leaving the college, to the professor's house, he was almost panic-struck on approaching the place, beginning to comprehend the whole affair.

Yet, in order that no one might be led to suspect the real truth, he walked into the house along with the rest, and on reaching a certain apartment which he knew, he beheld his poor tutor, almost beaten to a mummy, and chained down upon his bed close to the fire. His pupils were standing round condoling with him and lamenting his piteous case. At length it came to Bucciolo's turn to say something to him, which he did as follows: "My dear master, I am as truly concerned for you as if you were my own father; and if there is anything in which I can be of use to you, command me as your own son."

To this the poor professor only replied, "No, Bucciolo; depart in peace, my pupil, depart, for you have learned much, very much, at my expense."

Here his wife interrupted him: "You see how he wanders; heed not what he says; pay no attention to him, Signor."

Bucciolo, however, prepared to depart, and taking a hasty leave of the professor, he ran to the lodgings of his relation, Pietro Paolo, saying, "Fare you well! God bless you, my friend! I must away to Rome; for I have lately learned so much at other people's expense that I am going home"; and he hurried away, and fortunately arrived safely at Rome.